STILL POINT

STILL POINT

Deborah Weisgall

Crown Publishers, Inc., New York

Grateful acknowledgment is made to the following for permission to reprint previously published material:

Harcourt Brace Jovanovich, Inc. and Faber and Faber Limited: an excerpt from "Burnt Norton" in *Four Quartets,* copyright 1943 by T. S. Eliot and renewed 1971 by Esme Valerie Eliot. Rights outside the U. S. administered by Faber and Faber Limited, London. Reprinted by permission of Harcourt Brace Jovanovich, Inc. and Faber and Faber Limited.

Macmillan Publishing Company: an excerpt from "Sweet Dancer" from *The Poems of W. B. Yeats: A New Edition,* edited by Richard J. Finneran. Copyright 1940 by Georgie Yeats, renewed 1968 by Bertha Georgie Yeats, Michael Butler Yeats, and Anne Yeats; and an excerpt from "The Fiddler of Dooney" from *The Poems of W. B. Yeats: A New Edition,* edited by Richard J. Finneran (New York: Macmillan, 1983).

Published by Crown Publishers, Inc.,
201 East 50th Street, New York, New York 10022

CROWN is a trademark of Crown Publishers, Inc.

Manufactured in the United States of America

Library of Congress Cataloging-in-Publication Data

Weisgall, Deborah.
Still point / by Deborah Weisgall.
p.   cm.
I. Title.
PS3573.E39796S7   1990
813'.54—dc20   89–29850
ISBN 0-517-57629-5

Book Design by Shari de Miskey

10   9   8   7   6   5   4   3   2   1

First Edition

For Throop

Except for the point, the still point,
There would be no dance, and there is only the dance.

T. S. Eliot
"Burnt Norton"

STILL
POINT

I

THE SORCERER FLEW ABOVE THE BARE STAGE LIKE an evil bird. Black gauze wings trailed from his arms. An icy spotlight lit their balsa bones. Below him the dancers trembled on their toes, as if the surface of the stage rippled like water before a storm. Trombones blared dissonance; the dancers turned with the current toward the bleak light.

They leapt and fell back to earth, and their feet, laced into black shoes, gently struck the floor. That was the noise Rosalind Child heard, an earthbound thudding, feet striking the floor—the sound of dance. Dance every day—class, rehearsal, class tomorrow morning after one last entrance and the last pas de deux tonight with the Prince, Alexander Ives. Rosalind's white-powdered face shone with sweat; her black hair, loose for this last scene, stuck to her back.

Tonight was her first Odette, her first performance as the Swan Queen in Achille Perrot's new version of *Swan Lake*. Perrot himself danced the Sorcerer, and he was a sorcerer. He was a magnet pulling his dancers like the moon; he beat

1

his wings and hovered in an updraft, and the dancers raised their white arms; his feet trod space, and the dancers' white legs followed. Their bodies traced a sharp obbligato over the lush music. They wore white tights and leotards, no gauze skirts, no feather headdresses. They were women trying to fly, or they were enchanted birds trying to regain the shape of women.

Counting measures, Rosalind Child flexed her knees and inhaled on the beat. At her first entrance, she had been light-headed with apprehension, her breathing so shallow she did not know if she would have the stamina to dance. The orchestra had faded under the wind of her breath. The edge of the stage dropped into blackness; the theater rustled dangerously like the night forest where her prince hunted. A flash where a jewel caught the light—it could have been an animal's eye.

Fear had infused her limbs, lightening her. She had arched her feet, lifted herself to her toes, and gone on. The oboe's swan theme, with its ascending notes, had gleamed white like stones marking an airy path; she raised her leg and stepped onto them, one and then another. She had danced as if she weighed nothing, as if her legs were springs launching her and spinning her, as if her joints had been dipped in oil.

Dizzy exhilaration had replaced anxiety, an excitement as breathless as fear. She whirled in a pirouette, counting one turn, two, three, four. The Prince caught her. He lifted her; he lowered her so that she could not feel her toe meeting the floor. She tensed her body in its perfect line; her muscles burned, familiar pain that tonight flamed into pleasure. She had leaned like a lover on Alexander's arm; he found her balance. His face had lost personality; it had yielded to the music and the dancing. He was newly exposed to her.

Now, from where she waited in the wings impatiently to go on, the spotlight whitened a cone of air, and the wires holding the Sorcerer aloft shimmered like the strands of a spiderweb. Achille Perrot turned his head, his hooked nose a predator's beak, his eyes, black sockets, fixed on her. Her feet trembled; she was as much in his thrall as the dancers onstage.

2

Opposite her, stage right, the Prince entered and stopped, absolutely still. The Sorcerer froze; the dancers froze with him. Rosalind sensed Alexander's imperceptible crouch before he suddenly wheeled in wide leaps, one after the other, higher and higher. The Sorcerer tried to stop him; his wings blackened the stage like thunderclouds. The Prince leapt again, arms and legs parallel to the floor. He held the split, then thrust his back leg forward. To drums and cymbals he toppled the Sorcerer into blackness.

The wires trembled; they tightened and slackened; the Sorcerer's spot went dark. The Prince jumped six times across the stage, scattering the dancers in the corps with each landing; and Rosalind, the Swan Queen, stepped into her spotlight, into the Prince's embrace. He danced with her to harps; he held her by her arms, her waist, her thigh. He bent her in a slow geometry of love.

The brass grew louder and discordant; the trombones and tuba blared. Cymbals and kettledrums rumbled an earthquake. In a magnesium flash the Sorcerer erupted onstage, a man trailing wings. Odette spun in pirouettes, fixing her eyes on the Sorcerer to avert vertigo, triple pirouettes and doubles, three and two. Her loose hair whipped the Prince as she whirled out of his grasp. The Sorcerer beckoned to her, his fingers curved like claws.

The Prince seized her wrist and pulled her back, but Odette had lost her will and her strength to the Sorcerer. Her legs buckled, a long aching drop to her knees. One arm—one wing—flailed at his skeletal form. The Prince held her other arm behind her back; he held her upright until, defeated, he released her wrist and she slumped onto the floor. She collapsed with a snap, as if a tendon had been cut, her wing severed. Triumphant, the Sorcerer picked her up, wrapped her in his gauze wings, and carried her limp body offstage.

Achille Perrot's bitter old man's sweat enfolded Rosalind. Backstage she jumped from his arms and bent over, gulping breath. Her thin chest heaved; her ribs showed sharp enough to break her skin. The orchestra sounded rising harmonies; the harp unrolled heavenly arpeggios; this was the transcendent journey in the swan boat, in traditional versions when the Prince and the Swan Queen were reunited after death. Achille Perrot, breathless himself, the inside of his mouth livid against the white painted mask of his face, beckoned to Rosalind. This time his gesture carried no threat. In the dim light he caressed her head in praise. His hand, the veins protruding green like bronze serpents, revived her and sent breath and joy into her body.

That night her legs had lifted higher, her feet had beaten with new speed. The steps Perrot devised had been too hard at first, and she could not execute them. At rehearsal he had made her repeat them endlessly. She never dared plead for easier combinations; he never offered to simplify. Dancing in performance, fueled by fear, concentration, strength, and desperation, she had perceived a power in herself. It was new, and it showed, a gift from Perrot that electrified the theater's black space.

She started to kiss his cheek, but he had turned his attention from her to gaze at the stage where his dancer, the Prince, stood alone, desolate, defying the promise of redemption in the music, his back arched in a tight bow of despair.

Applause and shouts of "Bravo" cut short the last chords. The curtain fell with a dusty draft and muffled the ovation. The company crowded into the wings. The stage lights went on full. Perrot urged Rosalind out in front of him; she pranced onstage, dazzled, dazzling. The other dancers grouped behind them. The curtain rose, letting in the raucous noise: clapping, stamping, shouts. Rosalind flinched with fear and pleasure at the assault. His wooden wings dragging on the stage, Achille Perrot took her right hand and Alexander Ives her left. They led her forward, into the blinding, welcoming circles of light, golden now, mimicking daylight.

Sumner Loewen and his wife, Fanny, sat without applauding. "Achille was right," he muttered. "He won."

"What was that, dear?" His wife bent her head down to hear him. She remained six and a half inches taller than he; she had not shrunk with age.

"I said that Achille won."

"I don't see where it's a contest. He's supposed to win. The Sorcerer wins every time. That's the story." She repainted her mouth with thick arching strokes of lipstick.

Sumner Loewen frowned. "I could not understand why he insisted on dancing. I told him it was a mistake. I made a bet with him that it wouldn't work."

"What did you bet?"

"Champagne." Sumner shrugged. "He always wins when we bet."

"He was marvelous."

"But he's too old. He looks like Alexander's ghost. I thought it would be laughable. But it was very effective."

Fanny said, "The new girl was very good."

"Not bad," he agreed. "Small."

"She could be better than Caroline Harbison."

"Not better, Fanny, different. She has a different build; she's smaller but voluptuous. And she's much younger. When they're young, they have energy. You can't really tell what's behind it."

Fanny patted her bun, driving loose hairpins back in. "Poor Caroline. Too bad she hurt her ankle. There's something going on there between those two." She pointed at Alexander Ives and Rosalind Child. "It doesn't seem fair, does it? Dancers are so fickle."

"It is only the circumstances. Alexander is a very fine actor."

His wife pursed her lips disapprovingly.

Sumner Loewen capitulated. "I would have said, as you did, that there's no contest. Rosalind's a baby. But you know better, always."

The applause continued around them. Sumner Loewen listened. He never joined it; he wanted to be able to judge the audience and appraise its inarticulate enthusiasm. Later he intended to express more precisely his judgment to the dancers and to Achille Perrot. In some way, by applauding he felt he would be immodest; he would be applauding himself. He had been associated with the Perrot Ballet from the beginning, when Achille Perrot in 1946, new in America, sought him out. That was the story Sumner told: "Achille came to my office and sat himself down and asked me for ten thousand dollars to start a company, and I gave it to him."

The son of a textile merchant, Sumner Loewen had grown up in a household more affluent than cultured. His parents went to the theater and the opera and slept during performances; his father kept a stable of exotic motorcars in Manhattan, including a red Bugatti and a hunter green and gold Hispano-Suiza, and aspired to racehorses.

When he was eleven, after the family's annual appearance at the synagogue on Park Avenue for Yom Kippur, Sumner Loewen announced that he wanted to be a rabbi. His parents took his declaration seriously. His mother was not pleased; she feared that religion would only intensify Sumner's uncompromising and already somewhat self-righteous nature; moreover, she was unsure of what it was that rabbis did, where they were to be seated at dinner parties, what you could talk about in their presence, whom they could appropriately marry.

Sumner's father reacted more rationally. A businessman who understood humanity in terms of supply and demand, product and need, he saw that his son's spiritual needs, which he admitted to his wife he had ignored because he had few himself, were not being met. He also guessed that art could prove as satisfying as religion, and the elder Loewens came to the conclusion that the idea of having an artist for a son appealed to them. They could afford it, certainly. Sumner's father arranged for lessons: music, drawing, elocution. Sumner thrived. His father had him admitted early to a boarding school in Massachusetts; from there the boy went to Princeton and after Princeton, Paris and Berlin—briefly, because of the anti-Semitism there.

When he returned to New York, Sumner Loewen upset his parents again by asking to join his father's business. He explained that he was grateful to them because they had enabled him to learn that although he was talented—at anything you do, his mother interrupted. "But, Mother, only up to a point," Sumner explained sadly; he would never be the best. "You haven't given yourself the time," protested his father. "It would be a waste," Sumner answered. "I am a connoisseur and possibly a businessman." There was no place his parents could send him, no diversion they could invent to change his mind, and his father acquiesced.

Sumner had progressive ideas about how to run the business—communist ideas, his father felt—such as paying workers for vacations and days missed due to illness, but Sumner had become even more uncompromising and articulate and won the arguments. Within a year his father had a heart attack and retired, and the business, burdened with high-minded intentions, foundered, but during the Second World War the firm again prospered. Through an old friend of Sumner's from Princeton, the company obtained a contract to supply fabric for U.S. Army uniforms. After the war, Sumner hired a cousin to handle the day-to-day operation of the business, though he maintained an office to remind himself, he told his friends, who he really was. He bought paintings and sculpture, he invested in a literary quarterly although he did not approve of its contents, he went to concerts and plays, he underwent psychoanalysis, and he searched for an artist or an institution worthy of help.

He married a large, rich, lanky girl from Nebraska who had come to New York to study modern dance, but, more energetic at evening parties than at morning class, she had put her mind to searching for a husband instead. Unlike Sumner, Fanny never cleansed herself of a longing to perform. She called herself a dancer; all her life she kept her blond hair pulled back from her flat, pale Scandinavian face. Brunhilde and Alberich, people said, the Valkyrie and the dwarf. Sumner, with his pink, narrow face and pointed features and diminutive body, looked more womanly than his wife.

Sumner Loewen stood. Around him the audience was already on its feet for Alexander Ives. Tall, slender torso, wide shoulders, skin stretched tight over his breastbone above the neck of his black leotard, dark blue eyes outlined and shadowed in blue—onstage he was abstractly beautiful, not male, not female. Sumner imagined that if he touched his face, Alexander's skin would be dry and chalky like the limestone of an archaic Greek statue.

He recalled the nineteen-year-old boy with large hands and feet who had appeared in Perrot's class. Alexander was not then a good dancer, but Sumner loved him. Now that he was great, now that the audience came as much to see him as to see Perrot's ballets, now that the pleasure Sumner felt watching Alexander dance was as pure as anything he could remember, he was not sure that he loved him. What was it? There was, somehow, less to love, less for him. All he could tell himself was that the way Alexander bowed disturbed him; it was perfunctory, distanced, crabbed. Dangerously, Alexander had lost his desire to please. The audience would not notice. It mattered only to Sumner. Sumner cultivated desire of all kinds; it was what he choreographed.

Sumner scanned the theater, the satiated faces. The ushers had opened the exit doors; in the dark house they glowed incandescent like the mouths of caves. He saw a figure standing in the door nearest him, a tall, thin silhouette—from its shape an adolescent. The figure stepped back into the lobby lights, and he recognized the tight, older angles of Caroline Harbison's cheekbone and jaw. That was all they could do, Sumner thought, dance and watch dancing, and worry when they had to watch.

Achille Perrot came onstage alone; the theater shook with shouts and applause. He was as tall as Alexander Ives, but gaunt; his Sorcerer's costume hung loose on him as if his thighs had shriveled inside the Prince's black tights. He did not bow; he stood facing the audience, his black-shadowed eyes gazing more in confrontation than in acceptance of praise. He raised his arms, trailing wings, in an ambivalent gesture that Sumner read as dismissal, but which elicited more cheers. Perrot stood for a moment; then, as if yielding, he dropped his arms, his wings clattering, bowed abruptly, and disappeared behind the curtain.

The house lights went up. Applause gave way to the rumble of conversation. The audience filed past Sumner. He knew many of them. Ballet was a small neighborhood of New

York. The critic Gertrude Stella approached; her large bulbous face, flesh disguising bones that had once shaped spare and lovely lines, glowed happily. For critics, Perrot was a reprieve, an artist they did not have to judge but could interpret, about whom they could dance words, arabesques of metaphor. Gertrude Stella wrapped Sumner's slender fist in both of her chapped hands. Her ruby ring and red nails twinkled. "It is Achille's masterpiece," she whispered, her bulging blue eyes with yellowed irises searching for corroboration. "I've been waiting for years for him to do *Swan Lake.* I've been telling him for years it must be done."

Sumner smiled. "And now you have it, dear. Thank you so much for your persistence. Enjoy, enjoy."

Having maintained throughout his life a predilection for religion, he looked for contributors to the ballet, whom he considered his flock, his sheep. Some generous sheep gave without being prodded, from a sense of duty; Sumner shepherded the others to where they could smell and nearly touch the dance, where they could feel that they were getting their money's worth. It was like a zoo, like one of those natural habitats designed to create the illusion that one shared territory with impalas and cheetahs, but where the observer remained separated by an almost invisible moat. Sumner Loewen looked especially for Eveline de Charny.

The theater was emptying. Metal seat frames made a pattern of converging black curves against red plush upholstery, like a diagram of parallel lines meeting at some infinitely distant point in space. Sumner Loewen observed Eveline de Charny across the aisle a row behind him. He was an expert on beauty, an objective judge of women, unmoved by them, and he acknowledged that Eveline de Charny was magnificent. She was tall and buxom and large-boned. She stood like a dancer, head erect, spine stretched. She wore a black strapless dress, and the skin of her face and shoulders and décolletage glowed opalescent, as if embedded with refractive crystals. Her opulence was old-fashioned and bountiful and made the contemporary ideal of female spareness appear misguided. Looking at her, Sumner Loewen breathed deeply. She was monumental; she possessed the dignity of a

9

classical marble nude. Indeed, her dress seemed superfluous. Without clothes she would not, Sumner Loewen imagined, degenerate into an object of desire; she was too imposing— she could only be admired. She had told him that she had danced as a child; her father insisted she take ballet lessons. Twenty years later she had become passionate about ballet again and resumed dancing. At this point Sumner Loewen had to assume that it was an exercise in absurdity, but he could not be sure. Eveline de Charny's body seemed infinitely capable. In any event, he tended to forgive the excesses of the rich and to accept their notions of possibility.

She was, Sumner Loewen guessed, the sort of woman who posted a tally sheet and who expected a precise return on her investment, favor for favor, promise for promise. While that might have been a moral failing, it worried Sumner Loewen only because he did not see how it could give him a tactical advantage—she would certainly not feel the obligations she demanded of others. He probed for weakness—need, the longings that proximity to art could fulfill. He used himself as a model. Eveline de Charny was enormously attractive, financially, physically, and by relationship. Sumner Loewen, while cultivating Eveline de Charny, hoped also to encounter her father. Dancing and her father, possibly; those were her weaknesses.

Eveline de Charny's black hair was cropped to expose her long, muscular neck. Large gold disks hid her earlobes, and she wore no precious stones; she did not need them. Her eyes were black, her nose long and slightly arched, her lips wide and precisely red. As the audience left the theater, men and women gazed at her as if they ought to have recognized her; she had the actor's ability to draw attention to herself. She dabbed at one eye carefully with the tip of her forefinger, wiping a tear. Compressing his lips, Sumner smiled at her to show he shared her emotion. He tilted his head toward the front of the theater, toward the red door, upholstered like the wall, that led backstage.

"Take the car," he said to Fanny. "I'll find my own way home."

"I thought we were going to supper, to the party."

"I don't think so."

Defensively, Fanny gathered her mohair scarf about her shoulders. "What happened?"

"You don't want to eat; you told me so." Sumner stared at her sternly. "You told me you'd put on a pound or two."

Fanny shrank. "And what are you going to do?" she asked. Eveline de Charny approached them.

Sumner smiled, and for his wife's sake made his tight mouth seem as if he anticipated swallowing something bitter. He smoothed the edge of her scarf against her neck. "I must discover what makes Eveline de Charny hungry."

Alexander Ives waited for Achille Perrot backstage near the door leading to the dressing rooms. The black velvet curtains that shaped the stage within its cinder-block shell had already been raised. Members of the company milled around, elated. A new ballet, a new success. Dana Coelho, who had danced Hilarion, the Prince's friend, whooped and turned a cartwheel. He was blond and slender, with a boy's innocent face and curly hair, smooth skin, a boy's smooth, luminous body, hardly any beard, no guile. Dana, humming the swan theme out of tune, spun over to Alexander, grasped his waist, and tried to make him dance. Alexander resisted. Dana attempted to lift him like a wrestler, tilting Alexander back against his chest for leverage. Alexander hung limp.

Dana let him go. "Hey, you're no swan; you're a turkey!"

Alexander smiled. "Or a ham."

"A big one. Well"—Dana pretended to pout—"if you won't dance with me, I'll find somebody else, somebody lighter."

The corps de ballet left the stage, swans turned into dancers turned into girls. The girls watched Alexander out of the corners of their painted eyes, to see if he saw them, to see what he thought of them, to see if he was interested in one of them, since Caroline Harbison was injured. The company danced together every day, took class in the same room, rehearsed with one another in the afternoon; these dancers were the moving background, the little girls, the contours of their faces still soft, their bodies, some of them, still strug-

11

gling with baby fat. He differentiated among them as if they were fruits; he picked out the most perfect, the most unblemished, and sometimes he smiled at them, but even perfect Rosalind Child did not talk to him.

He was thirty-three, fifteen or sixteen years older than the newest kids, thirteen years older than Rosalind. He ached—his knees, his back—but he dealt with that; all dancers ached, even the young ones. He had his routines—his massages, therapy sessions, special exercises, whirlpools. But he was tired—tired before he began in the morning, tired during rehearsal, tired at night. It was not a physical exhaustion but a malaise, a dissatisfaction that ate at him and frayed the edges of his concentration as he danced, obeying Perrot, doing steps at his bidding.

Alexander listened in the darkness for Achille Perrot. Perrot, like a man securing his house for the night, remained on the stage after each performance until all the dancers had left and the stagehands had lowered the asbestos fire curtain. It was his custom, and the technical crew gave him his minutes alone. An electrician—Alexander didn't recognize him; he was a substitute, unaware of Perrot's habit—dragged the tripod supporting the heavy chrome night-light into the center of the stage and set it down with a clang. He switched it on, and Achille Perrot started and stared into it, like an animal blinded by a poacher's flashlight.

"Oh, Mr. Perrot!" the electrician exclaimed. "Excuse me. I didn't mean to scare you." He switched off the light.

"Turn it on," Perrot ordered.

"I would have warned you. I didn't know you were here," the electrician apologized.

"I am here. Thank you," said Perrot, his politeness thin over impatience. "Good night." He had put on glasses, black and thick-framed, over his makeup. The black-penciled outlines of his eyes flared over the tops of the frames. Alexander smiled; Perrot looked like a myopic pterodactyl.

The electrician scurried away.

"Perrot," Alexander said.

"So. They liked it," said Perrot.

"It was a big success."

"That gives me no pleasure, or you."

"That's not true," Alexander lied.

"Oh, it is. The applause does not interest you. Sumner says he can see it." Perrot smiled. His voice was high-pitched and breathy, and he spoke English as if it were French, placing equal emphasis on each syllable. "Our pleasure comes from what we know already. We know whether it was good or bad. What do they know?" He gestured at the asbestos curtain. "They are told that I am good, so they applaud. They know I chose Rosalind, so they cheer for her. What do they understand?"

"If the audience hadn't liked it you'd be unhappy."

"Unhappy? Not at all. I would be angry. There were years when they didn't at all like what I did. Now they like everything. Is there a difference in the ballets? No. If anything they are more difficult. They like this one because they know the music. They do not care about the steps. They do not understand." He took off his glasses and rubbed his eyes, smearing black on his fingertips. He shrugged. "Well. Isn't there a celebration we are supposed to attend? With Sumner's sheep? Sheep? They are wolves. They will eat us alive. But I cannot go like a dead tree." The night-light shone on the staples fastening his gauze wings to their struts.

"Perrot?" said Alexander.

The choreographer turned. "Alexandre"—he gave the name its French pronunciation—"you danced well enough, but—"

"You have corrections?"

"Not corrections, precisely. Your steps are perfect. It is not your steps; perhaps I should give you different ones. But you know how you danced. You do not need to hear that from me."

Alexander ignored the implied criticism. "Perrot, I have a ballet."

In the light Achille Perrot's head was a bird's skull, bleached and white, his arched nose a beak.

"I have a ballet," Alexander repeated. "I'm making a ballet."

"You?"

"Me."

"Why?"

"For the same reason you do. Because I hear the steps."

"That is impossible."

Alexander stepped back to the margin of light. "Why? Would you have preferred me not to tell you?"

White greasepaint smudged the neck of Perrot's black leotard. "No. I would have preferred that you not do it. For what?"

"For nothing. For myself. For next season. You have not announced any new ballets for next season."

"I do not have to announce anything."

"Look at it, please. Look at it when I've got it ready."

Perrot's neck was wrinkled and the skin hung loose; he seemed diminished, contracting inside his skin. "I'll look, but I don't understand what you are doing. You dance my ballets. People want to see them; this is where they come for my ballets and for my dancers, not for anything else. And as long as I am capable of making ballets with my dancers, that is what they will see."

"You just told me that you don't care about the audience."

"Certainly they care about me."

Alexander Ives lowered his eyes. "Should I take my ballet somewhere else?"

Perrot smiled. His teeth appeared yellow against his chalk-white makeup. "And continue to dance with me? I think not."

Alexander tossed his head, as if Perrot had looped a leash around his neck. He started to speak, but light rubber-soled footsteps, like the padding of a large cat, stopped him.

Rosalind Child walked with a dancer's duck-toed waddle. She had changed into leggings and an oversized shirt and high-top black sneakers. White streaks of scalp showed through her wet hair, which she had tied back from her face. Her skin gleamed clean and colorless in the hard light. Off-stage, her features lost their classic cast; they were young and tender, not fully formed; her nose was too long, her mouth too wide, her golden brown eyes too far apart, a blotch

14

bloomed on her cheek. In one arm she cradled a bouquet of red roses bound and tied with a red florist's bow; in her other hand she held a single rose. "Oh," she said, and blushed. "I'm sorry. I'm interrupting."

"We were finished," said Perrot. "What is it, my dear?"

Rosalind Child thrust the rose out in front of her like a candle. "I had these and I thought"—she looked from Alexander Ives to Achille Perrot—"I know I didn't deserve them all. Well, you weren't in your dressing room—I mean, neither of you were. I've been looking all over." Her voice—breath wrapped around a thin core of tone—was high as a child's. "Here! Thank you." She handed the rose to Alexander and quickly reached into her bouquet for another, but the flowers were tied too tightly and she could not pull one free. "Oh!" she exclaimed. "Oh, well!" and she handed the entire bunch to Perrot.

"No need, my dear," said Perrot. "I have had too many flowers. And these are your first." He pushed them back to her.

"Please," she said, "please take them."

But Perrot did not; he let them fall from his hands onto the floor, and he turned and disappeared, his wings rustling like winter branches in the wind. Rosalind stooped to pick up the roses. "I did something terrible. Oh, God, he's going to hate me!"

"It had nothing to do with you," said Alexander. He stooped and lifted her and her roses and put his arm around her. He pulled her against him and stroked her small wet head. "Nothing. Nothing at all. Believe me. Monsieur Perrot loves you. He chose you. You're his girl. He'll give you wonderful things to do."

Caroline Harbison and Sumner Loewen and Eveline de Charny arrived together at the upholstered door leading backstage. Caroline reached to open it, but Sumner Loewen slipped ahead of her. He bowed slightly. "My dear, how is your ankle?"

Her mouth widened, part grimace, part smile. "I'll tell you tomorrow night. I'm going to take class tomorrow."

"Isn't it a bit too soon?"

"Maybe, I don't know. I hope not. Of course it is, but what's the choice?"

"You mustn't push," said Sumner Loewen, and introduced Eveline de Charny, pronouncing the name in French, rolling the *r* deep in his throat.

"I'm honored. I've seen you dance many times," said Eveline de Charny. She spoke with a hint of an accent—her vowels back in her throat, consonants precisely articulated.

"Thank you," said Caroline, ill at ease in the front of the theater, where she did not belong.

"Tell me, Caroline," said Sumner Loewen, remembering his wife's prediction. "What did you think of the new girl, Rosalind Child?"

"She danced well, didn't she?" Caroline's face was smooth, her blue eyes clear and impenetrable. When she was nineteen, she had come east to the Perrot Ballet from Ohio, and during the years she had been in New York, Sumner had watched her open midwestern good nature close and harden over. He was relieved and somewhat saddened that it had. Not that Caroline couldn't reopen a bit when she wanted, but with him she was always contained now, always guarded. The dancers were all children when they came to the company; it seemed a pity that dancing toughened their spirits as well as their muscles. "And it's a beautiful ballet," Caroline added, surprising him with a sweet smile that came from a smaller town. "I have to tell Perrot." She opened the door a crack and slid through.

Sumner Loewen wondered if she had smiled because she wanted him to think she was not jealous. All dancers were jealous. He touched Eveline de Charny's arm. "I thought you'd want to meet Caroline. I'm sorry she was somewhat preoccupied."

"Why shouldn't she be? She's an artist. I understand."

Sumner Loewen did not think artists were sacred. They were like anyone else, he thought, although what they were was less well disguised. Sumner did, however, believe that the art they produced was sacred and rare; it was the ultimate alchemy, the basest human elements distilled through an

16

amoral sensibility, a sensibility that utilized experience without mercy.

"Artists are thieves and butchers," Sumner said with his elegant diction as he opened the door for her. "They take whatever they want and hack it up to satisfy their appetites."

Eveline de Charny should have been pleased. Sumner Loewen was outrageous, but not to everybody. This bon mot was a little gift; she would have something to repeat, a token of intimacy. But she did not smile in grateful acknowledgment. Instead, she took it as her due, as if Sumner Loewen, like the dancers, owed her entertainment.

Fluorescent tubes lit the backstage corridor in a green wash. Sumner Loewen took Eveline de Charny's arm and steered her aside as a stagehand wheeled a wooden scaffold past them. The top of the scaffold supported a wooden platform, and the lower level jutted out in back to hold a dingy mattress. The whole thing was painted blue, and one of the uprights was labeled with a black felt-tip pen: Death Leap, Act IV. The stagehand turned to stare at Eveline de Charny; her beauty survived fluorescence.

She read the label. "So that's how the Sorcerer dies."

"This, my dear, is how in real life he does not die." Sumner Loewen smiled. "This is the backside of art."

Eveline de Charny said, "This is a very spiritual thing for me, getting involved with the Perrot Ballet."

"I understand." Sumner Loewen nodded, tempering his irreverent tone. "And we're very grateful."

Dana Coelho, in white jeans, cowboy boots, and a denim jacket, strode by. Sumner Loewen summoned him. Dancers for a dancer. "Dana, come, I'd like you to meet a good friend." Dana grinned at Eveline de Charny; she stared at him, taking in his curls, his pug nose, his bright blue innocent eyes, his slender body; she stared at him avidly, past politeness. Sumner Loewen smiled to himself.

"Dana?" said Eveline de Charny. "You danced what?"

It seemed to Sumner Loewen that Eveline de Charny knew this boy.

"The Prince's friend," Dana said. "I had a couple of jumps, but if you blinked you missed them."

"No. I saw. I didn't recognize you."

Dana Coelho started to speak, but Eveline de Charny interrupted him. "You danced beautifully," she said, and turned away abruptly, cutting him off.

Dana shrugged and rolled his eyes at Sumner Loewen. "See you around," he said, but Eveline de Charny did not answer, and Dana turned and continued down the corridor.

Eveline de Charny's head was slightly bowed, betraying a slight looseness of the skin at her jaw—the first physical imperfection Sumner Loewen had detected. He gave her time to recover from her distress. He marveled at the transparency of her desire; it pleased and amused him. So few people these days dared to take blatant advantage of that prerogative of wealth, the privilege of lust. Eveline de Charny stepped over to a portable barre that stood against the cinderblock rear stage wall like plumbing going nowhere, extended her hand, and placed it on the railing. Sumner Loewen watched her, letting her collect herself. She wobbled, as if disoriented, then lowered her arm and looked at him. "Where are you taking me?"

"To meet Achille Perrot and then to the little celebration we're having for the premiere."

"I don't think I want to meet Perrot now." She spoke rapidly and her accent grew fainter. "I'm not ready, and there's no need, really. Maybe when I've done more. You've been very kind to me, Sumner, but I think I have to go. I've had an exhausting week, so much to do."

Sumner Loewen was taken aback. He might have been mistaken; perhaps Eveline de Charny had qualms and was not yet comfortable with simple lust. She strode toward the red door. Her legs were strong; they were not slender, but they were exquisitely shaped—round calves tapered to narrow ankles. She had a dancer's legs, but when Eveline de Charny was still, they retained their proportions and did not seem outsized like a dancer's. She was too beautiful to be a dancer, too smooth, too solid, Sumner in his distress could not help thinking as he trotted to catch her and soothe her. Yes, that should cancel her displeasure: he would tell her she was more beautiful than a dancer.

2

CAROLINE HARBISON PUSHED THE UPHOLSTERED door closed behind her, severing herself from the audience, from Sumner Loewen and the woman with him. She placed her injured foot deliberately, toe first, then rolled and pressed her sole against the linoleum floor, her dancer's walk. The ligaments in her ankle resisted; she maintained her alignment and ignored the stiffness, timing precisely the action of each muscle as if the injury did not exist. She calculated the pain and judged it incrementally less than it had been that morning. The pain was a real thing, a heap of gravel that had been dumped at her feet—on her foot—and which she had to work to remove inch by inch. The pain deformed her; it blocked her way. It made her ugly.

She believed herself beautiful only when she moved. Caroline was not vain. To dance she had to be beautiful; beauty was an aspect of her character, a moral state.

For a dancer she was tall and so thin it seemed there was

not enough volume inside her skin to accommodate her bones. Veins and ligaments protruded like ropes; she appeared to be translucent, the machinery of her body visible. Her calves were as thick as her thighs. Her skull lay just under the tight skin that stretched over the armature of her jaw, her cheekbones, and the plate of her forehead. Her brow and jaw were broad, her nose short; her mouth was wide, her lips disproportionately thick and sensuous. Up close, her features did not cohere. She needed distance. From a distance, across the space from audience to stage, she was beautiful.

Her eyes, overly large in that face almost without flesh, were a changeable blue-gray like a thundercloud. However, she was by nature steady and consistent, not stormy, and her eyes did not look for trouble. Not that she was placid, although she was reticent, and offstage she hid her emotions. Onstage she used them to dance. She had not danced for six weeks, and she felt as if she were going to go mad.

She blamed herself for the injury. She had been out of shape; the company had just returned from a month off, and during those weeks she had let herself get lazy and had not exercised every day. She had injured herself dancing Odette at the first rehearsal of *Swan Lake*. She had been eager to work on the ballet ever since Achille Perrot had announced the plan to stage it, at the beginning of the previous season. As a child she had grown up on *Swan Lake*, dancing pieces of it each year in her recitals, never dancing the great pas de deux because in Ohio there never was a boy to partner her. The ballet had marked her progress as a dancer, and her mother still kept Caroline's feather headdresses and her tulle skirts and satin bodices, each year a larger size, wrapped in tissue paper in a box in the attic.

At the rehearsal she had been exuberant. She was not given to reveal joy any more readily than anger or grief, but the music, condensed on the rehearsal piano, reminded her of her teacher's ungainly daughter playing it in the church basement. Caroline had waited at the back of the rehearsal room; Perrot was working with the corps de ballet. She remembered the old Russian choreography and loved it. She looked at herself in the mirror along the rear wall with the backs of the other dancers reflected behind her, looked at herself for once without judging, without assessing her body and movement, without thinking how to alter the shape and amplitude of each action, without her detached correcting eye. She looked and remembered herself at thirteen, when she had danced those measures. The music, the harmonies, had reawakened in her the pleasure of infinite potential, like a white arc, the high trajectory of a leap.

The old steps inhabited her bones. She leapt. She knew as her foot touched the floor that the angle was wrong. Her foot slid and her ankle twisted under her with a short crack like the click of a child's rhythm stick. She crumpled. The music stopped; the dancers, resilient children, crowded around her, frightened and intrigued by the possibility of injury. The ankle did not hurt at first, but when Caroline stood, it could not support her weight and she collapsed again.

Guy Pissarro, the Perrot Ballet's tiny dark-haired ballet master, raised her and helped her offstage and treated her ankle with ice until the doctor came and recommended immediate surgery to repair the ligaments and realign the tiny bone she had snapped. She spent the night in the hospital, waking groggy and nauseated from painkillers, to a vast bouquet of pink roses that Achille Perrot had sent. Alexander Ives came to visit her, bringing more roses, and told her that Perrot had replaced her as Odette with Rosalind Child, who had just that season joined the corps de ballet.

Caroline had expected to be replaced; by whom she did not care. After Alexander left she analyzed her reaction as minutely as she had watched her muscles in the mirror. She found traces of anger and bitterness, although she saw that Perrot had no alternative but to find another Swan Queen if the production was to go on as scheduled. Caroline was sure of herself, sure of her dancing, aware of her gift, her grace, and her ability to understand and control that grace. She had never before been injured, and at first the process of rehabilitation, the work of physical reconstruction—the sessions with the therapist, the hours in the whirlpool, the massages,

stretching, strengthening the damaged joint—completely absorbed her. But she was not dancing.

Not dancing corroded her. She had believed herself immune to dancers' fears—jealousy, fat—but inactivity made
her anxious and susceptible to those fears. Before the injury
she had watched Rosalind Child with delight; she observed
the young dancer's energy and reckless spirit with an almost
motherly admiration and had not felt diminished by the new
generation. She saw clearly what Rosalind lacked: resonance,
the experience to understand the space she had to dance in,
and the confidence to take her time in it. Rosalind's innocence was both refreshing and reassuring. Caroline had not
imagined her, or anyone else, a rival, nor had she thought
that she would ever worry about growing fat.

Both notions were stupid, she had thought when she
first came to New York to dance, although almost every
dancer was obsessed with them. If you danced you could not
gain weight because you used too much energy; if you were
jealous you wasted too much energy and could not dance.
Caroline carried east with her a midwestern straightforward-
ness learned from her mother, for whom good and evil were
always overt; what one did revealed who one was. Her
mother believed that people voted with their feet.

After a few months Caroline Harbison, in awe of the
neuroses that daily surfaced in other dancers—in everyone
she met in the city, a city that cherished obstructions, in its
streets, in the mind, and which loved darkness more than
sunlight—had begun to doubt her own reasoning, to worry
that she was lying to herself, to suspect that she was not
clear-sighted but blind.

Her jumps became crabbed; her balance grew precarious. Where she had been confident she became self-
conscious. She stayed after rehearsals to review the steps and
came to the company's studio early in the morning to do a
barre by herself before class. But her joints stiffened; she
suffered from a psychic arthritis. Perrot observed her, and
one morning as she tied her shoes, preparing for her solitary
exercise, he appeared, in black as always, but dressed to
dance, wearing ballet slippers, not the lace-up shoes he usu-

ally wore. In the slippers his feet looked like the knotted roots of an ancient tree, his bunions, boles, round and thick.

The room was as gray as dawn; Caroline had left the lights off. She stood rigid at the barre, the waist-high wooden railing that ran the length of the room. Perrot said nothing. At that time, black streaks remained in his curly hair. He was darker than the room. He crossed the floor and stood in front of Caroline, his back to her, placed his left hand on the rail, and counted slow beats out loud: one, two, three, four. He began the knee bends, the pliés, that started the progression of the barre, the basic steps, the vocabulary, the geometry of ballet.

His voice was soft and melodious, and the count became music. Plié in first position—feet form a straight line, heels touching, knees bend, heels rise off the ground. In second position—feet aligned, heels spaced a foot apart, deep bend, feet remain flat—grand plié. Caroline followed Perrot's feet, arms, the line of his body, and his balance as if she were doing the steps for the first time. Fourth position—feet crossed and parallel to each other, one twelve inches in front of the other, bend. Fifth position—feet crossed and touching, toe to heel, an open triangle between knees and ankles. She felt ease returning, and grace; she felt her joints loosen, the muscles of her back release. Tendu—in each position extend one leg to the front, side, and back. Rond de jambe— the toe traces circles to the front, side, and back, on the floor, and, the leg raised, in the air. She lightened. Perrot never turned to look at her, never glanced at her in the mirror. Passé—lift and bend one leg, the foot, toe pointed, alternately touching the front and the back of the other knee. Relevé—rise on pointe, onto the toes, balance.

When the barre was finished Perrot walked to the center of the floor, bowed, kissed her hand, and said: "*Ma chère* Caroline, you must remember that it is simple. You had forgotten, but dance is a simple thing."

The following morning he had arrived early again, wearing his tie shoes and carrying a geranium blooming red in a clay pot. He placed the plant on the floor in front of Caroline. "This is to remind you," he said. "This is what dancing is like. It is no more complicated than this flower." Caroline still kept the geranium, in more than a decade grown lank and leggy with a thick woody stem. It filled a window in the living room of her apartment. She watered it and fertilized it, but she could not bear to cut it back, and when she spoke to it as the indoor gardening manuals her mother sent advised, Caroline called it Achille.

Several times during the past month she had contemplated throwing the geranium away. She had come to see it as symbolic. What had happened to it was happening to her. Its leaves were flimsy and pale, its flowers sparse. Her inactivity seemed a rehearsal for the time when she would have to stop dancing permanently, when her days would not be filled with the obsessive, comforting repetition of the dance, its incremental approach to perfection of form, its calculus of movement. She could only imagine that time as something distant and awful, as black and incomprehensible as the edges of the universe.

Now, instead of dancing, she watched. When Perrot moved the rehearsals of *Swan Lake* from the studio to the theater, Caroline had filled the time between her sessions of physical therapy sitting in the auditorium watching. She had never watched Achille Perrot make a ballet because she had always been the armature on which Perrot constructed his dance. "Make a ballet"—she liked that phrase, as if the choreographer were a carpenter and the ballet a building: a single room or a house or a palace, a tower, a structure waiting for her to inhabit it.

Perrot worked quickly, the steps composed, chained in his head, ready for the dancers to realize. He rarely spoke; his hands and feet sketched the combinations. From the orchestra the process seemed magical; the silence surprised Caroline. On stage the turmoil of construction had surrounded her: panting, beating feet, music. Now she watched Perrot gesture, nod, incline his body slightly, and the dancers answered. As the shape of the ballet emerged around Alexander Ives and Rosalind Child, Caroline grew jealous. The desire to be onstage congealed in her throat and choked her.

She had not often watched Alexander Ives from the

audience, never for such an extended period of time. Watching him partner Rosalind and adapt himself to her height, her balance, she felt estranged from him, as if she no longer understood his body's meaning. From her new distance, his beauty, the spell of his dancing, unnerved her.

She and Alexander were lovers and had been since the first ballet they had danced together. Alexander did not belong to Caroline; what he chose to give of himself she accepted as a gift, or tried to, and wished for more. He angered her; she despaired of him; three times she had considered leaving the company on his account; she was unable to be interested in anyone else. He existed at the center of a cleared space, raked earth, a no-man's-land, which sometimes, when his blue eyes watched her with mixed desire and sadness, Caroline believed he yearned for her to cross. But always afterward he raked over her footprints. He returned her clothes if she left something at his apartment; if she forgot her toothbrush, she invariably found that he had thrown it away.

She wanted to leave traces. It was not that she wanted to possess Alexander; she could not. She had known that the first time she saw him, when he walked into the company class one morning in February at the start of rehearsals for the spring season and took his place at the barre. He gazed at each member of the company with his large blue eyes, curious eyes, naturally arrogant but fearful as well. Caroline returned his stare, and although he did not flinch and his gaze did not waver, his eyes grew blank, as if he had decided not to see her. Alexander stood apart; that space surrounded him as clearly as if he had marked it in chalk.

In his dancing, however, Alexander was hungry for space and danced as if he wanted to swallow it, erase it, and cross distances. Alexander then had not yet learned how to lift a girl to take advantage of her momentum or how to put her down without dropping her and drilling her toes into the floor. So Caroline did not consider him, and her straightforward soul mistrusted his aloofness. She had to acknowledge his potential: when he jumped he seemed to will himself to remain suspended longer than was possible. When he simply opened an arm, his fingers stretched into emptiness as if he searched for something palpable, yearned to snatch out of air some elusive substance—love—and pull it close to him.

Perrot kept Alexander in the corps de ballet for over a year. Alexander grew frustrated; he knew his ability, but he also knew his rawness and hated it. When Caroline arrived early at the studio to do her solitary barre, a practice she continued, to remind herself to dance simply, Alexander was there, too, sweating, dancing to his portable tape player. They nodded to each other, Alexander turned off his music, and they worked in silence, separate, ignoring each other. Every day before class, Alexander took a shower and changed into fresh rehearsal clothes; only Caroline knew how long he had already been dancing.

One day after class, Perrot told Caroline that he wanted to use her and Alexander in a small ballet, four two-part inventions by Bach. It was a problem he was trying to solve, he said, an experiment, something that might not work; it would probably look too small and would not carry across the proscenium. Perrot begged Caroline's pardon, flattered her, asked her to have patience, to indulge him. She protested that Alexander was not ready; she predicted that his inexperience would lead to an injury—hers, not his. She claimed that she was tired from dancing so many roles. Perrot shrugged.

He rehearsed them late in the day, after the rest of the company had left and before the dancers returned for the evening. They worked on a dim stage in the blackness of the theater—Perrot, Caroline, Alexander, and Harry Menard, the rehearsal pianist. No one came to watch them, and those hours began to seem charged, as if what they were doing was precious and illicit, only for pleasure. They could not get enough of it.

Caroline understood that her reluctance had been a premonition. Aversion and attraction: dancing with Alexander was fatal from the first day, from the first measure. At first she thought their congruence was due to their size. They were perfectly matched; on toe she was still shorter than he. But size alone could not account for the intensity of joy. It made her dizzy. In Alexander's presence her body moved with the sublime certainty of the music's counterpoint. Caroline did not believe in fate; at twenty, not knowing much about it, she hardly believed in love. Fate implied passivity and self-indulgence. Dancing with Alexander left her off balance, exhilarated, longing for him, and afraid and angry that she had lost something of herself.

It had not been so different for Alexander, Caroline saw when he came into the studio for the next rehearsal and looked at her, his blue eyes alternately helpless, ravished, angry. He did not greet her. When they danced, he avoided looking at her face and concentrated on the parts of her body he had to touch. But he touched her without hesitating, intimately, as if his hands were imprinted with her shape, as if in one day he had understood everything about the way she moved.

After the third rehearsal, they made love for the first time. Neither was performing that night, and together they left the theater and walked back to Alexander's bare apartment. They began tentatively; they knew how to make a ballet better than how to make sex. They were especially unsure of how to begin. They stood in the middle of the living room, the bed in sight through the doorway, and did not know how to get there. They did not know how to talk and fill time with words. Later they argued over who had made the first move, who had touched first, who had started their new dance.

They let what they had done show; they could not have hidden it. Harry played the Bach tenderly; he was happy for them, happier than they. They feared consequences from Perrot. He saw what they had become, with an ironic widening of his black eyes behind the black frames of his glasses. He never acknowledged that they were lovers. He withdrew. Perrot was angry with Alexander; he answered Alexander's questions brusquely, even rudely. He turned down Alexander's invitations for coffee or dinner, walked out of the room when he entered. Alexander was bereft.

"He was in love with you," teased Caroline. "You've left him. Leave me and you can have him back."

They saw Perrot only in class and rehearsals and at performances; he did not speak to them about anything other than the business of dance. His resentment, however, was specific and personal; his intentions toward them and dance never wavered. The Bach ballet continued. At their rehearsals the tone of the ballet became more intimate; the counterpoint, lines interweaving, echoed the approaches and retreats of courtship. Perrot, who normally worked quickly, who never hesitated, played with each combination, finding, like a lover, endless possibility and delight in Caroline's body and in Alexander's.

"He's using us," Alexander protested to Caroline one night, in her bed.

"But that's what we're for. We're his dancers."

"He's using our lives."

"He's using that we fit together."

Alexander turned away from her, his back a barrier, refusing to fit.

After *Inventions*, that first ballet, which Perrot decided to perform, and which the critics loved, the choreographer continued to use them together. What offstage they were to each other they perfected onstage, with Perrot's steps, until it became utterly beautiful.

When they danced together, there was no barrier of space or personality or fear. They became—they did not possess—each other. The dance became their romance, an iridescent bubble that held them inside its surface tension. There was no difference between dancing and making love. When both were ended, finished, the effort of each washed off without a trace.

Caroline often felt a fool; sometimes she felt blessed. What held them together was how they knew each other—by touch, by weight, by movement; what they knew, their incongruence of desire, she often thought, should have separated them.

Watching the rehearsals of *Swan Lake*, Caroline saw a shimmering tension surround Alexander and Rosalind Child. She wanted to ignore it and tell herself that she was hallucinating from boredom, but she was not in the habit of lying to herself. And it was true that this tension was not yet erotic. It was more a shared sense of timing, a mutual quickness of reflex: speed and exuberance. Alexander stretched Rosalind, lent her his size, the grandness of his movements. Rosalind, weightless, learned Alexander's tricks of suspension, and she transmitted to him her young energy, simplifying him so that his dancing revealed a new, boyish side. And he gave her the benefit of his intuition, his years with Caroline. Each day they grew surer and more at ease with each other. They grew into partners. The performance had been almost too painful for Caroline to watch.

She concentrated on detecting pain in her ankle. As she passed the large dressing rooms, members of the corps de ballet, showered and changed into their party clothes, acknowledged her with small smiles and quick nods, abbreviated bows. The door to Alexander's dressing room was open, the light on. Caroline looked inside. His street clothes hung on the rack; he had not been back to change. Down the hall, Rosalind's dressing room door was shut. Caroline knocked, no answer. She went in. The room was bare, as if Rosalind knew that she occupied it only temporarily. Her costume, white tights and leotard stained with makeup, lay crumpled in a pile in the middle of the floor. Caroline stared at it, at the darker marks on the legs and around the waist, makeup smeared from Alexander's hands and arms. Evidence of betrayal. Jealousy rose rotten in her throat and she slammed the door.

She ran along the corridor toward the stage, suffering twinges of pain as her right ankle took her weight. She leaned on the chrome bar to unlatch the heavy wide metal door leading backstage. Before she pushed, she hesitated, balancing on indecision.

The door opened toward her, and Caroline stepped back. With a rustle of balsa like dead leaves, Achille Perrot stretched out his winged arm to stop her from colliding with him. Caroline tripped and threw too much weight onto her ankle. She started to yelp and sought to suppress the sound. Perrot caught her and righted her.

"Caroline, *ma chère*, it is still painful?"

"Yes. No. I just tripped. My ankle doesn't hurt."

"I see."

"I'm better. I want to learn Odette."

Perrot nodded, scanning the emptied corridor. Caroline waited for an answer.

His black eyes focused on her. "*Ma chère,* do you think you are ready? Have you done a barre? Are you strong again?"

Caroline gazed back at him. "Try me." Her glance shifted impatiently over his shoulder into the black-curtained space behind the wings.

Perrot stepped in front of her, blocking the door. "Where were you going?"

She did not answer; she could not think of what to tell him. She never spoke to Perrot about Alexander unless it had specifically to do with a ballet. She raised her head and looked again over his shoulder. "Nowhere," she finally said.

"It has been difficult." Behind his glasses, his eyes magnified pity.

"My foot? Not really. The doctor said it's healed faster than he expected. I guess I'm lucky."

"That is not what I meant."

"I hate not dancing."

"Yes. So did I. That is why . . ." He swung his arms and fanned her with his wings. "But that is not what I meant, either." As he spoke he glided forward, backing her into the corridor. He let the door close behind him.

Caroline reached around him for the handle.

"He is not there," said Achille Perrot, raising his threatening bat-wing arm. "Do not look for him there, Caroline."

She did not believe him. The Sorcerer, he blocked her from what she wanted. She flushed with anger and lifted her hand to avert his arm. He caught her wrist. His bony fingers were hot and dry against her skin. She dared not pull away. "Then where is he? Tell me!"

"Let him find you. You know he will. He always does."

Perrot had never before acknowledged that she and Alexander were lovers. His tone was not angry; it was tinged with sympathy. Gently, he released her hand. A black winter tree, Perrot clattered down the hall toward his dressing room, leaving her. She left the stage door closed and waited in front of it, uncertain where to go, waiting to be found.

She was displaced, nowhere. Afraid now that Alexander would find her waiting, she headed out of the theater. Sumner Loewen, looking less dapper than usual, came in through the stage door, letting in with him a chill gust of wet wind. Caroline shivered. Sumner Loewen's pearl white hair, normally combed back from his high forehead smooth as a shell, had splintered over one temple. "It may be spring, but I wouldn't be surprised if it snowed." He smiled, distracted, regathering. "Are you waiting for someone?"

Caroline shook her head. "I don't know."

He nodded sympathetically. "We're in the same boat. Caroline, I must confess, our friend, the lady I introduced you to, left me in the lurch, overwhelmed by her sudden proximity to art. She literally ran away. I tried to chase her, but I'm not very fast." He patted his hair into place. "And poor Fanny went home with a migraine. So I am alone. I would be honored if you would go with me to the party."

"I'm not sure I should. I didn't dance. I don't have anything to do with this."

Sumner smiled, his lips together, the benign, knowing expression he assumed to herd his sheep and steer them toward the pleasures he could provide. "Of course you do. You are in the company. Everyone expects you. And you look so lovely." He took her arm and squeezed her hand in both of his. "My dear, you're cold. You need champagne." He led her to the door and turned to her. "For my part, Caroline dear, I can only say that I wish you had danced this evening."

Caroline Harbison, ashamed that he had assuaged her jealousy, let him lead her into the cold spring night.

3

THE KEY RESISTED THE LOCK. EVELINE DE Charny tried to force it and bent the key. She had told Atalanta to call the locksmith and have it repaired; Atalanta had forgotten. Atalanta often forgot. Eveline de Charny twisted the key again. It broke off in her hand. She hurled it down and it clattered like a coin on the sidewalk. She wanted to fire Atalanta, but she loved her. And Eveline de Charny forgot things, too; every day she forgot to tell her lawyers to complete the arrangements for Atalanta's green card, so every day Atalanta feared deportation to El Salvador. Eveline sympathized with Atalanta; she could understand the difficulty of her situation, the uncertainty. But it was a limit, and as Eveline de Charny needed limits, she imagined that everyone did. Having no green card kept Atalanta faithful, and Atalanta retaliated. Eveline de Charny expected that.

Nevertheless, this was infuriating. She was locked out of her own house. She rang the bell, leaned on it, let it scream.

She should have made the car wait; on the street, even East Seventy-eighth, she felt abandoned and vulnerable. If you were well dressed you were a target. She tightened her cape around her shoulders. Spring had only thawed the surface chill off the wind.

Light came on in the living room and projected a tall shadow grid onto the street. Footsteps, not quick enough, thumped down the stairs. Squat, her slanted black Mayan eyes half-open, ocher skin greasy from sleep, broad feet shoved into broken-heeled running shoes, Atalanta shut off the burglar alarm, released the dead bolt, and opened the door. The bare entrance hall was scarcely large enough for the two of them.

Eveline had been changing her house for several years. When she first bought it, she had workmen tear down its molded plaster ceilings, pry off the garlanded moldings, strip away the elaborate dark walnut paneling, and remove the carved Italian marble mantels—all the opulent Beaux Arts details. Demolition was expensive, but cleansing. She wanted no ornament, she told the many architects who had submitted plans; she wanted her house bare, she said, bare, close to despair. You want it to reflect the world, the architect she had finally chosen told her at his preliminary interview. You want your space to be merciless, but precise in its order. Yes, she agreed, and hired him without asking to see what he intended to do.

He had installed in her living room industrial windows salvaged from a factory in Long Island City that was being converted to condominiums. He had the cast-iron framework sandblasted so that it was a dull aluminum color. When she bought the house it had a formal garden, which was now a lumberyard, the rhododendrons whitened and stiff with concrete dust, the brick terrace pitted and cracked from stockpiling wood and stone. Throughout the house the walls were dead white; the few pieces of furniture, which the architect had designed for the space, were gray upholstered cubes; the carpet was gray; partitions were glass with polished broken edges. The architect had the formal stairway removed and the entrance hall converted into the ballet studio Eveline de Charny needed. The unpretentious entrance, he said, would only increase the drama of the living space upstairs.

Eveline strode into the cramped vestibule and tossed her cashmere cape on the stairs. Atalanta, climbing behind her, retrieved it. "Missy, you have a good time tonight?"

"Atalanta, you forgot to call the locksmith. I broke my key. I nearly froze."

"I do not forget. I call, but he do not come."

"Call again. When did you call? Last week? You can't expect them to remember an appointment for a whole week. They are not mentally equipped to do that. Make them come the day you call."

"I ask him, but he say he can't. His people don't come to work."

"Oh, Atalanta, please. I'm tired of excuses. I need that door fixed." At the top of the stairs Eveline turned and laid her hand on Atalanta's shoulder. "I'm sorry. I'm upset about something else. I did not have a good time."

Atalanta nodded commiseration. "What happened?"

Eveline de Charny's shoulders sagged a fraction, as if the weight of her precisely poised head and its heavy earrings had grown too great for them. "Come with me." She beckoned to Atalanta and crossed the spare living room into the kitchen. The steel counters were cluttered with brokerage statements, invitations, loose photographs, lists, scraps of paper with telephone numbers. The kitchen, as well equipped as a restaurant's, though Eveline de Charny seldom ate in, was not clean. Grime filmed its surfaces. This was her file room, and she did not permit Atalanta to shift the piles of paper.

"Did Ricky come?" she asked.

Atalanta nodded.

"No problems?"

Atalanta shook her head.

"Well?"

Atalanta opened a cupboard and took out a cereal box, opened it, pulled out a small white plastic envelope, and placed it on the circular island in the center of the kitchen.

Eveline de Charny smiled and sat on a stool tucked under the island. "That's a silly place to put it. What if the kids found it in the morning?"

"I knew it not be there in the morning."

Eveline de Charny laughed. "Are we that predictable?"

Atalanta shrugged and climbed a stepladder and reached to the top shelf and took down a smooth black onyx tile and a slender silver straw, which she handed to Eveline de Charny, who fished a leather case out of her evening bag and withdrew a silver razor blade. Atalanta pulled out another stool and settled her haunches onto it and propped her head on her stubby hands with their chipped painted fingernails. She watched as Eveline de Charny poured a portion of the cocaine onto the black tile and carefully chopped it to a fine powder with the razor blade. She divided the powder into two lines and snorted one of the lines with the silver straw. She pushed the onyx tile across the stainless steel counter to Atalanta and gave her the straw.

Eveline de Charny took her earrings off and dropped them on the counter. They clanged like untuned bells. Her face flushed and her eyes opened wider.

"Atalanta, this *Swan Lake* was so beautiful, I can't tell you. It was so simple. It was dancing, simply dancing. I've ordered tickets for the children next Saturday, and I got a ticket for you, too. You can take them. You'll love it; you've never seen anything like it. Genevieve and Louis got to sleep okay?"

Atalanta nodded and furled her brow.

"Don't worry," said Eveline de Charny. "I have a dress you can wear, from a couple of years ago. I'll give it to you in the morning so you have plenty of time to alter it." She reached for Atalanta's wrist and squeezed it.

"So why you not have a good time?"

"I danced in *Swan Lake* when I was a little girl." Eveline's voice, usually husky and somewhat loud, softened around the edges and became intimate.

"I forget that, missy."

"I always knew I could be a dancer. I should have been a dancer. Sumner—Sumner Loewen, you know him; he's called here. He's the Perrot Ballet's patron. Isn't that strange? He likes to be called the patron. He's so old-fashioned and elegant, and he works so hard at it, because, you know, he's Jewish. They work at everything they do, because they're afraid it doesn't come naturally. I love it. He told me tonight that I was more beautiful than a dancer. I don't know what he meant. He thought he was flattering me. I *am* a dancer. For forty-two, I'm not bad. Look."

She hiked up the ribbed silk of her dress and extended her left leg straight out from the stool, toes pointed, calf flexed; the nut of muscle above the inside of the kneecap protruded round and hard. "Feel that!" She placed her hand, her large square hand with long thick fingers and long unpolished oblong nails, on her thigh, on the solid muscle that curved from her knee to her buttock.

"Feel that, Atalanta!" Eveline lifted Atalanta's hand from the counter and pressed it against her leg. Atalanta's palm brushed nylon; her rough finger pads pushed into the hard flesh and caught the stocking's sheer knit, pulling a thread. She withdrew her hand and held it in the air, as if she were bestowing a blessing. "Very strong, missy, very strong!"

Eveline de Charny smiled. She ignored the black snag and lowered her leg. "I studied in Paris when we lived there. Daddy loved my dancing; he used to come and watch me in class. He would just appear and stand outside the door in the corridor so you could hardly see him, like a ghost, but I always knew when he was there. I loved those classes, Atalanta. I worked so hard; you have no idea how hard; you can't imagine." Her lipstick had worn off, and her lips were as pale as her skin; she seemed a statue speaking.

The clock over the cupboards read one-thirty. Atalanta gestured to the empty tile. "Missy, please."

Eveline de Charny shook out another small mound of cocaine.

"Thank you, missy, thank you. You are very nice."

Eveline's words came faster; she spilled yearning. "Once Daddy brought somebody with him. I was ten. I was tall, the tallest girl. 'Don't grow too big for the boys,' my teacher said. 'You are too talented. We will put weights on your head.'

Daddy stayed for the whole class, even though he gets bored easily. My teacher could be a real bitch, but she was like honey with this other guy. He was kind of seedy-looking and dignified at the same time, you know what I mean—like he had no money but tried to look expensive? So this man stares at me and I think, 'Who is he?' But he's with my father, so I stay still. 'She is a dancer,' the man says. 'She has a dancer's feet.' Then they turn around and leave without a word. When they're gone, my teacher says to me, 'That was the director of the Ballet!' Oh, what the director said—that I was a dancer—Atalanta, I can't tell you, it was like a blessing."

"That is very nice, missy." Atalanta had heard the story often and she loved it; it had taken on the quality of a fairy tale, meant to be repeated, awaiting its ending.

"Then, just when I was beginning to be good, when I was fifteen and ready to try out for the Opera Ballet and dance in that beautiful building, on that stage—Atalanta, can you imagine, they told me I would be accepted; I was going to be one of the rats; that's what they call the young girls in the corps de ballet—my father told me they were sending me to boarding school in America. It was my mother's idea, and my father didn't defend me. He knew what I wanted to do, but he didn't help. He said it was time I developed the American side of my character. Can you believe it? I had to stop dancing; I couldn't dance at that dumb school they sent me to."

"Maybe your father knew what was best," said Atalanta.

"For himself." Eveline de Charny lowered her head between her arms. Her fingers combed through her black hair, shooting it up in weary spikes.

Eveline said, "I didn't go to the party after the ballet."

"Why not? You were not invited?"

"Of course I was invited."

"Then why not go?" Atalanta persisted.

"Never mind." Eveline de Charny's voice regained its huskiness and volume. She regarded Atalanta and her eyes narrowed; she was beginning to feel foolish. She pretended to be finished with confiding. "It's none of your business."

"Okay, missy." Atalanta acquiesced. She opened Eveline

de Charny's evening bag and removed a cylindrical rosewood box about two inches high. She unscrewed the carved ebony stopper, tipped out a glass vial from the box, and carefully tamped the rest of the contents of the plastic bag into the vial. She headed for the door. "Good night."

"Wait. Remember that boy who was here the other night? That blond boy? You know, I met him at my father's?"

"Very handsome," said Atalanta, leaning against the door.

"Very spacey." Eveline de Charny stretched. "Sweet, though. He said he was a dancer, but I didn't believe him. Everybody in this town with a good body's a dancer. I thought he was just one of Aline's little friends. One of her knick-knacks."

"I don't like that lady, Aline," said Atalanta. "She a scorpion."

"Oh, she's all right. Daddy has to have somebody in New York." Eveline de Charny spoke possessively, proud of her father's appetite. "It might as well be Aline. At least she's not greedy. And she's a fabulous art dealer, not that she has to be to support herself. Maybe I was pretty out of it that night. Did he leave? I don't even remember what we did. I'll have to ask him. God, how embarrassing. Anyway, Sumner Loewen takes me backstage and we run into this Dana. He really is a dancer. I didn't even recognize him on stage. He was so good. I felt strange, like two parts of my life had crashed together, like the pieces didn't fit. I couldn't cope. Do you think I was overreacting?"

"No, missy."

"I'll call Sumner in the morning and apologize."

"Oh, missy, I forget. Amos Furst call."

"What did he want?"

"He want you to call him. He said he calling back."

"I called him days ago. I forgot what I wanted." Eveline de Charny nodded. "Anybody else?"

"That girl, that girl who paints her hair, Devon, she call, too. I tell her you out of town."

"That's okay," said Eveline de Charny. "I like her. I know you don't like how she looks, but she's really sweet." Atalanta swaddled her like an infant in a blanket of concern. She loved Atalanta. "Anybody else call? Did you forget anybody?"

Atalanta shook her head and then lowered her eyes and raised them sheepishly. "Oh, yes. Your father call."

Eveline de Charny bit her lip. "Oh, Atalanta, I can't trust you with anything, can I? Well, at least you remembered. You're sure, nobody else? Anything about the kids I should know?"

"No, missy."

"What did my father want?"

"He not say."

Eveline de Charny strode through the living room and climbed the steel circular staircase leading to her bedroom. Atalanta followed and stopped at the foot of the stairs. Eveline threw off her dress and her underwear and tossed them over the brushed chrome balustrade. At the landing she turned naked to Atalanta. Her body was white and smooth and of monumental scale: she had large round breasts with dark, sharply defined nipples, strong hips, the volume of muscle exercised so it pumped her skin smooth; her body was as hard as a dancer's body, but fleshed out, voluptuous, the bones, the effort, concealed.

Atalanta studied Eveline de Charny's body. She loved it with a mother's erotic bond, and she envied it; she could see in it no resemblance to herself. She scrutinized that flesh: the long thighs, the perfect triangle of black hair, the flat stomach after two children; she worshiped the perfection while she hoped for flaws. Eveline de Charny loved to let her look. Atalanta's eyes absorbed her and adored her; she flowered under Atalanta's eyes. Atalanta wished her to be nothing but herself; she saw the truth of her and accepted it. Eveline de Charny paid her to do so; this was a relationship on her own terms. After five minutes she turned away. "Atalanta," she called over her shoulder, "don't let the children wake me in the morning. You'll get them off to school, won't you? And when the masseur comes, just tell him to wait. I'm very tired."

When she heard Eveline de Charny lock the door to her room, Atalanta lifted the discarded clothes from the balustrade and carried them back to the living room. She unzipped her uniform, left it on the floor where she stepped out of it, and put on Eveline's evening gown. In the black reflecting factory windows, she admired herself. The dress was a bit long, the bust a shade too loose, the waist tight, nothing that could not be fixed; it was a beautiful dress. Atalanta did not want an old dress. She pulled at the seam under the arm, where the ribbed silk fabric was whitened from Eveline de Charny's deodorant. The thread gave, fraying the fabric slightly as it tore. Atalanta yawned and smiled. With her teeth she worked another five stitches loose. Her lady would throw the dress away; already it belonged to her.

Sumner Loewen stood at the entrance to the private room of the restaurant. He was comfortable in doorways; they set him slightly apart, half-in, half-out of the party, where he could be aware of the currents, the balance, the patterns of social migration. He greeted his sheep, he thanked them for their support; he stood guard to prevent guests from leaving prematurely, before they had had their audience with Achille Perrot, with Alexander Ives, before they had shaken the hands they wanted to touch.

The party had the air of a wedding; there were two generations: the older generation winter-tanned, richly dressed, marginally bored with the food and the company; the younger, the dancers, in their funky finery and glamorous bodies, admiring the elaborate hors d'oeuvres their elders ignored. The dancers occupied the corner near the piano player, who was performing polite jazz. The patrons clustered at the front of the room. From time to time, Sumner Loewen abandoned his position at the door and organized two or three patrons into brief safaris into the dancers' territory. Introductions, limp handshakes—Sumner was always amused that young ballerinas with their wiry forearms pretended to have no grip, only soprano giggles. Like antelopes they lifted their heads on their nervous, graceful necks and searched for an opening to escape.

Achille Perrot hovered in the space between dancers and patrons, separate from everyone, yet everyone was aware of him. He sat on a gilt chair at a small round table, his back against the wall, his long body in black trousers and black silk turtleneck sweater. Perrot looked like a religious ascetic. His thinness, his rigorous posture, his black eyes at once focused and vague; magnified behind his glasses, they widened like the aperture of a camera to notice the smallest material details, then narrowed to locate some private dimension.

Perrot sat apart, isolated with a kind of transcendent self-consciousness. There was a surprising denseness about him. It was startling to come upon him in the flesh. He was a man who existed as an idea, a genius; there was about him a sense of identity imploded, of intense mass. The distance surrounding him seemed critical, the margin of safety; inside it one might be sucked in by his gravity or by his consuming vision.

Guy Pissarro, the company's ballet master, shared Perrot's table, immune to the black force of the choreographer's personality. It was rumored that Guy Pissarro was the illegitimate mulatto grandson of the painter Camille Pissarro. A tiny dark man with a matador's posture, he had come to America with Achille Perrot. He was Sancho Panza to Perrot's Quixote, Leporello to his Don Giovanni. He rehearsed the corps de ballet; he comforted and encouraged the young dancers, his boys and girls; he rededicated them to ballet when Perrot's steps seemed too difficult and when the choreographer's capriciousness, his detachment, his lack of concern for their difficulties, made them doubt themselves and want to terminate their apprenticeship. Guy Pissarro was dedication personified, Perrot's acolyte, secure in his faith; he believed utterly in the nobility of dance and the genius of Perrot. He held in his memory each ballet Achille Perrot had made, and because he provided the only continuity, the only connection to it, it was assumed that he also knew Perrot's past.

Achille Perrot never discussed his life before his arrival in New York in 1946. "There is nothing to tell. I am as you see me. I am ready-made, like your American clothes," he told friends and journalists who asked, "and my history will be my ballets."

Gertrude Stella once challenged him. Perrot was not his

real name, she said. He had taken the name from the legendary nineteenth-century dancer, Jules Joseph Perrot, the partner of Marie Taglioni, and the teacher, lover, and partner of Taglioni's great rival, Carlotta Grisi. Achille Perrot smiled. "Perrot was a choreographer as well, known throughout Europe, who devised all of Grisi's solos in *Giselle*. I chose my name well, don't you agree?"

Gertrude Stella demanded to know his real name. Perrot laughed. "Why is it prohibited to apply one's powers of invention to oneself? I do not understand that. My dear Gertrude, my person, what I look like, my mannerisms—my identity, if you must—I am as much a fabrication as one of my ballets." But Perrot had laughed, and it was one of the few occasions anyone could remember his actually doing so. That laugh in itself assuaged a great deal of Gertrude Stella's disappointment, if not her curiosity.

In the beginning there were stories of imprisonment in a concentration camp, contradictory rumors that he had been a collaborator, reports that he was an illegitimate cousin of the Prince d'Orléans, pretender to the French throne. He kept a black mistress; he preferred Indonesian boys. After some years, curiosity about Achille Perrot began to seem inappropriate, even prurient in connection with a man who had so openly constructed an image of himself, from his name to his black clothes. Clearly, dance consumed him; the rest of life to him was irrelevant—not hidden, simply unimportant, not worth mentioning, a compendium of mundane details. Sumner Loewen reported that Achille Perrot had no life outside of dance, and the city's inbred ballet community, hearing nothing to the contrary, had to take Sumner's protestations as true.

Perrot sat at his table like a lion in a crowded game park. His champagne had gone flat. A waiter brought a fresh glass, which Perrot ignored as he watched the boys and girls. The members of the company, as they danced to the piano player's music, glanced sidelong at Perrot as if expecting corrections, knowing he could not help judging them. The patrons smiled at him as they talked among themselves of buyouts and the Caribbean and the Alps and Rockies and the peaks

and valleys of art and real estate, but none approached him
or attempted to draw him into conversation; without Sumner
Loewen's guidance they did not know what to say.

Sensing that the party had achieved an equilibrium that
no longer required monitoring, Sumner Loewen retired to
Perrot's table. As Sumner took a chair, Guy Pissarro rose,
bowed stiffly like a matador, and retreated. The pianist was
playing Beatles songs, written before many of the dancers
were born. Dana Coelho danced alone, bouncing on his heels
and waving his arms in perfect imitation of the loose, gyrat-
ing style of the sixties. A generation later, it seemed naive.
Dana's blond hair glistened; it was the color of aspen leaves
in the fall, and it rose and fell to the music's beat like leaves
in the wind.

"My new lady was quite taken with Dana," Sumner said.
The waiter brought a glass of champagne, which Sumner
quickly finished. "So taken that she ran away at the sight of
him. Bolted, literally. But she'll be back. We have plenty of
time. I have high hopes."

Achille Perrot's eyes flickered away from Dana to Sumner Loewen. "I am sure," he said. "So."

"The performance went very well. I have to tell you that
I was wrong. Not wrong to have doubts, but wrong to think
you couldn't overcome them. So, you won. What was it that
we bet?"

"I don't remember. And you never pay up." Perrot
shrugged. "And Alexander?"

"What about him?"

"Do you feel Alexander danced well?"

"Well? Of course. But by whose standards? His own?
God's? By my standards, which I admit are those of an am-
ateur, he danced brilliantly. By yours, which are higher than
God's, I gather he did not."

"Sumner, do not make jokes."

"What didn't you like? He was wonderful."

"No. Not wonderful enough. I am going to change his
part."

"The audience was happy."

"The audience would be happy if he stood still."

"What has he done to you, Achille?"

"Nothing at all." Perrot's black eyes magnified in indignation. "He was detached."

"Fanny said it was a pity Caroline was injured. Not for the ballet, but for her own sake." Sumner Loewen glanced toward Alexander Ives and Caroline Harbison, who stood side by side against the opposite wall. "It seems that they have found each other. It could be that Alexander missed dancing with Caroline."

"Caroline misses Alexander," said Perrot. "Alexander does not miss. He does not know what he does." Perrot pursed his lips. "Perhaps I am wrong; perhaps you are; I will see."

"You were dancing. You can't always judge. That's a problem when you dance."

"My dear Sumner, you are persistent. You have to admit I danced well. And still you would rather I didn't, although I don't know why. But your opinions are never completely invalid. I should not dance the Sorcerer. I do not think I will again. I was vain to think I could do it. Not that the steps are beyond me, but I must confess that I used to get vertigo on that scaffold, and I still do, only during performance, not rehearsal. Strange. It has gotten worse. Perhaps it is because I do not wear glasses during performances. In any case, I am too old, and I am afraid to fall."

Sumner saw Perrot's eyes deepen with fear behind the black glasses. He smiled to himself: Perrot the dramatizer, the actor, even in private conversation the consummate mime. "We get brittle as we get older," Sumner said.

"Perhaps. This will make you feel better—I will give the Sorcerer to Dana; he is afraid of nothing, and he is rather beautiful. It will be amusing to give him someone evil." Perrot removed his glasses. His black eyes shrank and sank into his face, a sudden aging.

Sumner Loewen was moved with pity, an emotion that sent a spasm of alarm through his body. Perrot put on his glasses. Enlarged, his eyes were masked again.

"Look at him." Perrot nodded at Dana Coelho, deflecting Sumner Loewen's attention from his own face.

Dana glowed with a need for delight. He flashed from dancer to dancer like a firefly. He chose partners at random, boys or girls. His blondness was luminous, exhausting. He bounded off the dance floor and pulled a boy back on with him. The boy was reluctant, no dancer. New to the company, he was officially Guy Pissarro's assistant, but his duties included public relations. "Our first bureaucrat," Sumner Loewen had called him, not without pleasure at the symbol of organizational growth.

The boy, Walter Mowbray, wore an oversized black jacket, baggy pegged trousers, and red high-top sneakers. His skin was pale, sunless white like an endive; he had flat blue eyes, stripped white hair. He bent his head and, embarrassed, looked at his feet and balked. Dana held his body still and moved his feet carefully so the boy could pick up the pattern. His eyes shot gaiety like sparks from a firecracker. Walter, charmed, forgot awkwardness.

"A sweet boy, Dana," said Sumner Loewen.

"An interesting dancer," said Perrot.

"We have good new dancers," said Sumner, finishing Perrot's champagne. "We have our pick. Such luxury. Remember when we had to take whomever we could get?"

Perrot smiled. "Your poor Fanny had to put most of them on diets. And poor Guy had to teach them what pliés were."

"Do you remember the boy who called them deep knee bends? You know, Achille, you should give the young ones more to do."

Perrot bristled. "Dana is the Sorcerer. And I made that little girl Odette."

"Because you had to."

Rosalind turned slowly in a circle, like a child blessed with exquisite balance and grace, entranced with spinning. She turned in her own pleasure, her eyes half-closed. Alexander Ives watched her, not ardently, Sumner Loewen noticed, but critically, studying her movement. Caroline, beside him, was watching nothing.

It was hard, Sumner Loewen imagined, not to watch Rosalind in her happiness. He was thinking that if he had

had a child he would have wanted a daughter like Rosalind, so small that she could remain a child always. But children were a risk Sumner had preferred not to take; their outcome could be difficult to control. "It will be interesting to see what happens to that Rosalind, how she dances in ten years." Achille Perrot did not answer. He seemed to be gazing at Alexander. "Do you think Fanny will turn out to be right?" Sumner said. "About those two?" He nodded at Alexander Ives and Rosalind Child.

"She is an oracle, Sumner, there is no question. And you and she have raised gossip to the level of art. I do not care. I only care how they dance, and I do not like his detachment; whether caused by love or corns it makes no difference to me."

A short man and a short woman interrupted Rosalind's dance. Sumner Loewen did not recognize them. They did not belong in this room; they were too wide; their wattage was too high. The woman's makeup covered her face like a thick clay slip, and her hair had been dyed too black. Her sequined dress encased her large curves like a glittering carapace, giving her the air of an electrified armadillo. Her companion's tuxedo, which pulled tightly through the waist, shimmered with the iridescent slick of a fabric extruded from hydrocarbons.

Sumner rose to divert the intruders. But Rosalind Child laughed and embraced them and let them envelop her in their eager, hot synthetic shine. Family. An aunt and uncle from Queens. Sumner sat down. Rosalind picked up her bouquet of roses, which had been wilting on a table, thrust it into the woman's arms, then took each by the hand and led them to Alexander.

Watching Rosalind spin, Alexander had been struck by sadness. The girl was not vulnerable; innocence made her impermeable. It seemed to him a quality that would never leave her, a congenital immunity he had never had and which he wished for. He envied that hard innocence; it astonished him. She is who she is, he thought as she approached. Nothing is hidden. He saw the traces of resemblance between her and the couple flanking her, and he marveled: she didn't want to be anybody else.

Rosalind said, "These are my parents. They've just moved from Florida to be near me."

Alexander extended his hand. "Mr. and Mrs. Child, I'm glad to meet you."

Rosalind's father's hand stopped short of Alexander's. His face and neck flushed red. "Surosky," he said. "The name's Surosky." He grinned in embarrassment, his mouth folding creases into his neck and chin, and turned to his daughter. "He doesn't know?"

"I don't know anything," Alexander said. "We don't talk; we just dance."

Rosalind cheerfully nodded in agreement and shrugged. "Perrot made me change my name."

Caroline slid to the left, toward the piano, separating herself from the conversation.

Rosalind's father said, "I had to admit he had something. I'd never heard of a ballerina named Surosky, not that I know anything about ballet. But Rose Mary Surosky? Even I can tell that it sounds wrong. What could we say when Rosie told us? Sure, her boss was right. And you want the best for your kid. You have kids?"

Alexander, abashed, shook his head.

"Well, when you do you'll understand. But I'll tell you, and I swear to God this is the truth, I was glad my mother was already dead so she didn't have to know what her grand-daughter had done to my father's name, and what I let her do." He extended his hand straight out to Alexander. "The name's Surosky," he repeated.

"It's a nice name," said Alexander.

"We just wanted you to know how much we enjoyed watching you dance with our daughter," said Mrs. Surosky. "You really do her justice."

"Mother," groaned Rosalind, "that's a horrible thing to say."

"No," said Alexander. "Thank you. It's a compliment."

The three of them stood awkwardly, beaming at each

other. "I think I know how you chose your name," Alexander said to Rosalind.

"I bet you don't. I named myself after a horse. When I was a little girl I had a book about a horse, and the owner called her Rosalind because when she was a filly she was as high as his heart, and I really liked that."

"Then I was right. That's from Shakespeare," Alexander said. "From *As You Like It*. Rosalind is the heroine, and that's what the hero says when he's asked how tall she is. 'Just as high as my heart.' " He took Rosalind by the shoulders and pulled her toward him until her head rested against his chest. "There. That's exactly as high as you are. It's what I would have named you."

Rosalind giggled and tipped her head up to smile at Alexander. Mrs. Surosky beamed at them both with maternal approval, seeing in Alexander's gesture a happy ending.

Caroline could not help the lurch of anger in her stomach. She loathed her jealousy. She loathed standing still. She swung her shoulders away from the wall and stepped onto the dance floor and placed her hand on Dana Coelho's arm, forcing him to stop. His bright blue eyes narrowed, annoyed at being distracted from Walter Mowbray; then they widened into concern.

"I want to dance," Caroline said.

"You're in the right place." Dana placed his hands on her waist. The pianist had progressed in time five years to "Norwegian Wood," and Dana rocked Caroline to the song's slow beat. She moved gingerly at first, though Dana smiled encouragement and urged her to more complicated steps.

"I'm worried," she protested. "My foot."

"You're fine. Just let go. You look like you need to." Dana's hands transmitted delight. His firefly smile lit her; he whirled her in intricate turns and dips. Her foot hurt, but it was nothing she couldn't bear. The pianist began "Lucy in the Sky with Diamonds."

"My song." Dana laughed. The other dancers gathered in a circle to watch them. The pianist increased the tempo, and Caroline and Dana danced, stamped, flung each other backwards and caught each other, spines rigid, torsos cantilevered out over the floor. Strands of Caroline's hair came loose from her knot and stuck to the perspiration on her forehead. Their mouths were open, for breath and to laugh. When they slowed down and stopped, the company applauded. Dana grabbed her waist and embraced her and whispered, "Do you want something else? I mean, you seem pretty down. I've got it if you want."

"You just gave me what I need." Caroline shook her head and looked over Dana's shoulder and saw that Rosalind and her parents had gone. "I'll be all right. Thanks. Go back to your friend."

"Your foot seems better," Alexander Ives said as Caroline took her place beside him.

"Rose Mary Surosky," she said.

"She wanted to keep it. Perrot said she couldn't join the company if she did."

"Tyrant." She accused Perrot lazily, from habit. "Dance?" she asked.

He shook his head. The energy of these women drained him: Rosalind's because she was impervious to desire, Caroline's because she was not. He watched as Dana, indiscriminate, flashed desire. Alexander responded with desire of his own, a bright pulse, on and off, finished, forgotten.

Caroline felt it. She turned away. Wanting to comfort her, Alexander touched her shoulder. "What is it?"

"Dance?" she repeated.

"Not yet."

She moved away a step.

"Stay."

"I think I should go home. I don't like what I'm doing."

To bring her back he said, "I told Perrot about the ballet."

"What happened?"

" 'You dance my ballets here.' " Alexander's quiet voice had become high-pitched and clipped. " 'People want to see them, not yours. This is where they come for my ballets, and for my dancers, not for anything else! As long as I am capable of making ballets, that is what they will see.' " He imitated Perrot's intonation perfectly; Caroline, despite herself, smiled.

"Well, at least he knows you're doing it. It's a beginning."

"And he said he'd look at it when it's done."

"But that's great!"

"It doesn't mean anything."

"You don't know that. It's the best thing he could have said. Come on, Alexander, dance. It felt so good. I've been still for so long."

"Then you'll be able to rehearse my ballet tomorrow?"

"I hope so. I'll try. I haven't even done a barre yet."

"Well, when will you know?"

Caroline, pent up, burst: "If you're so impatient, why don't you just ask Rosalind to dance my part? You're happy enough with her!"

Her anger, her desire, wounded him. "You don't understand. I made it for you. I'd have to start all over again with her, and I've already lost time waiting for your foot. If you didn't want to do it, why didn't you tell me a month ago?"

Caroline, near tears, said, "That's not what I meant. I do want to do it."

Alexander embraced her, lifted her, and she lightened herself, tightened her muscles to give him her balance. He rested her against his chest, pressed her to him, kept her close. She was higher than Alexander's heart, Caroline noticed, as he brushed her escaped hair back from her face. His familiar hand caressed her, his gesture perfectly tender.

They were being watched: by the patrons, by the dancers, by Perrot and Sumner Loewen. Their love was being watched. Their gestures possessed a musical power and engendered a state of yearning in those who saw them, making witnesses wish they could feel what Alexander and Caroline demonstrated. Sumner Loewen averted his eyes, distressed that he was not immune, and searched for discord.

"Dana, dear, there you are!" The woman's voice had been burned dark from cigarettes. Dana had reclaimed Walter Mowbray and taken him into the corner to show him a step, behind the piano where Walter's legs and self-consciousness were screened. At the sound of her voice Dana stopped still and half twisted in her direction. He held the pose, like a baroque statue.

She leaned her elbows on the piano. "You're in hiding. I was afraid you'd gone. I was so disappointed, and now I don't have to be." She smiled at Walter. "I'm Aline Barbour, a friend of Dana's. You're a friend of his, too, I imagine." Aline Barbour was compacted by age, her head with brittle golden hair like spun sugar too large on top of her tiny body; she had a doll's proportions. She wore a red kimono that fell almost to the floor; its back and sleeves were embroidered with chevrons in turquoise, white, and black. The colors echoed her white-powdered face, peaked black eyebrows, artificially blue eyes, and sharp-edged red mouth. She made a small moue, which contracted her lips into a raspberry, and raised an eyebrow in the direction of Walter Mowbray. She beckoned to Dana across the piano and turned toward the room's entrance without waiting to see if he would follow.

Dana obeyed and left Walter in the corner. Beyond the doorway in the dim light a man waited. He was extremely thin and he had jet hair and white skin, a long, dark mouth with a deeply bowed upper lip, and long slanted black eyes. He stood erect and haughty in his evening dress, as if it were a uniform. As Aline Barbour crossed the room, he smiled, showing widely spaced carnivorous teeth. When she reached him, he took her arm. He scanned the room and saw Dana approach; his eyes narrowed and his bony face resembled a jackal's.

Beside Sumner Loewen, Achille Perrot stiffened like an animal sensing a scavenger.

"That was Roland de Charny," Sumner Loewen said.

"I know that."

"Of course. Everyone does. I didn't see him at the performance. I should ask him to come in. I was not aware he was interested in ballet. Were you? I thought only his daughter—"

Perrot interrupted. "I do not know him. And I do not wish to know anything about him." He turned his back to the door. Sumner Loewen watched Dana pass through the knots of guests, smiling sporadically, his light flashing.

4

A T TEN O'CLOCK IN THE MORNING THE DAY turned suddenly warm. White sunlight thawed the sky and beamed on the schef-fleras and ficus trees the wholesale florists along lower Broadway had carted out onto the sidewalks to air after wintering in-doors. Among pots of daffodils at the entrance to the Perrot Ballet studio and offices, dancers dawdled in the sun before they went inside to class.

Amos Furst leaned against a narrow column of brick beside a store window and watched the dancers. The brick, sun-warm, heated his spine. He tried to slouch, but the danc-ers inhibited him. Slouch, he could hear them say. Slouch? A word they didn't know. What's a slouch? A South American marsupial? He leaned straight like a piece of lumber. He tried to appear nonchalant; he concentrated. The way to do it was to slacken your jaw and dull your eyes, to will them filmed over with dust or with images far more intriguing than what was in front of you. Nothing was. He loved dancers, desired them, their thinness, their self-absorption, their perfect posture. Little narcissistic daffodils, he thought. They glanced at him only to ascertain whether he noticed them.

They wondered who he was. He could look like anything he wanted; like any actor, he had studied his face to control expression: the small muscles at the corners of his eyes and his mouth, in his cheeks and forehead. He had practiced gradations of pleasure, anger, surprise, grief, pity, arrogance, satisfaction, remorse. Muscles for each. Amos Furst's natural expression was melancholy. He had chameleon green eyes, large and eager, and they were not unattractive; his nose was already too big, but he did not see it becoming a problem for another ten years, when it would begin its midlife growth spurt. His day-old beard suggested both passion and insouciance; his body was lean and he had learned grace. Those little girls were trying to decide if he was a dancer. He talked too much to dance.

Eveline de Charny was late. Arriving somewhere first, she believed, put her at a disadvantage. Amos did not know if he liked Eveline de Charny. She fascinated him. He had at first thought her more generous than she was, because of her enthusiasm. She had the habit of getting her way, but she was not smooth. She could be overly earnest, and she felt a bit guilty about her wealth, and that had appealed to Amos Furst. She was flamboyantly inconsistent and dressed her colloquial American speech in a French accent. She refused to introduce him to her children because, she said, she wanted to shield them from impermanence. When he asked her what her husband had been like, she looked puzzled, as if she could not remember. "He was handsome," she finally answered, "really handsome. That's all I cared about, so the kids would be beautiful."

Amos admitted that her body astonished him, although it was not thin. He shrugged his shoulders and narrowed his eyes, implying that he was jaded, that he had had many women. That would be a good piece to do—a stud, a man who attracted women the way garbage lured flies. Feet apart, pelvis forward, a slight southern accent—you expected southern men to be conceited and to have retained the old habit plus the balls to talk about women in bulk. Northern men—Amos Furst, for instance—had been trained not to.

Amos had not lacked for women in his time, though the indiscriminate urge had slackened and recently all but vanished. He had been afraid that he was starting to believe in the idea of love and had experienced intense loneliness, so he tried to think of Eveline de Charny as reassurance. She was at least five years older than he was, but her flesh was firm. Not a pucker, not a dimple in her thighs or buttocks, breasts shaped like those pairs he had practiced drawing in high school, curved scimitars spearing the sky. Enjoy, he told himself. Nothing to lose.

He had met her after a performance. She had come to see him on the second night of his week-long run. He had gotten reviewed; the paper had even published a picture. She came backstage alone and introduced herself. Eveline— he didn't catch her last name; he thought it sounded Irish. She was striking, with her close black eyes and cropped hair; she dressed plainly, but everything about her was fine. He knew that if he touched the fabric of her black dress it would be cashmere and that the leather of her pocketbook would feel like creamed skin. He was going out with friends to celebrate his good review, and Eveline, straightforward and disarming, asked if she could come along.

They walked to a restaurant in Chelsea. Eveline sat and listened to the wisecracks and plans for the future and complaints about money and laughed happily. She did not seem out of place; she seemed, Amos remembered, grateful to be included. When someone asked her what she did, she said that she danced. By early the next morning, although they had barely spoken, Amos Furst, rosy from wine, was quite fond of her. In the vestibule of the restaurant, as he helped her with her coat, which the label identified as cashmere, he asked her if she wanted to go somewhere else, with him alone.

"Where do you live?" she asked.

"Six or seven blocks away."

"Good."

He turned west, toward his apartment.

"Wait," she said, "my car's here."

Amos nodded as if he expected her to have a car. It was a small Mercedes. Her driver got out. She sat in the driver's seat; the driver closed her door and climbed into the back. Amos sat up front beside her and pretended that he was the fourth passenger in a taxi and calmly told Eveline his address. She drove to Amos's apartment. As soon as she stopped, the driver leapt from the car to open her door. He handed her out and sat behind the wheel; she told him he could go home and collect her at ten o'clock the next morning.

She insisted on keeping the lights on when they made love. She enjoyed seeing him admire her body. The next night she invited him to her house and sent her car for him. Amos was disappointed that the chauffeur did not let him drive. He ran his hand along the glass partition separating the stairway from the living room.

"Isn't that marvelous?" Eveline asked.

"Who is your architect?"

She told him.

Amos Furst shook his head. "There was a kid in my sixth-grade class who used to collect pebbles at Jones Beach and polish them in one of those electric tumbling machines; then he tried to pass them off as semiprecious stones. I thought maybe it was the same guy."

Eveline laughed. "You are very funny," she said. They made love again with all the lights on, and afterward she rang a bell and her Salvadoran maid appeared at the bedroom doorway with a tray containing a bottle of wine and fruit and cheese and bread. Eveline jumped naked out of bed and smoothed a space on the coverlet for the tray.

"Atalanta, this is Amos."

Amos clutched a pillow to his midsection and extended his hand to shake, not sure if he was more embarrassed by his own nakedness or Eveline's nakedness in his presence. Atalanta put the tray down, yawned, and wiped her eyes, and shook Amos's hand, studying his face like a mother reading a suitor's intentions toward her daughter. Eveline chattered about her plans for the following day. It was two in the morning.

"You woke her up," Amos said after Atalanta left the room.

Eveline, sitting cross-legged on the bed, dropped bread crumbs on the sheet. "Atalanta loves it. She's curious about my friends." She shrugged. "And anyway, it's what I pay her for."

She gave Amos money. It was a grant, she explained, for his art.

"I don't do art; I do monologues."

After a while, it became clear to Amos that Eveline de Charny did not care if he liked her or not. He continued to see her. "She's funny. She's up for anything. She's rich. She's kind, sometimes. Generous. Powerful—scary, too, you know what I mean? She can have anything she wants. For her it's no big deal. Write the check, pull out the plastic. She never learned to add. No need. And she's gorgeous. She's a good piece—of art or ass, I can't figure out which." He stood in front of his mirror and delivered a monologue to himself. "But what worries me is all this talk about art. This lady is into art. That's what she says: 'I'm into art, into performance.' Maybe she thinks I'm an act—I'm a piece of art, too. She's bad. That's why I see her."

He was only half-joking. Amos Furst did not try to conceal the base aspects of his nature. On the contrary, he studied them as he would a mannerism or a facial expression, but he wished he could contain his corruption within performance. Eveline de Charny was seductive. She would call him, and he would call her back three days later, but he always called, and they always met. This morning she had called earlier than usual and found him at home. He was pleased that she asked him to a rehearsal; it was becoming difficult for him to make love to her always in bright light. He wondered if hidden cameras recorded their encounters. He put himself in the sun, wishing it would bleach his soul.

*   *   *

In the studio, dust on the high windows diffused sunlight into a white scrim. The dancers tossed their satchels with their extra layers of clothing and extra shoes on the floor and stretched at the barre. They wore rehearsal motley: ripped tights, bleached, discolored leotards, bulky leg warmers, oversized sweat shirts with frayed necklines scissored below their collarbones. The girls in the corps de ballet had applied careful makeup, and their painted faces perched on long necks whose taut tendons like guy wires anchored their heads to their shoulders.

Rosalind Child was already at the barre when Caroline Harbison entered the studio a few minutes before noon. Rosalind watched Caroline's eyes; her limbs absorbed Caroline's jealous assessment. Used to jealousy, Rosalind Child applied it as liniment; jealousy loosened her. She arched her back, bending almost to the floor, then straightened and raised one leg and hugged her calf to her ear, leg perpendicular to the floor, preening. She did not understand why Caroline had come to this rehearsal, and she did not care.

"Why is she here? She's not in *Swan Lake*." A girl leaned forward and whispered to Rosalind's back, her breath moist as sweat on Rosalind's neck. "Is she? I thought this was for Dana. Maybe Perrot's putting Caroline in. Maybe you're out. Is that why he called the rehearsal?"

Rosalind, limber, doubled backwards once more, and, wisps of hair brushing the floor, she smiled; upside down her small mouth seemed to frown. "Don't you wish?" she said.

Caroline was ashamed that Rosalind, with her physical intuition, had read her. She dropped her dance bag in the back corner of the room, next to a meager ficus, its leaves white with dust, which had been given to the company by the florist downstairs. She took her accustomed warm-up position at the front of the barre where she could see herself unobstructed in the mirror and where she could blur the other dancers. The younger dancers deferred without openly acknowledging her, though they watched her surreptitiously to observe the extent of her recovery.

Unlike the members of the corps de ballet, Caroline

dressed sparsely for rehearsal, in pink leotard and tights; the only frays showed where she had cut the heels from her tights, revealing the callused skin. The nipples of her tiny breasts showed like twin moles through the thin material of her leotard. Caroline pointed her right foot, circled it, stretched carefully. She frowned at her reflection in the mirror and ran her hand along her inner thigh, assessing her turnout, imagining fat.

Alexander Ives entered the studio. Caroline did not break her concentration; working, they never acknowledged each other. He wore a gray sweat shirt and baggy gray nylon parachute pants with thick white socks over his ballet shoes. When she saw Alexander, Rosalind smiled and her eyes skipped quickly across the surface of the mirror to him. He ignored her. Caroline saw and was reassured, and despite jealousy, she pitied the girl.

At precisely noon, the door opened and Achille Perrot came in. The dancers abandoned their images in the mirror as he gathered their eyes to himself; his spare black-clothed body absorbed energy like sunlight. Harry Menard, the rehearsal pianist, opened his score and his can of Coke. The room quieted; the swishing of feet against the floor and the faint chirp of conversation ceased as the dancers, awaiting entrances, bunched along the walls of the studio as if in the wings of a theater. Dissatisfied, Perrot searched the room.

With a click of metal and the soft clatter of wood, Dana Coelho bounded into the studio. He wore an electric blue spandex bodysuit cut below his breastbone to reveal his golden skin; the contours of his muscles and the pouch of his genitals shimmered as the fluorescent light skimmed the shiny material. Dana held his arms out from his sides, the Sorcerer's balsa wings buckled to them. "I feel like a snow fence," he said loud enough to be heard. "And I hate snow." He stopped in the center of the room, turned to Perrot, waved his arms, and stamped his feet like a flamenco dancer. His wings rattled like castanets. The dancers giggled; even Perrot's mouth stretched across his face for an instant.

Dana stepped to the back of the room, muttering: "If I can't be the Prince, why don't you just let me be a Swan

Princess? I'd love to do that sweet little pas de quatre. It's much more my style." He jumped, knees to the side, one foot landing slightly later than the other, a percussive pas de chat.

"Let's do," said Perrot in his quick, high-pitched voice, calling the rehearsal to order, silencing Dana. The members of the corps tensed, heads poised, but Perrot raised his hand, releasing them. He bent over the pianist's shoulder and leafed through the score. Harry started a passage at the beginning of the second act, where the Prince comes upon the swans. Perrot shook his head. Harry flipped pages to the end of the ballet and played another passage. Perrot nodded and stopped him with a hand on his shoulder.

He gestured to Alexander, a tiny movement, a finger extended in the dancer's direction. Some company members sank to the floor, legs extended in front of them like limp dolls. Slowly Alexander came forward. In silence, Perrot led him through the first entrance; they marked the steps, elbows cocked, wrists limp, their hands dancing as if they were puppets. "Here," Perrot said, "here, I want more jetés." His fingers rose and dipped ten times.

Alexander frowned and danced his hands, counting. "I already do six. I can hardly fit six into the music."

Perrot shrugged. "But here I need ten. You must be desperate from the beginning." He smiled provocatively. "Ten. Otherwise it looks too easy, I think. Let's do." He turned from Alexander and beckoned to Rosalind.

She ran eagerly to the front, her shoes clopping like a filly's hooves. Caroline stepped into the cleared space at the back of the room. Perrot marked steps with Rosalind, leading her through the pas de deux to increase the number of her turns, the pattern of her small steps, her bourrées. Caroline shadowed them, counting, spinning, her lips, pale with concentration, drawn tight against her teeth. Rosalind saw Caroline in the mirror and stumbled and flung her arm awkwardly, a tiny panic that unbalanced her. Without losing the beat, she recovered and gazed intently at Perrot as if exorcising Caroline's reflection.

As Perrot stepped toward Alexander, Rosalind skipped beside him, eager to join the duet, but Perrot shook his head.

"Not yet, my dear. Be patient." Perrot nodded to the pianist and took Alexander's hand. The music began and, taking the part of the Swan Queen, Perrot walked Alexander through the pas de deux. He was as tall as Alexander; dancing a woman's steps he became suddenly languid and pliable. In his black clothes he seemed the shadow of a woman cast by a low light, the hollows of his face androgynous.

At the back of the room, Caroline danced alone, in the mirror a luminous pink edge to Perrot's black form, the substance whose shadow he was dancing. Rosalind did not watch but balanced on pointe, ready to dance, eyes vague, nodding to the music's beat. The pianist stopped. Perrot stepped back, took Rosalind's hand, and led her forward. She minced on her toes. He reached for Alexander's hand and joined it with Rosalind's, as if he were a priest performing a marriage ceremony.

"Now let's do," Perrot said.

"From Rosalind's entrance?" said Alexander.

"From your entrance," said Perrot.

"I can't do ten jumps in here. There isn't enough space. You need a bigger room."

"From your entrance."

Alexander shook his head. Harry Menard slouched on his bench and sipped his Coke. Perrot glared at Alexander, his magnified black eyes like a reptile's, unblinking. He nodded to the pianist.

The music began. Alexander, his shoulders high and tight, strode across the room and launched the jumps, angry explosions. The room filled with his energy. He gasped for air; with each jump, he flung his limbs parallel to the floor. When they contracted, they seemed to shrink space and pull the walls in closer. He leapt for the tenth time, and as he landed, his foot slid out from under him and slammed into the iron cross-brace supporting the piano. The instrument lurched on its casters into the pianist's stomach. His can of Coke wobbled and clattered onto the keys.

Alexander slumped over the piano, his face pressed against the ebony lid. Caroline ran two steps toward him and caught herself.

"That was excellent," said Perrot. "Just what I wanted."

Alexander remained still; his back heaved.

"Can you continue?" Perrot's tone was cordial, satisfied.

"I'm not broken." Alexander straightened. His face was white. Where his head had rested, sweat dampened the piano case.

"Let's do," Perrot said, and surveyed the dancers, "from your entrance, with the corps this time."

"Wait a minute," said Harry. "I can't play with Coke on the keys." He left the room and returned with paper towels and mopped the piano. Alexander pressed his foot, checking for bruises; he tested it with his weight. Perrot ignored him.

The girls flocked to their positions. Alexander, favoring his left foot, crossed the room. The pianist began again. Alexander started his leaps through the swans, but after three jumps he stopped. The music faded; the corps milled in confusion.

"You know I can do the rest," Alexander said, "but not now."

Perrot spoke softly, without concern. "If you cannot do a grand jeté fifty times in rehearsal, you cannot do it once in performance. Now, from the beginning."

Alexander remained in the middle of the floor where he had stopped. The corps had retreated to the sides of the studio. Backs to Alexander, they absorbed themselves in the mirror. Harry the pianist lit a cigarette.

Alexander said, "Then I won't do it." He strode toward the door at the back of the studio. "Get Dana to try."

"Can I?" Dana asked eagerly.

The door opened, and Sumner Loewen nearly collided with Alexander. Both stepped back. Sumner Loewen held the door and ushered Eveline de Charny and Amos Furst into the studio.

"I am sorry to interrupt," said Sumner Loewen. "Please, pretend we are not here."

Eveline de Charny wore a short jersey dress cut close to her body, black stockings, and red shoes with curved heels. As her foot touched the polished wood, her back lengthened and she stretched her neck. She blushed. Sumner Loewen nodded to Perrot and seated Eveline and Amos in folding chairs at the front of the studio in the corner opposite the piano.

Caroline Harbison felt the expensive currents emanating from Eveline de Charny, and the currents of self-consciousness as well. Eveline did not interest her; Caroline understood neither wealth nor the discontent it engendered. But, attuned to movement, she watched Amos sit. He was loose-jointed and gawky, yet controlled, a quality achieved, not a natural state.

Alexander waited at the door, watching Perrot for a cue. The choreographer hated public scenes; he reserved capriciousness for his dancers.

"From your entrance." Perrot relented. "You may mark, if you must."

Alexander took his position. The pianist struck hard the first beat of each measure and pounded the bass line. On the second and third beats he did not play the top line, but smoked and held his cigarette in his right hand. Alexander walked through his steps, moving limply between the ranks of girls, pushing them aside as if bored.

Dana Coelho unstrapped his bat wings and whispered to Perrot. Perrot nodded and shrugged. Dana trotted to the back of the studio, behind the corps de ballet, and began to dance the Prince's part. He jumped, high and accurate in the alignment of his limbs, exuberant.

Alexander glimpsed Dana behind him in the mirror and, like a horse that would race only when challenged, began to dance full out. He leapt and landed and leapt again, searching, longing. The members of the company grew silent and watched. Behind Alexander, Dana's dancing diminished to an exercise in technique.

Rosalind rose on pointe for her entrance; Caroline shadowed her at the back of the studio. "I thought we were marking," Rosalind whispered as she spun toward Alexander.

Alexander shook his head and took Rosalind's hand. She caught his energy, his urgency. Harry flipped his cigarette into his Coke can and entered the music; his playing buoyed the dancers and carried them on its long lines. The images of

Caroline and Dana danced behind Rosalind and Alexander in the mirror.

The tendons in Alexander Ives's arm strained as he balanced Rosalind Child in a bent leg turn. He let her go, they spun apart, and Alexander jumped, a jeté. Amos Furst recoiled, as if a lion had leapt in front of him. Alexander Ives seemed a beautiful creature, beyond gender, in his dancing as powerful as an animal, as desirable, as exposed and defenseless, grand and pitiable. In the mirror, Amos saw that Caroline Harbison kept her eyes on Alexander Ives and measured their distance and her steps to his, as if they were partners.

Rosalind and Alexander twined around each other in the slow cadences of the pas de deux; Caroline and Dana remained apart. Caroline altered her steps to execute them herself and maintain her balance alone. She and Dana hovered in the mirror, detached, abstracted from love.

The Prince and the Swan Queen joined hands; in the mirror Caroline's hand and Dana's hand, separate, floated above theirs. At the end of the pas de deux, Rosalind, her hands arched over her head and held by Alexander, stretched her leg in a high arabesque, then tilted her head and arched her back and raised her bent leg behind her until her toe touched her forehead.

Unsupported, Caroline's body tightened in circles, the tendons in her neck swollen, leg muscles hard blocks under her pink tights, her pink leotard maroon with sweat. Harry sounded the last note; Dana scrambled to the front of the studio for the Sorcerer's entrance.

Achille Perrot restrained him with a hand on his shoulder. Perrot was amused, his eyes narrowed behind his glasses, the creases in their corners magnified by the strong lenses. "That was very nice," he said, extending his arms in an embrace of the air that included all four of his dancers. Rosalind, close to weeping, turned away and rested her elbows against the barre. In the mirror her face was flushed, the perspiration on her cheeks beaded like tears. Her ribs heaved with her breath.

"I am pleased to see that you are feeling better, my dear."

Perrot smiled at Caroline. He inclined his head toward Alexander. "And I am pleased to see that the damage to your foot is not permanent. Now, let's do—"

"Achille," Sumner Loewen interrupted, "a moment, please. I would like you to meet Eveline de Charny."

Behind his glasses, Achille Perrot's black eyes widened with displeasure. His mouth compressed; the skin of his long upper lip whitened. He took her hand, bowed, and kissed the air above it. He peered questioningly at Amos Furst. "And who are you?" he asked.

"A clown, sometimes," Amos Furst answered.

"Not a clown, a performance artist," Eveline de Charny said. "An actor, a wonderful writer, a monologuist."

"Clowns are unhappy people," Perrot said to Amos Furst.

"True. Otherwise, why spend your life trying to laugh?" Amos answered.

Perrot smiled. "Perhaps if I believed in happiness, I would have been a clown."

Amos watched the dancers. Caroline Harbison remained in the rear of the room. Motionless, her body seemed scrawny, her calves outsized. Her forearms were thick, like an adolescent boy's, her feet large and boxy in toe shoes. When she danced she had been transformed. Rosalind Child unwrapped a stick of gum and began to chew. Dancers, Amos thought, were like any kind of illusion; you didn't get too close. But to Amos the dark side was irresistible. The point at which light and darkness intersected interested Amos. That point became the fulcrum of his monologues—the place where dance began, where Caroline Harbison turned beautiful, the place, in Eveline de Charny, where generosity gave way to greed.

"Monsieur Perrot," Eveline de Charny cut in, "thank you so much for letting us be here. It is a privilege. I hope we did not disturb you. It means a great deal to me to see you work with your dancers."

"It is only putting steps together; it is not very amusing."

"Oh, yes, it is, much, much more than amusing," Eveline

de Charny protested. "Watching this process, I feel as if I am entering your mind. You see, I am a dancer, too."

"Yes. Thank you." Achille Perrot bowed abruptly and turned away from her. "We will break for ten minutes," he announced to the dancers, and walked out of the studio.

"Oh, please, Perrot!" Rosalind called, but he ignored her. Her sharp shoulderblades poked from her back like little wing stumps as she rushed from the room after him.

Eveline de Charny glared at Sumner Loewen. "Did I do something wrong? Did I insult him?"

"Oh, Eveline, you know how capricious Achille is. It meant nothing. He has been working too hard, I'm afraid. You must know how difficult things are halfway through the season, a premiere, when everybody is already tired. It's really too much, but nobody can tell him that. You understand, of course, the pressure he creates for himself. I promise you, this summer we will have a quiet dinner, just the three of us. But come, don't worry. Let me introduce you to the dancers. Caroline you've already met. And I think you know Dana."

Eveline de Charny nodded coolly at Dana Coelho, as if she barely recognized him. Sumner Loewen observed that she glanced at Amos, claiming him, using him as a buffer. He backed away a step, denying her claim.

"I am late, I'm afraid. We have to be uptown," Eveline said. "Thank you, Sumner. We'll talk soon. Amos, let's go." She laughed indulgently to mask annoyance. "He wants to stay."

"I'll take you outside," Sumner Loewen said. "Our studios are so strangely connected that you'll never find your way out. Unfortunately we've outgrown our space."

After they left, Alexander put his arm around Caroline's shoulder. "I am pleased to see that you are feeling better, my dear." He imitated Perrot's clipped speech. "And since you are better, will you rehearse this evening?"

"If anybody's interested in me," Dana interrupted petulantly, "I'm busy. I have an appointment at nine."

"An appointment?" Alexander asked.

"I'm meeting somebody."

"Then how is six? Caroline?"

"I'll try."

"Cary, you weren't very nice to Rosalind," Dana scolded.

Caroline shrugged. "I want to learn the part. It had nothing to do with nice. And you weren't too nice to Alexander, either."

"It was your idea, really; you said so." Dana wrapped his arm around Alexander's waist. "You didn't mind, did you? I just wanted to see if I could do those jumps. I checked with Perrot."

"I don't care," said Alexander. "Do whatever you want. The part's yours if Perrot will give it to you. I'll even coach you. Tell him that, why don't you? I'm serious. Tell him I don't care."

Distance, Amos Furst thought, you need distance. Distance makes for beauty. The sky behind a pink twilight haze shone pale turquoise. Amos Furst stood with Eveline de Charny at the tall windows in the living room of her father's apartment. Fifteen stories below, trees in Central Park were leafing; tight-rolled buds like strokes of acid green paint had been daubed on the black network of branches. The apartment was at precisely the correct altitude, not so high that detail was lost. The windows on the south side opened onto a terrace planted with evergreens and dwarf flowering trees with delicate cascading branches hinting at bloom.

Roland de Charny's Chinese manservant refilled the empty champagne glass Amos had hesitated to put down. Every surface in the room was pristine and hard, vulnerable to stain: polished stone, glass, brushed steel. He ran his fingers across a blue-veined tabletop that had been sliced and polished from a rare mineral he could not identify. It was warm to his touch, not mineral cool.

Roland de Charny approached Amos and stood beside him at the window. He wore a navy blue business suit of fine light wool cut to emphasize his attenuated torso, his elegant posture. From behind he seemed a man half his age; frontally, the effect was ambiguous. His skin stretched artfully over his bones. It was etched with tiny lines as fine as those an engraver could incise with the sharpest burin. His large eyes glowed incongruously, like real eyes through the cutouts of a papier-mâché mask. Under his jaw hung a tiny wattle, a hint of age, a concession to time. Roland de Charny stood close to Amos, cutting his daughter out of the conversation.

"What is this blue rock?" Amos asked. "Is it some kind of lapis lazuli?"

"Wood," answered Roland de Charny. "Trompe l'oeil. I had it painted to look like lapis."

"Why bother?"

"Why not? Are you a literal man?"

"In a manner of speaking."

Roland de Charny smiled. "Do you like the view? What does it make you think of?"

"Actually, I was thinking of where I could put my glass. You have a very shiny apartment. Why? What should the view make me think about?"

"People who don't have it always answer money. Artists, especially, as if they disapproved."

"If I don't disapprove will that make me not an artist? It's beautiful. Is that good or bad?" Amos grinned at Roland de Charny and finished his champagne. "But to tell the truth I did think about suspending a wire over the park and walking across it. Any higher than this and I'd be afraid. I have acrophobia."

"I love the idea," said Eveline. "It would make a wonderful monologue. A high wire walker with acrophobia."

"No. Not a monologue. I would like to do it. Get out there."

"Without a safety net?" Roland de Charny raised one eyebrow.

"You would insist on no net, wouldn't you?" asked Amos. "If you subsidized it."

"It would certainly be more amusing without one." Roland de Charny had worked to erase his French accent, yet tiny vectors, marks of French-speaking muscles, radiated from his lips. He drawled his vowels and pronounced the *r* with the front of his mouth, not rolled in the back of his throat. Amos wondered if Eveline acquired her accent to spite her father's attempts at assimilation.

"Amos"—Eveline de Charny reclaimed him—"I want to show you Papa's collection before it gets dark."

A stele stood in a dark corner of the living room. At first in the dim light it appeared Mayan, crusted, intricately carved, but it was mufflers, several dozen rusted car mufflers crushed and welded together. "Daddy says that's to remind him of where he came from," Eveline said. "Exhaust systems."

"I beg your pardon."

"The family business. Exhaust."

"I see."

"Mother's father started it. It's diversified now, of course."

"Of course. Otherwise you'd be bored."

"You're making fun of me."

"Not at all. I admire the alchemy. Carbon monoxide into art. Not to mention into money."

Eveline took his arm and led him to an alcove off the living room. Lights concealed in the molding illuminated paintings of men and boys. Eveline identified them: "These boxing scenes are by George Bellows. This boy swimming is by Thomas Eakins. He got into trouble in Philadelphia in the 1870s for painting nude boys. Now, of course, those paintings are the hardest to find. This little sketch is Picasso."

"I recognize that," said Amos. "An early work."

"Bravo," said Roland de Charny. "It was one of the first things I bought. I didn't really like it; it seemed like a great deal to spend on something so small, but the dealer convinced me that it was worth it. He was right, of course."

Amos followed Eveline and her father into the dining room. Paintings hung in ranks from floor to ceiling. "I've always been drawn to the German Expressionists," said Roland de Charny. "They were exquisitely uncivilized." He pointed to a wall of colored drawings of men in evening dress with rodent faces and mistrustful eyes, women with bloody lips and large breasts and vermilion pubic hair, dead men, and dead dogs. "Grosz," said Roland de Charny.

"Yeah, scary," said Amos.

"Grosz is the artist, Amos," Eveline told him. "George Grosz."

"I know," said Amos.

"Remember the man you bought those from, Daddy?"

Roland de Charny nodded. "You were very small."

"He was pathetic. He smelled."

"These drawings were all he had. I bought them for nothing. It was just after the war. The man had been a friend of Grosz. A Jew. He'd managed to hide in Paris. I wonder how he survived and kept his paintings. Clever."

"He was disgusting."

"I did well." Roland de Charny smiled.

"Anything new, Daddy?"

"A painting and two sculptures, but the sculptures haven't been delivered. I don't know where to put them."

"Send them home."

Roland de Charny pursed his lips; the fine lines whitened. "I'm sure your mother would not approve. They are too obtrusive. They are made with barbed wire—among other things, of course." He addressed Amos: "My wife is much more refined than I am."

Amos nodded. He marveled at Eveline's composure before this plethora of art. It intrigued him that she could be so familiar with it, inured to it. It seemed to him the utmost luxury to possess art such as this. He assumed it was corrupting.

They returned to the living room. From the windows the last of the sun turned the new leaves bronze. Amos thought he could do a piece about an entrepreneurial artist. He would wear thin round horn-rimmed glasses with gold ear pieces. Tousled hair, a slouch and a swagger, vague eyes, breath in the voice, words like "negative" and "superimposition," "iteration." He would say "about" a lot: "I was interested in doing a painting about . . . about the reduction of line into color and vice versa." He would carry a calculator in the pocket of his plaid flannel shirt. He could get inside an artist.

What about a collector? Could he do Roland de Charny? There was not much space to maneuver inside his tight skin. The Chinese manservant announced dinner.

Eveline de Charny and her father talked about people whom Amos did not know, using first names, referring to unexplained scandals. He felt left out. "Eveline took me to the Perrot Ballet rehearsal today," he said.

Roland de Charny gazed at his daughter. "You have given money to Perrot?" he asked.

"Not much."

"How much?"

"A few thousand. It's all I can afford. Actually . . ." She hesitated.

Her father smiled.

Eveline de Charny continued. "Actually, I wanted to talk to you about that. About my trust."

"Have you seen the ballet company's budget?"

"Not yet. I didn't think it would be appropriate to ask."

"Who are its big contributors?"

"I don't know, besides Sumner Loewen."

"What is it planning next season?"

"Papa, the Perrot Ballet isn't a bunch of kids dancing in a church basement. It has a fabulous reputation. It's not going to disappear. And I've only just gotten involved. I don't know much yet. I met Sumner at a party, and we started to talk about dance. He invited me to a performance. It's fantastic."

"Perrot is not young."

"He's not going to die tomorrow, either."

"What do you want from this ballet company?"

Eveline finished her wine. "What do you mean? Nothing."

"Nonsense, my dear girl." Roland de Charny laughed. "You don't have to be modest in front of your friend. He understands these things. You want to control the company. If not, you are wasting your money."

Alexander Ives squatted beside a portable tape recorder on the floor in the rehearsal room. The tape whirred and clicked off. Alexander removed the tape and reversed it. His hair was matted and stuck to his neck and forehead in wet black commas. Caroline Harbison and Dana Coelho, slicked with perspiration, waited in the center of the room. They breathed together, as if still counting for the dance. Caroline felt a surge of fondness for him. The sky through the dusty windows was light blue, fading before it darkened. Dana trotted to the corner and turned on the light. The green fluorescent brightness dimmed their intimacy.

"I hope we're almost done," he said.

Alexander did not reply. He pushed the fast-forward button, played a phrase, then rewound again. "Ready?" he asked.

Caroline flexed her ankle and, frowning, rose on pointe. Dana stepped back three steps. Caroline hummed to herself and bounced. Her hands pranced, one over the other. "Okay." She nodded.

Alexander started the tape. It was an impromptu for piano by Schubert. The music sounded small in the room, mechanically shrunken. Fragments of dances: mood and tempo shifted with each phrase, languorous then frenetic, lyrical then angry. The moods were pale, as if heard through memory—yearning and passion, joy and loss, layered translucently one over the other, condensed—and kept alive—in memory.

Caroline Harbison jumped, a sissone; her feet tracked a parabola. She landed in a brief plié, raised her bent left leg in front of her, and rose on her toes in a long balance. She lowered herself, turned slowly on her heel, and lifted into a long arabesque. Just behind her, Dana followed her slow movements, outlining them with his hands, containing them; he never touched her. From the corner, Alexander began fast turning leaps; he circled Dana and Caroline, twice, three times, spinning in midair. At different tempi, fast and slow, the three dancers circled without touching, searching for each other. Then Caroline and Dana caught Alexander's speed, and the ballet became a maypole without ribbons: quick steps, intricate interweaving patterns.

Caroline began little jumps, miniatures of Alexander's at

his entrance; she changed direction, right, then left. She spun, turn after chained turn, then pirouetted; then whirled in faster chains, her toes drumming, skimming the floor, propelling her.

The music hesitated. Caroline stopped still, arms out. She revolved in one last slow turn, one leg extended, then drew her foot in to her other knee and lowered it along her calf. She contracted and crouched on pointe, her knees bent at right angles, her shoulders curled. The piano cascaded into descending scales. Abruptly Caroline straightened and arched her back, reversing her body's curve. Fiercely she thrust her arms back over her head and stretched her left leg behind her into a high, triumphant arabesque.

The music ended. The tape whirred white noise.

Alexander panted, "No! You're off again. That plié—that crouch—needs four counts. You take too long in the pirouette. Start the arabesque on the first count of the slow measure. Don't anticipate."

"The plié's murder to hold four counts, bunched up on my toes. I've got to get out of it sooner."

"Caroline, try. If you're not with the music it looks muddy. Try; I'll count for you."

Caroline looked doubtful.

"Watch."

Counting, "One, two, three, one, two, three," Alexander walked through Caroline's part. Counting, she bent her body through the combination with him: turns, pirouette, crouch, arabesque. "Okay?" Alexander asked.

"Okay. I see what you mean. But when you scrunch down, you do it on demi-pointe. If I did it that way it would be easy, or if you held me. Try it, Alexander; try it on pointe."

"Lend me your shoes."

"Sure." She knelt to untie the ribbons at her ankles.

Alexander caught her hand. "Wait, Caroline, don't. Try again."

He clapped and counted. Caroline exaggerated the start of each step, planting each one precisely on the beat.

"Right," said Alexander. "Now make it lighter."

Breathing hard, Caroline glared at him.

"Your ankle doesn't hurt, does it?"

"If it did, would you care?" Caroline, legs apart, bent from the waist, hands on her hips, stretching forward as she gazed at herself in the mirror, her eyes empty and mysterious as an animal's eyes. Alexander watched her as he rewound the tape. Caroline counted louder than the music; she spun, crouched, uncurled, and began to arch her back an instant before the tempo change. Alexander and Dana turned in diminishing circles behind her. Her standing leg trembled and she fell off it. "Damn. I can't do this. I have no preparation. There's no way I can get a balance. I need someplace to fudge, or you could at least give me a hand. All this not touching. What are you trying to prove?" The wistful music ran on.

"You know, Cary, you complain a lot." Dana sighed.

"Because there's a lot to complain about." She faced Alexander. "You don't know what you're asking me to do. I'm going to hurt myself all over again trying to do these steps. It's too early to dance on my leg anyway." She pulled the front of her leotard away from her body and blew down her chest and marched in a circle, her hips rocking and her feet turned out.

Alexander confronted her and took her by her shoulders. "You mean," he began gently, "that we're running late, you're bored, your ankle hurts, and I don't appreciate what you're doing for me. You doubt I have any talent for this, and you don't know why I bother to try making a ballet when I have so many ready-made ones to dance in. You wish I'd quit and resign myself to a happy old age soaking my bunions and doing Drosselmeyer in the Boise Ballet's Christmas *Nutcracker*. You want to go home. You want to soak your feet, and you think I owe you an apology. You're right, too. I'm sorry."

"Good," Caroline said, trying not to smile. She slid her heels out of her slippers.

Alexander caught her smile and magnified it, shone it back at her. "And you'll try this once more, won't you?" He turned, swinging his hips, and waddled away, his feet rigid, as if he were walking in toe shoes.

"You—" Caroline laughed.

"You—can always say no."

"No." Caroline tried to pummel him, but he caught her wrists in one hand and held her at arm's length and tickled her ribs.

"You're torturing me!" she shouted.

"I'll draw your bath. I'll massage your legs. I'll bring you supper in bed. And then I'll—"

"Enough. One more time and that's it."

She pulled the backs of her shoes over her heels. The tape machine clicked. Caroline counted. She turned, folded her leg, curled, and blossomed into the arabesque. Her standing foot shook with the strain, but she held her torso in a perfect arch. She tilted forward, her hips the fulcrum, until her knuckles brushed the floor.

"Yes," whispered Alexander, "yes, Caroline, yes."

The tape ran silently. The three dancers caught their breath. In the blue square of twilight that reflected off the floor like last light shining off water, Alexander, satisfied, embraced Caroline and Dana.

"Do not touch the surface," said Roland de Charny as his daughter and Amos Furst attempted to help him unwrap a large canvas. "It is sticky like glue. It is tar, like those pits in Los Angeles where the animals drowned. Disgusting. Jurgen Jaeger is a wonderful artist."

Tenderly he propped the picture against the living room wall. Clots of paint and tar crusted its surface. Scratched into the tar were sketched screaming heads, like the faces of the damned in a medieval Last Judgment. Immense trees, an *allée* to hell, dipped thick branches into the pit.

"I must hang it quickly," Roland de Charny explained. "The surface is intended to attract dust and acquire a patina. The work is not yet complete. It needs several months of dust."

"German dust or American dust?" Amos asked.

"I don't think that it matters."

Amos nodded. "Why do you collect?"

"Do you hunt?"

"Cockroaches."

"Well, then, you might not understand. Collecting is not dissimilar to hunting. I indulge in it for the pleasure of the moment of possession, for the moment it is mine." Roland de Charny smiled at Amos Furst. "Perhaps that was not the answer you wanted. Of course, I enjoy beauty, but beauty is only a commodity. Art is something else; it can be dangerous, as well. And the chase is fascinating."

A bell chimed in the apartment. Aline Barbour entered the living room. Black gauze harem pants draped forgivingly over her full hips; the pant legs were gathered tightly at her ankles to emphasize her small feet in blue high-heeled sandals. She wore a blue satin bolero and a matching blue turban. Her eyes were ringed blue, her mouth tinted orchid.

Roland de Charny kissed Aline Barbour on both cheeks.

"This is a friend of my daughter's," Roland de Charny said, introducing Amos Furst. Behind Aline Barbour stood Dana Coelho. He glowed, lion-colored. He smelled musky, tinged with the scent of flowers. Roland de Charny barely looked at him; he fixed on Aline Barbour's face the way a dancer, while turning, spots a fixed place to avert dizziness. His hand trembled as he reached out to shake Dana's. "And this—" he began.

"We've already met," Amos interrupted, and smiled at Dana.

Dana Coelho took Roland de Charny's hand and felt its tremor. It unsettled him. He thought at first that the older man was angry, but when Roland de Charny's fingers lingered against his palm, Dana felt his impatience, his anticipation. Eveline de Charny shook hands with Dana, too, coolly, and appraised him as if he were a new acquisition. She glanced at her father to ascertain that he understood what she knew, but Roland de Charny was not interested now in concealment. Dana stood awkwardly between Eveline de Charny and her father, unsure of whether they were in collusion.

"So you finally bought a Jurgen Jaeger!" Aline Barbour exclaimed. "A nice messy one. I'm jealous. But you'd better hang it quickly. They improve when they're covered with dust. Did you know that he and that awful dealer of his just broke up? Jurgen caught him with Carlos Castillo, that Cuban painter Duston just signed on. Not only were they in flagrante but Duston spent more on the catalogue for Castillo's show. So Jurgen's left him. I don't know what it's going to do to his prices. You should have waited."

"I haven't paid yet." Roland de Charny smiled. "I have this on approval." He turned to Dana. "My daughter and I were talking about your company at dinner."

Dana shrugged with shyness. "I just came from a rehearsal."

"Still *Swan Lake?*" Eveline asked.

"Oh, no. Nothing really for the company. A ballet of Alexander's. Alexander Ives." Dana smiled at Eveline. "You know."

"You do this for love?" asked Roland de Charny.

Dana shrugged again. "Alexander asked me. I guess so."

With a look that told his daughter and Amos not to follow, Roland took Dana's arm with one hand and Aline Barbour's with the other and led them into the living room. It was an expression Amos wanted to remember. Eveline chose not to understand; Amos held her back. "Who is that woman?" he asked. "She looks like one of those Grosz paintings."

"Aline? She's my father's mistress. They've been together forever. She's very nice. She has money of her own."

"And she buys younger men, too? Your father doesn't mind?"

"She doesn't buy people, Amos. Don't be silly. She knows everybody. I'm surprised you haven't met her. Do you want a brandy?"

"I would like to go," said Amos.

"It's still early," said Eveline de Charny impatiently, and headed toward the living room. Roland de Charny met them at the door and took his daughter's hands. "You must be tired, Eveline dear. I had no idea how late it was." He smiled at Amos Furst. "Come back and look at my collection again, when we both have more time, Mr. Furst. Your high-wire plan amused me." He led them into the hall.

"Wait," said Eveline. "Mother wants to know what my plans are. So I have to know when you are going home."

"She is having that reception, a benefit, for our little festival. I will go to Detroit for that. I may have to be in Japan next week."

"But I have to talk to you," Eveline said. "About the trust."

"Call me." He and Eveline smiled at each other, and he raised an eyebrow in the direction of Amos Furst. Roland and his daughter looked very much alike, with long arched noses and close-set eyes. Eveline carried more flesh, which made her appear ripe and adolescent beside her desiccated father. He kissed her on both cheeks. *"Amuses-toi, ma petite,"* Roland de Charny said, embracing her. "God help you. You are your father's daughter."

5

BLURRED BLACK-AND-WHITE IMAGES DANCED ON a television monitor. The music, turned up loud, was blurred as well, condensed; the orchestra sounded like an electric organ in a skating rink. Achille Perrot, his thighs sharp as pleats in his linen trousers, watched the ghost of a ballet. He leaned forward, perched on the edge of a metal folding chair; his hands echoed the steps. The monitor was in a small room without windows, the company's library, its metal shelves stacked with videotapes, notebooks, scores. In the blue television light, Perrot's face appeared lusterless and artificially pale, as if powdered.

Sumner Loewen opened the door and stood behind Perrot and watched. At first he assumed Perrot had not noticed him, and he was slightly alarmed, but Perrot broke his concentration to nod briefly. Sumner Loewen observed the choreographer closely for evidence of age; the future now seemed to him less particular, less a matter of next season's ballet and more an idea, a new shape, which he, as architect, was obliged to design. After a few moments, he said, "That was a fine ballet, those Strauss waltzes. Quite popular. When was that, Achille? I remember we got a big grant for it."

"It was the first year Alexander danced with me. You can see him." Perrot pointed; the ridged veins and tendons of his long white hand made the flesh seem an eroded landscape.

Sumner recognized the figure of a dark-haired boy in the corps de ballet. In the grainy picture his jaw was softer, the bones of his face less prominent, and his eyes rounder, his large hands outsized for his thin arms. "He was beautiful, wasn't he?" Sumner asked.

Alexander leapt across the screen. The jumps were uneven, their height erratic; the boy's instinct for the music made his technical shortcomings even more intrusive. Achille Perrot smiled sweetly, without irony, gazing at someone he once loved, a child. He pushed the pause button on the remote control; Alexander's image flickered in mid-jump.

"He was very bad at first. Do you remember, Sumner? You watched his audition, I think. Guy Pissarro did not want to take him. Poor Alexander. He wanted to do too much all at once. Triple pirouettes when he could barely hold a balance. That was his problem. I had to be careful, but I taught him. He learned what I wanted him to do."

"This was the first time he did well, and he wasn't perfect. Look at his arms. Hopeless."

Achille Perrot started the tape again. Sumner Loewen sat beside him, and the two men watched the rest of the ballet. Once or twice Perrot shook his head, dissatisfied with the choreography.

"I am thinking of using Webern and Schoenberg's orchestrations of these waltzes," Perrot said. "Perhaps in the fall."

"And you will revive this ballet on the same program? I like that."

"No revival," said Achille Perrot. "I do not believe in resurrection."

Sumner did not argue; it was not his habit to precipitate a confrontation. He noted Perrot's positions and maneuvered around them. The ballet ended; gray snow danced on the screen.

"Achille, we have received a gift of ten thousand dollars from Eveline de Charny. That is just a first installment, she says."

Perrot compressed his lips. "I do not think we should accept it."

Sumner nodded. "As far as you're concerned, every donation is a Trojan horse. Unfortunately, we've already deposited the check. It's too bad that you don't like Eveline; she worships you." His face grew concerned. "But she has questions. She wants to know about our budget, our plans for the future—endowment funds, for instance. Good questions."

"For you, good questions."

"She's thinking about giving a great deal of money. But I can't tell her about the future, our long-range plans, because we have none of those things."

"Long-range planning. Such an American idea, so confident."

"I am confident," Sumner said.

"As am I, but of the past, not the future. And I understand how difficult it is for you to tolerate me." Perrot goaded Sumner Loewen: "I would wish my ballets to die when I do."

"That will be difficult."

"Keeping them alive will be difficult. You cannot preserve space and time. Certainly you cannot preserve bodies. Those Strauss waltzes are dead. If we danced them now they would be completely different." Perrot shut off the monitor. He spoke fiercely, his magnified eyes fixed on Sumner Loewen. "I am too selfish to concern myself with the future. I do not care what happens after my death. I will be gone. I have no school. My method is too idiosyncratic to teach. My dancers learn it by osmosis. I do not believe in monuments. If I did I would have become a sculptor." He looked away for a moment. "But, my dear Sumner"—he pronounced the name as if it were French—"I understand your problem. We must pay the rent. Why cannot you make this lady think that the world will end after our fall season, and convince her to give vast amounts of money to ensure that it is gala?"

Sumner smiled. "I've already told her that we need more space, that our offices and studios are too small for the company and our projected growth."

"So you have not heard me."

"Indeed I have, but Eveline has not."

"Do you remember the first studio we rented, on Forty-third Street? It was large enough."

"But now we are twice as large. Our season is twice as long. Would you still be happy with twelve dancers? You could not have done *Swan Lake.*"

"I would have found a way, you know that." Suddenly Perrot laughed. "Now you will go home and tell Fanny that I am getting senile." He looked at his watch. "Sumner, you will enjoy this, I am sure; it will reinforce your strange hopes for a future. My Alexander has made a ballet which he wants to show me."

"I've heard about it," Sumner Loewen said.

"Oh?"

"We're not big enough yet for secrets. So you're going to watch it. No one seemed sure whether you would or not."

Perrot shrugged. "What is watching? An hour, nothing more. Time. If it will make Alexander happy, I will watch."

"What if he has talent?"

"My dear Sumner, that is his problem, not mine. And who am I to judge?"

Harry Menard rested his cigarette on the rim of his can of Coca-Cola and began to play through the first Schubert impromptu. Alexander, in his gray parachute pants, stood behind him, following the score. Caroline Harbison at the barre stretched through her long, methodical warm-up. Wearing his brilliant blue bodysuit, Dana Coelho spread his legs in a split. Several of the girls in the corps de ballet sat on the floor near the dusty ficus tree, their backs propped against the studio walls, their legs splayed in front of them. Surrounded by a litter of pink ribbons and scissors and thread, they sewed ties to their toe shoes.

"A little faster here," said Alexander, and he leaned over Harry's shoulder and played the passage himself.

81

"Hey! Where'd you learn to do that?" Harry exclaimed. He took a drag of his cigarette. The fingers of his right hand were nicotine yellow. "You're not bad. I've never known a dancer who could play."

"Nijinsky could. He played piano four-hands with Ravel."

"And I thought Nijinsky was an animal."

"He was. Pianists are animals."

"Well, in that case"—Harry smiled—"I have an idea: I'll dance; you play."

"Great. I'm tired of dancing. Move over." Alexander took Harry by the shoulders and pushed him to the bass end of the piano bench.

"Not so fast." Harry laughed and patted his soft paunch. "This animal is in lousy shape." He slid back to the center of the bench. "Tell me, are you sure Perrot's going to show up? How'd you get him not to fire you?"

Alexander shrugged and tapped a cigarette from Harry's pack on the music rack. Harry lit it for him. "He said he'd come. Maybe he won't."

"So what are you going to do with this ballet?"

"Dance it, for starters. Move over."

"Nervous?" Harry asked.

Alexander dropped his cigarette into the Coke can. It hissed. He sat beside Harry and continued to play.

Harry rested his hands across Alexander's, silencing them. "Here he comes. Break a leg, if you know what I mean."

Achille Perrot entered the studio, followed by Sumner Loewen. The girls put down their sewing. Caroline continued stretching.

Dana curled his legs under his body and, twisting slowly, rose from the floor like a cobra from a basket. He grinned and ebulliently greeted Perrot and Sumner Loewen. Alexander nodded to the two men and banged an ominous, resonating chord.

The door opened again, and Rosalind Child tiptoed into the room. Caroline shook her feet like a cat who had stepped in a puddle.

Alexander removed his baggy nylon pants. Underneath he wore black woolen tights and a black leotard. He moved to the center of the room and arched his back, until his arms nearly touched the floor behind him, as unaware of his sex as a panther rolling in the sunlight.

Harry lit another cigarette and turned to Achille Perrot. "Ready?" he asked.

"I cannot tell you." Perrot sat in a folding chair, his back to the mirror. "Today I am the audience."

Alexander nodded to Harry. The first impromptu began with a slow introduction for Caroline alone. She rose on her toes from a plié in exaggerated second position, her feet far apart, into a slow turn with one leg bent and lifted in front of her. As she danced and her limbs stretched, she grew. Her neck lengthened; her arms and legs reproportioned themselves and acquired grace.

The tempo quickened; the bass line ran in eighth notes, and Caroline's turns, interspersed with small, skipping leaps, increased in speed. Her body seemed to shed particles of glitter, a trail of light that traced a luminous memory of the geometry of her steps.

Dana Coelho followed her, dancing the high top line of the music. His leaps were condensed and athletic, a horse circling in a controlled canter. Caroline jumped and landed abruptly, as if offstage. Panting, her breath as loud as the music, she frowned at herself in the mirror and waddled across the back of the studio for her next entrance. With her fingertips she pasted loose strands of hair against her sweating temples. She seemed ungainly again, a bird landed, its wings folded gray, concealing their brilliant colors.

Caroline spun back onstage; she and Dana, approaching and receding, mirrored each other. They never touched. When the slow first theme reappeared and the music modulated to a minor key, Alexander cut between them, leaving a wake, rocking them. Dana and Caroline spun around him like trills, their feet beating, racing to catch the arpeggios. They danced, dream figures, searching for each other through a lake of memory rippled with illusion, where the time was always evening, just before dark.

Gnarled veins, shallow roots, knotted under the translucent skin of Achille Perrot's temples. As if he were singing, his lips parted, loosened, for once, from their ironic twist. He sat erect, hands flat on his sharp thighs. His face, as if remembering its past, took on the tautness and lift of youth. The darkness surrounding his eyes appeared to be a shadow cast by strong light and not discolored flesh.

Sweat ran down Caroline Harbison's back, soaking her leotard in parallel columns along the muscles of her spine. The dancers' smiles in the hot, green-lit room seemed grimaces. Their nostrils flared for air.

In the last manic impromptu, chromatic runs and arpeggios in triplets and sixteenth notes calmed for a beat and hinted at resolution, then rejected it and rushed on, frenzied. Caroline whipped between Alexander and Dana. Her straight leg speared the floor with each spin; she sped into chained turns, her feet stabbing in tiny quick steps. At the end, at the last rushing, descending scale, she crouched and rose in a high, sudden, angular arabesque, her extended leg nearly perpendicular to the floor, her back arched so acutely it seemed on the verge of snapping. The piano sounded the final low D.

"Curtain," gasped Alexander.

"That last business is a bitch," said Caroline with a triumphant smile. She opened her arms to Alexander, but he concentrated on Achille Perrot, expectant, his face flushed, vulnerable as a child's.

Sumner Loewen applauded. The girls in the corps de ballet applauded. Rosalind Child, sitting among them, stretched her arms straight in front of her to clap. Achille Perrot sat, his hands spread on his knees, his face absent, as if he were asleep with his eyes open. Harry found his cigarette, and an inch of ash fluttered to the piano keys.

The choreographer removed his glasses and rubbed the bridge of his nose as if he had just awakened. "So, you would like to know what I think?"

Alexander waited for his answer.

"It is an interesting beginning," said Achille Perrot. "I like that you use three dancers. I like the lack of balance. But the ballet is not simple enough. A natural mistake when you are beginning. You work too hard; there is no chance to rest. It makes me nervous. And worse, it is repetitious."

Alexander frowned and pushed his wet hair off his forehead. His blue eyes, pupils expanded, grew black.

Perrot continued. "The atmosphere does not change. In the last impromptu, you must have the dancers do something together. They must touch."

"That is the point," protested Alexander, "that they do not."

"I understand what you are trying to do. But you must have something. Anything, only a walk, perhaps, all together, holding hands. Yes, I like that." Perrot's hands formed a circle as he talked. "Here, let me show you." He spoke to the pianist. "Ten measures before the end of the last section, before the più presto, as I remember."

"How do you know the music?"

"I made a ballet to it once, years ago."

"I didn't know," murmured Alexander.

"How could you? It's young man's music, don't you think? Let's do." Perrot took Caroline Harbison and Dana Coelho by the hand and walked in a quick circle. They trotted after him. "There," he said, "no steps, only walking. You see?"

Alexander shook his head. The girls from the corps de ballet gathered their paraphernalia and quietly filed out; only Rosalind Child remained in the corner near the dusty ficus.

Perrot spoke patiently. "You cannot remain apart at the end. If not another walk, which I like very much, perhaps you only take hands. Do not use that arabesque; it is too predictable. It is too hard to do, so it is too showy. It begs for applause. You must balance Caroline, finally achieve a balance. You must make a picture we can remember when the curtain comes down."

"It's not impossible to do," Alexander protested. He turned to Caroline, who was sitting on Perrot's chair untying her shoes. "Cary, you can do that last arabesque without any trouble."

Caroline wiggled her toes, red and swollen from dancing. She avoided Alexander's humiliated gaze. "Don't ask me. I'm just the instrument. I do whatever I'm told." She shoved her feet into scuffed ballet slippers and walked out of the studio.

Alexander started to speak, but Perrot interrupted him. "My dear Alexander, you should not dance in your own ballets. You cannot see what is happening. You must make that choice, between dancing and making."

"I don't have any choice, as far as you're concerned," Alexander said. "You danced the Sorcerer."

"That was vanity. And I am not doing it again. And"— Achille Perrot touched Alexander's cheek—"I am not you." His long white fingers with their curved claw nails stroked the dancer's jaw. The gesture was tender and full of yearning. Alexander stood still, submitting. "I am sorry you do not understand," Perrot said. "I am only telling you the truth, nothing else." He dropped his hand and left the room.

Alexander Ives walked to the corner and pulled on his nylon pants.

"I loved it, Alexander." Sumner Loewen patted his shoulder. "Don't be discouraged." He smiled, his teeth long and white in his jaw; in his eyes the future shone as brilliantly as his teeth. "What else could you expect him to say? He is too much a perfectionist not to criticize, and he is too full of himself to admit that he likes anything he didn't do. His ballet to that music was very different. I know him. He liked it; just be patient. He needs time to get used to liking it." Sumner Loewen checked his watch. "Oh, dear, I'm late to meet Fanny. She will be furious. A dedication at the French consulate. What a bore. Have some sympathy." He inclined his head toward the door through which Perrot had exited. "It's difficult to grow old." He scurried from the room on narrow little feet.

Harry Menard closed the score and handed it back to Alexander. He hitched his wrinkled pants higher around his ovoid waist. "Maybe I should have danced. At least he couldn't have gone after you for dancing, too. Oh, well, next time . . . But, listen," he said as he left, "it could have been worse. He didn't have to look at it at all."

Alexander sat on the piano bench. Dana Coelho began to massage his shoulders. Alexander shook his head.

"Sorry," Dana said, and picked up his dance bag and caught the door before it swung closed behind Harry.

Hesitantly, Rosalind Child stepped toward Alexander until she stood beside him, between the piano and the bench. She opened her mouth to speak, but she had no words. She touched Alexander's cheek. It was Perrot's gesture, but its tenderness and desire were uncomplicated by yearning. Rosalind Child did not know impossibility. She drew her fingers along his jawbone and pressed to her chest her fingers wet with his perspiration. Alexander met her eyes, but his own were blank and distracted, elsewhere. Rosalind blinked and gazed at her own eyes, slanted in her face; she loved how they slanted. They were wide and young, steady in the mirror.

6

FROM THE LOW STONE WALL BORDERING HER acre of patio, Fanny Loewen watched her guests move about the lawn in patterns—dancing the choreography of her party. Parties were Fanny Loewen's art. She was, she believed, a consummate practitioner of party-giving. She understood details like the luxurious effect of the thousands of pink roses climbing over the patio wall; that morning she had had her gardener augment with cut flowers the gaps where the bushes had not bloomed sufficiently.

Parties aroused in Fanny Loewen enormous anxiety, frenzy, anger, self-doubt, frustration, and finally, pleasure—reactions similar to those of any producer before an opening. Fanny Loewen's parties, and Fanny Loewen herself, aroused in her husband similar emotions. Years earlier, after their first soiree—and Fanny had, to his embarrassment, called the affair a soiree—Sumner Loewen had engaged a housekeeper who implemented the details of their social gatherings, leaving Fanny the leisure to imagine them. Those elements that were unfeasible the housekeeper simply ignored. Although the housekeeper's presence did not eliminate Fanny's tumult, it did contain it and render it harmless.

At the same time he hired the housekeeper, Sumner Loewen, after a spiritual crisis, decided never to leave his wife. No one could make him happy—this he understood—and it was wasting time to expect happiness from a wife. He came to the conclusion that marriage, although the accommodations one had to make were inconvenient, had more advantages than its alternative. There would be no children. In the first place, children were unpredictable. And Fanny suffered from an excess of bodily fluid. Her kisses were wet; her palms, her face, and the soles of her feet perspired excessively; even those secretions which in abundance some men found irresistible left Sumner Loewen unmoved, if not slightly repulsed. Aside from that, he and Fanny, Sumner decided, were well matched financially, aesthetically, and spiritually—she was an intransigent innocent; he was not. He enjoyed their unlikely physical impression, the juxtaposition of her blond bulk against his rabbinical concavity.

Every year Fanny Loewen's lawn party inaugurated the Perrot Ballet's summer in the Berkshires. It was June, the spring season had just ended; the company was weary and danced-out. Everybody came to the party—the dancers, their friends, staff, favored donors, and, unofficially, some members of the press whom Sumner Loewen rewarded for a season of favorable reviews. Gertrude Stella was always invited. Sumner also asked a small contingent of aspiring balletomanes. These were much valued invitations, and it was understood that one replied to them with a donation. Sumner Loewen had learned early the cachet of exclusivity. One had to be invited to contribute to the Perrot Ballet; one waited to be approached. There was no board. Achille Perrot refused on philosophical grounds to form one, and Sumner Loewen saw no practical reason to diffuse his own authority.

He and his wife had built cottages scattered over their land—they owned several hundred acres—which they lent to the company's dancers for the summer. Their house crowned a hill, and its immense lawns sloped to a lake. Fanny had named the house Arabesque. In keeping with the name, she had added exotic touches to the vast shingled cottage. Over each of the front windows she had applied a mantle of wrought-iron filigree, which, a visitor once remarked, made the place look like a cancerous Mexican pot rack.

To one side, adjacent to the vast patio, she had added an arcade of pointed arches carved from soapstone, which doubled as a rose arbor. Here the roses bloomed in all colors—red, pale orange, yellow, white. Their smell wafted through the rooms, an olfactory siren song. Sumner Loewen hated the roses, not because he thought them gaudy but because their intoxicating smell made him melancholy and reminded him of points in his history when he could have chosen to live otherwise. Not that he regretted his decisions. As he grew older he did not like to remember choice. He preferred to see his life already shaped into an ordered, inevitable work of art; he preferred to forget the raw material.

But this afternoon there was no avoiding the roses, as there was no avoiding Fanny Loewen, wrapped in an iridescent silk robe and a turbaned headdress that played upon the Arabic theme of the house. Her presence occasionally tortured Sumner Loewen, and he endured it the way Indian holy men endured the torture of a bed of nails. It enabled him to achieve a higher state. When her excesses overcame him, he retreated to Achille Perrot's house down the road; it was an austere white New England farmhouse. As a courtesy, Perrot had converted part of the shed into a sanctuary for Sumner Loewen—a white room with plain walls, a bare painted gray floor, a pine bed, a pine writing table, and a dark green Windsor chair.

During the summer, the dancers in the Perrot Ballet were not on salary, but at Arabesque they lived for free. Fanny Loewen supplied food and laundry services. At one point, Sumner Loewen envisioned a summer festival, but Achille Perrot believed that the dancers needed rest, and he did not relish an audience in shorts and sandals looking for easy entertainment to accompany a summer night. Some company members toured in small groups and performed as guests at festivals. Alexander Ives and Caroline Harbison had done this for several years. Freed from the rigor and the arcane repertory of the Perrot Ballet, they danced the roles audiences recognized, in costumes audiences expected. They took with them Perrot's discipline, his insistence upon precision, his self-effacing deference to the shape of the music. They had been asked, together and separately, to assume the directorship of several regional companies, and one or two European institutions had approached Alexander. Together and separately, they had refused, and they limited their tours to no more than two weeks. Always they returned to Arabesque for most of the summer, and this year, because of Caroline's injury, they had canceled their tour altogether.

Sumner and Fanny Loewen had converted a large barn on the estate into a studio. Guy Pissarro conducted voluntary daily classes in the barn so that the dancers could stay in shape. Occasionally Achille Perrot took the class; sometimes he worked with a group of dancers to sketch a ballet or, as he said, to play with music. But summer, for the most part, was for rest. Fanny Loewen's desire to become the mother of all the company flowered. She gave dinners and organized picnics and barn dances. She invited dancers, individually, to lunch or to spend an afternoon antiquing. The dancers, many of them eager for mothers, especially mothers as generous as Fanny could be when she wanted to please, indulged her. They made fun of her, too, but cautiously, sensing that somehow she possessed power, even if it was simply the undervalued power of comic relief.

A string quartet made up of young musicians participating in a nearby summer festival played amid the roses in the cloister. A quarter of a mile away, in a gazebo the Loewens had built on the lawn, a dance band played. The small late afternoon breeze mixed sounds in delicate cacophony. The breeze also mixed seasons: the cold green smell of spring, the dryness of summer; it was a day on the cusp. The air smelled of time passing.

Costumed in harem pants as eunuchs and houris, barefoot aspiring dancers served champagne and passed hors d'oeuvres. They came from summer schools former Perrot dancers had established nearby, satellites orbiting the Perrot

Ballet. Aware of the presence of the choreographer, these boys and girls danced their jobs. They glided on their high-arched, bunioned feet, deferential, attentive to even the youngest members of the corps de ballet.

Most of the guests wore white. Fanny Loewen liked them to; she liked the contrast of white against the green lawn, the gentle blend of white with the pastel roses, the surprise of a white skirt against a spray of red blossoms. She watched the party. She imagined how people saw her—bountiful, grand, fabulous in her robe, blue shading to purple and red, her blond braid hanging down her back like a golden spine. She felt their admiration. Below, on the lawn, she watched her husband shepherd his guests, laugh, and listen and initiate conversations. Fanny Loewen felt her own isolation, the isolation of a creator.

She had reached the point where she was happy to watch her parties. She had set the stage. Now the themes of the drama emerged. She could not have spoken now; at this point chatter eluded her. Words fluttered at the edge of her brain. Words were as hard to catch as butterflies and as substantial, yet Fanny Loewen saw with clarity the shape of things. She saw into the future. It was a quality of hers, a power, the source, she knew, of her solitude.

Fanny Loewen watched Eveline de Charny cross the terrace, followed by Amos Furst. It was not difficult to guess what favors they exchanged, but nonetheless they were an unlikely pair. They were staying at Arabesque for the weekend. Sumner Loewen had invited them; Fanny had not. But she would have invited Amos Furst. She liked him; she recognized him; she had begun to read his name in reviews. He was making a reputation; he was a find. She liked his looks.

Fanny Loewen did not like Eveline de Charny; it was a visceral reaction to her posture, her orange dress clashing with the roses, her eyes, which craved attention. Eveline aroused in Fanny physical anger; Fanny begrudged the air she displaced. Maddeningly, Eveline de Charny seemed to want nothing from Fanny—in fact, seemed hardly to notice her. Fanny Loewen drained the last of her glass of champagne spiked with vodka. She saw too clearly; in Eveline de

Charny she saw herself and her fierce, thwarted desire to dance. It tortured her when she turned her vision inward, when, without meaning to, she shone a flashlight into her own eyes and saw into her own mind with helpless clairvoyance. Fanny Loewen had complained to her husband about Eveline, but he had insisted on inviting her.

Eveline de Charny, Fanny understood, had bought a house nearby in order to remain close to the Perrot Ballet during the summer. She had rushed renovations—her contractor was working on Sundays—but she would not be able to move in until the following week. Eveline de Charny, taller than the dancers and fleshier, made her entrance and paused, with brilliant instinct, at the top of the wide steps leading from the terrace to the lawn, at precisely the point where Fanny Loewen always stopped to make her own entrance.

Sumner Loewen opened his arms in greeting and led Eveline de Charny from group to group, introducing her to the painters, the writers, and the artists, understanding that she would feel demeaned if he took her to mingle with other patrons. Eveline de Charny strolled beside Sumner, placing her feet like a dancer, flexing and stretching the muscles in her bare calves, and she bent her head with its boy's hair to hear him talk. Fanny Loewen could hear him, too, without hearing him. She could see the bon mots bursting like pink bubble gum from his mouth.

Behind them Amos Furst was excluded from their exchange, yet he appeared happy enough. He had worn a white suit and a straw boater. To her surprise, Fanny Loewen saw him leap into the air and click his heels.

As always, the dancers congregated apart from the rest of the guests. They were lighter than the others; they wore fewer clothes, translucent layers that lifted in the wind. Gravity seemed to affect them less than it did other human beings. Watching them, Fanny Loewen began to feel the weight of age on her body as if it were strapped to her waist, unbalancing her, rendering her slow and ungainly. She held aloft her empty glass. A blond eunuch, instructed in her concoction, appeared with another.

Caroline Harbison arrived with Alexander Ives. She had pinned an innocent pink rose to her smooth knot of hair, and she moved with the ageless freshness of a dancer, with a dancer's permanent eagerness. Fanny Loewen tracked the pair as they walked across the lawn with their matched gait, their quick steps. Their feet hated to touch the ground. They moved like horses in a field, anticipating the direction and speed of the other. At the far edge of the lawn, Fanny Loewen noticed Rosalind Child; she stood on her toes and stretched her neck as if sniffing the wind for Alexander's scent. And Fanny Loewen saw Alexander Ives, his black hair refracting sunlight like a dark prism, search for Rosalind, sensing her before he saw her. Fanny Loewen smiled to herself, but not without regret. There could be no drama without injury, she thought; that would be farce. Pleased with her perception, she forgave Alexander.

Near Rosalind Child, Fanny Loewen saw Dana Coelho laughing and dancing, circling a boy with spiked black hair. The boy wore an oversize short-sleeved yellow shirt cut like a pajama top. It was printed with large green and red parrots clinging to vines that climbed the length of the shirt. Fanny Loewen could not place the boy, although she knew she should be able to. Sumner had wanted to invite him, she knew that. His identity flitted like a butterfly until she lunged and caught it. Of course. He was Walter Mowbray. But he had changed his hair; it had been white when she met him. Sumner had Guy Pissarro hire him. The company needed a director of publicity. Achille Perrot had been opposed on principle, but had been too involved with *Swan Lake* to object when it happened. Where *was* Achille? Fanny Loewen wondered with an irrational flash of anxiety. She had seen him earlier, dressed in his summer black, large and dark, riding the party's currents like a hawk, hovering in the shadows.

Achille Perrot had a cold. For a week it had besieged him with aching. It woke him at night, soaked him in sweat. A summer cold; Perrot's discomfort exacerbated his usual aloofness. He knew Sumner Loewen expected him, at a certain point, to greet Eveline de Charny and to say the obligatory pleasant words, but he felt a profound and intense desire to avoid her, as if he and she were two magnets with the same pole facing.

He retreated to the house, upstairs to Sumner Loewen's library. Its little balcony, railed in elaborate wrought iron, overlooked the lawn and the lake below. He watched the gathering through the balcony's open French doors. He lounged in the doorway, his hands in his pockets, his thin lips hinting at amusement, his bearing nonchalant, but he was feeling intense emotions. They exhausted him; he blamed his cold. He lacked the stamina for them.

He marked Alexander Ives's entrance with Caroline, as had Fanny Loewen; he watched Alexander catch sight of Rosalind Child. He followed Alexander, loving him, wishing to possess him, wishing to punish him for his arrogance, and hating him for assuming that his suggestions for changes were an attempt to possess. It was not simply that; he was unable to erase Alexander's ballet from his mind. He was as angry with its mistakes as with its promise. He was furious that Alexander had blinded himself to those mistakes by dancing. Alexander wanted everything at once.

It was Alexander's American need for innocence, Perrot mused, his American mistrust of experience, his American perception of the past as a treacherous pit, a trap. Americans, who wanted no past, were afraid to learn from it. But that was the unifying national premise; every American had escaped from a past. Perrot had, too, but not before he understood it, not before he measured the pit.

So Alexander would never be good. This infuriated Achille Perrot and soothed him. He was no teacher; he did not believe that his art could be transmitted, and he had had no desire to do so, until that afternoon weeks earlier when Alexander showed him his ballet.

Achille Perrot watched Alexander circle the grounds with Caroline. Perrot's love for the boy—no, Alexander was no boy, but grace, even in a dancer, rarely survived as it had in Alexander's body—his love for the boy made him tremble. Achille Perrot reassured himself; it was not love that made him shake. Recently he had felt cold, a chill deeper than influenza. It emanated from his bones. Perrot laughed at himself, remembering Rosalind Child in his arms during the first performance of *Swan Lake*. She had been cool and moist; she had smelled of talcum powder and pungent young sweat. She was heavier than girls used to be. No, he was weaker. He had confessed to Sumner Loewen his vertigo; he had not confessed his weakness. And his love, his trembling, was another symptom of weakness.

Carrying her young body offstage, he had felt himself to be the personification of death, an emaciated apparition from a Renaissance woodcut. Achille Perrot shook. Like death, he desired somebody young and warm, not from loneliness—he was not afraid—but from anger. He watched his dancers with a jealous yearning that froze his heart. He watched Dana Coelho bound like a puppy around that new boy Sumner Loewen had hired, that young monkey in his parrot shirt.

Achille Perrot considered himself. Under his black clothes there were creases in the flesh beneath his breasts; his skin gathered like crinkled cotton now in what had been the plump folds of his elbows and armpits. The joints of his knees swelled larger than the muscles of his thighs. Achille Perrot smelled the gagging staleness of age under the scent of the roses. Yet he imagined love as beautifully as ever; he imagined his body in the sweet postures of love; he trembled.

He watched as Eveline de Charny and Sumner stopped and greeted Alexander and Caroline. Their heads swiveled, scanning the grounds, the terrace, the house, with the exaggerated vivacity of people who do not wish to be talking to each other. Eveline separated from the others and moved on. Eventually, Achille Perrot thought, he would have to allow himself to be found.

Dana Coelho had taught Walter Mowbray to dance and to shed the shyness that made him clumsy. Dana had misunderstood Walter's flamboyance, which at first beguiled him— his bright clothes, the constantly varying hair color. He had thought Walter was a party boy, a fast good time. But Walter's loud clothes concealed a quiet soul. He lived in New

Jersey with his mother. He owned a parrot; when his older sister got married, she insisted that her new husband get rid of his bird, and Walter was the only person whom they could persuade to take it. At the end of the season, Walter brought the parrot into Manhattan to show it to Dana. Walter cooed over it, urged it gently to speak and to whistle; he had taught it passages from *Swan Lake.* Walter's gentleness intrigued Dana; that Walter had nothing to offer in return for Dana's body but affection enchanted him.

But he was not sufficiently enchanted to forget Roland de Charny. Dana saw Eveline de Charny approach, striding like a Percheron across the lawn, her muscles working under her smooth skin. He saw her as her father's accomplice, a female manifestation of her father's desire. He did not remember what they had done at her house or what combination of substances they had taken for inspiration. That both Roland de Charny and his daughter wanted him shamed him and intrigued him. Desire acted like another drug on Dana. He overlooked the old man's desiccated brown body, its tight potbelly protruding like a tumor. For beauty, Dana had Walter.

Being desired made Dana high; it lifted him from himself. He could not resist it, and he despised himself for it. In the brief periods when he was alone, when he was not rehearsing or sleeping or engaged in lovemaking, Dana Coelho almost suffocated with a despair that blasted him like heat from a subway grating. The despair filthied his system. He had come home from an evening with Roland de Charny and vomited. He kept his shame hidden; it was his secret. He feared that it was his truth.

He and Eveline de Charny embraced briefly and each kissed the air over the other's cheek. Dana vaguely remembered the heft of her sturdy flesh and felt a frisson of guilt. Eveline de Charny took Dana's hand, and they strolled together toward the back of the house, where pink-tinged clusters of tiny parachutes, the flowering mountain laurel bushes, echoed the deeper pink of the terrace roses.

Eveline talked of dancing, of the intoxicating pleasure of

the physical discipline. "You stayed that night, didn't you?" she said suddenly, turning to him and resting her hand on his shoulder.

"Yes, I think so," Dana said, and shivered as her fingers stroked his collarbone and grazed the skin at the base of his neck inside his shirt. "Don't you remember?"

"I wasn't sure."

She pressed his arm against her side, and Dana felt the familiar dizziness coming over him, the blood rush of response, the beginnings of the free fall. He commenced the mechanical gestures of pleasure, the small signs of acquiescence. His fingers brushed her bare thigh; he leaned closer to her so she could smell his body's freshness, so that she could more easily caress his resilient skin. He saw the small wrinkles at the corners of her eyes.

Eveline de Charny smiled. Dana saw that under their thin enamel her molars showed metallic blue from fillings. "I was foggy after that night," she said. "I was wasted. You said you were a dancer, and I didn't believe you. Nothing personal, but you never believe anybody at first. It was a coincidence to run into you backstage."

"Where are you staying?" Dana asked, his mind still on the mechanics.

"Here." Eveline de Charny laughed and pointed up the hill to the main house. "I hear you're going to Detroit to dance in my mother's festival. My father asked you?"

Dana nodded, embarrassed. "Do you mind?"

Eveline laughed, not understanding. "I couldn't care less. You'll love it. I brought something for you." She reached into the small pouch whose strap she had slung across her chest, between her breasts, defining the perfect aggressive shape of each one.

She pulled a small engraved silver box from the pouch. Dana opened it, exposing a finely worked gilt grate enclosing white cocaine. "It's the best you can get." Eveline de Charny smiled. "It's a present, no strings. Enjoy it. And put it away. Sumner is coming to take me to Achille. Go back to your friend. I'll see you after the festival. I'll be here."

*　　*　　*

Sumner Loewen admired Eveline de Charny. He enjoyed her carriage, the costly simplicity of her clothes. Her ample, glorious body astonished him. She reminded him of his wife before he married her, before they began the work of eroding each other into bizarre shapes like sandstone pillars in the desert. Sumner Loewen approached each of his patrons as if they were works of art. He suspended judgment and made every effort to believe about them what they wanted to project. In that way, his admiration was always sincere.

He observed that Eveline had recovered from her awkwardness with Dana Coelho. Dana's capacity for pleasure concerned Sumner Loewen somewhat, but it was that capacity which informed his dancing, which gave it energy and impulsion. Dancing was not safe. Art, for that matter, was not safe. It claimed its casualties, but so did the stock market, so did a life on an assembly line. The casualties of art were often spectacular, but often the victims left behind something of beauty. Its risks were not Sumner Loewen's concern. Dana Coelho was developing Eveline's connection to the company. "I want to know artists," she had told Sumner. "I am an artist." He was relieved that at least one dancer was willing to oblige.

"I am sorry to tear you away from Dana," he said as she approached.

"He's sweet, isn't he?" Eveline smiled.

"I worry about him sometimes. Actually Fanny does. He never stops."

"Dana? He just likes to have a good time. And he's got so much energy."

Eveline de Charny did not want to leave the part of the lawn where the dancers had congregated. Sumner let her lead. She stalked the dancers, her eyes on them while she talked, measuring their bodies. "Do you know," she said, "that I weigh the same today as I did twenty-five years ago, when I studied at the school of the Paris Ballet?" She rose on her toes, an automatic motion, as if unaware of what she was doing. Possibly she was. "I danced with the corps in one performance."

Sumner wondered to himself how much it had cost her father to place her in the corps de ballet. Certainly she had been striking; it would have been all the more important for her to dance well; she would have been noticed. Perhaps she had talent. He wanted to believe her, but about dance, despite himself, he maintained his objectivity.

"You must have had a very happy childhood," Sumner said. "You must have been close to your father."

"As close as it was possible to be. My parents were always traveling. They rarely spent time—what do they say now?—hanging out."

"How unfortunate for you. I can imagine you must have missed them. But life is never what we want it to be, especially when we are children. We always want more, but finally we make the best of it, don't you think? You are close now?"

"Yes, yes, of course we are." Eveline spoke quickly, rushing the words. She gestured with her hands and executed little dance steps while they walked, as if she were motorized. "We see each other as often as we can, my father and I. He's wonderful."

"Tell me about him. Tell me about your parents," Sumner said.

Eveline looked at him suspiciously, but Sumner's smooth, cared-for face, his large interested eyes, his aquiline nose, and his long teeth above his short pointed chin—every feature seemed to focus on her. "Families," Sumner said softly, "families fascinate me. Maybe because I do not yet understand mine."

"My mother is a saint," she said, "and my father in his way is a saint, too. They both believe in art, Sumner; I know it sounds strange, but it is the truth about them. They believe in art; it's their refuge. They believe in its healing powers, in its spirituality. It's their religion. They taught me to believe the same thing. It was a gift; I'm grateful to them. I don't know if I can ever do for art what my parents have done—especially my mother. I would like to. She has been very generous, in a creative way. For instance, she has a festival, the Arbroath Festival—she founded it and runs it herself—at home in Michigan."

"Yes, I know about it. One of the best. Small, first quality. I've often wished we could do something like that here. . . . Perhaps . . . with your know-how . . . Your parents are unusual in their harmony; they have done these things out of shared passion."

"They are like you and your wife," Eveline responded.

Sumner looked away, across the lawn to the gleaming sliver of lake. "We do appear that way," he said with a regretful smile. "We make an effort to appear that way. But it is an effort."

Eveline regarded him with her black, close-set eyes. "Why are you asking me about my parents?"

"I admire you," Sumner countered. "And because I admire you, I want to know everything about you. I wish you would bring your children. And your friend, Amos Furst, tell me about him. Oh, my dear, I nearly forgot to tell you—I saw your father at our party after *Swan Lake*. I didn't know he was interested in ballet."

"My father?" Eveline de Charny's arched black brows met when she frowned. "Believe me when I tell you that I don't think you want to get involved with my father."

Alexander Ives and Caroline Harbison stood together under a huge beech tree. The tree's leaves were still translucent; they had not yet hardened into summer's tarnished copper opacity. A cleared space surrounded the two dancers. The sun, shining through a gap in the branches, lit Alexander's face like a spotlight, shadowing his bones, his cheeks and jaw, the long line of his nose, the full curve of his lower lip. The sun's angle gave Caroline her stage beauty, the elegant slope of neck into shoulder; it enlarged her eyes. They both wore white for Fanny Loewen, somehow a white more absolute than what the other dancers wore; subtly differentiated, they were the preeminent dancers, and they had made their entrance.

Even the costumed waiters hesitated to approach and offer them champagne. As if he were the Prince, they waited for Alexander to summon them. When he did, a girl hurried toward them, gazing timidly on Alexander, her body welcoming his eyes, her toes grass-stained. He took two glasses and offered one to Caroline. She shook her head. She had felt his eagerness to escape as painful twinges in her neck and shoulders, a cramp in her leg. She could not hold him; she wished he would go.

"You were looking for Perrot," she finally said, to release him. "Have you found him?"

Alexander shook his head.

"Maybe he's in the house. Go look."

"Will you be all right?"

Caroline laughed. "Here? When have I not been?"

"I'll be back in a minute." Alexander bent down to kiss her, and she wished that lying would encumber him and make him clumsy. She watched him leave her, luminous like a white bird, and noticed with a cramp in her heart that he had the grace to walk toward the house. Rosalind Child waited in the other direction, in a cluster of girls near the gazebo.

Caroline Harbison moved into the shade and leaned for a moment against the gray bark of the beech tree. The trunk was scarred and healed like an elephant's hide. Stumps of pruned branches had been painted black; the tree had been husbanded and pampered. Its roots broke the surface of the grassless earth like half-buried gray ropes. Caroline waited, counting, giving Alexander enough time to circle behind her, furious with herself because she knew him so intimately that she could measure his stride as if she were counting to join him at an entrance, furious at her cowardice: she would never intercept him in his lie.

Slowly she wandered toward the house, holding her body with the careful posture that, when she was not dancing, concealed emotions as utterly as it revealed them when she danced. Fanny Loewen smiled at her as she reached the terrace. She opened her shimmering arms. "Caroline dear, how lovely you are! As lovely as today! So lovely." She fluttered her arms.

With her nodding head and her robe's dark iridescence Fanny Loewen resembled a crow more than a butterfly. Caroline recognized Fanny's state of exalted inebriation. Strands of hair had come loose from her braid and surrounded her head in a disheveled halo; her pupils had expanded with the intensity of her vision; the whites of her eyes were watery; her face was at peace.

Caroline Harbison was tempted to ask about the future, to ask what Fanny Loewen saw. "Fanny," she began, "tell me—" But she could not bring herself to ask. She realized that in a sense she already knew, and she feared confirmation.

Fanny Loewen cocked her head, like a bird disturbed at its feeding. She smiled. "I will, dear; I will tell you everything. You can see it all from here; that's why I stay here, to see it all. Glorious, isn't it? The perfect day. I asked for that, you know; I didn't think I was going to get it. They were predicting rain. Sumner thinks I'm ridiculous to ask, but look at the result. Absolutely beautiful. And this year everybody wore something appropriate, white, like little sails on the green lawn, like little clouds in the blue sky. Just what I wanted. Except for that person." She paused to search the grounds. "I don't see her. That person Sumner seems so fascinated with, the one with the French name. She came in an orange dress, a horrible orange that has nothing to do with nature—can you believe it?—up to here," and Fanny gestured vaguely at her pelvic region. "And she has nothing on underneath; she bounces like two basketballs. She calls herself a dancer, but you can't dance with a bosom like that. She came with a lovely young man, though. Amos Furst. Have you heard of him?"

Caroline shook her head.

Fanny nodded slowly, her bright, blurred eyes fixing Caroline with sudden sympathy. "Caroline, dear, don't you worry. Don't you worry about anything. There is an energy here today—I know, I can feel it. Go sit down. You look pinched; is your ankle still hurting? Go, dear, sit down." She drained her glass and swept away.

Caroline Harbison obeyed. Fanny Loewen in her obtuse optimism envisioned solutions. So much for the future. Just sit down, Fanny said. Caroline sat on the low terrace wall. Trees shortened her view and she could not see the pattern of the party; she could not locate Alexander now had she wanted to. She wrapped her skirt around her ankles and sat. There was nothing else to do until it was time to go home. She could go to the barn and do a barre, but Sumner, touring the grounds with an enthusiastic guest, would find her. Caroline willed herself still, her body and her eyes, and time would pass, without her noticing, until it was gone.

A figure crossing her peripheral vision distracted her. A lanky man wearing a straw hat brushed the corner of her eye and sat on the terrace wall twenty feet from her. She did not recognize him at first; she resisted looking at him, but he had caught her blink as she registered his presence, and he bowed his head to her. She nodded back, knowing who he was: Amos Furst, Fanny Loewen's lovely young man, and she ignored him.

His hat rolled on its brim down his arm. He caught it and flicked his wrist, and the hat flipped in the air and landed on his head. He grinned. Caroline smiled back briefly. His expression once again deadpan, he pressed his fists together in front of his face and opened and closed his fingers, rolling them in quick smooth sequence like a caterpillar.

Then he took three small clear balls from the pocket of his jacket and began to juggle them. His arms moved familiarly, fluidly through their small parabolas. Rising and falling, the balls sparkled in the sun like tears, like spheres of ice. At the apogee of their arc they vanished in the light. Amos Furst performed an abstraction of juggling, a dance. Caroline watched, intrigued. She reacted to his grace and wanted to reach out and catch one of the balls and join his game, and she wanted to cry; the emotions collided like the wakes of two ships.

He stopped and waited for her to speak. Caroline said, "Sometimes the balls disappeared and it seemed as if you were juggling nothing."

Amos nodded. "The idea to use Lucite came to me when I wondered which people watched, the juggler or what he juggles."

"And?"

"You tell me."

"Both," said Caroline. "Do you do this for real?"

"I did. My father disinherited me after my freshman year, and I earned my tuition juggling. I was a street performer."

"Is that true?"

"No. When he disinherited me I quit school."

"Why did he disinherit you?"

"He was in love. He'd finally met a nice girl, but she believed in things like austerity that he had always thought were marginally criminal. The first thing he did, he took away my car. Canceled the insurance. Then he cut my allowance because he decided that I was probably buying drugs with it anyway. Then he wrote a letter to the dean of students saying I was lazy and should be kicked out. And in the meantime, he gave me lectures every week on how I had to change my life. He wouldn't leave me alone. Finally I asked him what I had to do to get him off my back. As long as he was supporting me, he said, I had to listen. So I said, 'Dad, *you* listen. I'll make a deal. Cut the money and the crap. I've had it.' And he did." Amos Furst paused. "Do you believe me?"

"Yes."

"Don't. I made it up."

"I see."

"Do you?"

"Why not? Shouldn't I?"

"Do you mistrust me, then?"

Caroline laughed. "I hadn't thought about it."

Amos Furst began to whistle an ascending scale while he hummed a descending scale at the same time.

Caroline laughed. "Is whistling and singing what you do now? Don't you still juggle?"

"Verbally."

"You're good at it."

"Do you want to learn? I can teach you."

"Which kind?"

Amos tossed her a ball. Surprised, she caught it; it was heavier than she thought, dense like a crystal ball. She held it up to her eye. Through it, Amos Furst was upside down, remote. She threw it back to him, and, as she did, he set the other two balls in motion and incorporated the third into the circle. Delighted, she clapped her hands.

"Thank you," said Amos.

"Why are you here?" she asked.

"I came with Eveline de Charny."

Caroline looked blank for a moment. "Oh, that's right, the person in the orange dress that's upset Fanny so much. Are you—are you and she—together?"

"You're very direct," said Amos.

"Sorry."

"No, I like it. I came with her. I go places with her. She has introduced me to a glamorous life: limousines, champagne, air conditioning, indoor plumbing, silk neckties that cost as much as a suit. Are we together? Together? What's together? She likes artist types, performers. She wants to be an artist. She wants to make art. She's kind of a juggler, too. She's dropped me for the moment. She's off with our host. She's sweet. That's her word. I'm sweet, for instance."

"What kind of art does she want to make?"

"She's a dancer."

"Where has she danced?"

"Nowhere recently. She danced as a kid. She wants to again."

"She's too old to start over. Why does she want to?"

"Because she wants something she can't buy. How do we know that she isn't a dancer?"

"I can tell. It's a waste of time to want to do what you can't do."

"She's too old to dance like you do. For that you have to be like a vestal virgin and dedicate your life."

"It's not that holy. It's hard work."

"Who's to say that hard work isn't holy?"

"Are you a comedian? No. I remember. You told Perrot you were a clown."

"A postmodern clown. A step beyond vaudeville," he answered. "But I want people to laugh."

Caroline Harbison stood and, despite herself, her eyes searched the groups scattered across the lawn. She could not locate Alexander.

"At that rehearsal I saw," Amos said, "even when you were not dancing with him, you seemed to be. Maybe it was the mirror."

"No," said Caroline, "I'm always dancing with him."

Alexander Ives and Rosalind Child walked slowly to the margin of the lawn, behind the borders of high rhododendron and precisely edged beds of perennials—feathery pink and white astilbe, daisies, delphiniums carefully staked. They followed a path marked with slate stepping stones through glades of lily of the valley leaves growing under clusters of low yews and sheared cedar to another lawn edged with drifts of day lilies. The lawn became a field of high grass, thick and fragrant. Rosalind held her arms out from her sides, a child balancing, and tickled her palms with the tassels of the grass. She walked beside Alexander, so light on her feet that the grass sprang up behind her and she left almost no trail. They did not talk; their legs swished noisily through the grass.

Above the lake, the field gave way to an outcropping of rock. They followed the path down steps cut into the rock until they reached a wide ledge that dropped off steeply into the lake. The sun had heated the ledge. The rock bent where it entered the water, a trick of light. Schools of minnows, silver needles, glimmered under the water and poked little rings into the surface. Out of the wind it was quiet. The lake lapped silently. Sprigs of thyme sprouted in crevices in the ledge.

Alexander smiled and stretched and bent down and untied his shoes. He took off his shirt and pants. Rosalind observed. His body was golden; planes of muscle stretched over his bones, ridged along his ribs and stomach. It was hard, worked. His flesh was thin, barely tanned, tender. His body's shape was what was beautiful. When Alexander was naked he dived. Rosalind followed the green-white line of his body underwater until she lost it. Alexander surfaced fifty feet from shore, shook his hair out of his face, and beckoned to her. Without waiting to see what she would do, he swam away.

A black swallow—angled wings, split tail—skimmed the

water, and with a small slapping splash snared a mosquito. Rosalind dropped her clothes on the rock. She dived with a splash as precise as the swallow's, with the sound of a small stone. She swam toward Alexander. He trod water until she was ten feet from him. She raised her head. Their black hair was smooth and gleaming; their wet skin caught light; they were as glossy as seals. They swam together, separated by ten feet.

They swam in the light, skimming a crescent of shadow cast by trees over the water. They swam with slow strokes, kicking small wakes; they moved together, keeping their distance, in a wide curve back to shore. Alexander clambered up the ledge; underwater the rock was slippery with invisible algae. Rosalind followed him. She slipped backwards and fell into the water. She surfaced laughing. When Alexander offered his hand, she shook her head and pulled herself up.

Rosalind faced Alexander; she lifted her arms over her head and wrung out her black hair and watched Alexander study her body. She showed herself to him, to admire or to want—it made no difference. She made no effort at grace; her feet were a foot apart, her legs straight. Goose bumps started on her arms and thighs. How young she was, Alexander thought, how delicate, how smooth. The skin on her thighs was sheer; she had no marks on her, no blemishes. The tiny patch of hair between her legs thickened into a dark wet curl; her breasts swelled in perfect hemispheres; her nipples puckered into points. She was not vulnerable.

He turned from her and lay on his stomach on the warm rock. Rosalind lay a foot from him. Their hands could have touched, but they did not. They lay and listened to the wind above them, the loud fussing of squirrels in the dry leaves of the woods, the splash of swallows. Their closeness and their distance were unbearable. "We have to go," Alexander said, and stood. "We have to be back." Rosalind raised herself on her hands; the effort hollowed the muscles in her buttocks. She turned and looked at his erection. Squinting in the sun, she tilted her head up to him. He bent over and kissed her on the mouth. Her lips were cold. She took the kiss and smiled. There were spaces between her small teeth. They put on their clothes, and Alexander led Rosalind up the steps in the rock.

It was nearly seven o'clock. From the balcony, Achille Perrot had watched many of the guests leave, strolling down the lawn in the direction of the barn where they had left their cars. He heard voices in the house. Fanny Loewen instructed the housekeeper to set out the buffet for the best guests. He had to stay. Eveline de Charny. Gertrude Stella. Alexander, perhaps, and Caroline. Doors squeaked, the double doors into the dining room. Murmurs from Fanny Loewen; it had already been done.

Perrot shivered. He put the back of his hand against his cheek; his own flesh chilled him. Dampness rose from the ground, intensifying the scent of roses. The string quartet and the dance band had stopped playing; the musicians were packing their instruments. Dana Coelho sprawled on the ground, staring happily at the sky. Walter Mowbray, hair spiked like a sea urchin, sat beside him, keeping watch. Caroline Harbison sat alone on the terrace wall with her perfect dancer's posture. At the bottom of the lawn, where the day lilies had closed, Perrot saw Alexander Ives and Rosalind Child, walking with each other at too great a distance to be innocent.

The sun, setting behind the blood red leaves of the beech tree, dropped into a pruned space between the branches. It illuminated Achille Perrot; it flashed into his glasses and blinded him, lit him like a spotlight. It was too low to warm him. He backed off the balcony and shut the French doors and deflected the useless sun.

7

THE SHADES IN THE BEDROOM WERE DRAWN, DIF-
fusing the summer light to a white wash, eras-
ing shadows. Air conditioning filtered the
Detroit heat. Dana Coelho lay naked on Roland de Charny's bed. He gleamed blond as if
he were himself a source of light. His eyes
were jammed shut; his mouth gaped. Roland de Charny sat
on the edge of the bed, attentive to the boy's growling breath,
the spasmodic heaving of his chest, as if he were watching an
animal die. "It is only the cocaine," Roland de Charny whispered. "Your throat is numb; you cannot feel yourself
breathe, but you are breathing. Lie still. It will wear off."

But Dana sat up and swung his legs onto the floor. He
opened his eyes and hung his head. Dizzy, he stumbled into
the bathroom and found himself in the mirror. His pupils
were dilated, his face sallow; his lips were cracked and pale.
His nose was blocked. He gagged. He waited to suffocate.
Numb. His throat was numb. It happened with coke. It was
important not to panic and hyperventilate.

He knelt on the floor. The chill white marble shocked him like ice water, but he was too heavy to move. His heart was not sturdy enough to pump the congealed blood frozen in his limbs. He had to stop doing drugs. He was wasting himself; he could not face Roland de Charny straight.

He wanted to be sick and purge the old man from his body, but the door was open. Roland de Charny would hear. He could not offend him and rebuke his generosity. Roland de Charny, wrapped in a white linen bathrobe, smelling faintly of lemon, waited for him on the bed. Dana placed his hand over his belly and concentrated on pushing his diaphragm in and out. He willed himself vertical and shuffled back into the bedroom.

Sadness, the aftermath of love, sucked the air from the room. Dana opened a window, letting in the heat on the afternoon wind; he needed evidence of air. He lay back down on the bed and curled into a ball. Roland de Charny reached for Dana's wrist and pulled his hand from between his knees.

"The numbness is gone?"

Dana nodded. "Going."

"What can I do for you?" Roland de Charny asked, his face slack with tenderness. He stroked Dana's forearm.

"You do a lot."

"But it must not be enough. What else do you need? Tell me. What are you thinking?"

Dana raised his head. "Nothing. That—I was thinking nothing. I was thinking about dancing. About not dancing. I was thinking I couldn't dance."

"You dance beautifully. Have I done something to upset you?"

"It has nothing to do with you. I promise that." The truth of what he had said appeared to Dana. Roland de Charny could be anyone. If he were not in this bed, Dana knew he would be lying in another bed in another old man's house.

All his life Dana Coelho had been desired. It was his gift and his burden, and it was his pleasure and torment to return desire and to be worth desiring. He had to stop. His heart would give out; he would try to dance and he would collapse. His heart was malignant; it poisoned love.

"You know," Roland de Charny said, "I would do anything I could to make you happy." He pulled Dana to him, lifted him half upright, and rested the boy's head against his tight brown chest. The skin under his nipples sagged like tiny empty breasts. He patted Dana's back rhythmically, comforting a child. They sat for a quarter of an hour as the room grew hot from the outside air. Uncomfortable perspiration filmed Roland de Charny's skin; he loosened his embrace and looked at his watch. "Lunch is in half an hour. Please try to be there. Please"—he pointed to the drawer of the night table—"do whatever you want. Take whatever you need, but be careful." He caressed Dana's blond curls. "I must get ready."

The house of Roland and Benedicte de Charny was one of the last Frank Lloyd Wright designed before his death. It was never cataloged or listed as his work because Wright, who tyrannized his clients, could not dominate Benedicte de Charny. She knew what she wanted and she was determined to get it, she told him, because she was paying for it, and for him. One of Wright's assistants, the young man who executed the final drawings from Wright's sketches, claimed that the master had fallen in love with Benedicte de Charny.

She had spurned him and laughed at his proposals, at the glory he promised her. "What do I need you for? I have no desire to lie beneath you. I will be no foundation for you to rebuild yourself upon," she was rumored to have told the great man. Her rebuff, coupled with her relentless insistence that he take her desires into account when planning the house, the assistant contended, killed Wright. In blond Benedicte de Charny, seductive and irresistible, Frank Lloyd Wright saw death—the implacable, omnipotent force indifferent to his genius, a force that finally undermined his will to live.

It is known that the two spent many hours discussing the house and its philosophical structure. Benedicte de Charny had no interest in Wright's concept of the hearth as central to the home. "Perhaps this notion—this myth—of warmth is a necessity for other families," she said to the architect. "Perhaps other families require such illusions. Perhaps you do yourself. I do not. My family does not."

Benedicte de Charny was the daughter of an engineer, Magnus Arbroath, a Scotsman who developed an exhaust system that was licensed by all major American automobile makers. She was an only child, raised in Michigan by her Presbyterian father and Francophile English mother in an atmosphere of material austerity and spiritual conflict. Her father spent money only to keep the world at a distance. Her mother, for whom the feel of furs and silk and pearls was a religious experience, battled valiantly for possessions. Her husband gave her things grudgingly, often only as the result of her subterfuge; they were not always exactly what she would have chosen herself.

Although he had made his fortune from the excreta of automobiles, Magnus Arbroath could not tolerate the smell of the source of his wealth. He insulated his house from exhaust fumes by building it within acres of virgin forest. Visitors and tradespeople and family members left their motorized vehicles at the gate house. Clydesdales carted supplies, including barrels of oil for the up-to-date heating system. Matched teams of Hanoverian horses transported family and guests to the main house in red lacquered carriages. There were no exceptions to this policy; on one occasion, Theodore Roosevelt, upon having his automobile confiscated, mounted a carriage horse, ordered it unharnessed, and galloped bareback up the driveway. Magnus Arbroath's wife furnished the red carriages with mink lap robes, of which her husband approved, although he would not permit her to buy a fur coat. On at least one occasion she appeared at Severance Hall for a Detroit Symphony concert with a mink blanket draped about her shoulders.

She devised a family coat of arms, upon which a golden squirrel (for frugality) and an automobile muffler were intertwined. It was painted on the carriage doors, and she secretly ordered a set of Limoges porcelain emblazoned with the crest. She paid for the dishes herself out of the household budget by reducing the number of gallons of oil delivered each month for the central heating. Magnus Arbroath, during the last days of the month as the oil ran out, complained of drafts. His wife presented him with the bill for the balance of the dinner service; loving warmth, he had no choice but to pay.

Benedicte Arbroath was educated at a convent school in Normandy. It was a painful compromise for her parents. Her mother, alternating loud tantrums with weeks of reproachful silence, prevailed in her desire to give the girl a French education. While Magnus Arbroath acquiesced, he insisted on Normandy because it was close to England. Her teachers reported that Benedicte had a vocation for religion. She was devout; she took as her patron saint Teresa, who swooned with ecstasy at her visions of Christ. Upon finishing school, Benedicte went to spend several months in Paris with her mother's half sister. She soon displayed an equally intense predilection for the ecstasies of drinking and dancing.

When her parents asked—both had agreed that they would raise their daughter to be truthful and had succeeded in that—Benedicte assured them that she was a virgin. She added, however, that she did not intend to remain virgin for very much longer. She was in love, she told them, and she suggested that to avoid embarrassment they give her permission to marry Roland de Charny. He was ten years older than she, a witty, somewhat morbid aristocrat obsessively attentive to luxurious detail. All of his shoes were crocodile, and all of his shirts, including those he wore to play tennis and golf, were silk, their buttons perfect round pearls. At their first meeting, at the Ritz, he had ordered oysters and champagne, and Benedicte's mother, when she speared her first oyster, discovered that it concealed a pearl. Each of the remaining eleven oysters on her plate, when lifted, revealed another matched pearl. Benedicte's mother was charmed; she was completely won over when the following evening a superbly tailored silk blouse buttoned with six more pearls the size of overripe peas was delivered to her.

Roland de Charny's toothbrush handle was carved from rock crystal. He kept a room at the Ritz, where he had merchandise from the shops in the Place Vendôme sent around for his leisurely inspection. There was talk that he had ruined his father's fortune, yet it was an ascertainable fact that he had learned life's pleasures from his father, Ulysse de Charny; it was likely that Roland de Charny was only a junior partner in his father's ruination. His father had recently sold the family estates to pay debts. Magnus Arbroath's half sister-in-law had heard that, like his father, Roland de Charny had admitted to fathering at least one child out of wedlock. Magnus Arbroath confronted Roland de Charny with this damning information, and Roland de Charny, to Arbroath's unhappy confusion, was delighted that his future father-in-law knew of his exploits.

Magnus Arbroath returned to his sister-in-law's *hôtel particulier*, confronted his wife and daughter, and declared loudly and angrily that his child would never marry that morally and fiscally irresponsible, reprehensible Frenchman. His wife gently pointed out that his daughter would and that it was absurd to protest. Guessing that her father might not approve, Benedicte had consummated her relationship with Roland de Charny—only once, she assured her father, and in a perfunctory fashion—but thoroughly and at the correct time, and she was pregnant.

Benedicte had inherited her father's moral vigor; at the same time she sympathized with her mother's love of earthly possessions, so she did not condemn Roland de Charny for his fondness for luxury. She had also inherited her father's pragmatism, and early on understood how to get what she wanted. Roland de Charny had the liquid, yearning, unblinking eyes of a mystic; swooning like Saint Teresa, Benedicte could not see a representation of Christ without thinking of her fiancé. Roland de Charny was also an accomplished dancer, and in his evening clothes he gleamed with the ebony-and-ivory elegance of a grand piano.

Despite her attraction, Benedicte Arbroath would not have married the man if she had not believed that she had converted him, not from luxury, but from vice. Fidelity was only partly a moral issue; to Benedicte, possession was paramount. Even after her miscarriage, she had no second thoughts. They were married in Paris, at Sainte-Chapelle, on a bright day when the sun through the stained-glass windows studded her white dress with jewels of light. The couple would have preferred to remain in Paris, but in 1940 Magnus Arbroath, by closing Benedicte's account at the Banque de Paris, forced her and her husband home to Michigan. He had learned that Ulysse de Charny was suspected of sympathizing with the Germans. Foreseeing the United States' entrance into the war, and expecting to profit from it, Magnus Arbroath intended to spare his family a scandal.

In Michigan, Roland de Charny was at first horrified and then bored with the paucity of consumer goods, and with his sudden inability to buy what was available. Magnus Arbroath gave his daughter and her husband no money. They were living at home, so they were in no danger of freezing or starving. Roland de Charny, his father-in-law had decided, needed a job, and Magnus Arbroath hit upon material deprivation to wear down his son-in-law's resistance to that idea. Reluctantly, Roland de Charny entered the family business, predicting that his involvement would bankrupt the entire company.

However, he turned out to have a surprising aptitude for commerce. He had a salesman's instincts; he could project his own passion for possession, be it for pearls or a car muffler. While her husband was earning a reputation as a businessman, life became difficult for Benedicte de Charny. The balance of power in their marriage had shifted; Roland de Charny's salary exceeded Benedicte's reinstated allowance. And after her years in France, Benedicte found the United States somewhat limited, culturally and intellectually. She missed the irony of the French; in Detroit she read into conversations more than was there. For six months she sulked, until she grew tired of writing to her convent mates and reading their charming descriptions of wartime deprivation.

Quickly it became clear that Roland de Charny and Magnus Arbroath could never share territory. Roland and Benedicte went to South America, and, taking advantage of the available cheap labor decades before any other industrialist, Roland built factories to manufacture parts for Arbroath Exhaust, thus dramatically increasing the company's margin of profit. After the war, when the Japanese began to manufacture in South America, Roland de Charny invited their management teams to tour his modern plants; soon the Japanese cartels had contracted for versions of Arbroath systems in all of their automobiles.

Benedicte de Charny came to understand—although out of loyalty and a curious shame she never confessed this to anyone—that Roland de Charny, gifted as he was, could not have achieved his feats of expansion without her. Alone, people did not trust him; he was so polished he made them feel coarse, and he made them too aware of their own covetousness. His wife, with her famous posture and legendary moral uprightness, embodied the spirit of Magnus Arbroath. She wore simple clothes; she seemed plain as a nun beside the gaudy ladies of Brazil. She demanded from Roland de Charny a portion of his earnings, and once again she was richer than he.

At home, Benedicte became a presence in Detroit society. She gave parties featuring chamber music performances, during which guests were not permitted to speak. She and her husband were invited to join the boards of the symphony and the museum. Benedicte built bright playgrounds for children who lived in the new housing projects sprouting throughout downtown Detroit after the war. Prison camps, she called the projects, and commissioned artists to decorate their drab cinder-block walls. This exercise stimulated the project residents, who proceeded to cover their walls with their own designs, a development which Benedicte de Charny approved but which the Housing Authority, calling it subversive graffiti, did not. They began to whitewash the walls.

Benedicte retaliated by sponsoring an exhibition of abstract painting at the museum and juxtaposing with it photographs of project art. She gave an extravagant party to open the show, to which she invited the mayor and the chairman of the Housing Authority. It was not clear which were more shocking, the paintings or the photographs; an editorial came down on the side of the photographs because at least the subjects were recognizable. From this escapade Benedicte de Charny earned a certain notoriety, a reputation for danger.

She and Roland de Charny produced two legitimate children, a boy, Louis-Marie, and a daughter, Eveline. In 1947 they began spending summers at Roland's father's house in Brittany (which Benedicte's father had bought back for the couple as a wedding present). They sent both children to public school in Detroit for two years so they would not become snobs. This was hard for Louis-Marie, who was not at all aggressive and could not bear to be teased. When Louis-Marie and Eveline were in their teens the de Charnys spent three years in Paris so that the children would not remain uncouth. During this time, Roland de Charny moved Arbroath Exhaust into the expanding European market.

They appeared to thrive. Roland de Charny indulged in material extravagances, but they amused Benedicte. One of the intangibles that had attracted Roland de Charny to Benedicte was the potential of her sensibilities, and from the beginning of their courtship he taught her to be discriminating. She quickly developed her ear for music, and soon the de Charnys began to collect art as well.

It was inevitable, people said, that Detroit would prove too small for such a couple. Roland, especially, gravitated to New York and kept an apartment there. Benedicte de Charny understood how to shop in Manhattan and always arrived for part of the opera season, but she preferred Paris to New York. Her husband found Paris drab; he loved neon. Benedicte de Charny said that the more time she spent in New York, the greater her affection for Detroit grew. That statement, which she repeated at board meetings and dinners, was greeted with some skepticism. Some felt that Benedicte de Charny was, with characteristic dignity, trying to conceal a marital rift. All of their friends were on her side and said that they never liked her husband anyway. For some time there were rumors, originating with Magnus Arbroath's unsuccessful cousins, that in New York Roland de Charny's proclivities were more easily satisfied. Opinions varied as to what these unspeakable proclivities were; nothing was ever verified.

As she grew older, Benedicte's early impulse for religion returned. Her husband drove her back to it, the unsympathetic gossips reported; her supporters contended that she was like her father, that as a girl she had given evidence of a vocation, and her father's death had returned her to her original course. The truth contained elements of both versions. Benedicte was sorely disappointed in her husband and in herself. They had produced their children with great difficulty. Although Roland de Charny was a consummate seducer, he was not as expert at how to proceed after the moment of capitulation. He seemed dismayed by the process and by her nakedness. The unsatisfactory nature of their first union, Benedicte Arbroath suspected, was her fault. She was utterly ignorant, and certainly the political motives for that encounter were as strong as the physical ones, and perhaps more distracting. But that first time proved to be by far the best. Benedicte de Charny cursed her education and its inculcation of shame, although she never asked her friends whether their experience paralleled hers.

She wrapped her disappointment in a shroud of spirituality, testy and brittle like cellophane exposed to the sun. It caused her agonies, but finally she came to believe that she was more comfortable with the soul than with her failed foray into a more sensual expression of love. When, on his deathbed, her father confessed to her that the greatest joy of his life had been making love with her mother, that it was their bodies which united them well into decrepitude, Benedicte wept. His confession was cruel; she suspected he made it because he understood how things were with her husband and desired to nail his disapproval into her heart. He succeeded. His daughter was enough like him to have inherited his passions, especially the one passion he shared with his wife.

But then she wondered if he could have told her as a form of apology; perhaps he believed that she married Roland de Charny only because he was so strenuously opposed.

Perhaps he was trying to say, however indirectly, that he understood she might want to dissolve her marriage. That was out of the question, although he left his fortune to her alone. He died and his daughter continued to weep, not from grief, but from resentment and anger at her father for not warning her at the beginning.

This revelation stained Benedicte de Charny. Her father's knowledge of her intimate life humiliated her. To maintain self-respect, she needed to assign to her husband some moral worthiness, and she reviewed carefully what Roland de Charny had taught her. She had learned from him to care deeply about what was new. Now she realized what solace that could bring, what energy it required. Early on, she sensed a general resurgence of interest in religion, and this was a happy coincidence. Their home—at this time they still occupied a wing of her father's mansion—became a salon for priests, rabbis, gurus, Buddhist monks. Ecumenicism was discussed; plans were developed for a synthetic religion of the twenty-first century that would embody the latest developments in philosophy, medical research, and computer technology.

When he was fifteen, searching in the forest for birds' nests, their son Louis-Marie de Charny was shot by a hunter trespassing on the Arbroath estate. The man claimed that he mistook the boy for a mountain lion. He said he called out, and the boy climbed a tree. He had heard stories of a mountain lion in those woods, and he shot. Louis-Marie was tawny and lithe; he was reserved; he said that he wanted to be a naturalist, and he knew the forest of the Arbroath estate like an animal. Deer took berries from his hand—they were just like big squirrels, he told his mother. He knew where the foxes' dens were. He was surpassingly gentle; from the time he was born Benedicte felt the need to protect him. To her horror, when he was declared dead at the Grosse Point hospital, her first emotion was relief: finally the disaster she had always dreaded had occurred, and her vigil was finished.

A jury convicted the hunter of involuntary manslaughter, and he was sentenced to only three years in prison, which exacerbated the family's grief. The courtroom was crowded with spectators waiting to see how Benedicte de Charny would react, but she disappointed them all by not appearing. In truth, she could not walk. Her son's death paralyzed her; it was months before she regained the use of her legs. Six weeks after the sentencing, the hunter was found murdered in his cell, the victim, according to a spokesman for the prison warden, of an unexplained attack.

After her son's death, Benedicte de Charny could no longer bear to live in the old Arbroath house. The ghost of her father's happiness haunted it; the spirit of her son emanated from its walls like the smell of freshly cut wood. She had the forest cleared where her son had died, and that was where she decided to build her house. Its large cool white rooms spilled like the crest of a wave on a hill above Lake St. Clair. Mourning, she rejected every suggestion of opulence in the design.

Although Louis-Marie resembled Benedicte, Roland de Charny had been able to achieve an attachment with his son that he never could with his wife. It was almost physical; the two spent hours together walking and rarely talked. It did not disappoint Roland de Charny that his son was a quarry, not a hunter. It brought out a tenderness in him, as if he recognized himself in a reversing mirror.

After the loss of his son, he did not lose or gain weight; he did not talk about Louis-Marie and accepted condolences with minimum politeness. Sensitive to futility, he did not try to comfort his wife. He continued with his life; he attended the trial, but not regularly. He still took long walks through the snow and the thick underbrush, as if he were trying to track Louis-Marie. The following spring, when Benedicte de Charny began to have the forest cut down, he spent two months in New York and came back to Detroit only for short visits. It became a pattern—two months of each season away, one home—and it seemed to bring peace to both Benedicte and Roland de Charny.

In New York he became involved with that city's cultural life. He made significant contributions to several museums and performing organizations and served on the boards of two or three of the smaller institutions and one of the most prestigious, but his terms were short and he did not stand for reelection. Roland de Charny said that he lost interest, that the politics of art was petty and time-consuming. The truth, and he was powerful enough to prevent it from being generally known, was that he was a willful and somewhat petulant man in a city of similar individuals. Their interests and financial resources were comparable to his, and although none could match his style, which they held against him, their power had already been established for several generations. He did not care to cooperate with them and support their agenda, and he was outspoken, eloquent, on the subject of their provincialism. In retaliation, they booted him off the boards while continuing to invite him to parties and solicit him for funds.

With his characteristic bravura, he, through his wife, consolidated his cultural efforts in Detroit. He and Benedicte employed a discreet corps of public relations experts to ensure that their legend was secure and well known outside Detroit, especially in New York. Roland de Charny wanted that city to understand what it was missing. Under the de Charnys' guidance, Detroit became a center for avant-garde art of all kinds. Their Arbroath Festivals featured dance and other performance, often hybrid arts combining various media, always with a spiritual element. They attracted international attention, and what they were doing was often better understood in Europe than in America.

Roland and Benedicte de Charny did not appear to need the bolstering of a public relations team. They each possessed a strong character combined with the intellect, the social position, and the means to make their mark. They espoused art and social justice. They did not pollute their name with casual indulgences like liveried servants or week-long parties with delicacies flown in from other continents. Although Roland de Charny occasionally imported game from the estate in Brittany, he never made a point of telling guests where their meal had been grown. He had learned from his mistakes in New York how important it was to safeguard his reputation. He suspected that those boards which had not reelected him would have acquiesced to his demands and his plans for programs if they had not heard unsavory things about him.

Perversely, Roland de Charny, although he had not been able to gain the kind of acceptance he had originally sought, found that as a renegade he was even more desirable. He cultivated an aloofness, a disdain for the established cultural elite, while the public relations people kept his name pure. They identified revisionists, those who would contradict the de Charny image. They masqueraded as friends and silenced criticism with careful doses of exquisite hospitality; they arranged weekends at the house on the lake and small dinners in New York. Although Benedicte de Charny had mistrusted these friends at first, she came to appreciate their usefulness in keeping intact the idea of her marriage, the idea of delicate harmony she wished to protect, an idea that became more precious to her than if it had actually existed.

Roland de Charny had returned to Detroit for the opening of the Arbroath Festival. It was held in the old house and on the grounds of the Arbroath estate, where artists had erected site-specific installations. Inflated vinyl bladders swayed in the wind like tethered protozoa. Bulldozers sculpted an earthwork representing an interchange of an interstate highway two thousand years in the future. A team of workers wove a Mylar and canvas aerial maze.

Dana Coelho's dancing did not precisely fit the definition of avant garde, but the Perrot Ballet's reputation was august enough to transcend definitions and deflect suspicion. Roland de Charny occupied a separate suite in the house, with a living room and two guest rooms adjoining. In the years since the house was built, he had introduced elements of his own taste into his wing, most recently a small collection of plastic laminate furniture by Memphis, the Italian design firm. Its profligate decoration irritated Benedicte de Charny and gave her an aesthetic excuse to avoid her husband's rooms.

Dana had not announced what he would be dancing. However, since the Perrot Ballet as a company never toured and Achille Perrot refused to sell the performing rights to his

compositions to any other company, an audience of balletomanes nationwide was hungry to see anything connected to
him. Groups from throughout the entire Midwest had arranged pilgrimages to Dana's performances. Amos Furst,
sponsored by Eveline de Charny, was also scheduled to perform at the festival and was surprised when tickets sold well.

Roland and Benedicte de Charny observed the social
formalities of married life, and they enjoyed a certain super-
ficial ease in each other's company. Their shared disappointment with each other became a bond, as did their mutual
pleasure in newness and surfaces. It was a precarious connection, however, and when Roland de Charny was in resi-
dence, they preferred to have their daughter with them, as a
buffer. This suited Eveline de Charny, who knew that Benedicte did not approve of her; Benedicte did not believe in a
life ruled by unfulfillable desires. Eveline's visits coincided
with her father's. For that family, the triangle provided a
stable geometry.

This summer, despite Amos Furst's debut at the festival,
Eveline had daily postponed her arrival. In telephone calls to
her mother, she gushed over the Perrot Ballet, the extraordinary privilege she had been given to watch the sacred daily
rituals of the dance. Finally she announced she was not coming to Detroit at all. Benedicte de Charny demanded that she
take the next plane and mentioned her allowance. Eveline de
Charny arrived, but she was depressed and spoke of nothing
but the Perrot Ballet. Benedicte de Charny had inherited
Marcus Arbroath's suspicion of spiritual excess in anyone but
herself, so while she feared for her daughter and her obsession, she also mistrusted her. Moreover, Eveline possessed
her father's energy but, lacking his discipline and dispassion,
could not regulate it. Lack of control disgusted Benedicte de
Charny; after dinner the second night, Benedicte, wearied
and bored, capitulated and sent her daughter away.

Benedicte de Charny felt her husband's presence, alien
yet familiar, like a chronic condition whose symptoms she
had grown attached to. She had spent the morning in her
study reviewing finances. Recent declines in the market had
hurt the family, but not significantly; they had been able to

offset some losses because delays in the enforcement of environmental regulations were enabling Arbroath Exhaust to continue to manufacture obsolete, cheaper systems.

Simultaneously, their subsidiary, Arbroath Environmental, was developing the prototype of a device that reburned and compressed exhaust fumes; it reduced the detritus of a year's driving to a pile of small black pellets that resembled deer feces, the composition of which was related to petrochemical fertilizers. This intrigued Benedicte de Charny; it seemed religious in its simplicity, alchemical in its elegance. She made a note to herself to call the division president to ascertain whether their work was supported by government funds. She did not want to risk capital on such an enterprise.

At a quarter to one the doorbell rang. Benedicte and Roland de Charny had invited Gertrude Stella to lunch, in gratitude for her having successfully prevailed upon her newspaper to allow her to cover all the festival events; at an avant-garde festival, she had argued, everything has to do with dance. She had already filed an introductory story calling the Arbroath Festival the most innovative in the country and praising the de Charnys as the country's most enlightened patrons of the arts. Roland de Charny had ordered champagne for lunch.

Benedicte de Charny was dressed, as usual, in a simple dress with a loose top, which concealed her bosom, and a straight skirt that emphasized her narrow hips. The dress was sashed with a cord like a monk's cincture. She wore no makeup. Her golden eyes in her pale face were large and candid, intense and humorless, wide-set where her daughter's were close together.

Roland de Charny filled Gertrude Stella's glass so that champagne foam domed delicately over the rim. " 'Given this city's inertia, nothing as spontaneous and serendipitous as the de Charnys' festival could ever be accomplished in New York,' " he quoted. "I enjoyed that very much."

Gertrude Stella smiled and coughed as bubbles floated up her nose. In her full skirt and brightly patterned fringed shawl, which crossed over the bosom of her eyelet blouse, she resembled a madonna in a South American church, costumed by the faithful. "I find it instructive to occasionally leave the city. One gets so provincial in Manhattan, don't you think?"

"My wife does not even have to go to New York to find it provincial, do you, my dear?"

Benedicte de Charny said, "It is not a question of provincialism. I am sure New York is not provincial. It is crude and heartbreaking. I cannot insulate myself from the crudeness; I cannot hide from the suffering on the streets, so I do not go very often."

"You know Dana is dancing," said Roland de Charny, "and someone named Amos Furst, a protégé of my daughter's, actually, is performing, too. I hear interesting things about him. You have seen the installations? They might be a bit farfetched for you, but perhaps you'll find them amusing."

"Roland, you know I don't want to really criticize anything. It's all so perfect."

Benedicte de Charny shook her head at her husband's offer of champagne. "Tell me, Miss Stella, how do you decide what to review? Do you choose only what you are sure to like? Or do you attend what might be unfamiliar in order to broaden your perspectives? What *do* you like and dislike?" Her voice was light and girlish, ingenuous; she exuded curiosity.

"So many questions! I'm used to asking, not answering." Gertrude Stella was disconcerted. "What do I like? I keep an open mind. I like what's good. What do I review? I try to cover both the familiar and the new. But of course you always know in advance what will be good and what is a waste of time."

"Do you?" Benedicte de Charny raised her eyebrows.

"It's a small world, dance."

"How much do you get paid?"

"I love my work."

"You are not paid enough," said Benedicte de Charny.

Roland de Charny listened, half-embarrassed, half-amused. His wife's privileged innocence, which she put on like one of her righteous dresses, always irritated him. The maid announced lunch. As they moved into the dining room, Dana Coelho appeared. Roland de Charny covertly searched his face for traces of distress. But Dana had recovered from his despondency. Golden light emanated from him. His eyes were bright, the pupils large with enthusiasm; he moved with a puppy's quickness. He was high again and happy. Roland de Charny felt a moment's concern, a small sting of guilt like an insect's bite, but it was true, he thought, what he had said to Dana earlier: he would do anything to make the boy happy, happy immediately.

"What are you dancing?" Gertrude Stella asked Dana Coelho.

He told her: a program of excerpts from Perrot's ballets, and she was disbelieving. "I know that only Alexander Ives has permission to travel with these ballets."

Dana shrugged. "Well, I've been learning these parts, and Alexander's been helping me."

"I think this is extraordinary," said Gertrude Stella. "I think it means something. Tell me, is Perrot coming to watch you dance?"

"No. He stays in the country during the summer."

"Who arranged this?"

Roland de Charny smiled. "My wife and I have a great friend, Aline Barbour—do you know her? You must meet— she suggested Dana."

"I arranged the program myself," Dana said. "With Alexander. I asked Perrot, and he said he didn't care what I did with his ballets."

"That does mean something," said Gertrude Stella, and pulled her notebook out of her striped straw satchel and wrote herself a note.

"Is it a burden always having to guess what something means?" asked Benedicte de Charny. "If you want to know, why don't you ask?"

Gertrude Stella put away her notebook and adjusted her shawl across her bosom.

The maid served poached salmon to Roland de Charny and Gertrude Stella and Dana Coelho. She put a plate of vegetables and cubes of grilled tofu in front of Benedicte de

Charny, who maintained a strict vegetarian diet. Dana ate quickly, with a heightened appetite. His gestures were abrupt, as if his muscles moved with more force than he meant them to have. Roland de Charny rarely spoke to him, but directed his conversation to Gertrude Stella.

Benedicte de Charny addressed Dana Coelho after they had been served raspberries from a silver bowl. "Tell me about your family. Where do you come from?"

"California. The valley."

Benedicte nodded as if she understood.

"No," said Dana. "My father is a physicist. Was. He kind of cracked up. I don't know what he is now." His voice was as bright as Benedicte's, light over the words, unconnected to what he was saying. "My mother said that he burned out. She said that he ran out of ideas so he ran away. I don't know; I don't really remember him."

"How did you become a dancer?"

"The usual way. My mother took me to ballet lessons with my older sister. I liked it."

"Were there other boys in the class?"

"No. But I liked being around girls, I guess because of my mother and my sister."

"What will you do next?" asked Benedicte.

"Next? Dance tonight."

"I mean in twenty-five or thirty years, when you are too old to dance."

Dana laughed. "Do you think I will ever be that old? Do you really? Not me. I can't believe that will happen. I mean, I hope it doesn't."

Benedicte de Charny smiled at Dana's mirth.

"I hope you'll never stop dancing," Gertrude Stella enthused. "I've had my eye on you, and I think you have the capacity to really be great."

Dana Coelho recoiled. "But what about now?" he asked. "Don't you like me now?"

Gertrude Stella beamed. "I think you're marvelous. I'd like to do a feature on you—maybe we can talk later. Where are you staying?"

Dana blushed. "Here."

Gertrude Stella raised one penciled eyebrow. "That's quite an honor."

Benedicte de Charny smiled easily. "Yes," she said, *"we* are honored." Abruptly she rose and announced that she and her husband had scheduled a meeting at the house that afternoon of the Detroit Pan-Religious Council. "I *am* honored that you are here." She smiled at Dana. "I am looking forward to seeing you dance." She extended her hand to Gertrude Stella. "And I will be eager to read your interesting analysis. But I'm afraid that Roland de Charny and I must prepare. The council, you know, sponsors an international conference on ecumenicism. Miss Stella, I would be happy to send you information. You will find it interesting, something to write about, a refreshing change. We're including performances and exhibitions in the conference." She opened her arms and moved her guests into the hall. A maid opened the front door for the critic. "You are welcome to look at the gardens or the installations. Dana, I am sure you will want to rest." She watched him as he headed down the corridor toward Roland de Charny's wing.

Her husband waited behind her. Benedicte turned to face him. "You should never have brought him here," she began in her girlish, straightforward voice. "This boy. Why did you do it? Why do you flaunt him? Why do you want to show him to me?"

"I do not understand," said Roland, "and I think you have misunderstood me."

"I never do that."

"Dana Coelho came to Detroit alone. He is fragile. I wanted him to be comfortable. We have room in the house, and I did a favor for Eveline. She asked especially that I watch out for him. She's quite fond of him; they're good friends. We thought, actually, that you might like Dana. And you saw how happy Gertrude Stella was to have lunch with him. I thought she was going to eat him for dessert."

Benedicte de Charny smiled sweetly. Her face had an angelic cast. "She guessed that he was your dessert."

"I think not."

"She is not as stupid as she appears."

"She splits infinitives. My governess warned me never to split infinitives in English. It was worse than picking your nose at table, she said."

"I love you, you know." Benedicte de Charny's words stated a condition; they did not express affection or longing.

Roland de Charny took his wife's hand and kissed it. "I thought you had decided to love God instead. He seems a worthier match."

"I'm sure he is." Benedicte smiled with a trace of fond yearning, a remembered emotion, all but exorcised. "But I married you. And I have something to discuss with you. We do have some business."

She led him into her study and handed him a folder.

Roland de Charny frowned as he leafed through the papers. He stretched his long upper lip over his teeth.

"Do you know what she spends her money on?" Benedicte de Charny asked.

"She inherited my taste." He smiled.

"What about the checks made out to cash?"

Her husband tossed the folder on the desk. "I do not spy on my daughter. If you are so concerned, why don't you ask her directly what she does with her money? You are not afraid of asking questions."

"She has spent more than she should have to spend. Here are the statements from her trusts; she has spent more than the income. I wondered if you knew how. It occurred to me that you might be giving her money." Benedicte de Charny walked to the long window. The wind raised white-caps on the lake. Dana Coelho, tawny in the sunlight, crossed the lawn. Benedicte de Charny felt her legs grow numb, the paralysis of grief returning. Dana leapt and hovered like a gull above the water. His grace, his being alive, filled her with rage, but as she watched him, pity supplanted her anger. She fought the desire to call him inside and protect him.

She had long ago realized the limits of love, its ineffectiveness against danger. She had not loved much in her life, and she was glad of that. She took one step back from the window, testing her legs. Before she married him, her husband had made her want to dance like Dana. But Roland de

130

Charny, with his tight, dry flesh, did not inspire dance in Dana; she knew what did—a demon of destruction, beauty turned lethal, turned against itself. Benedicte de Charny reflected upon the limits of Christian mythology; it could be a Hindu deity, a spirit reincarnated and perverted in its return, that made Dana Coelho dance, that made Roland de Charny want him.

It wounded her, nevertheless, to see the longing in her husband's eyes, but they had agreed not to comfort each other. It would be better to remove the boy; he weakened her. "Please do something about him after his performance," she said. "I don't know what's come over you." She placed her back to the window so that light shone through her curly gray hair in a fuzzy halo. "And I don't want to know."

"You know," he said.

She felt short of breath, as if the paralysis were embracing her lungs. "Go on," she added, "go on. Go to him, love him, you poor man, for whatever that's worth to you."

8

ATALANTA, A WHITE APRON OVER HER BLACK dress, showed Caroline Harbison into the living room of Eveline de Charny's house in the Berkshires. Amos Furst stood in the center of a group of three of the younger company members. Sumner Loewen sat on a sofa looking ill at ease, and Eveline de Charny talked with a woman whose spiky cropped hair was dyed with several bright colors like a piece of cloth.

"This is my astrologer, Devon." Eveline de Charny introduced the woman to Caroline Harbison. Devon extended a white limp hand with long, knuckleless fingers. Her skin was sallow, her features small and bland, but her thin mouth stretched in a mischievous smile. Eveline de Charny added, "Devon's an artist, too—she's mainly an artist."

Large windows let in the afternoon light. The floor was bleached white, the sofas covered in white damask. Bouquets of white flowers—snapdragons, cosmos, daisies, zinnias—

were arranged on the low tables. Caroline sat next to Sumner Loewen, and Atalanta brought her a glass of champagne.

Sumner Loewen inclined his head toward Caroline and spoke in a low voice. "My dear, I must confess that I feel positively unfaithful. I was supposed to go to a crafts show with my wife this afternoon. A friend of hers makes silver jewelry, you know—swoopy shapes with hammer marks, brooches, hair ornaments. It's painful to contemplate. I told her I had a headache. If Fanny knew I was here, she would be furious."

"Fanny doesn't like Eveline," said Caroline.

"The competition."

"I can understand that."

Sumner nodded ruefully. "But they're really very different." He appraised the room. The closed windows looked out on bare earth rutted with tire tracks. Lumber was stacked under a blue plastic tarpaulin beside the exposed foundation. "Odd, isn't it, that she has the air conditioning on? Odd that she has air conditioning at all in the country."

Eveline de Charny's property in the Berkshires abutted Arabesque. She had altered an old farmhouse and added wide windows and trapezoidal skylit turrets that rose like periscopes from the roof. The clapboards had been painted steel gray. She had sent her children to spend the summer in France with their second cousins, and she threw herself upon the company as if it, collectively, were a lover. But Eveline de Charny never gave herself completely to any one lover, and it was the same with the Perrot Ballet. Friends and protégés visiting from the city wandered the grounds of Arabesque in their downtown black. She invited dancers to lunch or dinner, and to Fanny Loewen's distress the dancers went, charmed by Eveline de Charny's appearance, intrigued by her hard-edged style.

Eveline de Charny kept a calculated, respectful distance from Achille Perrot. If she wanted to watch a rehearsal, which she frequently did, she asked Sumner Loewen to go with her, knowing that Perrot would not waste energy on a confrontation. The dancers laughed at Sumner Loewen, at the hours he spent at rehearsals, and it began to irk him; he preferred performance. He had never enjoyed the labor of process.

When Guy Pissarro taught morning class, Eveline de Charny often took it—he lacked the courage to refuse her. She wore black tights and a leotard, and her amplitude dwarfed the small, thin dancers. She stayed only through the first part, the exercises at the barre. She took a place in the back of the studio, and when the dancers moved to the center for the enchaînements, the combinations of steps, she left.

In every class, she maneuvered to find a place with a clear view of Caroline Harbison. Eveline mimicked the angle of her wrist, the carriage of her head. At first, Caroline Harbison was annoyed—Eveline de Charny's eyes on her itched and burned like poison ivy. She thought to talk to Perrot or to Sumner Loewen, but, retaining a midwestern faith in fairness, she could find nothing concrete to complain about.

At the barre Eveline de Charny was competent, her alignment excellent, her legs strong and tireless. Despite herself, Caroline Harbison began to admire Eveline de Charny's diligence and determination. She could not come to the center of the floor; she lacked balance. She could not be a dancer, but she was not ridiculous.

When Eveline de Charny discovered that Caroline Harbison came early to the studio to warm up, she began arriving early herself. They greeted each other; they chatted. Eveline de Charny asked Caroline Harbison to her house for a Sunday lunch. "And bring Alexander, if you'd like," she said. "It's casual, just some friends. Amos Furst will be there, for a while; he's flying to Michigan that night for the Arbroath Festival."

"Where Dana's dancing."

"It's my parents' thing," said Eveline. "Amos is perfect, just what they want, a little fringy, but great reviews; he's getting a reputation. He liked you. He said you'd talked at Fanny's party. That was out of another century, wasn't it?"

"So is Fanny. It was wonderful watching Amos juggle— he's very good," Caroline Harbison said.

"He's sweet. I don't know why he makes such a big deal

out of juggling. It's only a part of his performance now. He's evolving."

Caroline Harbison came to lunch alone.

Sumner Loewen patted her hand. "I must go, in case Fanny comes home early and becomes suspicious. I will leave you young people to each other. My dear, I'm happy to see that you and Eveline are getting to know each other." He rose. "And how is Alexander?"

Caroline gave him her icy smile. "He's fine."

"Eveline said he would be coming."

Caroline shrugged, her smile unbreaking. She had not seen Alexander to invite him. She stood when Sumner did.

Sunday lethargy permeated the room, insulated from weather but not from time. Devon and Eveline de Charny had disappeared. Atalanta circled the room with a plate of pastries. Only Amos Furst took one. He separated from the young dancers and crossed to Caroline Harbison.

"You're going to Michigan?" Caroline asked.

"In a couple of hours."

"Show me what you do."

Amos laughed, embarrassed. "I can't do that. I can't do my characters here."

"Who are they?"

"You can describe them in two words, but it won't mean anything. A dog psychiatrist who's an ex-marine." He stood with his back arched, his legs apart, and his arms dangling at his sides; the backs of his hands faced forward. "A professor of philosophy," he continued. His chest seemed to contract, his eyes narrowed, and his ankles loosened so his legs lost sturdiness. "He discovers his university's body-building equipment." He straightened and the volume of his muscles increased. "Beyond the brain. It goes on."

"You change yourself into different people."

"The physical part is just the beginning. Then I talk. But it's hard to talk *about;* it's like asking you how you dance."

"You studied dance, didn't you?"

"Sure. Not a lot, but some."

Eveline de Charny and Devon came back into the living room, arms linked. They were giggling, stoned. Eveline took

Caroline's arm. "Sorry to have deserted you," she said, leading her to the girl. Amos followed. "I want you to see Devon's work." Devon sat on the floor, her short skirt hiked up around her hips. Her legs were winter pale, and purple bruises discolored her soft thighs. She fidgeted; her gray eyes gleamed with energy.

"Show Caroline your portfolio, Devon," Eveline de Charny said. Devon sprang up and pulled a black leather envelope from behind a sofa and opened it on the floor. In it were mounted glossy color photographs, all of Devon naked. Her body was painted to match her Technicolor hair. She stood, she lay down, she sat, she faced the camera, her back was turned. A parrot posed with her in most of the photographs, perched on her shoulder, on her hip, on her left breast, between her legs, on her head; its wings blended with her patchwork hair.

"Dana's boyfriend has a parrot," Caroline said.

"We must introduce them," volunteered Amos.

Eveline de Charny ignored him and knelt beside Devon, resting her chin on the astrologer's shoulder. "I'm arranging a show of her work," Eveline explained. "Devon takes all of these pictures of herself by herself. She has an assistant paint her body where she can't reach."

Devon interrupted. "But he does it from a diagram. I've planned it all out beforehand, and I watch him in a mirror to make sure he paints exactly what I want. That's the hardest part, planning it out, the diagrams. Doing the photographs is easy. I have one of those little cords with a button at the end. I snap when I'm ready." The woman's voice was rough, the vowels flat and midwestern. Her teeth were stained from orthodonture, her cheeks childishly full. "I call what I do 'autoerart,'" she added.

The dancers gathered behind Eveline de Charny to see the photographs. Eveline explained: "Devon has a performance piece we're working on, too, partly live, partly on video, where she paints herself and gets herself painted. The parrot's in it. We're developing the format, incorporating his guano. I'm doing the movement."

Devon giggled. "The parrot really freaks people out. We'll let him fly around. Where he stops nobody knows. Kind of like a wheel of fortune, you know?"

"When is the show going to be?"

Eveline de Charny smiled. "Soon. This fall. Devon's art is important."

Caroline Harbison wondered how Devon could have traveled such a distance from the Midwest. She could see her as a cheerleader, pert and peppy and innocuously sexual; she had excavated pits of urban darkness into her flat innocence. Caroline was fascinated. How long have you been away from home? she wanted to ask. Do you wash your hair out before your parents visit? Do they visit? Do you let them? She kept silent, unwilling to confront.

"Amos," Eveline de Charny asked, "what do you think?"

"The whole thing is cosmic," he said neutrally. "She looks like a photograph of Jupiter." He pointed to her solar plexus in one photograph; it was painted red, matching a spot in her hair. "Jupiter has one of those. It's called the red spot."

"Really?" Devon smiled. "Kind of sexy. I never thought of that."

"And you're an astrologer?"

"Amos," exclaimed Eveline de Charny, "I have a fabulous idea! We really need somebody else in this piece we're working on—somebody to create drama. What about you?"

"You mean I get to wear cardboard rings around my waist like Saturn?"

"If you want. I don't care. What I was thinking is that we could paint you, too."

"I don't think so," he said.

"Why not?" Eveline de Charny pressed him.

"You're not into paint?" Devon asked. "It feels great. Cool, then kind of sticky, like you're covered with mud. Paint's mud, did you know that?"

"No!" Amos shook his head, pretending amazement. "That's really too bad. I'm allergic to mud. I used to have to have antimud shots when I was a kid. They hurt like hell."

"Won't you do it, please?" Eveline urged. "For me?"

"Eveline, I'd do anything for you, but honestly I don't have time. There's the Arbroath Festival, and then . . ." He hesitated.

"You have nothing on after that. Nothing yet."

"I think I do, part of a series this fall at Lincoln Center."

Eveline de Charny looked disappointed. "Oh," she said, "I see. Well, I thought we were going to do something. I've already started finding a space. I've talked to a few people, and they're interested. They'd love putting you with Devon. I mean, clearly this is more important to you. I can't blame you, I suppose, but I wish you'd told me. I feel a little silly."

"It may not happen."

"I see. Of course not. It doesn't matter." She had withdrawn and turned her attention back to Devon.

Amos started toward Caroline, then changed his mind and left the room.

Caroline remained, light-headed from the champagne and the cooled filtered air. Nothing could cleanse the atmosphere of malaise; she felt detached, unanchored, isolated on the white sofa. The young dancers stayed away from her; it was up to her to approach them, but she lacked the energy. On the floor, Eveline de Charny and Devon laughed as they leafed through the portfolio. Caroline Harbison felt scrawny next to Eveline de Charny, wan and monochromatic beside Devon's rainbow vitality. She wished she knew where Alexander Ives was so she could be with him. She stood up to go.

At the front door Eveline de Charny caught up with her.

"What happened to Amos?" Caroline said.

"He's too sensitive for his own good." Eveline shrugged. "But you. Are you okay?" Her voice was low and sympathetic.

"Why shouldn't I be?" Caroline was surprised.

"Well, you came alone. I could have killed Sumner for asking how Alexander was. He's a sweet man, I love him, but he's not very aware sometimes."

"Oh, that was all right. Everybody always asks me how Alexander is. As if I should know."

"It's miserable, isn't it? The worst part is not knowing, because then you imagine all sorts of things."

Caroline nodded. She bit her lip. Despite herself, she was close to tears.

Eveline de Charny put her arm around Caroline Harbison's shoulder. "You never let yourself go, do you?"

Caroline shook her head. "I don't know what you mean."

"You're afraid you'll crack? Well, you won't. The first time I met you, after the premiere of *Swan Lake,* I wanted to ask how you could bear to watch that ballet with Alexander and Rosalind Child. You're strong, stronger than you think. Believe me. You'll be fine."

"I don't know about that."

"I do." Eveline smiled. Her black eyes shared Caroline's distress. "I know it's easy to say."

"It's hard," Caroline told her, "hard to do. We have a lot of time behind us."

"Time is the worst. You forget what you were like before."

"There isn't really a before, it's been so long."

One of the young dancers entered the hall. Eveline de Charny opened the door and embraced Caroline.

"Well," she said, "there's always an after. Don't forget that."

The sweet smell of hay lingered in the barn at Arabesque, mixed with the odor of dancers' powder and sweat. Chaff dust like invisible insects pricked their necks. Their rehearsal clothes were soaked. Sweat gleamed on Achille Perrot's white face, giving his powdery skin a waxen cast. His black linen trousers hung limp and wrinkled, and a dark triangle of perspiration spread across the back of his black shirt, between his shoulderblades. The barn's large windows were all open, but the wind was capricious, teasing with coolness, then dying off. A specimen beech tree shaded the barn. The leaves had turned opaque, the color of clotted blood, and they wilted in the afternoon. The sun was lowering, still hot; where it shone through the leaves and the windows it beamed shafts of heat onto the barn floor.

Achille Perrot saw Eveline de Charny pacing back and forth outside. She wore what she called her Arabesque costume—a short denim skirt and a tank top, pink ballet slippers on her bare feet. She hovered near the barn, glimpsing the dancers through the windows when the light let her, dancing with her own steps to the piano, satisfied, oblivious. Even Achille Perrot had come to believe in her obsession. In the last weeks he had felt his scorn for that obsession as well as his aversion to her diminish somewhat. Her persistence worked at him; though he was unmoved by her physical presence, he tolerated her as he would a stray dog, simultaneously flattered and resentful at having been singled out. Occasionally, when he saw her spending so much money and effort and getting nothing for it but the empty time to wait for him and watch him, he pitied her.

Perrot was having difficulty concentrating. He could not focus on the ballet; the heat distracted him. He loved heat; it loosened his joints and his spirit. He was always cold now, and to sweat was a luxury. The heat, these long days, thawed his memory as well: this light, the smell of bodies and hay, the clean and bitter scent of rosemary carried by the teasing wind. The original owners of Arabesque had imported rosemary bushes from Provence and planted them on the south side of the barn where, sheltered, they wintered over.

American smells were so different from European smells that when he first came to this country he feared he was losing his memory and becoming, through the loss of familiar odors, an amnesiac. Here was no sense of accretion, no compost of lives. In America everything was too new. But occasionally a smell would touch him: rankness in a narrow street in Greenwich Village that reminded him of the Left Bank, olive oil heating in a pan. The rosemary outside this barn ravished Achille Perrot and inundated him with memory, like music.

It was a particular day he remembered: hot, time suspended in the stasis of midsummer. Achille Perrot was visiting Olivier Abravanel, his closest friend, during school vacation at the Abravanels' summer house in the Alpilles, near Avignon. Olivier had a twin sister, Odette; they had met because Odette also studied at the opera school of ballet. The school's director suggested that the Abravanels take an in-

terest in Perrot. They were generous people who encouraged the friendship with Olivier and treated Perrot as
another son. Perrot was eighteen; this day was the twins'
seventeenth birthday. There was a celebration planned for
the evening, and Perrot and the twins had been sent away for
the afternoon.

It was a gift, the request to disappear for the afternoon.
The Abravanels insisted that their children study even during the summer. The three of them left the house after lunch.
After the darkened rooms of the stone house, the day's brilliance blinded them so they could see only the present, only
desire. Heat wrapped them like a sheet; white and smooth, it
flattened against them as they walked.

Odette wore a pale blue dress and sandals; her heels,
sturdy dancer's heels, were pink. Achille Perrot remembered
the sun on her pale calves; her skin was so smooth that it
shone. A white arc of light followed the curve of muscle.
Olivier wore wide-legged khaki walking shorts like an En-
glishman, and the blond hair on his legs gleamed; the sun
picked out details of their bodies and lit them, displayed
them to each other's eyes. They were beautiful children, and
Achille Perrot was conscious of his own beauty as well, his
darkness—the dark rainbows the sun made in his curly hair—
against their fair hair and skin.

They walked indolently, as if they had no place to go and
all the time in the world. They passed through the kitchen
garden behind the house—tomatoes heavy and green, tiny
eggplants—and unlocked the gate in the garden wall, which
led to a field. The earth was rocky, the soil barren and burning beneath the soles of their shoes. Gray rosemary bushes
grew as high as their waists. They rubbed their hands against
the branches of silver needles until their palms and fingers
were infused with pungent oil. The field bordered a little
river where they went to bathe, a tributary of the Rhône.
Shallow-rooted willows screened the banks and let the sun
through in white stripes. They took off their clothes, and the
three of them swam in the slow current in the sun, their
bodies insulated from its heat.

They pretended not to see the rings of desire that rippled with each stroke and each kick. Odette's unripe breasts broke the surface. Olivier's sex and Perrot's were buoyant and small in the water. It was a birthday, and they felt inside them the premonition of age. They grabbed at childhood as if it were a lifebuoy; they clung to their disbelief in consequences. On shore they lay naked in the moss under the willows.

Achille Perrot remembered that he lay between Odette and Olivier. He touched Olivier's waist, his soft, cold skin, the taut, oblique muscle that tapered to his hip. He reached for Odette and felt her skin, identical in texture to her brother's; her thin, muscled waist swelled to her hip. The twins lay still and let Achille Perrot, between them, touch their stomachs, their thighs, their cold nipples hard from the river, the blond hair between their legs damp from swimming. Then they turned on their sides and put their hands on him. Crickets like violins played tremolos. The water and the breeze through the willow leaves combined in rhythmic white noise, and the wind carried the smell of rosemary. Achille Perrot remembered their positions, the ballet of their arms and legs. The three of them tasted each other's saltiness and sweat and the bitter algae flavor of the river water. They entered each other. They rolled into streaks of sunlight to see each other more clearly. Brother and sister, friend; they had wanted this for weeks; Odette and Olivier had wanted each other for years. Achille Perrot led the dance, led them to each other and diverted them to himself.

They lay under the willows all afternoon. As they returned through the field they rubbed their hands against the tall rosemary to erase each other's odor. What they had done was locked in the languorous heat of the afternoon, in the smell of rosemary, in a valley of memory. Perrot felt no guilt, but how could they not, he wondered, unless they blamed him? They had to cease loving him.

He had shown them their own desire. They had stretched childhood past recovery, and in doing so they would have to break their friendship. Innocence, however beautiful its loss, had to seem to them now an illusion, a trick of light through water, a suspect state. They had to hate him, although they were too generous to admit it and would go through the motions of love, growing clumsier and more reluctant. The three of them remained inseparable throughout the birthday party that evening and laughed and drank champagne together and danced, and both twins kissed Achille Perrot on the mouth before they went to their separate bedrooms to sleep.

Achille Perrot was the agent of beauty and of loss. What they had done they could not forget. Through his cold regret, Achille Perrot saw more clearly than they. To try to repair their friendship would shatter the memory, and to him the memory was already more precious. The following morning, although he had been asked to stay for another week, Achille Perrot left the Abravanels.

Despite the sign requesting no smoking in the barn, the English letters embellished with tails to make them appear Arabic, Harry Menard lit a cigarette and offered one to Alexander. The smoke settled around them. "This is for atmosphere," Harry said. "The music doesn't work without smoke, don't you think?" He played quickly through a part of the music, an Anton Webern setting of a waltz by Johann Strauss. "You need that cabaret effect, you know what I mean? A small room. Cigarettes. Sullied innocence."

"You know about smoke, but what do you know about sullied innocence?" Alexander teased.

"I've had my share," said Harry Menard. "I may not look it, but I have, in my day."

The Abravanels were dead, Achille Perrot thought, dead in the war. This music prefigured war. He walked Alexander Ives and Caroline Harbison through the duet, a complicated structure of lifts and balances, dips and spins to waltz time—one, two, three, one, two, three—an abstraction into triangles, a dangerous sharpening of the padded edges of Strauss's music. Perrot was not pleased. The dance lacked the sense of evil, the premonition.

It needed additional dancers to unbalance it and give it tension, to clarify the three points of the triangle. It needed another part. He shook his head and Harry stopped playing and looked at his watch. "We've been at this for a while," he said. "Maybe it's time to quit."

Perrot nodded. "Yes," he said. "I am sorry."

"For what?" Caroline Harbison asked him, surprised.

"We have not been very productive." Perrot never admitted mistakes to his dancers. He pulled a red handkerchief from his pocket and wiped his face.

Harry Menard folded his music. "Hot enough for you?" he asked. Alexander Ives and Caroline Harbison began to pack their gear. Caroline's callused heels were pink. Alexander's hair was flattened against his head as if he had been swimming. Perrot studied the dancer; the lines of tendon and muscle defined his limbs and torso as if they had been drawn in black charcoal. Those lines had been worked and hardened into a beauty more touching and more tenuous than the effortless grace Alexander had possessed when he was younger. He had made that dancer, Perrot thought. Why, then, could he not shape Alexander's dances?

"A moment, please," said Achille Perrot. They looked at him. "Do you have appointments now? Are you busy?"

"I have a meeting with the lake," Alexander Ives said.

"Then perhaps you will stay for a few minutes."

Alexander hesitated.

"Of course we will," Caroline said quickly, putting down her dance bag.

"I assume you mean me, too," Harry asked.

"If it would not be inconvenient."

Harry shrugged. "I'm no swimmer."

"Caroline, my dear," said Achille Perrot, "could you please go to the center?" He leaned his elbows back against the barre. "Alexander, come here, next to me, and watch, please. Watch Caroline. My dear, let's do, in fifth: plié, relevé, demi-pointe. Then in second: relevé on pointe. Harry, please."

The pianist played the Webern waltz. Caroline Harbison bent her knees, brushing the floor with the knuckles of her right hand, then rose quickly onto the balls of her feet, dropped again, did a plié in second position, straightened onto her toes.

"Let's do: glissade, tour piqué, on demi-pointe, then again on pointe."

Harry began playing a passage from *Giselle*. Caroline glided sideways across the floor, extending first her right leg, then her left, and landing in a plié; she repeated the glide, but touched ground on the ball of her right foot with her leg straight, bent her left foot up behind her knee, and turned twice. The third time she launched herself on her toe to turn; seemingly weightless, she spun five times and came down on her heel, grinning. "Five!" she exclaimed.

"Watch her balance," said Perrot. "Watch the difference. On pointe it changes. She has to be forward. She is more precarious, but she is able to do so much more. She is free of the earth."

Caroline repeated the sequence and Alexander nodded.

"This is very simple," said Perrot, "but you must understand. Caroline, my dear, let's do, again."

Caroline obeyed. Achille Perrot moved through the architecture of ballet; he had Caroline Harbison perform each exercise balanced on the balls of her feet and then on her toes. He showed how each step had to be prepared, how the glissade provided the momentum for the turn. He had Caroline turn from a standing position; the result was different, the impression one of strength, not of lightness. He had her do slow balances, stretching her leg into an arabesque, first with her foot flat on the floor and then on toe. "Watch the axis of her body," he said to Alexander. "You must help her with the steps to find that balance. Too much forward motion and she will topple. You must conceal a rest in the steps, a pause." Perrot progressed through turns and jumps. Some combinations Caroline Harbison could not do gracefully; when Perrot altered the steps slightly, when he added a step or delayed a step by a beat, they became possible. The adjustment—impulsion or pause—enabled her to balance or turn or leap.

He continued, telling Caroline in his soft voice, "Let's do, let's do," chaining steps, his own inventions, passages from *Giselle, Swan Lake, Sleeping Beauty*, choreography by Fokine, Petipa, his own namesake Jules Joseph Perrot.

145

"Let's do," said Achille Perrot. "Harry, the Webern. Alexander, please, let's do. She waltzes and you lift her." His hands danced the passage. Alexander reached for Caroline. Their arms twisted about each other; their legs intertwined. Caroline fell backwards into Alexander's hands, and he caught her and found her balance and launched her into turns.

"Let's do," said Perrot, and Caroline danced with Alexander's support and without it. They danced with an instinct for each other, for each other's space, the fall of weight, the trajectories when they leapt. They felt it, this love, golden and darkening. It propelled them and infused them with its own balance.

Achille Perrot choreographed it. His power filled him with ambivalent pleasure, bitter and pungent as rosemary. He remembered the pair when he first coupled them, giving them his desire to dance. Now he gave them small, melancholy steps, like the diminished music with its dissonant harmonies that mourned the end of gaiety. Perrot felt, as he never had, excluded from love. He felt an ominous desolation; he saw himself not there, erased, danced out.

He saw the other part, and he began to dance it. He circled Caroline and Alexander. He cut between them, fast turns, whispering the combinations as he danced. Cold sweat started on his body, chilling him in its evaporation. He flitted past Alexander, diverting him from Caroline, he spun back and placed his hands on Alexander's shoulders, asking to be lifted. Alexander, from habit, began to respond, then caught himself. "What are you doing?" he panted.

Perrot shuddered and stood still. Harry Menard stopped playing. "Alexander," he said, breathless, his soft voice ragged with a despair he tried to disguise as impatience, "it is not important for you to dance now. You understand how to partner. You must watch."

Outside, the day had lost color; the lawn and the beech tree, the trunks and leaves, the sky, took on the monochromatic blue of evening. Perrot continued to make Caroline dance. "Let's do." He gave her too many steps. The third part was not one person. It was two parts, a boy's and a girl's; he was both.

The part he wanted to see now was the girl's. He tried it on Caroline, though it was not for her; it was for somebody smaller and younger. Perrot made quick combinations, exuberant, cruel in their relentless speed, invulnerable; he made her impersonate Rosalind Child.

Alexander Ives watched Caroline Harbison dance. Perrot, working for himself, no longer spoke to him. Alexander leaned against the barre and studied Caroline—her feet, her body, her arms, the mechanics of her dancing. He watched her, excluded himself now, impatient with stillness.

Finally it grew so dark inside that Caroline's shape lost definition. "So," Perrot said to Alexander. "You understand. That is how it is. That is how a woman dances. If you do not know how, you cannot go on. Thank you, my dear." He bowed quickly to Caroline, as if they had just finished a waltz.

"Does anybody want to go into town and get a pizza?" Harry Menard asked, but nobody answered him, and he folded his music and scuttled out of the barn. The screen door banged.

Perrot turned to Caroline and Alexander. "Go now. I have work I want to do."

Fireflies darted under the trees. The warm air was dense with flowers, the intense night scent of nicotiana and the heavy smell of roses. The lights went on inside the barn and cast yellow parallelograms on the lawn. From inside Caroline and Alexander heard the piano. Achille Perrot began to play the Webern waltz himself, listening for steps.

They walked toward the lake with their arms around each other, the image of lovers. Bullfrogs belched their midsummer chorus; crickets trilled. Caroline, exhausted, leaned against Alexander's shoulder, and he took her weight.

"Why did Perrot do that?" Alexander asked.

"To show you. He did it for you, so you'd learn how a woman dances."

"But why?"

"Why? Maybe he thinks you've got talent. Maybe he just wants you to know how. Maybe he thinks it will make you stop wanting to choreograph when you find out how hard it really is. I don't know."

"You don't think he wants to frighten me?"

"I don't understand."

"Saying to me, 'Look, Alexander, this is what I know, and you don't.' "

"Maybe it had nothing to do with you. Maybe he was just working out ideas; you know, reminding himself of all that old stuff."

Alexander dropped his arm from Caroline's shoulder. "I have been thinking about leaving the company."

Caroline lifted her head. "And going where?"

"Anywhere. I could go anywhere."

"That's true." Her voice was without inflection. "So why don't you? What's there to think about?"

"If I went, what would you do?"

"What does it have to do with me? Maybe it would be the best thing." She wrapped her arm more firmly around his waist. "What would you want me to do?" she asked.

Alexander did not answer. She loosened her arm, and he continued to walk. Caroline followed. A whippoorwill called. "I haven't heard a whippoorwill for years," she said quietly. "Listen." The bird called again, whistling its name over and over. "Whippoorwill, whippoorwill," Caroline sang. "I haven't heard that since I was a little girl in Maine. I thought they were extinct."

"Maybe Fanny imported one for atmosphere."

"I could believe it. We rented a camp on a lake for a month every summer. We'd drive from Ohio, me and my parents and my older brother and the cat. It took us a day and a half. We'd drive straight through. My parents let my brother drive illegally. The cat always went nuts and screamed the whole first day. My father said he was going to kill it and I'd cry. I remember when we got to the bridge in Kittery at the New Hampshire state line we all cheered. The toll was a dime, and it meant that we only had two and a half hours to go. I loved it in Maine. I drew pictures of the lake all winter. I swam every day. We did puzzles and played gin rummy. My father taught me poker. Did you know I could play poker? I bet I never told you. I didn't dance at all. My mother worried about that, but I didn't care." Caroline laughed and said, as if the thought had just occurred to her, "If you left the company you couldn't come here every summer. I'd miss you."

"Do you think I'm serious?"

"Aren't you?"

Alexander let Caroline go ahead of him through a field of lilies, blossoms closed for the night. The weak light illuminated her long legs. She walked with a deer's nervous delicacy. At that moment Alexander loved her, but he could see past her, past the near edges of that short part of time to where it dropped off into blackness, to where he was alone.

That void was his recurring fear and his one certainty, a sensation he remembered from before words, which vibrated in his stomach and whirled on the inside of his eyelids. He danced against the edge of blackness; it encroached upon him, and he danced to keep it back: the emptiness of the theater, the emptiness in his own heart. There was for him no permanence. The audience that applauded him one moment from the blackness would hiss if he stumbled. He dreamed before performance that his knees had locked and he could only jerk jointless across the stage. To forestall the dream he danced as if he did not care. He tried to learn Perrot's contempt for the audience as he learned Perrot's steps, but in his fearful vision, the audience was one man multiplied, the hiss one sound. Perrot's magnified scornful eyes gleamed cold as onyx from every seat.

"And Perrot danced just to show me he could," he said to Caroline. "Just to remind me he was a dancer."

"Or to remind himself. He seemed strange tonight, did you notice? Maybe he knows what you're thinking. Maybe he was trying to keep you."

"He wouldn't care if I left."

"He loves you."

Alexander shook his head. "He's jealous of me."

"You're younger than he is. And you still dance. But he loves you. He'd never tell you. He wouldn't ask you to stay."

"He never knew his father," Alexander said, "like me."

"How did you find that out?"

"He told me, a long time ago, when I first joined the company. He told me he spent years looking for a family to belong to. He said that was why he liked triangles. I shouldn't have used three dancers in my ballet."

"What else did he tell you?"

"Nothing. I left him for you. Remember?"

"You never left him. You're still here."

"Maybe."

"You two hold grudges. You wait for each other to do something wrong. Why did he tell you those things?"

"He sees everything in mirrors. I looked like him. He thought I was like him."

"He wanted you to be his son."

"No. No. But he told me what it was like not to have a father. He told me I would have to invent myself. He told me it was a gift, not anything to feel sorry about. I was free."

"I have nothing to invent; it's all still there," Caroline said. "I used to think my childhood was boring. Not used to, I still do. All I can tell you about is poker and my cat. That cat died when I came to New York. Perrot is right, I suppose."

"No. You were lucky. It's not so frightening."

"What isn't? Sometimes it is. I feel so limited. I can't imagine. There are things I can't know about you. I can't know what to say to you."

"But you know how to be. I don't. I'm afraid."

The western sky retained light, an indigo wash above the trees. Overhead the stars were beginning to come out, and the dust of the Milky Way.

"What are you afraid of?" Caroline asked.

"Everything. It's the way I am."

"It makes me want to fix you."

Alexander put his arm around her shoulder and pulled her to him. "You'd be wasting your time."

She rose on her toes and stretched her neck, looking back over her shoulder. "Are you telling me to go away?"

"No." A shimmer of panic crossed Alexander's eyes. "I'm warning you about me."

Caroline pulled away angrily, then regretted her anger. He was not lying to her; he was telling her that he could not change. But she knew that however hard she tried to hold Alexander's warning in her mind, from habit and desire she would ignore it.

"Would you come with me if I left?" Alexander asked.

"I thought you weren't serious."

They had reached the lake and climbed down the rock steps to the ledge. The bright half-moon shone a white track across the water.

Alexander spoke: "It was hard for me to watch you dance."

"Why?"

"I hated being still."

"So does Perrot."

"He still dances. Why does he say I can't?"

"He's different."

"How?"

"He's a magician." She laughed. "You're a dancer. Maybe he wasn't as good as you are. I wonder why you want to make ballets so badly."

"Don't you want to?"

"I never thought about it."

"You don't feel like a trained monkey sometimes, out there doing what he tells you to do? 'Let's do. Let's do.' You don't think about what *you* would do to the music?"

"No. It's my fault, I suppose. I don't imagine. I don't invent."

"I imagined somebody else dancing with you. I hated it."

"You're lying," said Caroline.

"I'm telling the truth."

"Then I wish you were lying." He was contradicting his own warning. She sat down on the rock. She supposed that he did not feel much different from the way she did: limited, unable to be otherwise. "Where's Rosalind?" she asked.

Alexander shook his head. "I have no idea. She's not around, I don't think."

His indifference cheered Caroline. "This looks like a set for *Swan Lake*," she said.

A pair of Canada geese glided across the moon's path. Their wakes cut black wedges in the small silvered waves.

"Goose Pond." Alexander grinned, then masked his face with the abstracted expression of the *danseur noble*. He stretched his neck and flapped his arms and, honking the swan theme through his nose, danced an angular solo on the ledge. Caroline laughed and, when he offered her his hand, rose and bowed low to him. She flexed her feet at right angles to her legs; her elbows were bent, her shoulders thrust forward, her fingers splayed. They danced like a pair of demented loons. They sang and howled and hopped up and down until they frightened the geese. The geese, beating their wings against the water, raised their breasts from the lake. Their honks drowned out Alexander's accompaniment. With a frantic splash, they took off; flying low, they skimmed the dancers' heads. Caroline and Alexander ducked and felt the rush of air from their wings in their faces.

They collapsed laughing on the rock. "That big guy was Perrot," Alexander panted. "He lured us to the pond and changed himself into a kamikaze goose."

Their arms around each other again, they walked back through the field to Caroline's cottage. The moon lit cold colors: the tall grass white with gossamer gauze, the black leaves of the beech trees. Down the hill, yellow lights from the barn still streaked the lawn, and faintly the waltz reached them. Caroline held her door open for Alexander. He went to the refrigerator and found a carton of ice cream. Caroline, chilled and stiff, took a bath. When she was finished, Alexander showered. Caroline waited for him at the kitchen table in the dark, watching the moonlight reflect off the table's white enamel.

Alexander came out of the bathroom and stood behind her. He placed his hands against her sides. His fingers curved around her ribs. He lifted her, and she lightened herself for him. He turned her to face him and untied the rope of her bathrobe. He was naked, clean and gleaming; his skin shone white in the moon. He kissed her mouth and her neck. His hair dripped water on her breast as they began their other practiced dance.

They moved together into the bedroom. There were no curtains on the windows; the night light entered and with it the smells of the night, pines, dry grass. An animal rustled, a raccoon. A mile away a dog barked. An owl hooted. Alexander made small humming noises as he touched her body and partnered her. Caroline watched him as he danced. His eyes were slitted open; she saw crescents of white beneath his lashes. Inside her, he seemed remote as the moon.

He had gone inside himself. He moved to his own rhythm, his own dance. She pulled his hips against her so that his hipbones hurt her thighs. She wanted to change his dance, alter his steps, but he held her in his balance; inside her he moved until she was helpless. This was where she became afraid, where she wanted to stop following, unable to cross his distance. But this was his love. This was all he could do, this pleasure, all he could give. Let's do: invitation, command. And lonely as it made her, Caroline danced, her eyes wide open watching his white slitted eyes, which now saw nothing.

9

CAROLINE HARBISON SLEPT HARD IN SELF-defense. She dreamed of Alexander Ives with her in Maine, secure in the long days of remembered summers; she dreamed that she danced with him to new music, steps she did not know. She dreamed that the cat escaped through the open car window on the Kittery bridge, and she awakened at first light, rigid with anxiety, to Alexander leaving the bed. She rolled on her back and reached for him. She grabbed, hoping to catch cat fur, but her hand found pillow. There was no cat, she realized; the cat was dead. She let Alexander go. She shifted back to her side and pretended to fall asleep again and waited until the door closed behind him. She stretched, trying to enjoy the newly empty space in bed. It was just after five, and the deep orange-pink dawn was already whitening, but her anxiety did not clear.

She lay in the bed for half an hour and watched colors return, blue and green, blue sky, green leaves, the simple summer colors. She went to the bathroom. She had purple shadows under her eyes. She turned off the bathroom light so that she couldn't see her drawn skin as she brushed her hair and pinned it on top of her head. She dressed in rehearsal clothes. When she got to the barn, her sneakers were soaked. The studio was smoky from the night before. Caroline opened a window and found the tape recorder. She pulled a tape from her dance bag, put it into the machine, sat on the floor, and listened to the Webern arrangements of Strauss waltzes for chamber orchestra.

She played the music through once and rewound the tape and played it again. While it ran, she put on her toe shoes and rubbed her feet in the resin box in the corner. She stretched at the barre. The room was chill, damp as the outdoors; her joints were stiff. Her ankle had swollen. Yesterday she should not have continued dancing for Achille Perrot, but yesterday it had not hurt.

She accused herself of lacking the strength to admit weakness. Let's do, and she did. She began a barre. Sweat started on her back, between her breasts. She moved to the center of the room. She began to put steps to the music, waltz steps back and forth across the room. She added turns. One, two, three, one, two, three. What next? She had waltzed, she had spun. She tried little steps, glissades, low leaps, sauts de chat. Cat jumps. Cats again. Cute steps, little boring steps.

She held out her arms for a partner and waited for Alexander to cross the stage in two or three high, ballooning leaps and embrace her to take her into his dance. She tried to imagine what he could do. The music ran on. She could not imagine.

The sounds were dark and imploded, the harmonies compressed, diminished; the music spoke of misery she could not imagine. Not with her happy childhood. It was a shortcoming. She had been happy. Happy meant something to her, something palpable, an attainable state, a smell of dinner, a clock that marked predictable hours. Her mother was happy with her children; her father was happy at his job. His business. He owned a carpeting store. He loved rugs. Their house was always beautifully carpeted wall to wall in thick, tufted broadloom of the finest quality. She remembered her father's pride in those words. Every room except the kitchen had carpet, even the bathrooms. But when Caroline began to dance, her father ripped up the new beige wool broadloom and refinished the den floor to give her a place to practice. She had been wanted.

She was not happy now. She fixed on the moment she awoke, panicked, helpless, the cat in her dream gone, Alexander gone from her bed. Now she was with the music, arranged in the twenties, Perrot had said, on the brink of catastrophe, and she tried to move to it. One, two, three, one, two, three, the lilting rhythm contradicted the unresolved harmonies. Her feet kept the waltz time, her upper body tried to cancel it. She moved in a slow circle, her arms out, empty.

What next? Anything: a piqué turn, a passé entrechat. No. Perrot had her do those yesterday. She leapt anyway and in midair rapidly shifted her feet into fifth position, right front, back front. No. That combination was from *Giselle*, from another time, when dreams and death were white, not bloody. She could not imagine. The waltz maddened her. There was no "Let's do" in her head, no impulsion to invent the next combination of steps. She spun in a fury, small fast chained turns in a diagonal across the room: step half-turn, step half-turn.

The waltz ended. The tape machine clicked off. Caroline Harbison continued turning to silence. Her feet drummed the floor. She reached the corner and spun back again. Her head whipped around. She focused on the trunk of the beech tree outside the window, spotted it to avert toppling from dizziness. Her arms opened and contracted, wrapping her body to increase speed. She panted; her legs were burning. Back and forth she spun. She could no longer see the tree; tears blinded her eyes.

Caroline stopped dead. The room continued to reel on a skewed axis. She sat on the floor and sank her head between her knees.

She could not imagine. She longed for someone to come in and rewind the tape and tell her what steps to do. The steps would show her how to feel; given an outline she could color it in, neatly, perfectly. She felt contempt for herself. She loosened the ribbons of her shoes and rubbed her ankle. It needed ice to reduce the swelling. She wiggled her swollen toes free from the constricting satin boxes of the shoes. Her sneakers were clammy on her hot feet.

Outside, the day was already midsummer slow, indolent with heat and the sun's long arc. Caroline longed for Alexander and for his dance. "Let's do," she said aloud, hoping for an answer.

As he drove up the driveway, Amos Furst saw Caroline Harbison leave the barn. He stopped the car. Her dark hair had come loose and hung half-uncoiled along the right side of her neck. She walked deliberately and did not turn at the sound of the slowing engine. She was being ungainly, deliberately not moving like a dancer; she let her head droop and concentrated on watching her feet swish through the grass. The sun shadowed the large vertebrae at her nape. She was worn, Amos Furst thought, worn beautiful, like driftwood.

Beside Amos, Dana Coelho slept in the passenger seat. His head was back, his mouth open. His breath burbled in his throat. They had flown together from Detroit, a night flight immediately after Dana's last performance at the Arbroath Festival, and they had driven from New York. Eveline de Charny had asked Amos to bring Dana back to Arabesque, a favor, an opportunity for Amos to atone for the error of having found a job without her help. Wanting to restore himself to her good graces, he had said he would. She kept a ledger, and this would pay her back and put her slightly in his debt. But he was angry at Eveline de Charny for asking him to shepherd a person he barely knew and angry at himself for feeling that he owed it to her to do it. He had protested: Dana could take care of himself, but Eveline had pressed him. "Support Dana," she said. "Dana needs support; he needs nurturing. It's the least you can do."

"I'm not the nurturing type," Amos had answered.

What did he want Eveline's good graces for? he wondered. Was it the luxurious feel of the glamour that padded her life like sable, or was it Eveline herself—the tantalizing flashes of heart? Or did he simply want to go back to Arabesque?

Amos had watched Dana's performance at the Arbroath Festival. He had seen Dana dance in rehearsal in New York and had enjoyed his exuberance; in Detroit he hardly recognized the dancer. Dana danced recklessly, launching himself into each leap as if it were the last he would ever take. It amazed Amos, the abandon with which Dana danced. He stretched his body farther than it should have gone, thrust his legs higher, arched his back at breaking angles. For the evening's final segment, he danced the part of the Prince in the last pas de deux from Perrot's new *Swan Lake*. He had overwhelmed the girl he danced with. Uncertain in her steps, she was almost incidental; he barely helped her through her balances. Instead of celebrating his lightness, his gift to leave the ground, in this last piece, Dana Coelho had seemed to be desperate, protesting his inability to fly. There was an element of fear in his dancing, and anger at the tyranny of gravity. He leapt across the stage, hating the floor, hating the descent, terrified of landing.

Afterward Amos waited to accompany him to the airport. The taxi idled outside the little theater on the Arbroath estate, spewing exhaust fumes through the acres of trees. Amos was sure that they would miss their flight. Dana emerged, finally, moving slowly, breathing with an effort. He wore a jacket into the hot night. Roland de Charny came with him. The older man shook hands cordially with Amos and congratulated him on the excellent review Gertrude Stella had given his performance. "He is a chameleon; he becomes his characters; he ages thirty years by changing his walk. His humor subtly twists reality," she had written. "You're never sure if you should gasp with horror or if you should laugh." Roland de Charny continued to talk to Amos—"Give my regards to my daughter when you see her"—his eye on Dana, unwilling to remove his hands from the door and let the taxi go, although the airport was forty-five minutes away. They ran through the terminal and down the loading ramp, which lifted away as soon as they boarded the plane; Roland de Charny must have had the flight held.

After takeoff, Dana reached into his nylon duffel and pulled out a notebook. He wrote in it, and when Amos surreptitiously tried to read what he was writing, Dana grinned and wrapped his hand around the top, like a child preventing his classmate from copying. When he finished, he stowed the notebook and wrapped himself in a blanket, though the plane was overheated. Amos asked the weary stewardess if she minded if he opened the window for a breeze. She did not laugh.

"Did you like my dancing?" Dana asked over Pennsylvania.

"It was incredible," said Amos. "To tell you the truth I was shaking at the end."

"I wasn't sure I was any good."

"You were."

"You're not putting me on?"

"Why should I?"

"Eveline told you to. She told you to say nice things to me. She's very protective. She worries."

"You're strung out."

"A little high. It was awful, wasn't it?"

"It was spectacular. You shouldn't do this to yourself."

"Shouldn't do what?"

"Drugs," said Amos.

"Everybody does."

"Maybe."

"I'm glad you're here. I hate being alone. Especially after a performance, but I had to leave tonight. I had no place to stay. Mrs. de Charny wanted me gone. I liked her, though. She's a strong lady. I feel sorry for Eveline, with a mom like that. Tough act." He shivered. "Damn. I'm coming down. You wouldn't have anything with you?"

Amos shook his head. Dana pulled the blanket tighter around his shoulders and stretched out on the seat. His head grazed Amos Furst's shoulder.

"Do you want another blanket?" Amos asked.

Dana shook his head. "But you're very nice."

Amos laughed. "Are you coming on to me?"

"Only if you want."

"I don't think so. It's nothing personal."

"I just wanted to thank you."

Driving from New York, they got lost on the small Berk-shire roads after the last New York State Thruway exit. Amos, frustrated at the prospect of wandering around the Loewens' compound after he had finally found it, thought to catch Caroline Harbison to ask her which was Dana's cottage, but he hesitated to call through the still air. He continued up the driveway. Amos saw Alexander Ives cross the lawn beside the barn. He looked at his watch; it was just eight. Dana hugged himself tightly in his sleep and rocked unconscious against the doorframe. Amos was exhausted himself. The metallic odor of jet fumes permeated his clothes and skin.

He drove a quarter of a mile farther up the driveway and stopped again where a dirt track branched off. He shook Dana harshly until he opened his eyes. "Look. Do you know where you are?" he asked. "Are we near your place?"

Dana nodded groggily and closed his eyes and fell back against the headrest. "This is it. My driveway. We're here."

"Wake up," said Amos. "You've got to get out. There's something I have to do."

Dana, his eyes glazed, stared at him. His head seemed heavy enough to fall off.

"Go on," said Amos. "You're fine. You need fresh air and a shower, and you need to clean up your act. I'll bring your luggage by later."

Dana shivered. Amos reached in front of him and opened the car door. Dana wiped his eyes with his fists; they were teary with sleep. His mouth was loose and lush, un-guarded. He sat up and rested his hand on Amos's thigh. He smiled, a gentle, grateful expression, and leaned over and kissed Amos on the cheek; Dana's lips touched delicately. "Thanks," he said. "I don't think I could have made it here without you." He opened the door.

"Be careful," Amos said, his voice, despite himself, con-stricted with tenderness. "Wait. Get back in. I'll drive you."

"No, this is good for me, like orange juice." Dana grinned and gripped the doorframe and swung himself out of the car. He waved and stepped unsteadily down the track, his linen clothes crushed, his curly hair dulled with travel, deflecting sunlight.

Amos Furst backed the car up and parked it below the barn. He ran across the lawn to catch Caroline Harbison. He called her name, and she started and gazed at him quizzically as if she could not remember who he was.

"Amos Furst," he said.

"I know. I'm just a little spacey."

"You're up early."

"Well, the sun gets up early," she said, and continued walking. "I couldn't sleep." She kept her head down and marched heels first. He noticed the fine dark hair stuck to her neck, the gleam on her nose of sweat not yet dried.

"You've been dancing."

"Not exactly."

He walked with her. "Where are you going?"

"Home. Back to bed."

"Can I go with you?"

She raised her head and glared at him.

"I meant, can I walk you home?"

"Sure, if you want." Caroline Harbison walked quickly. Her calves bulged; despite her thinness, her muscles had an athlete's bulk; unlike an athlete's, her face was pale and thin-skinned. The vertical vein dividing her forehead protruded. The sun was already high and the air still; the breeze had not yet come up. Caroline bent over and pulled off her sneakers. She wiggled her long, muscular toes in the grass. Their joints were red and inflamed.

"Why were you dancing so early?" Amos asked.

"I told you I wasn't exactly dancing." They walked silently until they reached her cottage. Like the others the Loewens had built, it was a gray-shingled one-story oblong. A small peaked gable sheltered the front door; the steps were two slabs of granite scored with the drill holes by which they had been quarried. Caroline stood on the top step, her hand on the door. "Good morning, good-bye," she said.

"Don't go."

She smiled and shifted her weight away from the door. "Okay. What are you doing here? Visiting Eveline?"

"I brought Dana back from Detroit, from the Arbroath Festival. He's not in great shape."

"He likes to party," said Caroline. "He's a kid. Did you see him dance?"

"It was scary. Beautiful. He was right on the edge. You wanted to catch him before he fell."

Caroline nodded. "He makes me feel like that, too." She sat down on the steps and put her head in her hands. "Sometimes I don't blame him." She lifted her head. "Why did you bring him back?"

"Eveline de Charny asked me to. I did it for her."

Caroline nodded, indifferent. "She was angry at you."

"Yeah. I'm orbiting out of her sphere of influence."

"Is she really like that?"

"She likes her gravity, that's for sure. And she feeds you that garbage about how artists need nurturing like kids, but they're better than kids because they don't grow up. She could get a dog and it would do the same thing."

"That's nasty. What did she do to you?"

"You were there. She wanted me to get naked and tie-dye myself like Devon. And I'm angry at myself because I'm trying to make up with her."

"She wasn't serious about Devon."

"Yes, she was. She doesn't see the difference in what we do. Performance artists, she calls us both, so we mix and match. No, *she* mixes and matches."

"She's been nice to me," said Caroline. "I like her."

"I didn't say I don't." He stretched. Caroline appraised his shape, the way dancers watched other dancers. "Caroline," he asked, "if you weren't dancing, what were you doing?"

She furrowed her brow, and she tried to pin her hair back up but it came loose again and fell around her shoulders. "Would it be enough for you if you were just an actor? Or just a clown?"

"Just an actor? What is 'just'?"

"I mean if you didn't make up what you perform."

"Probably not. Why?"

"How do you imagine what you do? How do you come up with it?"

He shook his head, abashed. "I don't imagine anything. It's all around. I see it. I look for it. I play. I try things. Sometimes they work, sometimes they don't."

"Show me."

"How?"

"Be somebody."

"That takes a long time to do. I can't just be somebody."

"Try, please."

"Why?"

"I want to see."

"All right. I'll be Alexander Ives." He stood straight, tilted his head at a dancer's perfect angle, and extended his arm toward Caroline in a round gesture of yearning. His eyes were wide and anxious, his lips full. He stepped toward her until his fingers almost touched her shoulder. Abruptly he straightened his arm and thrust his hand palm outward. His mouth tightened, his eyes dropped guiltily, and, when he raised them, his gaze had shifted from Caroline to a point past her.

She was struck, wounded, but she smiled at Amos. Her expression was opaque, polite, her bearing distant, remote as Alexander's could be. "Then what?"

"Just that. Then what? I'd have to work out a voice. Soft, maybe, kind of tentative, because dancers don't talk much. I don't know. It's not something I can just do any more than you can just make up a dance."

"Then what," said Caroline.

"I told you; I don't know."

"No, 'Then what?' That's the question you ask yourself, isn't it? I can't ask it. 'Then what?' I freeze." She wrapped her arms across her chest.

"What were you trying to do?"

"Make a ballet. I couldn't. Alexander said, 'Don't you get tired of doing what he tells you to do? Don't you want to make up your own steps?' So I tried." She looked at him accusingly. "You make it sound so easy."

163

"It takes practice. I've been doing this for years. I was awful at first. There's nothing wrong with not wanting to."

"I don't think I want to." She lowered her head. "But I think, then what will I do? With my life, I mean."

She curled her toes around the edge of the granite slab until the joints turned white. Amos Furst touched her loose hair where it fell against her face. She brushed her hair back, beyond his reach. Her gray-blue eyes were cloudy. He turned to look and, although there was nobody behind him, he saw as clearly as she whom she was looking for.

"You're not asking about dancing," he said.

"I am."

"So Alexander's a dance?"

She glared at him.

"Sorry," he said. "I can't help it. An exit line. It just takes practice."

Alexander Ives noticed the fresh white crescents of resin on the floor, the repeated diagonals. The air in the barn smelled faintly of Caroline's powder. In the tape machine he found the Webern-Schoenberg waltzes. The patterns of resin were not what they had been dancing with Perrot. This morning, he realized, she had already been in the barn, trying to make steps. He stretched wearily and felt the memory of her body against him, its sharp known angles, the edges of his love, his fear.

He wished she would leave him so that he would know what it would be like without the balance she gave him. That, he realized, was the truth: Caroline balanced him; she kept him from falling. Even the wish that she would leave him sent a current of panic through his chest. He could not leave her; she would have to do it.

He played the tape of the Webern-Schoenberg waltzes. Back and forth she had gone. Alexander imagined her whirling on these diagonals, and he ached with pity for her. Perrot had moved them in circles. Alexander remembered Perrot dancing. He spun out quick, light steps, weightless. He remembered the rapid tapping of Perrot's feet, eighth notes, six to every measure of the waltz.

Alexander understood that Perrot had been making those steps for Rosalind Child. If Rosalind Child had been at Arabesque, Perrot would have had her in the barn with them, Alexander thought angrily. Perrot saw into his life, opened up his heart, and took what he saw for himself. Perrot was going to make Rosalind Child whirl in and out of Alexander's waltz with Caroline, interrupting them. Alexander hated Perrot's eyes that saw into lives and reduced them to steps, patterns on a stage.

Alexander began to dance Perrot's choreography. He saw the spaces Rosalind Child would fill, imagined the accuracy of her stepping between him and Caroline, circling the constricted patterns he and Caroline Harbison made. What was Rosalind to him? Alexander wondered. She was so light and young that she frightened him, so certain of her body and unconcerned with consequences, unacquainted with need. When she walked she hardly bent the grass. Her body could have been cut from marble and refined and polished until no imperfection, no trace of work or effort, remained; it was dangerous in its smoothness, its impermeability.

Through Caroline's translucent skin as she danced every effort showed, every thought, every wish for love. Rosalind reflected light and dazzled. Alexander stopped the tape and ejected it from the machine. If Perrot could not have Alexander, then he would take Alexander's desire; he could expose Alexander by giving him the steps to dance his own life. Alexander wanted his own steps.

He suspected that Perrot knew him better than a father, had taught him more than a father could. But he also demanded more fealty and required more love; he became more jealous. Alexander Ives did not understand how to survive fathers.

Alexander's own father, a poet, had fled to Italy within months of Alexander's birth; the infant's chaos, its dislocation of order and of time and affection, had unnerved him. Alexander was five before he knew his father was living; until then there existed in his image of life a cold hole where his father should have been, an absence colored black in the shape of a man beside his mother.

A package arrived in the mail one day adorned with foreign stamps, addressed to him in large, exuberant handwriting with the street and number of the house where his family had lived when he was born. The parcel had been forwarded twice, and the brown shiny wrapping paper was ripped. His mother bit her lip when she handed it to him; he smelled her anger. She let him unwrap it, but stood over him ready to snatch it away in case it proved dangerous. Inside was a book. One of the first pages was blank except for the words "To Alexander." He could read well enough to recognize his name, which, printed, seemed both familiar and strange, but the book lacked pictures and disappointed him. "These are your father's poems," his thin, dry, bony mother said bitterly, and after he had looked at his name and studied his father's name on the cover, bigger than his and repeated on the front inside page, he could not understand it.

He pestered his mother about his father, but all she would say was "If he wants to tell you about himself, he can come back and do it. I won't. God knows what I'd say, and I'd be right, too. But I won't stop him from seeing you, if he ever decides to do that. Don't be surprised if he doesn't, though, I'm warning you." His father never came back and never wrote or telephoned, although two more books arrived from Italy, one when Alexander was eight and another when he was seventeen. The last book had a photograph of his father on the back inside flap of the dust jacket. The man was a prefiguration of himself in twenty years: handsome bones closer to the skin, cheeks hollow, the long nose stretched, more pronounced, lips thinner, skin lined, gray strands mixed into his black curly hair. His expression was yearning, as if he were asking for love or answers from his anonymous readers. The biographical sketch said only that he lived in Italy. His publisher was English. Alexander read the poems; they were dense with obscure references to medieval philosophers.

One poem Alexander understood had to do with him. It took the form of an interrogation, and he—the son—was the inquisitor. In it the poet explained the limits of love in terms of the vast blackness of space. Why do you not love me? the inquisitor asked, and the poet answered that conception was a random act, like the impact of a meteor on earth. *"What could be born out of that black and burning shock?" the poet asked. "What of me? Of me there was not enough, no molten core, Only brittle rock."*

A few months later, Alexander found in a magazine a lengthy article praising the book. "He is a poet of renunciation," the reviewer explained. There was another photograph, a snapshot; here the poet wore shorts and hiking boots and squinted into the sun. He stood on a mountain, at the edge of a cliff, and he leaned out over it toward a rock face in the background—layers of heaved, striated rock resembling a striped Bedouin cloth. The poet pulled away from the camera, his head back, black hair glinting in the light, laughing. Alexander wrote to him in care of his London publishers, but never received a reply. Soon afterward, his mother got a call from a friend who had learned that his father had been killed climbing in the Dolomites. It was as if her husband had just left her. She wept for hours. Burned dry with hot new anger, he did not join her or try to comfort her.

He stretched again, then bent with his head between his knees so his palms touched the floor. He took a tape of the Schubert impromptus from his pocket, put it into the tape machine, removed his shoes and socks, and stood in the middle of the floor listening. Caroline's resin prickled his bare feet like sharp sand. He began to mark a woman's steps—the combinations Perrot had given Caroline to do the night before, the old steps Perrot's nineteenth-century namesake had made for Carlotta Grisi as Giselle at the Paris Opera. Alexander walked through his own ballet, seeing now where he had given Caroline too many steps, or too few, how one did not chain into another, how another provided no impetus or no balance for the next.

He danced with her and held out his arms for her, and he could sense the contraction of the muscles in her waist and thighs as he reached for her and lifted her, as he steadied her in turns. But they would not touch; he wanted his ending. At the end he wanted her to balance herself. She had to. He wanted to change the truth that she balanced him.

He wanted nobody to touch. He danced his own part, altering his steps to match her new ones. He danced Dana's steps to the high notes; he danced airy desire, Dana's body pliable with delight, coiling like a cool snake. Alexander was delirious with invention, and at that moment he understood Achille Perrot, his ruthlessness born of love.

The tape stopped and he started it again, and once again. He lost his sense of time; it existed only within the music. On the floor, the sun shadowed the squares of the small-paned windows. Alexander danced in and out of the barred light. Steps spun out of him; the veins in his temples throbbed with pleasure; his face was flushed. Perrot had given him a father's gift. Perrot gave him steps. Alexander tilted back his head and laughed as he glided and turned and leapt, inventing.

A shadow blocked the sunlit grid. Alexander stopped dancing; his chest heaved. Laughing, he looked out the window, half expecting to see Caroline, come to dance with him. But it was Achille Perrot, blocking the light, his eyes black holes, his nose a hawk's beak. Alexander froze, abashed that Perrot had seen him joyful, as if that would make the old man take back what he had given. He looked at his watch: ten o'clock, the hour Perrot came to work. Alexander willed Perrot to go away. Perrot nodded at him, acquiescing, and turned aside. The sun struck his face, and he smiled at Alexander, a smile at once jealous and complicitous. He backed off, letting the sun shadow bars again, leaving Alexander behind them.

Returning to his car, Amos Furst approached the barn and looked through the window. Alexander Ives was dancing. Except for white shorts, he was naked, and his chest and face gleamed with sweat as if they had been oiled. The thud and brush of his feet when he jumped and glided across the floor almost drowned out the music.

The dancer's grace threatened Amos. He wanted to run; he wanted to capture it. Alexander Ives seemed an animal inside the bars the sun cast on the floor; he seemed too big for the room. But as he crossed from corner to corner, he was vulnerable, too; self-absorbed, innocent of danger.

Watching him, Amos Furst instinctively crouched out of sight. His body was wound tense. He prepared to leap—a hunter stalking his quarry. His heart raced and sweat started. His breathing quickened and grew shallow. He hyperventilated, matching Alexander Ives's fast breath, spellbound by the dancer's grace. Amos shivered as he realized that this was how Roland de Charny had described hunting: it was all for the moment of possession, the moment of identification, the sexual longing to enter and be entered. And Amos understood Caroline Harbison as well, her desire to be possessed by beauty; there was an exquisite moment when to be possessed did not differ from possessing.

Amos Furst drove to Eveline de Charny's house.

"Missy still asleep," Atalanta said as she opened the door. "You want to go to her room?"

Amos laughed. "And wake her with a kiss?" He shook his head. "I'm no prince. I want to go to my room, to sleep, too. Alone, please. Just tell me where it is. And if I wasn't supposed to have a room, maybe we can find me one."

Atalanta tilted her head. "You want separate room?"

"Yes."

"What I tell missy?"

"That's my problem, don't you think?"

Atalanta shrugged and let him inside.

"She's done a great job with the house. Do you like it here?" Amos asked.

Atalanta shrugged again. "A house is a house."

"Have you been out?"

She shook her head. "Where?"

"Into town. For a walk, anywhere."

"I walk here, all day." Atalanta looked at her feet in her broken sneakers. "Missy needs me."

"I'll take you to town. You should see it. Lots of stores, a nice white church. What America is all about. Maybe we'll go later, after I clean up."

"But missy—"

"Missy owes me one."

Atalanta crossed her arms over her chest. "You feel sorry for me?"

Amos considered her. "Yes."

Atalanta turned away from him. "Then I not go." He followed her up the stairs to a small room under one of the turrets. The room, painted in a luminous gray lacquer, was already hot from the sun through the skylight. She pressed a button in the wall. A motor whirred, and the skylight opened. Atalanta started to close the door behind her.

"Wait," said Amos. He put down his satchel, and she watched him with her arms crossed. "Atalanta, do you feel sorry for me?"

She looked at the floor. Her dark cheeks flushed, but her Indian eyes, when she raised them, had narrowed with mirth. She nodded vigorously. "Yes, yes," she said, and turned to go.

"Wait." Amos stopped her. "Why?"

"You want many things. You want from her. You don't like to want, but you don't say no. And then you get mad at her."

"So do you."

"I do. I do. But I take care of her." Atalanta gazed at him. "She is a lonesome person. You should go to her."

"Because if I don't, she'll take it out on you."

Atalanta shrugged and laughed.

"What is it about her?" Amos asked. "What does she have that makes us want to keep her happy?"

Atalanta gazed at him like a conspirator. She crossed the room to the bed and stroked the bedspread. It shimmered under her dark stubby hand; its silvery gray perfectly matched the walls; it was part of the luminous effect. "Feel," Atalanta said to Amos.

The bed cover was finely woven, silk filaments combed

softer than feathers. The texture surprised Amos; he drew back as if it were alive, as if the material aroused him. Then he realized what Atalanta was showing him, its richness.

"She has," Atalanta hissed. "She has." She closed him inside the room.

10

HEAT CLOGGED THE CORRIDORS OF THE PERROT Ballet's offices in New York, accumulated over the summer, thick and gluey by the end of August. It precipitated a layer of grime on the corps de ballet as they returned to the studio for the first day of rehearsal for the fall season. They sat on the floor where the air was slightly cooler and pressed the backs of their legs for relief against the linoleum tile and sewed ribbons and elastic onto their new toe shoes. They gossiped like a flock of migrating birds, chirping that they dreaded class, complaining that they were out of shape.

Their twittering reached Achille Perrot through the closed door of his office, interrupting the music in his head. He was eager to begin rehearsing. Time was compressing for him, and movement became urgent. Memory distilled into steps. He saw dances. He was unable to sleep. When he closed his eyes, the dances began. He was afraid of how much time it would take to translate what he saw in his mind onto bodies. He lay awake, conscious of every minute, aware of the imperceptible lengthening of the August nights, while the days continued hot and clear, deceiving, pretending they were not shortening.

The increasing darkness angered him. It shrank the space he occupied; it squeezed the air out of him. From his dust-filmed window, he saw Sumner Loewen's maroon car halt, blocking traffic. Horns honked. Sumner emerged serene and waved the chauffeur on. The day was hazed with heat, the sky dull white; Sumner Loewen wore a dark suit; he was a man accustomed to air conditioning. The wholesaler across the street hosed down his sooty plants. Sumner Loewen, his feet in shoes so bright they seemed varnished, minced over the ribbons of water that meandered down the sidewalk and into the gutter.

As soon as he heard the knock, Achille Perrot called, "Come in." Sumner Loewen, slightly flushed from his exertion, closed the door behind him.

"I do enjoy that sound," he said with a smile, inclining his head toward the humming air conditioner. "On a day like this it's quite musical. But don't you think we need offices with central air? These appliances seem so makeshift." He put his old-fashioned accordion briefcase on a chair and took out a large envelope. The label bore the address of a law firm, five names of diverse ethnic origin in Roman capitals separated by commas. "Achille, I hate to bother you with my business while you're just getting down to yours, but something has come up."

"Long-term plans?" Perrot asked. He leaned against the wall beside the window, avoiding the air-conditioned draft. The skin of his face was white and dusty, translucent like the window glass; his lips were brown, as if he had stained them ocher.

"No, quite short-term, actually. It's—"

"Sumner, I have some business to take up with you as well," Perrot interrupted. "Guy has had an inquiry about Alexander's little ballet. It seems that people have been talking about it. Miss Gertrude Stella called to say that she is anxious to see it. I am not sure what there is to see; I am not sure if it still exists. She also asked, Guy tells me, what the ballet means. I assume she was not interested in an explanation of its allegory. It is her impression that this little exercise of Alexander's indicates a fundamental change in the company. What do you think she is talking about? And how does she know about the ballet? I do not think Alexander told her. He would not be so self-serving, do you think?"

Sumner Loewen saw that Perrot was affronted, but anxious as well; he squinted as if his vision were failing. Even magnified by his strong lenses, his eyes seemed to be receding; the direction of his gaze was shifting to what danced in his mind. Sumner Loewen felt a surge of pity for Perrot like that which he had felt after the first performance of *Swan Lake*. "No," Sumner said, "he would not. But everyone talks. I don't have to tell you that. Dana, probably. He and Gertrude were in Michigan together a month ago, I understand. Nothing stays quiet for long."

Perrot smiled at him. "Perhaps you are right. We shall say nothing and leave Gertrude Stella frustrated."

"I'm not sure I'd want to do that. I could take her into my confidence and explain that everything is still very tentative, and we would appreciate her discretion. She'll understand; she'll love it."

"No," said Perrot. "What will happen will happen. I do not care what she writes." He turned toward the window again. The white light flattened his face and turned it into a mask. "But, Sumner, nothing is tentative."

Sumner Loewen opened his mouth to reply and decided against it. Perrot cared nothing for the intricacies of maintaining the company, for the need to cultivate Gertrude Stella. "Achille," Sumner Loewen began again. His voice was conciliatory. "We have had a gift."

"I congratulate you."

"This building has been sold."

"That is no gift."

"It is. The building is ours, in a manner of speaking." Sumner Loewen took the papers from the envelope and placed them on the table between himself and Achille Perrot. It was a lease; Sumner Loewen pointed to a paragraph at the bottom of the first page. Typed in the blank for the amount of yearly rental was the figure "$1.00."

Perrot said, "Who bought the building? Whom did you organize to buy it?"

"Nobody. I was completely surprised. I had nothing to do with it. It was Roland de Charny."

Achille Perrot's lips compressed. "That is unfortunate." He picked up the lease, turned the pages, and gazed at the signature.

"I'm not comfortable with this, either," Sumner Loewen said. "I don't understand it."

"You were eager to recruit him, if I remember. You have become an uncle to his daughter."

"But I had no contact with him." He pointed to the lease. "This was the first I heard of what he had done. It was delivered to my office. I would never have encouraged this. It worries me; it's too close. I'll have to be careful. I know he's difficult."

"As am I."

"But you and I want the same thing." Sumner Loewen smiled.

"We used to," said Perrot.

Sumner Loewen ignored Perrot's answer. "I don't understand why he didn't buy it and give the building to us outright. He would have benefited from the charitable deduction—not as much as in the past, true—or he could have written it off as a real-estate loss. It does him no good to hold on to it."

"Perhaps he wanted to become our landlord while appearing to be our benefactor."

Sumner Loewen paused and smoothed his white hair back from his forehead, preparing for the confrontation. He placed his smooth pink hands on the table. "You could have avoided this," he said.

"I? How? I have no interest in the building."

"That's the point. If you have no interest, how can I ask for contributions? You barely acknowledge the donors. You speak to them twice a year. People know you want only ballets; to make you happy, they give money to produce ballets, but for nothing else. We could have owned the building years ago if you'd been interested."

"But I am not interested."

"Then we won't survive. Things have changed. They're more expensive, for one. Secondly, it's not enough anymore just to be good. You don't understand that."

"I don't have to," Achille Perrot said impatiently. "For me, I have enough. I am satisfied." He smiled at Sumner Loewen and rested his long white hand on his friend's shoulder as if to soothe him. "We have had this difference for a long time, Sumner. You want the future. I do not. You are correct: all that interests me is making ballets, which is very much in the present." He handed the lease to Sumner Loewen. "But we must move our offices. That is unfortunate. I cannot afford the time. Roland de Charny will be difficult to control. Perhaps another company will move here. He can be its benefactor. But I cannot work in this building if he owns it. I will tell Guy to look for new rehearsal space immediately."

"Aren't you being a bit irrational?"

Perrot smiled. "He can raise the rent. Sumner, you have been too greedy, and it has reversed—backfired."

"You don't believe me when I say it was not my idea." Sumner Loewen gazed at the choreographer, his thin, elegant nostrils flared, his mild eyes icy. "No, Achille, I think that you are the greedy one."

Achille Perrot shook his head. "Since when is it greedy to want nothing?"

He took off his glasses and rubbed his eyes. His face seemed concave, collapsing, and Sumner Loewen could not hold his anger against this new inwardness of Perrot's. Loss supplanted anger, loss as oppressive as stagnant heat.

The door opened a crack and Guy Pissarro thrust his small, close-shaven face into the office. "I am sorry to disturb you," he whispered, "but Miss Eveline de Charny is outside."

Sumner Loewen nodded. "I forgot that she was coming. Guy, please tell her I will be right with her." He had started to get up when the door opened and Eveline de Charny appeared beside Guy Pissarro.

She placed her hand on the tiny ballet master's wrist, pushed it down as if it were a turnstyle, and entered the office. She stopped two steps into the room and paused, hesitating at the sight of Achille Perrot without his glasses. They unnerved her, his eyes unprotected.

Achille Perrot admired Eveline de Charny's entrances. She possessed the instinctive timing of an actress and the capacity to dominate space with her presence. He resisted the urge to applaud. Her height, her posture, her stark coloring, black hair and black eyes, and spare clothes—today a short black dress cut to reveal the strong muscles of her arms and legs and shoulders—she was so unlike a dancer.

She was built for tableaux, for poses. He rearmed himself and put on his glasses. He mistrusted her; he mistrusted her stillness.

Like an actress, she was attuned to her audience, and she saw that she had created an effect that left her the room to apologize and put them in her debt. "I didn't think I would be disturbing you," she said.

"You are not," said Sumner Loewen. "We have finished."

Eveline de Charny smiled, a distant, all-purpose expression, tantalizing with its hints of warmth. "I would like to speak to you, Achille," she said, and blushed slightly as she uttered the choreographer's first name.

Achille Perrot's eyes narrowed. As if she were not in the room, he said to Guy Pissarro, "Has Dana come to the studio? Do you know where he is?"

"I have not seen him."

"He's in town," Eveline de Charny volunteered.

Perrot shrugged. "Then he will be here when he is ready. I hope it will not be too late to use him."

Guy Pissarro nodded and left. Eveline de Charny advanced a step toward Achille Perrot and said, "Sumner asked me to come and watch class this afternoon. I know that you don't object to that, but I want to push you a bit further. I want to ask you whether it would be possible—whether you would permit me, once, to take your class." Her smile intensified, to draw him in. "Guy has let me take his classes, but, well, I want to know what it is like to dance for you. I would stay in the back. I would not expect you to correct me." She faced him, erect, at once imperious and supplicating.

"Those are your conditions?" Perrot asked, his voice edged with sarcasm.

Sumner Loewen hurried to intervene, to assuage her. "My dear Eveline, Achille and I appreciate your passion. It flatters us. And I have to tell you that you are looking extremely well. Your summer in the country suited you."

"It was the creative atmosphere," said Eveline de Charny, her eyes still on Perrot. "It was a precious time for me."

He did not return her gaze; he seemed suddenly abstracted. She waited for his answer and surveyed the room, glancing at the framed costume sketches on the walls, the scores piled on a long cabinet. She picked up the envelope from the table. "Those are our lawyers," she said.

"Yes."

"I haven't asked them to send anything to you."

"Your father has." Sumner Loewen smiled. His voice was light, as if his words were inconsequential.

"What has he done?"

"He has been extraordinarily generous. He has bought this building, and he is leasing it to us for one dollar a year. The entire building. We have the room we need to expand. We are quite touched, as you can imagine."

"You have accepted the terms?"

"We had no idea it was happening. The deed arrived on my desk this morning."

"And you are quite touched instead of quite suspicious? You haven't asked why he did this? What he really wanted?"

"I'm not sure that concerns us."

Eveline de Charny laughed. "So you are going to accept the gift?"

"We are in the business of accepting gifts."

She nodded. "Like the Trojans?"

"You sound like Achille. We are not naive," said Sumner Loewen.

"No?" Eveline de Charny moved away from the table and stood in the center of the office. Her face under her tan had grown pale, and the fine lines from her nose to her mouth had sharpened. Her voice was deep and her accent had vanished. "My father is doing this to discredit me with you. He cannot bear to see me succeed in this city when he couldn't. He is a jealous man. He does not like to be outdone. He knows how I care about the Perrot Ballet. He enjoys cutting me off from what I want. He made me stop dancing when I was sixteen—I know how petty this sounds, but you have to pay attention. You don't know him. There is nothing generous about him; he's interested only in himself. Now you'll be nicer to him than you are to me; he'll force you to."

"I don't know how your father could cut you off from us," Sumner Loewen replied. "He does not control us, or you. He can't turn us against you."

"He controls all of us," said Eveline de Charny. "I gave him the papers having to do with the company that you gave me. I thought he was going to release trust funds to me to donate to the company. I don't know why I was so gullible." She laughed. "So maybe he's taught me something." She looked down at Sumner Loewen. The color had come back to her face; she spoke as if she had resolved the issue. "I'll buy it from him. I'll buy the building—through lawyers, of course, so he won't know I'm doing it—and I'll give it to you outright. He'll make a profit. He won't be able to say no to a profit. I'll talk to my mother; she'll help me. I know how to make her help me. I'll buy him out."

"Why don't you take some time to think that over, to decide if that's something you would sincerely like to do—if it's something you can afford? We're in no hurry. And Achille has been reminding me that our purpose is to produce ballets, not to invest in real estate. The company has a future, and I assure you that you will be a part of it." Sumner Loewen looked to Achille Perrot, inviting his corroboration. But Perrot remained impassive.

Eveline de Charny turned to Perrot. "And you have what he wants, too, you know. I'm warning you. You have your dancers; they're devoted to you. My father has to buy whom he wants. Do you know where Dana Coelho has been? With him, with my father. He was—he is—a bad father, a bad man. He is a man without love. He is cruel. He is not like you."

Achille Perrot left the window and approached Eveline de Charny. He touched her forearm gently with his long white fingers, ghostly against her brown skin. She flinched as if his fingers burned her. "You are wrong," Perrot said.

A siren wailed on the avenue. Perrot waited until it faded downtown. "You are wrong. I am very much like your father. I am sure that is one of the reasons I enchant you. Don't be offended. Of course you are enchanted. It is not that you are silly or weak; you are an enchantress yourself." He smiled, his teeth as long as a skull's. He stretched his black arm in a graceful, compelling arc, the Sorcerer beckoning. "It has been charming; it is charming to be chosen, I must tell you. But I would not have been a good father. I am not very patient, and I am jealous, too. I am not very good at love."

"You love your dancers," Eveline de Charny said. "I see that."

Achille Perrot shook his head. "No. I have trained them. My dancers could have been dogs or horses. My father trained horses, I understand—I never knew him. If I loved my dancers as human beings, if I loved their souls, I would be lenient with them, and I would be incapable of making them do what I want. Perhaps you could say that I love my dancers, but only for what they can do. Not for themselves. Do you understand?" He paused for a moment. A dance came into his head; he saw what he was saying in a dance. Dancers, like horses, stepping in a ring, a manège, circling Alexander or Dana. The dance spilled out, draining him, exhausting him. He closed his eyes, watched it for a moment, and continued. "When my father found that a horse did not serve his purposes—perhaps it lacked strength or it was too small or it refused to jump or it grew too old—he sold it. He was not sentimental. He loved his horses as long as they were useful. I am like that with my dancers, and your father, I am sure, is like that. I am sure that he loves only what is useful to him. Do you not see the resemblance?"

Eveline de Charny stared at Perrot. "No. Not at all."

"Look at me," teased Achille Perrot. "Do I not look like your father? I do. It is plain to me, although I do not like it. I should look like him. You do not see it? You do not see that he is my brother, my half brother?"

Eveline peered at him and nodded, wanting to see. Sumner Loewen's expression mixed astonishment and amusement.

"You understand that I never knew my brother. I only imagine what he must be like. My mother showed him to me once, when she took me to Brittany to try to persuade my father to see me. He would not. I was not useful; neither was she any longer. It was humiliating for her. I feel about Roland de Charny rather the way you do: he had and I had not. I am not even sure he knows that he has a half brother. I think my birth was a matter of some pride to my father, but my life held no interest for him. He did not give me his name, so I felt free to take one of my own. I find it ironic that Roland de Charny wishes to become involved with the company; I find it ironic that you do."

His fingers remained on Eveline de Charny's arm. Her distress had cooled; in her black eyes gleamed identification.

Perrot shook his head. "No. This will not change you," he said. "This relationship is merely a piece of information. Useless. It does not resonate. It implies nothing. Perhaps in my life it implies something. It is a memory, and memory is material. But for you, it has no meaning. It does not affect you. I repeat: it will not change you. If I thought it was important I would not have told you."

"Of course it changes me," said Eveline de Charny. "How couldn't it?"

"You are not a part of my life," said Achille Perrot.

"But you are a part of mine. You already were; now you are even more."

Perrot turned away from her. "I only tell you, Sumner, so you will understand that I have not become, as you say, irrational when I insist we move. I need my distance; I have earned it. I do not want to be beholden to anyone." Achille Perrot picked up the envelope and handed it to Sumner

Loewen. "My father was a hunter, and what he desired above all was possession. I am not so different, and Eveline is correct—neither, I am sure, is her father."

He paused and laughed, a high-pitched sound like a hawk's keen; it expressed no mirth, but only his awareness of a kind of absurdity. "And what I have told you may not be true," Perrot added. He shivered. "Memory is only material, and memory lies. It is impossible to know. It would make a good story; the symmetry is appealing. Perhaps your father is not my brother; perhaps I saw him once from a distance and decided that he could well be. Perhaps my mother, when she told me who my father was, lied. She could have."

There was another knock on the door and it opened slightly. Once more Guy Pissarro stuck his head through the crack. "I am sorry to disturb you again, but it is three o'clock," he said. "It is time for class."

Achille Perrot bowed to Sumner Loewen and to Eveline de Charny. "You are welcome to watch," he said coolly. "But dance? No. I think not."

The dancers hurried ahead of Achille Perrot down the hot corridor to the studio, glancing back at him over their shoulders. They were the newest members of the company, the least sure, alarmed that Perrot and not gentle Guy Pissarro was taking their first class. They had counted on Guy Pissarro's giving them an easy barre and simple balances. Normally Perrot insulated himself from the frustrations of the beginning of the season. But he was impatient to see dancers in front of him in daylight, impatient to begin moving them to his designs.

When Achille Perrot entered the rehearsal room, Rosalind Child had been at work for an hour. Sweat darkened her leotard, and her cheeks were flaming beneath her pale makeup. She had not danced in several weeks, and she worried that she had lost strength and speed.

She had left Arabesque following her swim with Alexander and had flown to Florida to stay with her grandparents in their bungalow north of Miami. Love had covered her like a swan with white wings, and she had fled from its dazzling weight. She swam back and forth in the tiny screened-in pool behind the Florida house, and the image of Alexander Ives shimmered before her in the turquoise water. She could not remember him clearly; he appeared to her always refracted, his body reduced to planes of light as sharp as glass. They cut through Rosalind's mind, through her glaze of self-possession.

Rosalind understood being loved, but until Alexander, she had experienced loving only as gratitude for being loved. In Florida she danced gracefully to her grandparents' adoration, their gentle acquiescence to her small appetite and late hours. In the mornings they tiptoed past her door and whispered to each other; after they were asleep Rosalind swam in the thick humid night, in the sweet rotting smell of Florida vegetation. She heard Alexander's name over and over as she swam to its rhythm. She pretended that he was going to fly south himself on white wings and find her and fly her back. She remembered the feel of his hands as he held her, dancing, and she wanted him. She sent a postcard of flamingos to the company at Arabesque with the date of her return. She knew that Walter Mowbray would put it on the bulletin board in the barn and that Alexander Ives would see it. He would love her.

Achille Perrot was pleased to see that Rosalind Child was taking his class, pleased that she had already been warming up. He smiled at the sheen of concentration on her face. He could begin. He had a dance for her.

The portable galvanized-pipe barres had already been arranged in the center of the studio. Achille Perrot nodded to Harry Menard and proceeded carefully through the barre as if this were an elementary class. The dancers were slow, their timing imprecise, their energy diffuse. Perrot noticed tiny faults in their placement. One stood with her back swayed; another tilted her shoulders too far forward. Perrot marched down the file of straight small bodies and corrected postures that were fractions of an inch out of alignment, his lips compressed in a frustrated frown.

As the class was finishing pliés, the door at the back of the rehearsal room opened and Alexander Ives came in. He wore street clothes, white pants and a white shirt and sneakers. Golden from the summer, he leaned against the back wall, preparing to watch. Rosalind Child knew as the door opened that Alexander was in the room. She blushed, a rush of blood that infused her chest and arms as well as her face.

Achille Perrot saw. His eyes flickered to Alexander, then to Rosalind Child. Perrot shivered, as if the door opening had let in a draft of freezing air, not heat from the corridor. Alexander Ives's presence reminded him of the shortening days. Perrot felt his heart constrict. He reached Rosalind's place in line. As she bent, he pushed her knees outward; she had let them fall slightly forward. She wobbled under the pressure of his hands and continued her fondu: she held the foot of one bent leg behind her ankle, while the standing leg dipped in a plié.

"One moment, please." Perrot raised his hand and stopped the pianist in the middle of a modulation. Harry Menard slumped on the bench and lit a cigarette. Perrot strode to the front of the room. "Ballet is geometry," he began. "Let me remind you. In first position and second position your feet must form a straight line. In fourth position and fifth position they form two straight lines, which are parallel. At all times your knees are directly above your feet. Have you forgotten this during your vacation?" The dancers straightened their backs and lowered their eyes, waiting out his tirade. Harry Menard frowned and dropped ash on the floor and ground it into the wood with the toe of his shoe.

"Let's do," Perrot said.

The pianist balanced his cigarette on the edge of the music rack and played two measures.

"No." Perrot interrupted again. He pointed at Rosalind Child. "Look at you!" His voice was a whisper white with anger. "Your feet. Your knees, they are practically touching. You are standing like a cow. In three weeks you have forgotten more than I can ever teach you."

Rosalind Child recoiled. She twisted her head and arched her back as if she had been struck. Her face red with shame, her eyes glassy with suppressed tears, she gazed at her legs in the mirror, mystified.

Perrot turned his back on the class. Alexander Ives watched the old man's face in the mirror. It was not angry, but fearful and pained, grieved at imperfection. His eyes, reflected, met Alexander's, and Perrot looked away.

He finished the barre perfunctorily, hardly glancing at the dancers. "Let's do." He announced the exercises in a voice that was barely audible. The dancers picked up the barres and moved them to one side, then broke up into three groups for center work. The room had grown damp with sweat; the smell of powder cloyed. The girls' backs and chests glistened from dancing and from apprehension.

Perrot gave them combinations, at first condescendingly easy. As each rank finished, the next began; the dancers moved to the front of the room in waves. Their energy broke against Perrot. Rosalind, her wide mouth pouting and stubborn, joined every group and found a place in the middle of each rank where Perrot could not help but notice her. He gave more difficult combinations, quick jumps with beats followed by turns and rapid shifts of direction, intricate footwork, passages from the dances he saw at night. Many of the dancers lost the beat and had to stop halfway through the combination and retreat to the back of the room. Perrot impatiently clapped the rhythm with his hands.

Rosalind Child executed each combination almost perfectly. She danced full out; although she was small her movements were large, too grand for the confined space. She ended each combination at Perrot's feet, braking her momentum. She gazed at him each time, her hot face tilted up at him, her wide-set eyes both supplicating and challenging. He studied her body coldly, noticing the small flaws. He did not speak, but she knew what he had seen: her back too arched in a jeté, her foot in a passé not tucked precisely behind her knee, her wrists flopping in a series of glissades. But he was giving the combinations to her, repeating in a different order the steps she had missed, acknowledging, despite himself, her effort.

His eyes revealed no pleasure. He watched Rosalind Child, but he also watched Alexander Ives, who was leaning against the back wall, learning from these steps how to train dancers, learning combinations. In the hot rehearsal room, Perrot felt cold. Ten minutes early he silenced the pianist and walked out of the room, leaving the dancers milling about like animals in a corral.

"Well, that's all, folks," said Harry Menard as he folded his music and lit a new cigarette. The dancers picked up their gear and left the room.

Alexander Ives stayed. Rosalind stood in the center of the floor, her back to him, her elegant neck exposed, her legs slightly tensed, suggesting vestiges of movement. She prolonged the exquisite moment of being watched. She raised her eyes to Alexander in the mirror behind her. In his white clothes and with his bright black hair, he seemed luminous as a swan. Rosalind Child counted beats and pivoted and he stepped toward her, into the rising arc of her arm.

Outside the ballet company's studio the day's white glare had softened to a tired yellow haze. A stew of smells simmered over the scorched street: hot frying oil, subway fumes, stale sweat, the dry yeastiness of a bakery, and the green humidity of watered vegetation from the wholesale florists.

Rosalind Child smelled damp, like a misted plant, her hair wet and slick from her shower, and she wore loose white gauze pants. She had put on fresh makeup, and her face in the oblique light had a smoothness and finish that made her seem both young and old. She and Alexander Ives walked side by side, not touching. The distance between them vibrated like copper wire. Rumpled office workers passed them and stared; the dancers seemed charmed and neon cool, glowing with the currents of sex.

They walked around the corner to a restaurant with a Caribbean blue neon sign, Exuma, in its window. Members of the company went to Exuma often after rehearsals and performances. Alexander Ives and Rosalind Child stopped there now to prolong not touching. When they arrived, the restaurant was empty. Clustered at the bar, the waiters in bright blue and white shirts greeted them by name. Alexander led Rosalind to a table in the back of the long room, under the air-conditioning vents and the loudspeakers.

Reggae spilled almost subliminally from the sound system. As soon as they sat down, the bartender increased the volume slightly. Alexander ordered a beer and Rosalind a Coke; their drinks came with translucent blue and green plastic swizzle sticks in the shape of swordfish. Rosalind, delighted, asked the waiter if she could have more. He came back with an array—mermaids, sea horses, dolphins—which Rosalind, with great concentration, arranged on the table in front of her.

"Did you see what Perrot was doing to me?" she asked Alexander. "I mean, I was much better than the other kids. I know I haven't danced for a couple of weeks, but I did stay in shape. It was just little things. My knees weren't perfect, but they were pretty good. Did you see that girl in front of me? She was the one who looked like a cow." Her wispy voice with its singsong inflections skimmed over the surface of words.

Alexander said, "It could have been because I was there watching."

"So what? I was trying so hard." She gazed at him with her wide-apart eyes, focused clearly, Alexander saw, on herself.

"He's impatient. He's hard on everybody."

"But I didn't know what I was doing wrong."

"Nothing, probably. Tomorrow I'll bet he comes in and tells you he wants to make a ballet on you."

"How do you know?"

"I just do."

"Well, it's a strange way to show it. I mean, was I all right, or was I really as bad as he said?"

"What do you think? You know how you were. He was giving those combinations to correct you—he was helping. He knows you can be perfect. He's not a nice man. He's not going to hug and kiss you."

"Are you in this new ballet?"

"Maybe."

"It's hard," Rosalind said. "I get so discouraged. It's like you're on top of the world one minute and the next you're nowhere."

"Perrot does that. It keeps us guessing, so we never stop trying to make him happy. It keeps us off balance." He swallowed his beer. "It's hard to take." He put down the glass. "I might leave the company."

Rosalind Child did not hesitate. "You can't do that. I don't want to dance with anybody but you." She looked at him adoringly, and he saw his reflection in her wide eyes. He remained still, to let her believe that he was what she wanted to see, that he would be to her precisely what she imagined. He would be noble and generous, he would protect her, he would love her absolutely. In a way, he thought, he was irrelevant. Who he was—his particularity—was beside the point. She was impermeable in her will and oblivious to the discrepancies of reality. And he was almost what she saw—he danced, every day, what she wanted.

Alexander considered going. He would earn more; he would be under fewer constraints. He could do whatever he wished, and that stopped him: he did not know whether he would fly free or drop like a stone.

Rosalind played with her swizzle sticks, hooked the mermaids and the sea horses in various combinations around the rim of her glass, and asked his opinion of the arrangements. The music grew incrementally louder and beat over their heads, a steel band on tape—resonant oil cans, drums, and tambourine. That was an automobile disk brake ringing like a triangle, Alexander imagined; he and Caroline had spent a week in the Caribbean the year before, swimming during the day and dancing to steel bands at night. They had gone to the island of Exuma. Caroline had loved it—empty time, the sun and water, the dancing. The wind had kept Alexander awake at night.

Alexander got up and eased his body into the music's beat, loosening to remembered soft Bahamian heat. Rosalind watched him for a few moments and then joined him, and they danced between the tables in the dark at the back of the restaurant. A ballerina, she wanted to leave the ground. She wriggled like a spider, all arms and legs. Not like Caroline, who unscrewed her taut dancer's joints and, to this music, laughed and forgot Perrot's discipline. Caroline understood that this dancing was earthbound; it took its strength from staying low.

But he could show Rosalind. "Watch me, Rose Mary," he said. "Get down."

His heels barely left the floor, and his legs absorbed the momentum of the bounces and kept it concentrated in his thighs; his arms hugged his sides, elbows bent. Wrists cocked, fingers splayed, his hands took her in to him, asked for her. His energy gathered in his hips and stomach, rose to his shoulders, and sank again. The rhythm was a fast heartbeat, pumping him with strength.

"Get down, Rose Mary," he repeated. "Get your arms down. Get low. Stay down. Get your feet flat on the floor."

He seemed transformed, his power less abstract, more capable of overwhelming Rosalind than she had dreamed while swimming in Florida behind her grandparents' safe house, and she was frightened and eager, both. She obeyed him. She approached his opened hands and let the music's beat enter her spine, contract it with its tension, straighten it in release. She planted her feet on the floor parallel to each other, abandoning the artifice of turnout, and let her small body bend in the music's rattling wind.

The volume grew louder. The waiters pushed tables aside and gathered to watch. Rosalind's gauze pants clung to her legs as if she had been swimming. The dark circles of Alexander's nipples showed through his thin damp cotton shirt. He crooked his elbows like a white bird's wings. They jumped low, disdaining height. Alexander clapped his hands over his head and Rosalind followed. He led her and she went with him; he thrust the dance low into his hips and bent over her, covering her with his white bulk.

He looked away, dropping her, suddenly indifferent. The circle of onlookers separated, and Dana Coelho leapt into the clearing. "There you are." Alexander smiled. Dana whooped and clapped and cut in front of Rosalind Child and shimmied, brushing Alexander's chest. His hair was lustrous even in the dark restaurant; it emitted its own light, its own charge. Dana laughed and his body shook convulsively. His lips were parted and his tongue gleamed between his teeth.

Alexander caught Dana's high and laughed with him. The two dancers mirrored each other, twisting their bodies like snakes; their hips and shoulders rotated as if they were boneless. They bent backwards until their thighs and torsos were parallel to the floor; they straightened and arched their backs, then whipped them forward, waving like palm trees in a hurricane. Rosalind, at the margin of the circle, seethed at their congruence.

Dana's pupils were dilated like a cat's catching light. He pounded his feet and clapped his hands and shouted. He sprang into the air and landed crouched on all fours. The onlookers shouted and stamped to the frenzied beat. The atmosphere had turned apprehensive, eerie green as if a storm were approaching. Rosalind, excluded, could not bear to look. She retreated behind the ring of watchers and danced by herself. Dana Coelho pounced, and Alexander feinted.

Dana spun until he staggered with dizziness. He blinked, his eyes unfocusing. He was drenched with sweat; his breath rasped as if he were choking. He sank to his knees, tried to get up, and fell again. Alexander caught him and locked his arms around his chest. Dana could not balance. Alexander dragged him to the table and put him into a chair. Dana slumped, still laughing.

"Easy, easy," Alexander said as if Dana were an agitated horse. "Quiet now. Easy."

Dana tried to rise, but Alexander pinned him down. "Cool out. You can't go anywhere."

Dana laughed, quick high gasps like sobs. He tried to squirm out of Alexander's arms and tossed his head and pushed against the table, but Alexander kept him down. He asked a waiter to bring a glass of water and fed it to Dana.

"I was having a good time. You're stopping me."

But he finished the water, and Alexander felt his resistance slacken. Alexander said, "You're strung out."

"I'm happy." Dana laughed. "I'm rich. I have my own company. I'm free."

"What are you talking about?"

"He said I shouldn't have to dance for anybody but my-self. He says he'll give me money, for me and whoever else I want. Do you want to dance with me?"

Alexander laughed. "You're not serious."

"I am."

"Who's going to give you money?"

"A friend."

"What have you been using?"

"Little pills. Happiness pills. Magic." He reached out and stroked Alexander's shoulder. "They're perfect." He smiled. "I'm so perfect. I'm going to fly. Want to see?"

"Sure," said Alexander. "Go ahead."

"Not here. It's too low here. You have to get higher. You want to be happy? You're a good person, Alexander. I love you. But I have to go; I have to go, you know." He giggled. "I'm late for a date. I hate to be late. I have a date to fly!" He giggled, listened to himself, and, liking the sound, giggled again. "Fly high. Come on, Alexander." He giggled, but the pulse of his laughter slowed, and his voice quieted.

The onlookers had dispersed. Rosalind Child stood be-hind Dana, still dancing, sullenly, airborne and spidery again, the currents between her and Alexander cut. Her wheeling arms spun an insulating web. Alexander beckoned to her; she shook her head. He shrugged. She approached. Without taking his eyes off Dana, Alexander touched her waist. That he knew she would come back angered her, and she spun away from him and sat opposite Dana, her chair pushed away until it touched the table behind her. She crossed her arms in front of her chest. Alexander kept a hand on Dana's forearm, holding the younger dancer down. But Dana was exhausted. His golden skin faded, became sallow, and lost its glow. He smiled at Alexander, but his mouth spread into a grimace.

Rosalind Child avoided looking at the two dancers, jeal-ous of their intimacy, angry at Alexander's concern. She wished Dana had flown. She saw Walter Mowbray enter the restaurant and waved with staged enthusiasm and called in her tiny voice, "Walter, we're here."

Walter Mowbray approached the table. He was swathed in layers of loose white linen: a white T-shirt, a baggy white jacket, oversized white pants cinched at the waist with a braided leather belt; its excess length hung down the front of his trousers like an arrow pointing to his groin. The tips of his hair had been tinged tomato.

"Welcome back, sweetie," he called to Rosalind. "You look wonderful! Home cooking—not that you've gained an ounce! How's your grandma and grandpa?" He leaned over to embrace Rosalind and saw Dana opposite her.

"Oh, Jesus," he moaned. "What's happened to you? Where've you been?"

"You're not his date?" Alexander asked.

Walter shook his head and began talking to Alexander as if Dana were not there. "Oh, no. I'm never his date. I'm when he doesn't have one." His hair burned orange as a sodium flame. "I don't know how I stand it. I'm a masochist, I guess. I'm too nice. I shouldn't do it. I shouldn't put up with him. I know I'm self-destructive. I should just tell him to get out. That's what everybody says—just tell him to go. But, I mean, I know why he does what he does. It has nothing to do with me, you know. I know how he feels about me, but still, what about how I feel? Doesn't he ever think about that?"

Alexander shrugged. "Ask him. Whatever he's done, he's coming down. I can take care of him if you want, if you were doing something else."

"I wasn't," said Walter. "I worked late and was going to get a hamburger, but I don't need to eat." He sat down next to Dana Coelho and touched his shoulder. "What's up?"

Dana blinked his blue eyes and smiled his lightning-bug smile. "Oh," he said. "What are you doing here?"

"I'm here because I knew I wouldn't run into you. I was hungry. You tell me you're not going to be around, so I believe you. But you're so out of it I bet you don't even know where you are. Tell me, where are you? Who am I? Do you even recognize me?" Walter tried to keep his tone light and teasing, but anger hardened it.

Dana closed his eyes, as if Walter Mowbray's voice were

too bright. "Hey, ease off. You're Walter. See? I know." He stood gently, so as not to dislodge parts of himself, and shook off Alexander's hands. "There's nothing to get upset about. I'll be back at the apartment later. That's what I want to do, and I'll do it. Trust me, please."

"Right, trust you. That's an old joke. Give me one reason why I should."

"Because I want you to, and you will." Dana rubbed Walter's shoulders. "You're so tight. Chill out, all right? I like your hair."

Walter smiled up at him in gratitude. "Thanks. I just had it done this afternoon, for the new season, for fall—you know, like for the foliage." He pronounced the word as if it had two syllables.

"Come on, I'll drop you at home, so I'll know where to find you later." Dana waved to Alexander Ives and Rosalind Child and bowed like a ballet cavalier; followed by Walter Mowbray, he walked carefully from the restaurant, as if he could not trust the surface upon which he stepped.

Rosalind Child shook the ice cubes in her empty glass. She did not look at Alexander. The memory of his dance with Dana Coelho stayed before her eyes, and she envied it. All her life she had worked for lightness; tonight she yearned to be planted in the ground. The music had changed; the loudspeakers broadcast slower music, calypso melodies vibrating on electric instruments. Alexander reached for Rosalind's hand, asking her to dance. She resisted; he pulled her up.

He danced with her as if she were a doll, and he lifted her off her feet with each slow step. This was what she had imagined: his body's heat, his smell of clean cotton and soap, the sound of his heart. She was as high as his heart, she remembered. They danced as much to the random rhythm of talk as to the Caribbean music. The restaurant had become crowded, and the tables around them were filling.

Rosalind recognized a group of dancers at the front of the long room, near the bar. She pulled away from Alexander, shy about being seen with him, yet pleased, too, eager to flaunt him. Alexander had been dancing with his eyes half-closed. When she lifted her head from his breast he looked at her as if he had just awakened.

"Where is Caroline?" she asked.

"I don't know," he said. "She was here, but then she went back to the country for a few days. I think she's supposed to come back tomorrow. I haven't really talked to her much."

"Have you seen her?"

"To dance, that's all for a while."

"Why?"

"We're like that."

"Like what?"

Alexander opened his palms and spread them apart, empty. It was inevitable, he thought; everything flew apart. That was entropy, the state of chaos toward which the universe was spinning. He embraced Rosalind and pulled her back to his heart. Her hair smelled like peppermint, her skin like lemon. Ephemeral smells, young smells that carried no history, smells that would wash easily off his own skin. Alexander closed his eyes again. A waiter jostled them.

He opened his eyes to get his bearings. At the front of the restaurant, over the heads of the waiters and the crowd milling at the bar, he saw Caroline Harbison. He loosened his embrace, leaving Rosalind off balance. She steadied herself, turned around, and saw Caroline Harbison. A thrill of guilt shivered through Rosalind's body as she smiled in triumph. Caroline, her jaw clenched with anger, her eyes clouded with misery, gazed at the girl.

Alexander pushed toward the front of the restaurant, but by the time he got there Caroline was gone. She had seemed to him a vision, like Odette appearing as the Prince betrayed her with an imposter in *Swan Lake*, an image that the Prince could not see because it was too late. Alexander ran outside into the close, humid night. She was not on the street. He stood at the entrance to the restaurant, in the thick hot blast from the air conditioner over the transom. Caroline could have gone home; she could have gone to the studio to work at the barre. He thought to follow. He started down the street and stopped. He did not know what he would do or what he could say. He could deny nothing and promise nothing. She had appeared and vanished. It was too late.

He returned to the restaurant. Rosalind sipped a fresh Coke ornamented with four swizzle sticks.

"Let's go," he said, and threw bills on the table without asking for the check.

The night was deep blue lit by neon and headlights. The air was acrid with fumes. Alexander hailed a cab. It had no air conditioning. The radio blared brassy swing music. The driver regarded them in the rearview mirror. The back of his neck was thick and creased and covered with grizzled curly hairs. He turned uptown on Sixth Avenue, tires screeching, and twisted his head; his jaws pleated into his neck. "Like this tune?" he asked in a smoky, rasping voice.

"Sure," said Alexander.

"This is my kind of music," the driver continued. "The wife and I, we used to go dancing every Saturday night. Forty years, we did this."

"Amazing," said Alexander.

"The wife, she loved it. You should have seen her. She could have been a pro. You like to dance?"

"It's okay," Alexander said.

"Every night she made us practice to the radio."

"You have to practice."

"That's what she said."

"Otherwise you lose it."

"Yeah. Well, she's dead."

"I'm sorry," said Rosalind in her whispery voice.

"Hey, no sympathy." The driver turned the radio louder. "Satin Doll" roared like a siren up the avenue. He looked behind him again, at Alexander Ives and Rosalind Child sitting close together on the backseat. "I'm crazy about this tune. You know, we were married forty years. The wife, she loved to dance. Every night, dance. But she wouldn't go to bed with me. No offense, miss, but that's the way it was. Dance is all. I hated it. The only thing in life is sex. You got it, everything's great. You don't, forget it." He paused. "Sorry, miss, beg your pardon."

"That's okay," said Rosalind, "but I bet you did love your wife."

The taxi swerved as the car ahead shifted lanes. "Nope. You'd lose. I stayed with her, sure. What else? It was habit, that's all." He banged the syncopation of "Satin Doll" with his palm against the rim of the steering wheel.

Alexander had him drop them on the corner of his street. His apartment was in a brownstone with thick mahogany doors and a white tiled entranceway. Rubber treads, dust embedded in their ridges, covered the steps, which tilted toward the stairwell. Alexander unlocked his door and pushed a switch controlling a standing lamp in the corner. Rosalind stood at the threshold.

"Such an empty room," she said. The floor was light wood. Nothing hung on the walls. There was a white sofa and two white canvas deck chairs, and on the floor along one wall Alexander had piled elaborate stereo equipment. The tangled wires collected dust.

"It's all I need," said Alexander.

He passed her and crossed the room and opened the window, which had no screen. The yellowish tender ends of locust branches rustled against the windowsill in the greasy breeze. Rosalind stepped into the center of the room and held out her hands to him. He embraced her and, humming "Satin Doll," he began to dance with her. "No," she said and pulled his head down to hers and kissed him. He smelled white, of talcum powder and smoke from the restaurant.

He kissed her mouth and her neck and the knob of her collarbone and loosened his arms and led her into the bedroom. A wide arch, no door, separated it from the living room. His bed, with white sheets and two pillows, rested on a low platform. A red telephone and lamp sat on the floor to the left of the bed. He switched on the lamp.

Alexander Ives unbuttoned Rosalind's shirt and unzipped her gauze trousers. She stood straight, letting him. He undressed himself and tossed their clothes below the foot of the bed. He studied her body and she studied his. This time she saw him clearly. The first time naked, he had seemed a rush of wings, brilliant in the water. She reached for his hand and covered her breast with it. Her nipple hardened against his palm. He picked her up and laid her on the bed and stretched out beside her. She watched his hands as he made love to her. She stroked his hair and shivered when his tongue licked her nipple. Her limbs were hard, her skin polished. He ran his fingers through her curl of pubic hair and gently tugged apart her thighs. His fingers separated the ridges of flesh, opening her, drawing out her wetness. Once again she covered his hand with hers.

"Wait," she said, and moved his hand back to her breast. "I haven't done this before."

He held her until a film of sweat spread between their breasts and stomachs and thighs. He kneaded her back between her shoulder blades; he ran his hand along her spine and held her buttocks, as small as a child's. He foresaw blood on the sheets between her legs, blood on his penis. He would possess her. His mind ran to Dana Coelho, to Achille Perrot, to Caroline Harbison at the barre in the hot studio. He could not imagine beyond suffocating blackness and a white roaring that drowned music and love's dance. He rolled away from Rosalind. The acid wind on his damp body made him shiver. Rosalind lay on her side and kissed him, his lips and neck and collarbone, as he had kissed her. She darted her head lower and like a sparrow pecked at his nipple. "Do you like that?" she asked.

"Yes," he said, although it had given him no pleasure.

"I'm ready now." She took his hand and placed it back between her legs and nudged his fingers into her. "There," she said, contented.

Alexander shook his head. He wanted to sleep. He embraced her and slung his leg over her hipbones. His penis was soft against her thigh.

"What did I do wrong?" she asked.

"Nothing wrong. You're very pretty."

"Was it Caroline?"

"And Dana, and Perrot, and me. You, too."

She tried to twist away, but Alexander held her to him. He stroked her cheek, his fingers soft as feathers. "Stay," he whispered. "Stay, Rose Mary, stay. Please. Let me hold you.

Stay with me. We can't be closer than this; we can't be closer than when we're dancing. That cabdriver was wrong. He doesn't know."

"But I want you," she said.

"You have me."

Choking with disappointment, Rosalind Child felt his heart against her ribs and his breath on her forehead. Caught in her desire, pinned beneath his weight, she held on to him while he slept.

I I

Y<small>OU'RE LOOKING THIN, SWEETHEART,"</small> R<small>OSALIND</small> Child's mother said to her. Darlene Surosky stood in the kitchen of their new house in Queens spooning mayonnaise into a steel bowl of grated cabbage. Outside on the deck, in a fine rain that whitened the air, with long-handled tongs Rosalind's father flipped the chicken parts sizzling on his new propane-fired barbecue. He basted the chicken with ketchup marinade using a matching long-handled basting brush. Rosalind had bought him the set of barbecue tools as a housewarming present. He was cooking lunch in the rain to please her; she dreaded having to taste the sticky, spicy, fattening meat.

Darlene Surosky's stocky hips were encased in sturdy cotton shorts, and a tightly wrapped jersey top revealed the structural details of the brassiere supporting her cantilevered bosom. She sprinkled raisins, dense with calories, into the bowl and stirred the coleslaw and frowned at her daughter. "You look tired, too, Rose Mary, and you're upset. I can tell.

Did something happen in Florida that you haven't told us? Grandma says that Grandpa has started to say strange things. Is that it?" She put down her plastic mixing spoon and reached out to smooth Rosalind's hair away from her forehead.

Rosalind Child stepped back from her mother's hand. She hugged herself and rubbed her upper arms. The day was oppressive and warm despite the rain, but she was cold. "Oh, Mom, they were fine. I didn't notice anything strange. It was great. I had a great time."

"So what's wrong?"

"Nothing." It turned Rosalind's stomach to watch her mother mix the coleslaw.

"You do look thin."

"Mom, I'm supposed to be thin. Perrot told me I have to lose weight. And I'm out of shape."

"If you lose any more weight you won't have any shape to be out of. You believe everything that man says like he was God? It's true he looks like the Holy Ghost." Darlene Surosky picked up the bowl and thrust it at Rosalind. "Here, taste."

Rosalind shook her head.

"I thought you loved coleslaw."

"I do, but not today."

"So you don't want barbecued chicken, either?" Darlene Surosky flushed from rejected love.

"Mom, please!"

Darlene Surosky put the coleslaw back on the counter and turned and embraced her daughter, holding her hard in her arms. Rosalind did not yield, and her mother relented and let go. "Honey, I don't want to force you to eat. If all you wanted was to borrow the car, you could've just said so. We'd do anything for you, you know that."

"I wanted to see you guys, too. I miss you." Rosalind smiled gently and fluttered her hand over her mother's shoulder without touching her.

"You didn't even get a tan in Florida," her mother scolded.

"I'm not supposed to. What if I have to wear a costume that shows the lines?"

Darlene Surosky nodded and regarded her daughter's tight face. "So what are we supposed to do with all this food?" She considered and called out the window over the sink. "Brian! Brian! Take that chicken off the grill. We're going to have to freeze it! Your daughter's on a diet." She turned back to Rosalind. "So, Rose Mary, you're not going to tell me what's going on?"

"Well, Perrot got mad at me."

"For what?"

"I hadn't danced for three weeks and he could tell."

"So that's enough to make you mope like this? What are you, his slave? I don't like it. Who does he think he is? Doesn't he know how good you are? Why don't you tell him? After all you've done for him, if you want, I will!"

"Mom, I've got to go." Rosalind shivered with anticipation; she rubbed her upper arms to erase the goose bumps.

"Where are you taking the car?"

"To the country. You know, to Arabesque, where I went at the beginning of the summer. A lot of the kids are still there."

"You don't want even a cookie for the trip? I made rum balls for dessert." Darlene Surosky reached for a tray covered with tinfoil. "Is that handsome young man going to be there? Maybe you want some cookies for him?"

"No." Rosalind shook her head and lied. "He's not there. And he's not young." Her stomach had contracted into a knot of desire. At the studio that morning, Guy Pissarro had told her that Alexander Ives had left for the country. She wanted to tell her mother that she was in love and that she was going to find Alexander Ives. "That handsome young man." Her mother approved of Alexander. However, her mother would not approve of what she was going to do. "Let him come to you," her mother would say. "Play hard to get. Let him come to you."

As Rosalind drove north it began to rain heavily and her father's big Chevrolet aquaplaned over the asphalt of the Taconic Parkway. She turned off the Taconic onto the short spur of the New York State Thruway that joined the Massachusetts Turnpike. The car bounced over the patched concrete roadbed. Despite the rain, it was still hot, and the windows fogged. The windshield wipers squealed; the fan rattled.

When she entered Massachusetts, the clouds thinned into shifting layers of mist like tulle. Patches of soft blue shone through drifting holes in the clouds. She left the highway and drove through the steep little valleys in the foothills of the Berkshires. The public radio station in Amherst reached the car on top of hills and lost it in the hollows; bursts of music interspersed with static. The music was something she had performed at the beginning of last year while she was still in the corps de ballet, something ordered and baroque; Alexander Ives and Caroline Harbison had danced the leads. Rosalind Child switched the station to clear, loud rock and let its hard beat drive their image from her head.

She rolled down the window, and damp air rushed in carrying the smell of conifers and grass. She cut the radio as she turned off the main road for Arabesque. She would find Alexander at his house, expecting her; she would open her arms and he would come into them, and it would be done, simple. She heard the music from *Swan Lake* in her head, tremulous high strings and harp; that was the accompaniment.

The roads glistened from the recent rain; little rivers braided down the shoulders of Arabesque's main driveway. The dirt road leading to Alexander's house was pitted with puddles, and the car gently splashed through them. On either side of the road, the brown floor of the forest was mottled like a tiger with stripes of black shadow and streaks of amber evening light. Goldenrod and leggy purple asters, bent from the storm, hung over the granite steps of Alexander's cottage. A car was parked in front of the house, its fenders splashed with mud.

Rosalind got out. The metal chunk of the door closing frightened a fat woodchuck, which rose on its haunches and folded its front paws in a quick prayer before it waddled away. She opened the door of Alexander's cottage and went inside. The house was empty. There was a coffee cup on the kitchen table and a nylon duffel bag in the bedroom, but she saw no other evidence of Alexander.

She went back outside and stood on the cottage steps. From down the hill, she heard music: *Swan Lake*—the sounds in her mind amplified. Enchanted, Rosalind listened. Her legs tensed and released; the steps danced in her muscles. The chords were blurred and tinny; they came from a tape recorder at full volume, from the barn. Splattering mud against her calves, she ran down the hill to Alexander.

The barn windows were open, and as Rosalind Child approached, she heard the sound of feet, like pebbles thrown against wood; she heard two dancers. She peered through the window. It was gray inside; no lights were on, and the sun was setting behind the hill. The mirror was black; it reflected the sky through the door as a white trapezoid. She saw the shapes of the dancers—shining skin and streaks of white that caught the light thrown from the mirror. The loud music rattled the tape machine's speakers.

As he spun near the mirror, Rosalind Child recognized Alexander. He was naked except for a white dance belt that circled his hips and rose between his buttocks. Caroline Harbison had to be the other dancer, Rosalind thought, and she wanted to run away, back to her father's car and her mother's kitchen to avoid seeing Caroline's body, to avoid seeing them with each other. The oboe theme called like a bird. Her own body knew the steps; she resisted her cue and held herself motionless and stayed outside, watching to find faults in their love.

Alexander stopped dancing and crouched over the tape machine. Rosalind could hear his panting as he stopped the music and rewound the tape. The wet grass had soaked her feet through her sneakers and thin cotton ankle socks. She moved to the sparser grass beside the barn's high stone foundation and brushed against the pungent rosemary bushes near the entrance. The music began again. Alexander faced the mirror, his back to the door, and marked three measures before he began to dance full out.

But it was not his music; it was hers. Alexander spun in place; his left leg shot parallel to the floor to give impetus to his turn. He bent his supporting leg into a plié, and as his heel touched the floor he brought his other foot to his knee: passé. He straightened his standing leg, rose high on his toes, and turned while stretching the bent leg out parallel to the floor. Rosalind followed the mechanics intently; her body knew the count, knew the effort, knew how many fouettés remained. He had completed the second of thirty-two. Alexander Ives was dancing her solo, the Black Swan's great solo, Odile's thirty-two fouettés, in the third act, when she invaded the palace and began her seduction of the Prince.

The Prince approached, lured by Odile's beauty, by her impersonation of the Swan Queen. Rosalind saw him in the mirror. Dana Coelho, wearing a dance belt, too, stretched his bare arm and invited Alexander Ives to come to him. They touched hands and began their pas de deux. Rosalind felt the shock in her own fingers. In frenetic chromatic lines, Alexander danced Rosalind's steps. Dana's hand spanned his waist, caressing him, giving him balance. Alexander's leg knifed high behind him in sharp arabesques. His torso was pliable and tender. His arms had lost their bulk and arched delicately overhead.

Rosalind crossed her arms in front of her stomach. She stared at Alexander's alien body with longing and disgust. Her heart pounded as loud as the dancers' feet. She flushed and gagged at the impossibility—and the beauty—of what she saw. She was afraid, as if she were witnessing something forbidden; and simultaneously she was transfixed with desire. She could not stop watching.

The two dancers were beautiful beyond gender. They possessed a terrible, magical power, and they were possessed by it; Rosalind saw that, and she pitied them. She wanted them while they horrified her. She wanted to stop their corrupt dance, and she wanted to join them. Dana Coelho bent Alexander Ives backwards over his thigh until Alexander's wrists touched the floor. Gently he raised Alexander. Dana's face was ardent, surrendering. Rosalind wanted to cry out for them to stop. She could not bear to stop looking.

She opened the screen door and closed it silently behind her and stepped inside the room. It was hot with their bodies and humid from the rain. The dancers did not notice her presence. She stood in the darkness against the wall and watched. Alexander seemed weightless, an apparition. He needed strength to return to earth, not to leap. He finished the pas de deux with a string of double pirouettes. Dana followed him, the Prince in the thrall of the Black Swan, bracing the spinning shape of Alexander's body within his outstretched hands.

To tambourine and discordant, triumphant brass, Dana lifted Alexander Ives and started to carry him across the room. But Alexander was too heavy, and Dana staggered under his weight. Alexander rolled out of the boy's arms and landed on the floor on all fours. Dana began another dance; he straddled Alexander's back and sat on him and kicked his feet into the air. "Now you carry me!" Dana laughed.

"No." Alexander laughed back, and he reared and tried to throw Dana off. As Alexander raised his head, he saw Rosalind. A slight tremor of alarm shivered through him. With a small rueful smile, he rose to his knees. Dana tilted backwards and staggered when his feet touched the floor. "Rose Mary," Alexander said when he faced her on his knees. "What are you doing here?" His voice was sorrowful, and soft and intimate, gorged with seduction.

"I came to be with you," Rosalind Child told him; it was what she had planned to say.

Alexander nodded. He rose and turned away. Rosalind watched the hollows of his buttocks as he walked. His gait held vestiges of femininity; he seemed a great distance from her. He picked up a towel that had been slung over the barre and mopped the sweat off his face and chest. He put on his gray sweat pants and draped the towel around his neck and returned to her and kissed her on both cheeks. She let herself fall against him. Alexander took her by the shoulders and righted her as if she were a weighted clown on a midway. "Well," he said.

Dana Coelho had retreated to the center of the room. In the darkness his golden body was dimmed. The music ran on; the swan theme played fast and urgent. Odette—her image, the Prince's memory of her—appeared at the win-

dow, trembling in a frantic bourrée, and begged the Prince
not to betray her, not to break his vow to marry her. Mes-
merized by Odile, the Prince could not see her.

With the heat of his will the Sorcerer welded the hands
of Odile and the Prince, betrothing them. Cymbals and blar-
ing brass drowned the oboe, the vision of Odette faded, and
the Sorcerer revealed that Odile was his daughter disguised
as the Swan Queen; he had tricked the Prince into betraying
Odette. The act ended. The tape hissed and clicked off.

Rosalind gazed at Alexander. "What were you doing?"

"I wanted to see what a girl's balance was like," Alexander said.

"Hard to keep," Rosalind answered.

Alexander laughed. "I have to learn."

"I don't believe you."

Alexander stood on one foot like a crane and massaged
the arch of his other foot with his thumb. "It's true."

"Why?" asked Rosalind.

"To make ballets. I have to know what you can do and
what you can't. I have to know."

Rosalind nodded doubtfully. The room had darkened;
in the mirror the sky had glazed ice blue. Dana Coelho stood
reflected like an apparition in the glass, nearly invisible.

"Alexander," Dana said.

Alexander Ives did not turn around.

"Alexander," Dana repeated. His voice was pinched and
desperate to be heard and answered. "Alexander." A draft
blew in through the screen door, the northwest freshening
after the storm. Dana, almost naked, shivered. He opened
his mouth to speak Alexander's name again. He had never
not been loved. He was beautiful; love was an act quickly
over; there had never been a need not to do it.

Alexander raised his eyes and stared at Dana and Rosalind in the mirror. He did not want to touch them. He
wished that the darkening evening would erase their images.
He wanted the solitude to dance his desires out. Desire's
actuality frightened him; it was only the idea now that he
wanted. He felt Dana's desire and Rosalind's desire, sharp as
needles, puncture him and draw his blood.

Dana could read the disengagement in Alexander's eyes. Alexander flinched, as if the pain were all his. Dana hoped he saw regret as well; he wondered if it was a trick of the dim light. There was not much about himself, he thought, to regret. He was brief. He felt Rosalind Child wishing him gone; she stared him away; she pushed him out the door. Alexander did not resist her.

Dana snatched a sweat shirt and sweat pants from a pile of clothes in the corner of the studio. When he spoke, his voice was high with doubt and bitterness. "You didn't tell me there was another shift, Alexander. Don't you think you scheduled us a little too close?"

"I want to keep dancing," Alexander said to them both.

"I'm here," said Rosalind.

"Go ahead. You two dance." Dana spit the words at Alexander. "It doesn't matter who you dance with, does it? I'm out of here." He ran from the barn, slamming the screen door behind him. The door bounced once, like a raucous tambourine.

"I didn't know," Rosalind said.

"Know what?" Alexander asked curtly.

"About Dana."

"What is there to know?" he challenged.

"I chased him away. Are you sorry?"

"There's nothing to be sorry for. You're here now. That's the way it is."

"If that's how you feel, then I can go." Rosalind wavered. She had come for him. She thought to leave the barn and drive away and make him chase after her. But he would not do that, she knew. Since she was already here, he would have to love her.

"I'll dance with you," she said. The mirror had deepened blue like the swan lake at twilight, the hour when the birds resumed the shape of women. She took off her sneakers.

She knelt in front of the tape machine and pushed the play button. The fourth act began, high notes like the spume of waves, a white froth of emotion. Her loose hair fell over her face as she danced barefoot the first measures of the act, the moment Odette saw the Prince, who had betrayed her. Rosalind danced the old gestures of love—Odette's delight at seeing her lover, and her despair, knowing they were doomed. Her outstretched arms reached for the man while her feet propelled her backwards.

From behind her, Alexander circled her waist. He tilted her so that in order not to fall she had to raise her left foot in back of her and sink into a plié in preparation for a pirouette. She rose and spun, twice, three times, four times. She frowned and pulled away from him, breaking the turn. She heard a car travel down the driveway toward the main road.

"I don't know what you're doing," she said. "That isn't the step. It's wrong. Leave me alone."

"Follow me. I've been playing with this. I'll tell you the steps to do. Arabesque." He held her waist and pivoted her torso forward. She lifted her leg and stretched it perpendicular to the floor. "Fondu." He lowered her body as she bent her standing leg. The music diminished in her mind as Alexander told her steps. He bent her backwards over his thigh and lifted her horizontally, set her on the floor and rested her head against his breast. She felt his heartbeat throb against her temple, and she embraced him. He lifted her out of that embrace into another, so that his head pressed against her heart. Her hands circled her head over his. She dropped them and caressed his face, and she bent her head over his and kissed his lips.

As he lowered her she saw that his eyes were half-closed, white crescents. His hands slid along her ribs, beside her breasts, preparing for another lift. He launched her, and Rosalind leapt.

He caught her under her thigh and carried her. She could have been flying. Her bones could have been hollow like a bird's. She arched her back, in love utterly pliant. Alexander set her down and let her go.

The music ended and the tape wound on in a rush of white noise—wings or wind. Panting, Alexander and Rosalind faced each other. She raised her arms to embrace him.

"That's enough," Alexander said wearily.

Rosalind dropped her hands to her sides. She stood in

front of the door in the breeze and bunched her hair in one hand and fanned her neck. The sky was diffused with gold, a cold sunset, a premonition of fall. Alexander left her and crossed to the corner of the room.

"Do you have something I can borrow? My top is soaked." She pulled off her shirt and mopped the sweat from her breasts.

He tossed her a sweat shirt. When she put it on, it hung almost to her knees.

"Come with me," said Rosalind, and she took his hand and led him from the barn. Outside more light remained. The shadows of the beeches barred the blue grass with black stripes. They crossed the lawn beside the closing day lilies to the path leading toward the lake.

"Swans are nasty birds," Alexander said. "Did you know that?"

Rosalind shook her head.

"They're vicious. They bite."

Rosalind stopped and pulled Alexander to a halt with her. "Why was Dana here?"

Alexander hesitated. "To dance."

"Did you ask him to come?"

"I wanted to work on my ballet. I had ideas I wanted to try."

"Do you love him?"

Alexander laughed. "Of course. Who can help loving him? But—"

"But what?"

"Don't you always say 'but' after 'love'?"

The high grass in the field had been mowed, and new growth brushed their ankles. They climbed down the path to the water. The evergreens at the far end of the lake were black and one-dimensional in the twilight. A thin gray wisp of cloud bisected the orange sun for a moment. The water rippled violet and green and gray; near shore it was still, translucent. The ledge had dried after the rain; little puddles remained in depressions in the rock. Beside it purple loosestrife and dusty pink clusters of joe-pye weed, tall wildflowers of the end of summer, hung over the margin of the lake.

Rosalind Child undressed and dropped her clothes on the ledge. "Here I am," she said to Alexander. Her flesh reflected the last light like water. She tugged at Alexander's shirt, pushing it up under his arms. She pressed her body against his, her lustrous skin, her cold hard nipples. She loosened the drawstring of his pants.

Alexander let her undress him. They lay down together on the ledge. Rosalind wrapped herself around him like a little snake, and she licked him, her tongue as red and hard as her nipples. He smelled her peppermint scent; her hair tickled his body like silk fringe. She flickered on top of him. She held his penis in her mouth with voracious innocence, tasting it, relishing her power to harden him. He moaned, and she smiled; her sharp teeth nipped him. A jay screamed a warning, and a squirrel chattered and scampered away through the brittle underbrush.

She lowered herself over him and nuzzled her small round breasts into his lips. He gave himself up to her, to her darting, weightless pleasures. She gripped his hips between her thighs. "Come into me," she told him. She opened herself for him and he put himself inside her. He grasped her waist, the heels of his hands pressed against her small flat belly. He was afraid to hurt her; he was afraid of her. She was having him. She gasped and recoiled. He held her above him, but she pushed back down, their bones hard against each other. She shuddered, her body tightened, and then she began to dance over him, arching her body above his like a white bird. He closed his eyes and let her take him, and he felt her wetness flood him, and in the midst of his own pleasure he feared it was blood.

She lay still on top of him. He rolled her off. She snuggled beside him. There was no blood, only love's whiteness. The rock was hard against his back.

Rosalind stirred and slung a leg over his groin. "How can Odette go back to the Sorcerer?" she asked. "I mean, after she's had the Prince?"

"She has no choice. That's the story. Love doesn't last." Alexander played with her long black hair. He looked at the dark water beyond her head. "You can't change the story."

"I can," Rosalind told him, sure as a child, her voice breaking with vehemence. "I can."

"You can only tell it over and over. It's always the same."

She sat up and looked down at him. "Do you love me?" she asked.

"Of course. How couldn't I? Who couldn't?"

"I love you," she said.

Alexander smiled at her and pulled her down to him. "No, you don't." His blue eyes were dark with recognition. "You're talking to yourself."

"No," she protested. "But—"

"Yes. Love, but . . . I know." Alexander kissed her and then drew his arm out from under her head and dived into the water. Rosalind stretched. Love's weariness made her slow. She felt complete, in possession of Alexander. The sun had set. The sky was now fuchsia, and the west wind carried under it a chill. A bat flitted over her head. Alexander surfaced far out from shore, where the water was dark green in the shadow of the firs. His head gleamed at the center of concentric circles of expanding bright rings; his black hair caught the last of the light.

Rosalind Child stretched and put on her clothes and waved once in Alexander's direction and climbed the rock steps away from the lake. She walked lightly, filled with him, as if he were an element as buoyant as helium. She was filled with a new elation that pumped through her heart and lungs and flowed into her bloodstream, a pure physical happiness that she suspected had nothing to do with love.

12

EVELINE DE CHARNY'S HOUSE WAS DARK; THE blank factory windows reflected the streetlights. Dana Coelho rang the bell. There was no shelter over the door, and rain soaked him. The city air was thick as soot; it was like breathing mud. Dana rang again, and after the red light at the corner had cycled green and yellow three times, a light went on in the stairwell and Atalanta opened the door and peered around the side.

"Missy is not home," she said.

"I need to see her. When's she coming back?" Dana started to walk in, but Atalanta blocked his way.

"She not say. All she say is that she not home."

"I need her," Dana said. "Tell her I need her."

"I tell her, but she not home. What you want?" She frowned.

"You know."

Atalanta shrugged. "Too late. You go home."

"I don't want to."

"She pay me to say she not home and to let no person in. You a person. Go." Atalanta shut the door and turned off the light.

Atalanta trudged upstairs to the kitchen and picked up the supper tray she had prepared and carried it to Eveline de Charny's bedroom at the top of the circular stainless-steel stairs. Atalanta knocked on the door, put the tray on the floor, and waited.

"Who was that at the door?" Eveline de Charny called.

"That boy Dana. He want to see you."

"You sent him away?"

"Yes, missy."

The maid listened for Eveline de Charny. She thought she heard her breathing; she felt her presence on the other side of the door, waiting, as she was.

"Thank you, Atalanta. You can't come in," Eveline de Charny said, dismissing her. Atalanta retreated, striking her heels against the stairs so that the metal clanged like cracked bells.

Atalanta had been closed out of the room for a week. Eveline had gone to watch the Perrot Ballet rehearse and had come back home and barricaded herself in her room and told Atalanta to bring her meals on a tray. She had made telephone calls; then, after three days, she had left the house dressed in a black suit, her physical flamboyance sobered, her hair tamed and smooth, and she had locked the bedroom door behind her. Upon her return in the late afternoon, she had withdrawn again to the bedroom without any explanation.

Eveline was sloppy; she needed Atalanta to organize her. The maid had tried ploys to get into the room and clean it and reassure herself that Eveline de Charny was healthy. She had said that the soup had to be eaten immediately; she had pleaded stacks of sheets and towels that had to be put away. She had tried a direct approach: "I worry."

"I'm fine," said Eveline de Charny. She had an appetite; each tray set in front of the locked door was replaced with the dishes empty, but Atalanta dreaded the complaints of gained weight that were certain to follow. Eveline de Charny had not exercised; Atalanta would have heard the thumping and pounding through the floor. She had also canceled her ballet lessons, her masseur, her manicurist, her secretary, her therapist, even the plant maintenance service. The television had played constantly, early in the morning, all night. Her children were due to come home in three days from their summer visit to their French cousins. Atalanta hoped that Eveline would emerge or had arranged to postpone their arrival. She considered calling the doctor, but she was sure that Eveline de Charny would not let him into the room.

She told everyone who called that Eveline de Charny was not in, and that she did not know when she was coming back. She kept a log of calls and delivered it into the bedroom along with the meals and the mail. Sumner Loewen had sent flowers, which Atalanta also passed in. They came back, pulled from their vase, wilted, with the next meal tray. The mail had been interesting: messengers delivered thick envelopes with engraved return addresses from her lawyers and her brokers. Ricky, a glossy young man who wore white ostrich cowboy boots, came to the door almost every day. Atalanta took him to the hall behind the kitchen and paid him with hundred-dollar bills Eveline de Charny passed to her under the door. She expected to be invited to share, but she was not.

The lawyers' and brokers' letters also frustrated her. Normally Eveline de Charny left her correspondence strewn about, and Atalanta read the bottom line; she knew how much money Eveline de Charny had available for her use. Eveline de Charny had tried to explain her financial situation to Atalanta. Her mother and grandfather had established trusts in her name, but they had placed complicated restrictions on them, and there was only a limited amount of income available for Eveline de Charny to live on. Theoretically, she explained, she had money, but in reality she had little access to it.

"They are incredibly controlling, my parents are, especially my mother," she had said to Atalanta late one night at the end of the summer. "For her, money is everything. So my money, it's like a mirage, you know, out there in the desert. You see it, and it's beautiful, only you never can get to it. I could do so much good if I had that money. They're afraid of the competition. My parents, you know, have never really forgiven me for moving to New York. They wanted me home. My grandfather made my mother come home from Paris. They enjoy doing things like that."

"Explain to me, missy," Atalanta had said. "What you do with more? You already a rich lady. You have everything you need."

"No, Atalanta, I don't," Eveline de Charny had answered. "It's not so much the money; it's that they dole out my life to me like an allowance."

Five more days passed. The children's return had been postponed. The mail continued to come, and the telephone calls, and Ricky. Sumner remained solicitous and announced to Atalanta that he was returning Eveline's calls.

Dana Coelho came back to the house, and Eveline de Charny told Atalanta to let him in. He climbed the stairs to the bedroom and remained there for several hours. The television blared, and Atalanta could not hear what they said or what they did. When he emerged, she tried to grill him. "How is she? What did you do?" she asked as she followed him down the stairs, but he was high and laughed and told her nothing.

Atalanta tried to listen in on the telephone conversations, but Eveline de Charny detected her presence through an echo in the line and threatened to fire her. Atalanta was deeply affronted; she was ashamed to care so much for this selfish, moody, privileged woman. She began to think that it was time to leave, but she could go nowhere without her green card. And if she left, Eveline de Charny would have nobody to help her. Atalanta could not leave her alone; Eveline was really a little child who needed to be watched over. Also, she paid very well. Atalanta was compensated for her affection, for indulging Eveline de Charny's whims, and she enjoyed Eveline's habit of measuring love with money and gifts. She was profligate with gifts. But there had been no gifts lately, and she had turned on permanently the intercom that linked the bedroom with the rest of the house and had tuned it to the kitchen and Atalanta's bedroom. Atalanta was outraged. If Eveline de Charny was so lonesome that she had to listen in, why didn't she open her door?

After Dana left, Atalanta went back upstairs. She had set a kitchen stool outside the bedroom door. Eveline de Charny shouted her name. She opened her mouth to shout back, but realized that Eveline was shouting into the intercom, as if Atalanta were in the kitchen.

"Missy, don't shout," said Atalanta. "I am right here."

"Stay away from my door!" Eveline de Charny warned. "I know you're out there."

"I will not go until you come out. I worry."

"Oh, Atalanta, I'm hungry. Please bring me something to eat." Atalanta went to the kitchen and defrosted a frozen mushroom pizza in the microwave oven, put it on the dinner tray, delivered it, and clanged down the stairs. As soon as Eveline de Charny retrieved her meal, Atalanta resumed her post outside the bedroom door, indispensable, keeping watch.

Eveline sat cross-legged in the middle of her bed, the pizza cheese wrinkling beside her, the dirty sheets crumpled around her like a gray linen nest. Her black hair rose from her scalp in stiff, dull tufts. The sash of her thick terry-cloth robe, gray as the sheets, had come loose; she wore nothing underneath. Her spine slumped, her breasts drooped. Brown shadows ringed her close-set eyes. The room smelled of perspiration and rancid perfume. Her hands shook. She rummaged through the sheets for the remote control and switched from the news to the music video channel. Her ears rang from the television, and her mouth tasted sour from the stale words rattling out of the box, but she could not bear the silence when it was off.

Over the manic chatter of commercials she listened for the doorbell. Her supplier had promised a delivery this evening. Her nose ran and she felt her depression mounting. It was a physical sensation, a burning flow like lava that traveled from the back of her head forward and spread down onto her chest.

The doorbell rang and Eveline heard Atalanta's feet clatter down the stairs. She would die without Atalanta. Who would bring her food? Who would answer the door? Atalanta sat outside her room like a jailer. Eveline hated her.

"Bring it upstairs!" she shouted into the intercom.

Atalanta knocked. Eveline scrambled out of bed and nearly blacked out. A flash, as if lava had spouted from a fissure within her head and blinded her. She bent over and braced herself against her thighs. The flesh on the inside was congealing into curds of fat. She waited, head down, until her vision returned, then hurried to the door. The floor was strewn with papers and clothes. She trod on them, enjoying the softness of crushed silk under her sturdy feet, and grabbed the plastic bag that Atalanta had left in the hallway. She tapped out two lines onto the stained marble counter in her bathroom, inhaled them, and waited for the viscous, burning depression to recede.

Her head cleared. She saw Perrot before her. He spread his black sorcerer's wings, and his long white hands danced, inviting her, giving her possibility. She sat on the floor and rearranged the papers in a ring around her. She was out of cash. Her mother had instructed the bank not to advance her any more funds. Interest on her loans already came to more than half her income. When she tried to borrow through other banks she had been turned down. She had pledged to buy the building for the Perrot Ballet; she could not raise the money.

Her father had not returned her telephone calls. He had allied himself with her mother against her. Eveline hated them.

Hatred was a pleasure. White and light, clean, it illuminated her. She saw herself clearly, the unlucky survivor. It was her fault she had not been slender and tawny, shy as an animal; it was her fault she had not been shot, and they punished her. She was wild with humiliation. Early in the morning, dozing, she had visions more vivid than dreams: her parents were dead, dismembered and violated. No one had done it; her wish alone had been powerful enough to murder them. Their faces were disfigured, their skeletal bellies white as fish, their blood splashed like murals on the white walls of their cold house; blood spilled down the lawn into the lake.

When she awoke, however, her pleasure in her vision ebbed like a drugged high. She awoke to their loss, she realized that she loved her parents, and she was left depressed. She had options, though; she was beginning to see that. She could move back to Michigan and join in her mother's life and good deeds. Her children would blossom; her father could take her son Louis as his own. She should have stayed at home with her father this summer. Leaving had been a mistake; her parents, depending upon her for the appearance of harmony, had retaliated.

Sue them, her lawyers had said when she met with them. You are in your forties, they told her; you are old enough to control your assets. You have certainly reached the age of responsibility. The structure of the trust would not survive a court test. They coerced you into signing documents when you were twenty-one; they threatened to withhold love if you did not do what they wanted. You had no idea of your rights; you did not have benefit of counsel. To avoid the publicity they would probably settle. She picked up the letters outlining the case. Litigation would only take two or three years. After the initial retainer, the lawyers would proceed on a contingency basis: thirty percent of assets recovered if it did go to court. It would be a landmark case, and the firm would be honored to represent her.

Eveline de Charny pulled at a wedge of pizza, extruding strands of cheese, which dipped in gluey parabolas over the sheets. Tomato sauce spattered on the bed. The pizza was cold and inedible, the cheese tasteless, the mushrooms soggy, the sauce pocked with dried oregano. She took the tray and tilted it at the crammed wastebasket. The food bounced off the crumpled papers and fell face down on the rug. Eveline returned to the bathroom and snorted another line of cocaine, and another. Her face flushed; her fingers tingled. She stretched out on the bed, infused with incandescent bubbles. She turned the sound of the television low, so the percussion on the music videos was a subliminal rumbling, felt more than heard, like a subway deep underground.

She dialed her mother's telephone number in Michigan. It was an hour earlier there, just after dinner, the perfect time to call. A servant answered, a voice Eveline did not recognize; her parents changed servants often.

"Mrs. de Charny is meditating, and she cannot be interrupted. Who, please, is calling?" The voice sounded Indian, clipped and dark, singsong like a raga. Benedicte de Charny had long been fascinated with Hindu cycles of reincarnation.

"Her daughter," Eveline replied. "It's extremely important."

"Would you like to call back, or would you prefer to have Mrs. de Charny return your call tomorrow morning?"

"Tell Mrs. de Charny," Eveline began in a voice cultivated and cold, mimicking the Indian's colonial cadence, "that if she does not come to the telephone immediately, I will kill myself."

An electrical click at the other end: the telephone on hold. Eveline held on. She turned up the TV volume and the songs rattled in the room. She sneered at the girls with tiny thighs who leered at the camera over their smooth adolescent shoulders. My body is as good as theirs, she thought. Two songs had played by the time her mother answered the telephone. Eveline lowered the volume once again.

"My dear," said Benedicte de Charny, "couldn't you possibly have waited? My ecumenical conference opened this evening. We were all sitting. In half an hour Hasidic dancing will begin. Would it be possible to talk tomorrow?"

"No."

Benedicte de Charny sighed, resigned to the interruption. Eveline could imagine her mother, with her monk's dress and halo of white hair, her slender calves and swollen ankles, sitting in the white library of her house, gesturing to the servant to bring her a cup of macrobiotic twig tea. Her forehead would be furrowed in a slight frown of boredom and concern that did not extend to her serene yellow eyes. "Well, Eveline, go on, then," Benedicte de Charny said, her voice patient.

"Are you in the library, Mother?"

"Of course."

"I thought so. Are you drinking tea?"

"I asked Hari to bring me some."

"His name is Hari, like Truman or Krishna?"

"He just arrived. A victim of the flood in Bangladesh. He was a professor. His wife died from typhoid. Terrible circumstances."

"I'm sure he'll make a wonderful butler. Mother, you have cut off my money."

"Hardly, my dear. You have overspent."

"I need money, Mother."

"I don't understand. How can you possibly need money? You must have a budget."

"I bought the house in the Berkshires; it was in terrible shape and had to be redone. I have renovations on this house, which are nowhere near finished; they're driving me crazy. I have the children's school bills—you know their father contributes nothing—and they need lessons and clothes. I don't even know how I can afford the plane fare to get them back from Paris. I'm going to have to ask your sister-in-law to buy their tickets. I have donations I've pledged to give, and I have to buy food so we can eat. I have nothing left."

"Eveline dear, you have an income that is more than adequate for all of those things. Frankly, I'm unclear as to exactly how you're spending your money. It seems that a great deal goes to cash. Most of your checks, for instance, are made out to cash. Maybe you could explain? Why don't you prepare an accounting of all of your expenses and send it to me? Then maybe we could make some sort of adjustment. But now I don't really see the need."

"Mother"—Eveline de Charny's voice was heated, erupting—"do you enjoy controlling my life? Does it give you pleasure to sit in your house and know that everything I do, every penny I spend, comes from you?"

About most things, Benedicte de Charny was straightforward, and she was a woman without guilt. "Yes," she replied. "Yes, I do. Yes, it does. Otherwise I wouldn't do it."

Eveline de Charny felt close to suffocation. Hot lava blocked her breathing. "Mother," she pleaded, "Mother, I have pledged to buy the building that holds the Perrot Ballet offices and studios. I want to do it. I love the ballet; I want to be able to help them. I want to help Achille Perrot. They need me to do this, and I could, if I had my money. It would be easy if I had my money. It would be nothing."

Her mother considered. "I understand your infatuation with the Perrot Ballet. I have condoned it. I have defended it to your father, who feels it is excessive, but this scheme sounds a bit grandiose. I can't imagine that they need you to buy them a building."

"Defended it to Father? He thinks it's grandiose? Who do you think I'm buying the building from? Of course Father thinks it's excessive, because he wants the company for himself. He bought the building and offered to lease it back to them. Achille won't work there if Father owns it. Father wants to control the company, and that can't happen. I can't let it happen! He's trying to take it away from me, and I can't let him."

Benedicte de Charny was silent. Her daughter thought she heard the small chink of porcelain against her mother's teeth.

"Do you know who Achille Perrot is?"

The silence continued, then another chink.

"Mother, are you there?"

"Of course."

"Do you know who Achille Perrot is?" Eveline de Charny asked.

"Your tone is so portentous, my dear."

"Achille Perrot is my uncle! He is Father's illegitimate brother. Father wants to own him; Father's jealous of him."

"Half brother, if anything. I'm not surprised. Your grandfather was promiscuous," Benedicte de Charny said calmly. "Notoriously promiscuous. He boasted. That was one of the reasons Magnus Arbroath opposed my marriage to your father."

On the television screen in front of Eveline de Charny, an androgynous young man gyrated and sang. His hair fell in black curls to his shoulders; his lips were shapely and gleamed with lipstick and opened and pursed closed with a sucking, kissing motion; his delicate jaw was hairless, his eyes narrow and slanted, his pants and jacket studded with sequins. His voice, what she could hear of it, ululated like a coyote's. She looked down at her body, exposed where her bathrobe opened. After a week of inactivity, it was flaccid, her stomach bulging and creased, deep folds under her breasts. It carried too much flesh. It was too much a woman's body. She yearned to be a boy.

"There's another reason Father bought the building," Eveline said. "Do you know what it is?"

"I'm sure you'll tell me," said Benedicte de Charny impatiently.

Eveline de Charny shouted into the telephone. "He's in love with a dancer. Dana Coelho, that boy who came out and stayed at the house and danced at the festival! Don't you know? Haven't you known this about him?"

"I'm sure you're wrong, dear. You don't understand. Before we were married, your father had quite a reputation as a ladies' man. It's hereditary."

"You're lying to me! You know. You knew."

"Eveline dear, you really don't understand." Benedicte de Charny's voice remained reassuring, as if she were containing a child's tantrum. "Knowing is not important. You must have learned that. What you know means nothing; it's what you do with what you know."

"You won't admit the truth, then."

"That's hardly how I'd put it. Admit? What is there to admit? What would its purpose be? Do I want pity? Do I want to leave my husband or force him to leave me? Do I want to humiliate him? Or myself? Or you? Is that what you want? Is that the truth? What if this piece of information, which you seem to think should horrify me and which should make me do something—and that something, as far as I can tell, is to give you money—is simply not relevant? And is impossible to prove?"

Eveline de Charny began to laugh, long, high, helpless sounds that could have been sobs. Her eyes ran with tears. She curled herself into a ball on the bed and hugged the telephone to her.

"My dear, what are you doing?" her mother asked.

"Laughing."

"Well, good. So. I'm glad. You must be feeling better. Really, there wasn't anything to be upset about. But I must get back to my meditation. You know how important it is for me to be there. Send me an accounting of your expenses, and I promise I'll look at it as soon as the conference is over. I really do think, though, that the building is a bit much. Frankly, I'm surprised that your father bought it. Automobile sales declined over the summer, even Japanese sales. I would have been more cautious, to see whether it's a trend. I would have waited to see how Arbroath stock recovers in the fall. That's not your concern, though, dear. I'll talk to your father about putting the building back on the market. It certainly is out of the question for you to buy. I won't mention to him that you were thinking about it." She paused. "I miss you, dear. I wish you were here. You would enjoy the conference. It's very spiritual, and you would be a big help to me." She sighed.

The boy in the music video ended his song on his knees, his legs spread, sequins winking across his crotch. Eveline hung up the phone and changed the channel. The weather-man pointed at symbols of clouds and rain and the sun. Tomorrow would be cold, unseasonably cold. Wear your new fall outfits, he was saying. Expect a blast of Canadian air.

Eveline de Charny turned off the television and got out of bed. Kicking clothes and papers aside, she crossed the room and opened the door and stood in the doorway, her bathrobe open. Atalanta perched on her stool, a bottle of nail polish braced between her chubby knees. She glanced at Eveline de Charny, at her magnificent body, lax and gray with drugs and confinement and lack of sleep. She sniffed the sweet, filthy smell. She opened her arms, and Eveline walked into her embrace. Atalanta patted her back while she sobbed.

"Missy, you don't look so good."

Eveline de Charny said, "Maybe you should clean the room, Atalanta. And don't let go of me. I need to be held."

"I hit bottom; that's what happened. I just hit bottom. And I realized I wasn't doing anybody any good, especially myself. I don't know what it was. Stress. I have so many things to worry about. My dancing, my son and daughter. It's hard being a single parent; there's so much nurturing you have to do with no support. It's a terrible responsibility. I was feeling cut off and isolated. You know, overwhelmed."

Caroline Harbison nodded sympathetically.

"But you can't know, really." Eveline de Charny smiled a maternal smile. "You don't have children."

"I didn't see your children with you this summer," Caroline Harbison said.

"Oh, they were in France visiting their cousins. But just because they're away doesn't mean that you stop worrying about them. Actually, it gets worse." Eveline de Charny, seated in one of the upholstered gray cubes in her living room, extended one leg out straight and pointed and flexed her foot, observing the muscles of her calf and thigh contract and stretch. Her toes were newly polished red. She wore black tights and a low-cut leotard and had draped a large red and gold silk paisley shawl over her left shoulder and across her chest and tied it under her right armpit. She sat perfectly upright, maintaining her dancer's posture, projecting opulence, even in dance clothes.

Words came out of Eveline de Charny's mouth upright, too, syllable by syllable, without cadence, as if memorized. "It was my mother who pulled me out of it. She's a wonderful woman—so much energy, and at her age. She just finished organizing and running an ecumenical conference with the Detroit Pan-Religious Council, a month after the Arbroath Festival. She really is amazing. Caroline, you'll have to meet her when she comes to New York. You would really like each other—you're both so pure. So I thought to myself, what good am I doing? Nothing, really. Nothing like her. I mean, she and my father have really made a difference. Not only in the arts, but in public housing, helping minorities. It really made me stop and reassess my life, talking to my mother. Of course I'm going to continue with my dancing—I've already worked for two hours today—but I have to do something bigger, too, something beyond myself. That's the secret of my mother's energy. So I got this idea to set up an agency for artists who are young or aren't really mainstream. People who arc hard to package and sell, so they have trouble getting managers to pay attention to them. People like Amos, you know, who had a really tough time getting established. And Devon, and dance companies that have to perform in church basements. You know what I mean." As she spoke she worried the corner of her paisley shawl, wrapping and weaving the fine material around her long, sturdy fingers.

"It's a good idea, I think," said Caroline Harbison. "But I don't know what you need me for. I don't know anything about managing artists. I don't know why you want me on your board. All I can do is dance." She smiled and shrugged her shoulders. "That's a beautiful shawl," she said.

Eveline de Charny looked down as if she had forgotten what she was wearing. "Oh, thank you," she said absently. "Caroline, I need your name. I'm setting this up as a non-profit organization, which is the way it should be; only the artists should get anything out of it. And everybody knows who you are, everybody respects you. Amos gets the same kind of respect, but fewer people know him. And Sumner, well, people would kill to have Sumner on their board."

Eveline de Charny smiled and gazed at Caroline, her black eyes warming, quickly gentle. "Listen, you think about it. I'm pushing because I'm so excited about the idea. You're much more prudent than I am. You're not impulsive. Take your time. I didn't mean to overwhelm you. I haven't even asked you how you are, how things are going." She hesitated, scanning Caroline's face. "How things are with Alexander," she added.

Tiny unhappy lines fanned out from the corners of Caroline Harbison's mouth. "When I hurt myself last spring, I thought I was ugly because I couldn't dance. So now I'm dancing. Rehearsals have started; I've got a lot to do. I try not to think about anything but dancing. My ankle's getting better. I guess I'll get better, too. It takes time, but whenever I see him I have to start all over again."

"You're a very strong woman." Eveline de Charny stood and stretched, arching her back vertebra by vertebra, enjoying Caroline Harbison's admiration. "Did you know that I have a studio downstairs, a ballet studio? I had the architect make me one. Would you like to see it? You'll be jealous, I promise. I'm dying to show it to you." Eveline de Charny slid her feet into ballet shoes. She rose and bent forward from the waist and reached for Caroline Harbison's hand and led her downstairs.

A wall of glass brick facing the sidewalk lit the studio; the brick fragmented the figures of passersby. On either side of the door, the wall was mirrored, and the door was mirrored as well, the edges of the glass beveled to minimize distortion where the panels joined. A barre was fixed to the wall across from the entrance. Eveline de Charny pushed a panel in the fourth wall, opposite the glass bricks, and it slid open to display an elaborate sound system. She put a compact disk into the machine and tossed her paisley shawl over the barre. Music began; the Tchaikovsky Violin Concerto emerged from concealed speakers, its notes sharp, immediate bites of sound. Eveline de Charny stood in the center of the room and closed her eyes and swayed to the music, entranced.

She lifted her arms and waved them about like sea grass swept by a tidal surge and swooped from one corner of the room to the other, bending her torso from side to side. Her steps were half ballet, half low to the ground, modern. She doubled up and straightened; she leapt. She was very strong and achieved surprising height. Dancing, her size increased. She seemed pneumatic, a parade float, puffed by gaseous emotion, features exaggerated and straining against the distended envelope of her skin. She could not be dismissed. She was fervent in her dance, and her imperious eyes remained fixed on Caroline Harbison, forcing her to watch as if she were the only mirror in the room.

Caroline could not laugh; Eveline de Charny moved with enough skill to save her dance from being ludicrous. She held her body correctly. Her legs turned out; her arms formed a rounded arc. Caroline Harbison stood rigid, her shoulders pressed against the cold mirror. Blasting sound clogged her lungs; the sound seemed separate from music, an electronic assault, and the dance she was watching seemed an exercise in raw need, unrelated to the music's decorum and grace. Eveline de Charny danced around the room; gesture layered on gesture, a string of exclamation marks losing significance.

Caroline Harbison felt like a voyeur, compelled to watch, a witness to the exposure of Eveline de Charny's ungainly soul. At the same time, with a shiver of terror, she felt as if she were watching herself dancing in a distorting mirror. She recognized the fury in Eveline de Charny's face, the wild frustration, the uncertainty as to what steps should come next, the inability to imagine them. She felt fraudulent, ashamed, kin to this woman; she understood her too well.

She shuddered. The room's air conditioning was turned up full. Eveline de Charny was perspiring. During the cadenza she spun; one turn followed the other without variation. She ran in uncertain, dizzy circles; she leapt in place as the violin played octaves.

The first movement ended. Eveline de Charny, her chest heaving, eyes gleaming with exhilaration, faced Caroline Harbison. "What did you think?" she panted.

Caroline crossed her arms in front of her chest. "I don't know what to say," she hedged. "I was very impressed."

"Really? Are you telling me the truth? I don't want you to lie! I want to know what you really think. I know the truth. I'm too old to dance seriously; I missed too many years. I know I'm not bad, but I want to know if you think I have potential, especially as a choreographer."

"I can't tell you that," said Caroline Harbison.

"Why not? You saw what I did. Was it good?"

Caroline was afraid to say no; it was as if Eveline de Charny questioned her own frustration; she had touched her own suspicions of failure. "I can't judge. You have a lot of energy. You work hard. But I don't know."

"Would you want to dance that?"

"I don't think I could. It was too eclectic. I'm not a modern dancer."

"What do you mean? It's not a question of classical or modern. Is it good? I'm asking you because we're alike," said Eveline de Charny. "We're both artists, we're both women, we've both been through a lot. I understand you; you have to understand me. You can help me." She reached for Caroline Harbison's hand.

Caroline recoiled from the touch and the identification, and from the word "women." This was a quality of womanhood she hated: the sloppiness, the self-indulgence Eveline de Charny had permitted herself to dance, calling it expression. Caroline smelled her sweat; it seemed incongruous, as if such a technologically sophisticated room should have an efficient exhaust system.

Eveline de Charny stepped back. "I'm sorry. I had hoped—" She interrupted herself and held herself erect, regaining the posture of dignity, bestowing a request like a favor. "I had hoped that you would work with me."

"How? I can't," said Caroline, helpless. "I only know steps, nothing else." Caroline Harbison had become a dancer by exercising the personality out of her body in order to dance someone else's steps; trying to attain that degree of self-denial would not occur to Eveline de Charny. How could Caroline criticize that? Caroline herself could be criticized. Her own aspirations might be too limited, the range of her own life too narrow. Caroline had pared herself down so that she existed only when she moved. She had disciplined herself to love only when she danced.

"I have to go," Caroline said. "I have to rehearse this afternoon. I'm sorry I can't help."

"Stay." Eveline de Charny smiled. "I'm so hot—I must be bright red." She made physical effort the excuse for shame's flush. She had not built up enough debt; she had not paid out enough to Caroline to buy what she wanted. She had not made herself sufficiently alluring. For a moment she hated Caroline, and she welcomed hatred, anticipated its release. But Caroline, she realized, would not care if Eveline hated her. Caroline wanted nothing from her. Eveline de Charny did not know how else to keep her. "Stay, please. I've made you uncomfortable. I've pushed you." She opened the studio door. Caroline started for the hall as if sprung from a prison. Eveline added: "But I'll put you on my board?"

Caroline Harbison, unnerved by her identification with this woman, guilty for having judged her, hesitated. "I don't know what I'm supposed to do. I don't know how much time it would take. I don't have any money to give."

Eveline de Charny laughed. With her instinct for how others perceived her, she sensed Caroline's guilt, and her own advantage. Her laugh was easy and generous. She did not block Caroline's way. "You don't need to give money. I do that. I'm good at that." She inclined her head and raised it quickly, her eyes lit with an idea. "Wait," she said, "one minute." She ran up the stairs. "Atalanta!" she called. "Atalanta! I need you." In a moment she returned with a flat package wrapped in glossy pink paper. "Caroline, this is for you. I just remembered I had another one. Open it."

Caroline unwrapped the package. Inside was a paisley shawl like the one Eveline de Charny wore, but colored blue and green and violet. Caroline started to protest.

"It's yours," said Eveline. "I don't need two. I always go too far, with people and with clothes. I see something and I think I'll never find another one, so I get two. I want you to have it. Please, because you've been so sweet. Now go." She opened the door.

Caroline Harbison stooped and put the package on the floor, trying not to accept it. Eveline de Charny picked it up and thrust it at her. "It's yours. If you don't take it I'll throw it away. I'll throw it out the door onto the street. And thank you. Think about it—I'd love to work with you."

Caroline Harbison started toward Fifth Avenue, to go back downtown. She felt tainted for taking the shawl and weak for wanting it, ungenerous for not agreeing to do what Eveline de Charny wanted. She did not notice Dana Coelho until he blocked her way so that she nearly collided with him. He was incandescent and golden; he radiated heat and nervous delight.

"Cary, what are you doing here?"

"Visiting your friend."

"I didn't know you knew Eveline."

"Just from the summer. Dana, I haven't seen you for a while. Where have you been? What have you been up to? What are you doing here? Does Eveline want you to be on her board, too?"

"What board? I've been around—here, in the country, back and forth. I haven't felt like getting back to work. Has Perrot been looking for me?"

"Yes. He asks every day. He's not happy. It would be a good idea if you showed up tomorrow."

Dana laughed. "Maybe I will, maybe I won't."

"Don't you care?"

Dana shrugged and grinned.

"Why not?"

He shook his head, not telling.

Despite herself Caroline Harbison asked something else: "Have you been with Alexander? Have you seen Alexander?"

"I've seen him." Dana put his arm around her and frowned.

"How is he?"

"Dancing. That's what he's doing a lot of. Dancing."

"Who with?"

"Don't worry. Just me." He laughed. "Don't be jealous."

Dana rang Eveline de Charny's bell. Atalanta opened the door. He ran up the stairs to the living room.

Devon, her hair disheveled, was coming down the steps from the bedroom. She yawned. "What time is it?"

"One-thirty, you lazy thing." Eveline de Charny smiled. "Dana!" She kissed him on both cheeks.

"What was Caroline doing here?" he asked.

She laughed. "Oh, a project, some ideas I had. I'll tell you about it. Nothing you'd be interested in. Charity. Don't worry. I wasn't corrupting her. Listen, I don't have anything for you, only a little coke. The good stuff isn't coming for another couple of hours, maybe not until tomorrow. Devon's been waiting, too. It's scarce; everybody wants it. I feel awful disappointing you both. Tomorrow I'll give it to you. They promise me it's fantastic." She smiled. "Guaranteed to make you happy."

"But I can't tomorrow."

"Why? What are you doing?"

Dana cast his eyes down. "I have an appointment."

Eveline considered. "I see." She looked at him as if she had solved a large problem. "Well, then, I know what to do. I'll meet you at my father's, early, before he gets there. He's flying in from Mexico City, isn't he? That's what Aline said. I haven't seen him in a while. I'll bring it with me." She put her hand on his arm. "But don't go. Why don't we finish up what we've got? I feel the need to party."

The florist next door to the Perrot Ballet had stocked the sidewalk with green and brown plastic pots of chrysanthemums—yellow, lavender, rusty red, and maroon flowers, daisy mums with white spoon-shaped petals and yellow centers, Fuji mums whose white blossoms exploded like fireworks. Sturdy plants, the season's last flowering. The chrysanthemums made Caroline Harbison sad, reminding her of time passing, a summer already gone, although it was just September. For years she had not dreaded the passage of time, not since she had hoarded the hours of the last week of summer vacation with a child's regret at the loss of empty days.

For years nothing had changed, so she had had no reason to hate time. She danced. The season, rehearsals and performances, began and ended, the summer began and ended, the season began again. She learned new ballets and practiced old ones. She loved Alexander as best she could.

Now that circle had broken. Dancing could not keep it round and keep her out of time. She looked through the door of the big studio; it was empty, afternoon class finished.

She passed Guy Pissarro's office. Walter Mowbray sat at his desk beside Guy's, leafing through a sheaf of glossy photographs.

"Caroline," he called, "want to see your program book picture? They just came back."

"Sure." She entered the office. "Walter, you've changed your hair again. You're a blond."

"Only the ends. I wanted to look like I spent two weeks at the beach, not in New Jersey house-sitting for my sister. And that orangy red, I don't know. It was okay for a few days, but it was a little hot. Hot is definitely not cool."

"It looks nice. Maybe I should bleach my hair."

"A little lighter around the face. It would definitely give you a lift."

"You think I need one?"

"I meant psychological. Hair color has a lot to do with mind-set. I read an article about it."

Caroline nodded and picked up the photographs. On top was a picture of Rosalind, her hair fanned out behind her, skin blasted white with strong frontal light. Her large pale eyes and full lips and tiny nostrils were set like jewels in a luminous oval. Walter looked over Caroline's shoulder. "Not bad," he said.

"She gets a big picture. She's been promoted?"

"Didn't you know?"

Caroline shook her head. "Well, she looks better than in real life. You can't see the zits."

"Meow. Aren't we jealous."

Caroline glared at him. "I don't know. Maybe I'm sympathetic. We could all look better in our pictures than in real life. But then it would be hard to look in the mirror."

Walter stepped in front of her and fluffed her limp hair out from her face. "That photographer makes everybody look marvelous. I wish I had an excuse for him to do me. Not that you don't look fine in this." He held up Caroline Harbison's photograph, a conventional full-length portrait taken by the company's photographer. She was leaping in a jeté, legs extended, back arched; her face, she thought, revealed too much of the effort.

"It's okay," she said without enthusiasm.

"So if you're not happy, next year go to this guy. Too

bad it's too late now. Lines, shadows, everything disappears. You'd look great."

"Walter. A little blond around the face. Lines and shadows. Good grief. What have I done to you?"

"Sorry, dear, nothing personal. It's me, I've been having a tough time myself. Mr. Loewen has been acting weird. Perrot walks around like he wishes we'd all drop dead. But they tell me that everything's fine. And Dana—Dana's my problem. He's missed rehearsals; he's never around. He's gone for days and nights. Not that I expect anything from him, but I guess I do. Perrot's ready to fire him."

"I saw Dana this afternoon."

"Did he seem okay?"

"A little hyper. I only saw him for a minute, at Eveline de Charny's."

"It figures. I mean, I don't care what he does—it's his business who he wants to hang out with—but I think he's out of control. He's never off the stuff. She gets it for him."

"Maybe you should tell Perrot what the problem is?"

"Dana would kill me."

"Do you want me to talk to Dana?"

"Sure. I mean, it's no big deal. Only if you see him, you know, only if it comes up, and don't let him think that I told you to."

"Tomorrow. I think I have a rehearsal with him tomorrow."

"Caroline, do you and Alexander have any idea what's going on around here?"

She shook her head. "No," she sighed. "I don't. Nothing as far as I know. And Alexander and me—you know about that. Everybody does. That's nothing, too."

13

ACHILLE PERROT STALKED HIS DANCERS; HE observed them, measuring them and arranging them. The members of the corps had already lost weight; in class they were growing stronger.

As Perrot passed by, the dancers ceased their chatter and suggestive touching. The boys stretched. Submissive animals, they displayed their stomachs and the surprising bulk of their shoulders. Their muscled calves bulged in their leg warmers. The girls' self-absorbed eyes in their small, poised heads looked inward, wondering how Perrot would judge them. Those who had not been in class when he corrected Rosalind Child had found out about what happened, and the story had grown and become exaggerated: Perrot had struck her; she had burst into tears and called him a terrible old man; Alexander Ives had defended her. There was much gossip about Rosalind Child and Alexander Ives.

Perrot heard it. He heard the stories about himself and

Rosalind Child as well. Gossip rebounded off the walls at the Perrot Ballet and acquired a momentum of its own, a self-propelled echo that reached everyone's ears. There were stories about Alexander's ballet; in the corridors the dancers debated what that meant, especially in light of reports that Alexander Ives was unhappy at the Perrot Ballet and had talked about leaving. There were stories that other companies had invited him to join them in any capacity he wanted: to dance, to choreograph, to serve as artistic director. "Is that true?" Guy Pissarro asked Perrot. "Is what true?" Perrot replied impatiently. "That he wants to leave or that he will?"

Rumors about the purchase of the building proliferated; nobody was sure who had bought it; everybody knew that Achille Perrot did not approve. Many thought the new owner was Eveline de Charny, while others insisted it was Sumner Loewen. Achille Perrot had always enjoyed rumors, baroque truths; it amused him to see them grow like crystals. But the rumors about Alexander angered him because he had not been their source; he was too proud to ask Alexander, or to ask anyone, even Guy Pissarro, to ascertain the truth. And he was angry with himself to realize how badly he wanted Alexander to stay.

As he stalked the halls, Perrot watched the dancers covertly sizing him up to detect deterioration—a stoop in his posture, perhaps, a vagueness in his eyes. Like children, they feared change and hated weakness, yet change and weakness excited them.

As Alexander Ives strode through the corridor on the way to class, the company members paused in their conversation and glanced obliquely at him. They smiled, they stretched, they straightened, they quieted their chatter. Alexander Ives saw, and his blue eyes, when he and Achille Perrot met at the door to the big studio, were wary. Perrot was disappointed; he would have liked to see some pleasure in Alexander's face at the dancers' submission, if only to justify his anger at Alexander and his outrage at his own diminution. Brusquely he hustled the dancers into the room ahead of him.

Alexander Ives took class with the rest of the company.

He assumed no preeminent place, but stood near the back of the room. He gazed at himself in the mirror, absorbing his own image. Perrot watched. He watched for vulnerability and hoped for awkwardness; he hoped to see Alexander's precise technique grown lax, to see his wrist droop carelessly, and he hoped for his beats, the quick, flickering motion of his feet, to falter.

Perrot remembered the boy whom he had made into a dancer; he remembered how he had loved him. He remembered how one of Alexander's moves could shock him with its beauty. The moment when a leap or a turn passed from roughness to a finished state—it was a moment of illumination as transient as an eclipse. The magical corona shimmered briefly and engendered in Perrot a permanent love. Perrot suffered the consequences of love: what was loved existed indifferently beyond possession, past death. He could not help wishing that Alexander had been a creation only of his mind, an illusion that would fade when he did.

Perrot felt tattered, worn from years of supremacy. Alexander Ives was sleek and smooth, in his prime. He never faltered, never grew lazy. He executed each element of the geometry of the barre perfectly, each combination, each balance.

Alexander's gift was surprise; Perrot had seen that, too, from the beginning. A gesture, an emotion, would burst suddenly from his reserve, from that part of himself he kept distant, a part he himself was unaware of. It would happen without any visible preparation, like a leap launched with an imperceptible flexing of his knees. His challenge, Perrot understood, had been to train Alexander without blunting the surprise, which meant keeping from him the secret of his own beauty and loving Alexander as if love were arbitrary, though Perrot always loved for a reason.

Perrot loved for what love let him do with his lovers; it was not to be loved in return. He had been jealous of Caroline, not only because she had taken Alexander away from him, but because he feared that she would make him lose artistic control of the boy; he feared that in loving her, Alexander would free his locked emotions. But he had not.

Perrot had used them together; her knowledge and his power. Alexander's distance from himself was unbridgeable; his art, therefore, was safe.

Finally the air conditioning had chilled the building's corridors; by this morning they had become cold. After class Achille Perrot went to his office intending to play through the score of Webern and Schoenberg's orchestration of the Strauss waltzes, but instead, he stood by the window watching the traffic on the street, clogged and raucous again after the summer. Below him, he watched his dancers emerge from the building and blink at the bright day. They moved lightly down the sidewalk through the lunchtime crowds of plodding pedestrians.

Restless, Perrot left his office. In the corridor he shivered. He walked through the boys' dressing room. It was empty. The big rehearsal room was dark. He continued down the hall to one of the two smaller rooms. The sound of a piano reduced on tape reached him faintly, and he peered through the small wire-gridded window cut into the door.

Inside the room Alexander Ives was working with Caroline Harbison and Dana Coelho. Perrot was relieved to see Dana. Guy Pissarro had told him that Dana was afraid he was going to be fired—another rumor, displeasure embroidered. He decided to talk to the boy after Alexander finished. Something was wrong, some failure of love, some trouble with Roland de Charny, that affected the boy's dancing. He watched Dana in his blue bodysuit, his magnesium energy brilliant even in daylight. He could love Dana Coelho.

Achille Perrot imagined loving Dana with an old man's craven love. He would be grateful; he would want to give gifts and comfort and be reassured. That was how Roland de Charny loved the boy, Perrot realized with scorn. It was ironic after a lifetime of possessing to come to that, to be grateful to be possessed. If he wanted love, Perrot thought, it was to use for his dances.

The dancers repeated a passage several times. After each repeat, Alexander Ives ran to the tape machine and rewound the cassette. He gave them variations on the steps, experimenting with the effect. He had learned, Perrot noted with pleasure, and that pleasure surprised him. His new combinations exploited Caroline Harbison's elegance and her translucence, the length of her limbs, the flexibility of her body.

Something else had changed: Alexander did not love Caroline anymore. He could not see her with such clarity if he still loved her. Oddly, Perrot felt no triumph, no vindication of his old jealousy; only regret, sympathy for Caroline and pity for Alexander. What Alexander had had with Caroline, whatever love, was more than he would ever have again, Perrot knew, and for a moment he wondered if he, in his considered isolation, had been jealous of the connection, not the woman.

The longing, the pain of separation that had seized Achille Perrot at the beginning of the summer, had diminished. He had grown used to the constant chill, the slow removal, the awareness of short time that intensified every emotion, like the sun through a magnifying lens.

He tested longing. Through the small window he gazed at Alexander Ives and Dana Coelho; he fixed his eyes on their bodies, their youth. He saw the delicate pattern of hair on their chests, the smooth muscles of their necks curving into their shoulders, the hollow of their buttocks, the high arches of their feet. He touched with his eyes Caroline Harbison's pliant back, her long, narrow waist, her concave stomach, and the rise of bone at her groin, the sharp lines of her collarbones and shoulder blades, the little cap of muscle where her arm joined her shoulder.

Desire remained, but it was apart from him, separated; distilled, intense, and pure like a memory—and, like a memory, reordered and bearable, finished. Perrot shivered. Although the corridor was cold, he knew it was the music that chilled him now; the music was an answer to death. Perrot heard in the music what he was beginning to understand—what he felt himself now—the urgency of memory in the presence of death.

Inside the room there was a chill as well. The light through the high dusty windows seemed white and winter

pale. Perrot watched Alexander Ives and Caroline Harbison
dance with each other and marveled at the familiar transformation. Without touching, each gave the other balance. In
each other's presence they took risks. Their dark hair and
blue eyes matched. Their bodies as well as their spirits com-
plemented each other, and each endowed the other with
additional grace. It was an accident that they matched, a
fortunate physical accident. But the delight and astonishment with which they encountered this accidental congruence had vanished since they no longer translated it into love.
Their dancing ached with the agonizing process of becoming
unattached.

So, Achille Perrot thought, it is over between them. He
would use their unhappiness in his ballet, in his waltzes. It
was what he wanted.

The last chords of the Schubert impromptus sounded
from the rehearsal room, faint and tinny under the pounding of the dancers' feet. Within minutes, Caroline Harbison,
out of breath, pushed the door open. She nodded quickly at
Perrot, hardly noticing him in her hurry to leave. He caught
the door and held it. Dana Coelho stood over Alexander Ives
as he crouched before the tape machine while it rewound.
They both panted, recovering from the dance. Dana regarded Alexander with impatience and expectation, and Perrot saw that the trouble was not Roland de Charny but
Alexander. As if Dana's gaze weighed him down, Alexander
Ives did not rise; he listened intently to the whirring tape.

Dana's hand hovered above Alexander's shoulder, close
enough for Alexander to feel its electricity against his skin.
Alexander contracted and ducked out from under Dana's
reach. A safe distance away, he confronted Dana. On Alexander's face was desire, and suspicion. Dana watched Alexander, Perrot saw jealously, the way Alexander used to look
at him, with selfish hope and a kind of gratitude, as if he
knew that what Perrot could give him would help him more
than he could benefit Perrot.

In love there was always calculation. Alexander did not
see that. His loneliness had not scarred over; he picked at it

and kept it raw. He would never enjoy what love could be used for, and this mitigated Achille Perrot's jealousy. It angered Perrot, too; if Alexander learned from him, he wanted his pupil to be worthy and not to fail. He wanted Alexander to learn the cosmic ruthlessness of play.

"Take him," Achille Perrot said as he entered the room.

Dana Coelho clenched his hand into a fist. Alexander Ives arched his back as if he had been struck. He did not look at Perrot. "What do you mean?" Alexander asked, his voice trembling with mistrust.

"Do what you want. You want him," Perrot answered. "Why not?"

Alexander Ives crouched again and removed his tape from the machine. He got up and turned his back on Perrot. He crossed the room and pulled a sweat shirt over his leotard.

"I'm not like you." Alexander's voice was pinched and angry, prohibiting intrusion.

"No." Perrot, defeated, turned to Dana Coelho. "We rehearse tomorrow at eleven. You will be there, finally? I have a part for you. I have missed you. Because of you I have not been able to begin."

Dana glanced at Alexander's back as if offering an explanation. Perrot shook his head. "The reason does not matter. Reasons are unimportant." Perrot frowned. "We don't have very much time. If you are not there I will use somebody else."

Achille Perrot left the studio and returned to his office. In the hall Walter Mowbray accosted him. As he walked, the bleached ends of his hair rose and fell like a small patch of wheat. He held a sheaf of pink message slips in his hand. "Mr. Perrot! Mr. Perrot! Wait. I've been looking for you. I've been getting these calls and I don't know what to do with them. I mean, I don't know what to say, so I tell them to call back later, and then they do and I still don't have answers. Listen, really, I hate to bother you, I know how busy you are, but I need your help."

"What are your problems, then?" Perrot asked most impatiently.

"Well, first, Gertrude Stella is bugging me about Alexander's ballet. She wants to know what it's about and when she can see it. Like, Guy told me to tell her to call Sumner Loewen, but she says Mr. Loewen has no idea when Alexander will let people watch. And Alexander looks at me like I'm Looney Tunes when I ask him, so what should I do? And then she wants a fall schedule, but I don't think there is one, is there? And she gets mad at me and says there has to be one, there always is one, and as soon as there is she has to get it first. She's always first. And she wants to do a big piece on the company in time for the opening. Then, what are all the rumors about the company's building and its new endowment and its long-range plans? She says Sumner Loewen's been teasing her about them, but she wants to talk to you before she writes her piece. So what should I say? And she wants to know why you're letting your ballets out. I guess she means what Dana danced this summer. She asked me if you really let Dana take those ballets or if he stole them. I mean, I know you let him, but she's not going to believe me."

Perrot smiled. "Mr. Mowbray, when Gertrude Stella calls again, tell her that you asked me everything she asked you, and I told you to tell her that nothing is happening. There is no ballet by Alexander Ives. There is no building. There is no endowment. There are absolutely no long-term plans. For that matter, there is not even a fall schedule, but you can tell her that of course we will send her one immediately, when it has been prepared."

"And it isn't true about Dana, is it? Is that why you're going to fire him?"

"He had my permission, but that is of no interest to anyone. It is another question you will not answer. And if Dana is at rehearsal tomorrow I will not fire him."

"Are you happy?"

Dana Coelho grinned. The capsule lightened him, made him incandescent.

"It's good, isn't it?" Eveline de Charny's dark eyes gleamed with kindness. "That's what I want," she told him. "Yes. That's all I want for you. I love seeing you happy."

He believed her, and he followed her through her father's apartment. Her black heels sank into the white carpet like black birds' feet, but she was too big, she couldn't fly. She would let him do anything, though; she wanted him happy.

"These are my favorites." She stopped in front of paintings of naked women and skull-headed men in dark jackets and striped morning pants. "I love these. I want my father to give them to me."

Vermilion, chrome yellow, acid green, cobalt—the angry colors penetrated the happy light Dana emitted and soured it. "That man looks like Perrot." He shivered.

"And like my father," Eveline said. "Don't you think? They're almost the same, you know."

She was crazy, but so what? Naked women colored like nightmares and the black-suited men who dreamed them—as Dana gazed at them, those figures, locked into their flat plane, tried to escape it, tried to embrace him. He recoiled, cornered. Eveline de Charny steadied him. "You don't like them? Then come on. We don't want you seeing anything you don't like."

She took his hand and led him into the living room. "Remember that?" she asked. "The Jurgen Jaeger. My father's new picture." She crossed to the dense black-tarred canvas hung opposite the window. Faces hazed with a film of dust screamed at him from inside the painting, but Dana was safe, the tar pit sucked at them; they couldn't touch him. Eveline stroked the picture's surface, and the tip of her finger came away stained black. She rubbed her finger against her upper lip and stroked the painting again and smeared black on her cheeks, like the shadow of a beard. "Whom do I look like?" She grinned.

"You look like your father."

"Do you like that?"

"I don't know. I'm not sure." He closed his eyes.

"I would do anything to make you happy," she said.

The room smelled of sulphur. Dana Coelho went to the window with the night city below him. He followed the waves of white headlights and red taillights as automobiles stopped and started to traffic lights in the park. White lights, red lights, green lights, yellow lights—it was poetry. Alexander had read him poetry, which he had not understood; it was too complicated. Now he could make up his own. It was better. He giggled. It was a kind of music. He could dance to his own laughter. But Eveline de Charny had put a tape on her father's sound system. "This is the music that goes with ecstasy," she told Dana. "This is what you have to listen to. It's a whole thing, a gestalt."

"What's that?"

"Never mind. Will you be all right if I leave you alone for a minute? Listen. Just feel good."

And, alone, he did. He opened the window, and the soft, dry wind cooled the room. Up here, the air even smelled good. The filthy exhaust stayed below. The city noise was music, too. The horns and sirens mixed with the tape; and, every once in a while, as if on cue, someone shouted, and it all blended into a perfect chord. Eveline touched his shoulder. He turned from the window. She had put on one of her father's suits. Its buttoned jacket strained against her breasts, the seams of its pants puckered at the inside of her thighs. She danced large in front of him; her voracious smile—lurid red lips, livid mouth—filled her face below her dense black hair, between her blackened bearded cheeks. She reached for him and, terrified, he reared back into the music and the clean air, where, safe, he laughed again and said words: red light, white light, love light. He was part of the music; it all made a luminous whole.

"I don't mean to frighten you." Eveline said, retreating into the darkening room. "Are you happy?"

"Oh, yes. Thank you, yes." In the clean air Dana felt redeemed and weightless, as if there were lights shining inside him, illuminating his spirit, showing him possibility and his own goodness. He had lost track of that, his goodness, and suddenly here it was, a soul, a bird, an aerodynamically designed white thing.

Nobody could touch his soul, nobody's dried out pathetic grateful old body could contaminate it. Even Alexander could not get near it. Alexander could use some of this. It would lighten him up. Tomorrow Dana would give him a capsule. They could go to the zoo after rehearsal. This would be a good thing to do in a zoo. They were animals. Alexander could be a panther. Dana was a bird. An egret or a golden eagle. Perrot knew he was a bird and made him the Sorcerer. He loved to fly. He loved to swish above the stage, looking down at the poor heavy girls in the corps pretending to be swans but not fooling anybody. His balsa wings billowed in the currents of air under the lights, the harness tight across his chest.

He had never told anybody; maybe it was time he should. Tomorrow, he would. He would tell Perrot, that poor old man who needed wires to fly, who needed him to make dances, he would tell Perrot why he was so important to the company. They had never had a dancer like him, and it was time they knew it. He didn't need that heavy harness, those padded canvas belts, those stupid annoying straps you had to buckle around your crotch that crushed your balls. He could fly by himself. He understood air. He could see the currents, updrafts and downdrafts; he could actually see them, here, outside the building. He danced. When he danced he was so light and so happy that his feet did not dent Roland de Charny's thick white rug.

"Dana," said Eveline. "Look at me."

He didn't want to, but she had made him happy. He was grateful; he had to look, he owed it to her. She had taken off her father's suit. Her heavy naked woman's body filled the room; above it her man's face ogled him. He couldn't bear seeing her, seeing her father in her. She—he—they weighed him down, and he wanted to fly.

"Don't make me!" he said, yearning for the white light, red light, the sweet air above filth. She would go away; if Eveline wanted him happy, she'd leave him alone.

But she said: "What about me?"

"You don't want me," Dana said—everything was clear, from his altitude he could see everything. "You want your father."

She shook her head no and hovered close behind him; she stroked his neck. Her greasy fingers marred his whiteness. Her man's face scorched him. She smelled like pitch.

Her naked breasts gunned him down; her nipples smoldered like the muzzles of guns. She was too bright, like those women in the paintings on her father's walls—red lips, flaming pubic hair. She wanted to burn him up; her arms around his neck branded his skin.

Her hot breath seared his cheek. "I want to be happy too. You have to make me happy."

He saw how—she wanted him consumed, she wanted him to become as light as his soul. That was perfect. That was what he wanted, too. It frightened him, but now fear acted on him like desire. It demanded a dance. He bent into it. He broke away from her and leaned out into the cool healing sky. Eveline's fiery mouth smiled encouragement. He lifted off. He was airborne.

Alexander Ives and Caroline Harbison warmed up at opposite ends of the barre. Rosalind Child had taken a place in the middle, equidistant between the two. Each dancer paid assiduous attention to reflection. With her hand resting against her inner thigh, so slender it seemed she could span it with her hand, Caroline monitored her turnout. Rosalind adjusted the angle of her right wrist. Alexander slowly raised one leg until it was perpendicular to the floor.

At eleven o'clock, Achille Perrot entered the room with Guy Pissarro. He glanced from dancer to dancer.

"Dana is not here," he said to his ballet master.

Guy Pissarro nodded unhappily. "Let me make a telephone call," he said. He trotted from the studio. Achille Perrot sat on a folding chair in front of the mirror. Harry Menard played through the first waltz and lit a cigarette. "Summer again," he said to the room. "Going to reach eighty today."

"The dust on that tree is appalling," Perrot said, pointing to the ficus. "Would it be too much to ask someone to water it?"

"I will." Caroline Harbison ran out and returned with four paper cups from the cooler. She poured water into the plant's parched soil. A puddle spread on the floor. Guy Pissarro followed Caroline Harbison into the studio. He looked

at Perrot and shrugged unhappily. Perrot, his mouth compressed in annoyance, scanned the room. He pointed to a
boy in the corps, a redhead with a blunt, freckled face, who
sat against the back wall. "You," he said. "I want you to
dance."

"Kevin," said Guy Pissarro.

The boy shook out his legs nervously and joined Alexander Ives, Caroline Harbison, and Rosalind Child in the
center of the room. "Let's do." Achille Perrot spoke to them
while his hands danced.

Harry Menard began to play. The familiar Strauss melodies burdened with twentieth-century harmonies became
world-weary. They had lost their exuberance; lust had corroded romance; a bright gilt ballroom shrank to a murky,
subterranean nightclub.

Achille Perrot played with threesomes. This was not a
dance for two couples; he made it for two triangles. Alexander, Caroline, and Rosalind; Alexander, Caroline, and the
boy Kevin. Rosalind danced a quick obbligato—delirious little turns and fast childish straight-legged leaps above the
bitter harmonies. She dipped and spun and enfolded her
body in her loose black hair and thrust her flat, thin hips
seductively forward as she skipped across the floor. She
darted between the other dancers, cutting their connections.
Kevin, trying for Dana's speed, missed beats; he counted out
loud.

Caroline's steps remained slow, weighted with pain, difficult balances and twisted postures. Reluctantly, Alexander
held her in her balances, lured by Rosalind and the boy.
Perrot had Alexander leave Caroline to partner the others.
When he came back to her, their feet relentlessly repeated
the waltz step—one, two, three, one, two, three. They
bounced as if the rhythm were alien, as if the expansive waltz
they used to dance eluded them. The two young dancers
teased Alexander and tormented Caroline.

Achille Perrot worked quickly. He had mapped the ballet in his mind; he made few changes. He leaned wearily
against the piano and whispered and gestured each combination impatiently as if he expected the dancers to know

already what he wanted them to do. The room was sharp with anxiety. Alexander Ives and Caroline Harbison moved like puppets through Perrot's configurations of desire. Caroline Harbison's mouth compressed, her jaw clenched, and her face reddened with shame and anger. Perrot had appropriated her heart.

At the end of the last piece, Perrot nodded. Those dancers who had been watching applauded. Harry Menard dropped his cigarette into his Coke and crushed the can. Guy Pissarro patted Kevin on the shoulder and praised his performance. Caroline Harbison walked to the wall and gripped the barre with both hands and hunched her shoulders over it.

Rosalind Child was exuberant; she skipped across the floor toward Alexander Ives. Alexander stepped back and nearly knocked her over. He gripped her shoulder and steadied himself. He smiled and he reached around her neck and gently picked up her hank of black hair and twisted it around his hand.

Caroline saw the gesture in the mirror as she bent over to take off her toe shoes. Jealousy rose inside her like nausea. She made herself watch. It was no more painful than the dance; it was the same thing. She stared at Alexander's hand wrapped in sleek hair, stared at it for meaning. She realized that there was nothing to be jealous of, nothing or everything. She knew Alexander. She knew about Rosalind, Dana, the next dancer. She saw nothing new. But she saw Alexander in a new way.

That gesture of Alexander's—its grace, the tenderness with which he wrapped that girl's hair in his hand—was finite. It was complete in itself; it did not resonate. It meant nothing. Alexander Ives was profligate with gesture. He was a dancer and repeated the combinations of love again and again, repeated them like music, refining them each time. His dance, his gestures, only became more beautiful.

More beautiful, Caroline thought, than the real thing. That was what she could not give up.

Alexander dropped Rosalind Child's hair. The girl hovered near him like a hummingbird, believing him sweet. Caroline stayed where she was, transfixed, in Alexander's thrall, and she slowly wrapped the ribbons around her toe shoes. Alexander gathered his gear, anxious to quit the room where the geometry of failed love patterned the air. Before he could leave, Achille Perrot stopped him with his long fingers on Alexander's upper arm. "So. When are you going to show me your ballet again?" When he smiled, his lips retracted above his long teeth, as on a death's-head.

"I didn't think you were interested," Alexander said.

"I always have been."

"Why? To change it?"

Achille Perrot went to the piano and played a yearning dance tune from the first of the impromptus, then interrupted it with one of the disillusioned Strauss waltzes. "It might be interesting to see the two ballets together." He rose unsteadily from the piano bench. Alexander Ives stepped forward to lift him. Abashed, he checked himself. Achille Perrot rested against the curve of the piano, glanced at Alexander angrily, and laughed once, a deep, ironic sound, an operatic expulsion of breath. He started toward the door. As he reached for the handle, the door opened.

Walter Mowbray stood at the entrance. His face was white; the blue veins pulsed at his temples. With his spiked, bleached hair, he looked like a mask of grief. His hands had cramped into fists. He remained where he stood when Perrot gestured at him impatiently to move aside and let him pass.

"If you have a message from Dana," Perrot said, "you are too late."

Tears coursed down Walter Mowbray's face. He tilted forward as if he wanted Perrot to take him in his arms.

Achille Perrot backed away. "Well, what is it?" he asked. "What on earth has happened?"

Walter Mowbray choked. "I got a phone call. Here." He opened his fist; it held a crumpled pink message slip. He tried to smooth the paper. "Here is the number. It was the police. A detective. He was very nice. Very understanding. What a terrible thing to have to do. Call people."

The shuffle of ballet shoes against the floor died down. Caroline Harbison stepped behind Alexander Ives, as if his body could block news. Walter Mowbray bent his head over the message. "It says—this detective told me—he called to say that they found Dana. This morning, they found him. The doorman recognized him. They took him to the hospital, but—"

"But?" Achille Perrot repeated.

Alexander Ives said, "He's dead. He's dead. How? Tell!"

"He jumped out of a window. That's what they said. That's what they think happened. It's consistent, they said, consistent with his injuries. They have to do an autopsy, of course." Walter Mowbray folded his hand over the pink paper to make it disappear. His voice rose into a high wail. He slumped in the doorway, his knees drawn up to his shoulders, his gilded head fallen into his hands.

Caroline Harbison opened her arms to Alexander Ives and he embraced her: a gesture of comfort. Alexander was shaking. He whispered, "Oh, God, he tried to fly."

14

THE UPPERMOST LEAVES OF THE MAPLES IN CENtral Park were red. It could have been the sunset, but the clouds were yellow; the leaves burned red, changing already. The capricious September weather had turned cold again; in Westchester there had been a frost. Roland de Charny could not feel the temperature through his well-insulated window. He looked down, his hands locked behind his back, and considered the distance to the ground. It was unimaginable. Dana Coelho could have been a bird, a leaf, a brick. Dana was inanimate, dead. Roland de Charny gagged. He had not seen Dana dead. He could not imagine him dead, only dying. It was terrible to imagine him dying, to hear the impact against cement; it was worse than to see him crushed and limp, dusty from soot. He would have preferred to see the body graceless and cracked and to feel the blessed superiority the living feel for the dead—pity and revulsion first, then triumph and tenderness, and finally relief. He had felt that even for his son, for Louis-Marie.

Roland de Charny swallowed. His bile was bitter and abraded his teeth. He felt revulsion for himself. He turned away from the view. He had always been afraid of heights; as a child his father had tortured him by carrying him up the spiral stone steps in the turrets of the house in Brittany and pressing him against the ramparts to look out on the countryside. The father exclaimed over the beauty of the green fields; the child shrieked. The torment ended when Roland de Charny learned to swallow his screams, destroying his father's pleasure.

He recalled vividly his black satisfaction in that destruction—a victim's triumph; now it was his daughter's triumph. The sun shone behind him so that his face was shadowed; it was impossible for the others in the room to see the hatred with which he gazed at his daughter, who had destroyed his delight and whom he had to save.

"I have no idea why he came here." Roland de Charny's voice was subdued, his vowels clipped; in his agitation his accent surfaced. "Of course I knew him. I knew him through Aline. Dana was a good friend of Aline's. She is such a sympathetic person." He addressed the long white-silk-upholstered sofa where Aline Barbour, her face and clothes complementary studies in black and white, sat between Benedicte and Eveline de Charny. Appropriately, in her costume black predominated; a black turban hid her spun-sugar hair, and her eyes, smudged black, simulated mourning and a becoming lack of sleep. A white lace jabot cascaded between the lapels of her black jacket.

Aline Barbour smiled sadly to acknowledge Roland de Charny's compliment. He continued. "Dana was a charming boy. Always cheerful, gay, if you will forgive the term, in the old-fashioned sense. And quite talented, too; he danced this summer at the Arbroath Festival. We counted it quite a triumph to have him. I wish I had taken the opportunity to know him better. We had lunch once, with Gertrude Stella."

Sumner Loewen occupied a low armchair that formed a right angle with the sofa. His skin, pleated in tiny vertical lines, draped over his bones like fine crimped silk. "Yes, he was a brilliant dancer. We at the Perrot Ballet are distraught.

You were not at the memorial service? No. No reason you should be. Perhaps you did not know there was one. His family took the body home. They wanted a private burial, but we felt we had to do something, for the dancers, for the company."

Roland de Charny nodded. "He was troubled. Aline would tell me; she was quite concerned about him; it seems he confided in her. I've been told that he was having trouble with Achille Perrot—that he was going to be fired, in spite of his talent. Perrot, I understand, is a difficult man. Demanding and arbitrary. That was probably the immediate cause of Dana's suicide. You would agree, wouldn't you?"

Sumner Loewen leaned back in his chair. "I understand how difficult—I hesitate to use a word as crass as 'embarrassing'—this must be for you. If it was suicide, why would Dana have chosen your apartment? No, I would not agree with your suggestion. Achille Perrot had no intention of firing him; Dana knew that." Sumner Loewen's voice was quiet and his enunciation delicate and sharp.

Roland de Charny flinched as if he had been nicked by a razor. "Clearly it was a suicide; there is no question about that. He jumped."

"Why did he? I do not know. I am asking for help."

"I assure you, Mr. Loewen, you are not the only person who has asked. I wish I did know. But I was not here at the time. I flew in from Mexico City and spent the evening with Aline. That has been, to use your word, somewhat embarrassing." He glanced, ashamed, at his wife. Benedicte de Charny nodded with reserved sympathy at Aline Barbour, acknowledging the difficulty of her position and praising, with an almost imperceptible glance, her husband's performance. She had doubted that he retained the will to carry it off.

Eveline de Charny smiled. The smile teased her mouth, twisted it open. She struggled to keep sober, but a laugh escaped, a mirthless huffing. She was bloated; since Dana's death Sumner Loewen understood that she had been taking heavy doses of antidepressants. She kept her hands clasped in her lap, but Sumner Loewen noticed that they trembled—

an effect of the drugs. She wore no makeup and her short boy's haircut showed gray at the temples. A tear rolled down her cheek. Her mother reached across Aline Barbour's lap and squeezed Eveline's hand, silencing her.

Benedicte de Charny spoke in her clear, honest girl's voice: "If it should come up, I understand that Aline will have to testify that she and my husband were together. It will be difficult for me. Not so for my husband; at his age it will be something to be rather proud of, I imagine." She glanced at him with a measured mixture of anger and resignation. "But that probably will not be necessary. My people—friends in New York—tell me that there will be no further questions about Dana's death. What happened seems, unfortunately, too clear. He was on drugs, cocaine and some new drug that is supposed to make one ecstatic. It might be a consolation that he died happy."

Sumner Loewen nodded, marveling at the woman's detachment, intending, at least for the time being, to equal it. "I'm glad to see that it has been out of the papers for the last few days. I wanted to thank you for that." He smiled at Benedicte de Charny. Her head, with its white halo of hair, seemed disembodied in the fading light, marble pale, a Roman bust of an aristocratic matron, severe, secure in her power, certain of her duty.

Sumner continued: "Of course, we've still got some problems. It is unfortunate that Eveline's maid—what is her name? Oh, yes, Atalanta—spoke to the police. She supplied a great deal of information that will be difficult to prove false." Sumner Loewen shook his head sympathetically at Eveline. "It's so hard to find decent help these days, don't you think? But it seems that her immigration status was not quite legal— your lawyers, Eveline, never completed the paperwork for her green card—so she had some problems. Maybe the police could be convinced that she's been lying to ingratiate herself with them. Maybe it could be pointed out that she was threatened, that she was coerced into giving her statement. Mrs. de Charny, what do you think?"

Benedicte de Charny's mouth pursed disapprovingly. "We found out that she'd been dealing in drugs. She denies it, of course, but we traced her supplier. Eveline's been very upset; she trusted Atalanta with the children."

"I see," Sumner Loewen said. "Unfortunate woman. And one of our dancers said that Dana had visited Eveline the day before; she thought it was to discuss the organization of an artists' management foundation that Eveline wanted to organize—a very good idea, by the way—but the dancer said that Dana knew nothing about it when she asked him." He sighed. "There's nothing incriminating about a visit, though. It isn't really important; you were interested in underwriting a performance project of his, weren't you? That's correct, isn't it, Eveline?"

Eveline de Charny nodded. "With Devon, another artist. Body art and dance."

"Yes," said Sumner Loewen. "That's very good. Devon was there that day, too, I understand. She was there when Dana arrived."

Sumner Loewen smiled sympathetically at Eveline de Charny. Her thwarted spirit intrigued him. He considered himself somewhat responsible; he had given her access to the real thing—real dancers, real dance—and instead of uplifting her, the exposure had made her unable to avoid seeing her own shortcomings. But facing one's limitations happened to dancers as well as to patrons. It had happened to Fanny, and she had not broken. Eveline de Charny had; Fanny had predicted it. It was painful for Sumner Loewen to see Eveline like this.

She had confessed, almost. She had telephoned him, weeping, before her mother arrived and took control. "I was just trying to keep him happy," she had said.

"How? What did you do?" Sumner Loewen had asked her; he'd wanted to know if she had stretched out her hand to keep him inside or to launch him.

"I don't remember," she had sobbed.

Sumner was weary. Dana's death had disrupted the company; it had disrupted him. Sumner Loewen preferred death followed by resurrection—a bounce off a mattress, the certainty of a repeat performance. He knew he was ridiculous to believe in the insulation afforded by art. He knew he was a dapper, precious little man. But he believed in art; these people believed in money. Money bought love and insulation and peace and preserved innocence, and Sumner Loewen intended to make them pay. This evening, he had these people where he wanted them. "You might be interested to know that some friends of the company have discovered that the doorman who was on duty when Dana arrived here—the person who let him in, who claimed that he also let Eveline in—my friends have discovered that this man has a criminal record. He lied about it, of course, when he was hired; it will not be difficult to disprove his statement."

"Yes. My people have found the same piece of information." Benedicte de Charny smiled. Her yellow eyes were clear and large, as innocent as always. In the oblique light from the large window they seemed like a lion's eyes, or a devil's eyes. Her gray flannel dress with its cord sash resembled a monk's habit. She sat forward on the sofa, her legs together. Sumner noticed that her ankles were slightly thick, swollen, possibly from water retention; water retention was beginning to bother Fanny.

Benedicte de Charny maintained the posture of a young woman, her back straight and righteous. "My dear Mr. Loewen," she began, her pursed lips appraising and worldly. "You have been very kind and very helpful. Under the circumstances, to be honest, which I hope we are all being, I cannot see why you would want to help us. So I must ask you just what it is you want from us—what we can do for you. It seems that our people have done a good job. There are no loose ends."

Sumner Loewen took a breath, emulating surprise, and placed his hands together in front of his face to form a little tent, fingertips touching. He was an accomplished speaker; he understood cadence and silence, and he had studied the uses of facial expression and gesture. "Ah," he said. "Yes. I have another piece of information that I must tell you about, a distressing one. I had thought you and your people knew about it already, but perhaps not. It is, again, unfortunate, but Dana Coelho kept a journal, faithfully—if I may use that word, which certainly, according to this diary, does not apply to his other activities." Sumner Loewen raised his eyes to Roland de Charny's. "A friend of his found it, a sweet boy, Walter Mowbray, who works for us. Dana wrote everything down. His appointments"—and Sumner Loewen glanced again at Roland de Charny—"his conflicted feelings, everything. He was a meticulous young man. You never saw that side of him; we did. We watched him work. We watched how carefully he prepared every role. In this journal he even noted details of his drug use—you must have been aware that he was quite a consumer of drugs—his sources, for instance."

Sumner Loewen paused and gazed at Eveline and then at Benedicte de Charny. "How odd," he mused, "that Dana was so tormented while he seemed so happy. He *was* happy, I believe, part of him. It is a mysterious thing. If only the balance had been slightly different. Achille Perrot thought highly of Dana; he had planned important roles for him. They started rehearsals of one of the ballets the day he died. Dana knew, of course. He was eager; he says so in his journal. Yes." He paused again. The hermetic silence in the apartment struck him; silence in Manhattan was, he thought, an ultimate luxury. He liked the room's acoustics, they were just resonant enough. "Not very many of us know that this journal exists. It is explicit. It would be painful to us all if it were to be made public." Sumner Loewen shook his head and touched his brow with his pointed forefingers as if he were praying. "I am sure," he said, his small, cloudy eyes meeting Benedicte de Charny's round ones, which now revealed a trace of confusion, "that we all want the same thing."

Benedicte de Charny tilted her head, indicating a question. "You want . . . ?" she invited his proposal.

"I want peace," Sumner Loewen said. "Forgiveness. Time to heal. A means to fulfill dreams."

"The building," Benedicte de Charny said.

"And maintenance. Maintenance, a healthy concept, don't you agree? At my age, I have been thinking a great deal about the future."

"It will be an anonymous gift, of course," said Benedicte de Charny. "There will never be a connection to any of us. And perhaps, Sumner, if there should be any further inquiries, you might say that since my husband was very much interested in the Perrot Ballet, you had given Eveline some information about the company—financial statements, budgets, et cetera—which she was delivering to her father that evening. It was quite early, however. You remember because you brought her here in your car and then waited to take her home."

Sumner Loewen smiled at Eveline de Charny. "Certainly I will put my regard for your daughter on the record. She has been a loyal friend to the company. She deserves loyalty from us. Now, how shall we proceed?"

"The assignment of the deed can take place almost immediately," Benedicte de Charny said. "It should be a sale, I think, for tax purposes; we could use the loss. You could pay us one dollar. The transfer of funds for maintenance must be arranged through our lawyers in Switzerland. That will take some time. I hope you don't mind."

Sumner Loewen nodded. "For what amount did you say the transfer would be?"

Benedicte de Charny smiled. "I did not say. I thought to surprise you."

"The only surprises I like are the surprises of art."

"Two million."

"Four, I think."

"Swiss francs or dollars?"

"Dollars, of course."

"Our lawyers will call to confirm your bank's name and your account number."

"That is very generous of you." Sumner Loewen stood and took Benedicte de Charny's hand and bowed over it. "I am sure that Achille Perrot will be extremely grateful for all you have done."

Roland de Charny spoke. "I am sure that he will not be."

"But why?" Sumner Loewen furrowed his brow.

Roland de Charny from his whittled height looked down at compact Sumner Loewen. "I would not be grateful."

Sumner smiled. "You were grateful to that boy, to Dana. He said you were. He wrote in his journal that you would do anything to keep him happy."

257

Roland de Charny flinched.

"Are you ashamed?" Sumner Loewen permitted himself the question.

"He was a beautiful boy."

"Forgive me," said Sumner Loewen. "Perhaps there is no difference between shame and love."

He ignored Aline Barbour and bent down and took Eveline de Charny's hands. Sumner Loewen noticed with sadness that her long, sturdy fingers were uncared for, the nails uneven, the cuticles dry and ragged, scabbed where she had bitten them. She had been splendid; it was a pity. "I understand that you will be going away for a while," he said.

Eveline nodded.

"Bless you," Sumner said. "Bless you. And let me know as soon as you are back."

Sumner Loewen turned slowly, examining Roland de Charny's collection of art. He indicated the painting by Jurgen Jaeger over the sofa; its sticky tarry surface was acquiring a mellow gray patina, cottony like mold. "An interesting work. It seems a bit dirty," he said. "But perhaps that is intentional. Hard to know these days when one is being made a fool of, don't you think?" Sumner Loewen shook his head. "I have to admit that, visually, my taste runs to older art. Much safer, I believe. Easier to know what's good. You might have been able to teach me about the new. It's a pity we had so much unpleasant business to discuss. I would much rather have talked about aesthetic problems, and I'm sure you would have, too."

The sun, setting behind the towers on Central Park West, shone horizontally into the room. Sumner Loewen sighed. He hoped to die at sunset; he reminded himself to choose the music for his funeral.

The Chinese manservant appeared to show him out of the apartment. Roland de Charny, his skin tanned like leather by the low light, walked as far as the entrance to the living room. At the door Sumner Loewen, ever conscious of effect, turned. "You were right, you know, about Perrot," he said. "He will not be grateful. He won't care, at best; at worst he will be angry. It might comfort you to know that what you are giving, you are giving to me, not to your half-Jewish bastard brother, if that is what he is, which I doubt. Achille Perrot invents everything. The past, his ballets—there's no difference to him. You could easily be part of that invention. But I am grateful for what you have done, and I thank you."

Roland de Charny did not respond. His eyes were opaque, the absent sockets of a carved stone mask.

15

I READ ABOUT DANA," SAID AMOS FURST.
Caroline Harbison worked at the barre in an empty rehearsal room to no music. The fluorescent lights cast green shadows in the corners of the room; the high windows were black. Ignoring the mirror, Caroline raised her left foot to her knee in a passé and took a long balance. "How did you find me?"

"I knew you'd be here. This is what you do. You dance to get things out of your system."

"I said I would talk to Dana. You warned me about what was happening to him. I told Walter I would talk to him. I didn't. I was too upset about my own stupid life."

Amos Furst leaned against the barre. He saw himself in both the mirror and the black windows. The windows reflected his reflection in the mirror; the mirror, his image in the windows. As a child he had set up mirrors to multiply reflections; they had been his understanding of infinity, and of dance, too, as exemplified by the Rockettes.

"I didn't see what good it would do, anyway, to talk to him. That was stupid, too, wasn't it? Lazy." She extended her left leg in an arabesque. Once more she took a long balance.

Amos asked, "Do you want comfort?"

She lowered herself to her heel and shook her head. "No. I'm doing comfort. Anyway, I don't deserve it. I wasn't especially close to him. But I liked him." She continued her exercises.

"Do you mind if I stay?"

Caroline Harbison shook her head. "No."

Striking the floor, the hard boxes of her shoes hammered like hooves. She danced to the night noise from the streets: sirens, shouts, whining tires, the hiss of air brakes, the growl of diesel engines, the hoot of exhaust.

Amos Furst sat on the floor in front of the mirror. Caroline Harbison's face was clear of expression, serene and abstracted, detached from her body's effort. Dancing, her neck lengthened, her legs and feet achieved perfect proportions. She finished the barre and moved to the center of the room and began from memory combinations from Perrot's ballets. She hummed the music to herself and covered the floor with her steps, counting, forgetting real time.

Suddenly she stopped and stood with her feet turned out and her hands on her hips. "Maybe we all liked him on drugs. I mean, lots of people do drugs. They get strung out, but nobody dies."

"Except when they do. What happened? Was it an accident? Did he fall or did he jump?"

"I told the police that I'd seen him at Eveline's the day before, but that doesn't prove anything. At first I heard rumors that she was there when he died; now the police say she wasn't. Who knows? Drugs. What is that? An accident or suicide?"

"Either. Both," Amos said.

"Alexander read poems at the service. Here." She fished the program out of her dance bag. "Listen: *'For the good are always merry, Save by an evil chance, And the merry love to fiddle, And the merry love to dance.'*"

As Caroline Harbison read, she raised herself on toe and stepped to the rhythm of her speech. "That was Dana. And then Alexander read another one: *'If strange men come to the house To lead her away, do not say That she is happy being crazy; Lead them gently astray; Let her finish her dance, Let her finish her dance. Ah, dancer, ah, sweet dancer!'* The poem's about a girl, but it doesn't really matter, does it? I'm sorry I don't read very well. Alexander does."

"You read fine."

Caroline shrugged. "I feel as if he's still here." The memorial program had a picture of Dana Coelho on the front; Dana, exultant, jumped into black air, legs bent under him, one arm white above his head, long, luminous fingers pointing like a candle flame. "You know what Alexander said when Walter told us? Poor Walter, he found out first. The police called the company and he answered the phone. Alexander said, 'Oh God, he tried to fly.' "

She slid the program back into her bag. "I don't know why I'm keeping this. Well. He's in every ballet. Was. It's going to be hard to replace him." She paced the floor on her toes, walking like a deer on tiny hooves. "Poor Alexander. He made his ballet for him."

"Where is Alexander?"

Caroline Harbison came down flat on her heels. "I don't know. I didn't talk to him at the service."

Amos Furst looked at Caroline standing facing him. He saw her without movement—her thin thighs, bulging calves, red heels where she had cut away the material of her tights. Her breasts swelled only slightly larger than an adolescent boy's pectoral muscles, and her eyes were too big for her face, the skin around them thin, abraded from makeup. "When you're still," he said, "you look human. When you dance, you're transformed."

"If I do not dance," she said, "if I'm still, I'm not beautiful."

"You believe that."

"Yes."

"And the point is to be beautiful?"

"Always."

"The only way I'm beautiful is when I'm talking. Then you don't notice my face too much."

"Are you making fun of me?"

"No. Not at all. I'm thinking how lucky we are, that you can move and I can talk. What if we couldn't?"

"Dana was beautiful when he was still. Alexander is beautiful when he's still. They're the lucky ones. I'm doomed to dance."

"I like you when you're still."

"You wouldn't look twice at me if I didn't dance."

"Would you care if I didn't?"

She rose again on her toes, lengthening her legs, and balanced herself into perfect proportions. What would I do, she thought, if Alexander came into the room now? What is the difference between the gesture and the feeling behind it if the gesture is beautiful? The point is to be beautiful. She imagined Alexander pushing open the door to the studio, his blue eyes dark with mourning as he held out his hand to her, an invitation to dance, to love. No difference. What would be the nobility in not going to him? What would be the victory? She started across the floor, her satin toes shimmering in the flat green light.

"Stay still," Amos said.

She sank.

"The point is transformation. That's what is beautiful. That's what you do."

Caroline extended her hand. "Come here," she said. "Dance with me."

"I can't. I didn't study enough. I didn't get into partnering."

"Try. Just support me. Come here." She took his hand and began to walk around him in a circle. He felt the muscles in her fingers contract, the tension in her forearm as she rolled up on her feet and stood on toe. She began to raise her leg. Her arm shook. He tried to steady her but could not. He braced his arm against his side, but that shortened his reach and threw her forward. She hopped toward him on toe to keep from tipping over. Holding her was a trick of balance, not strength, and he did not know the trick.

She pulled her fingers out of his grip and took her own balance in the center of the floor.

"I am not Alexander. I am not a dancer," he shouted in frustration. Sharp shards of words splintered against the windows and the mirror. "I cannot dance the way you would like. I cannot dance with you. I am not clumsy, but I am not a dancer. I cannot be steady as a crane to hold you while you move because you're worried that if you stop you won't be beautiful. I want to know you, that's all. That's why I came here. I wanted to see you. Actually, I wanted to talk to you, and I wanted to see how you were feeling. That's why I came. Maybe to talk about Dana, maybe not. That was an excuse, I think, but if I'm going to be honest I have to say that I was hoping you'd want comfort. Then I could have told you wise things like don't blame yourself, and I could have put my arms around you. I want to be with you and to see what happens when I am. That's a risk."

He paced the rehearsal room in his black sneakers. "At least with Alexander you know where you stand."

"That's not fair."

"It's true."

Caroline turned away from him and looked at him in the mirror. "Are you putting me on? Are you acting out some character?"

"I'm being myself."

"You asked me to be still. That's not myself."

"Only for a few minutes."

"It's like dying."

"No, it's like resting. It's not permanent. I'm not asking for anything permanent."

"Who dares to ask for that?" said Caroline.

"Clear the space! Move away!" The stagehands released the crossbars securing the backstage cargo doors, letting in a glaring parallelogram of daylight that stained the dusty concrete floor. The dancers, preferring darkness, avoided stepping into the bright space. A truck backed up to the door, restoring twilight. Its slatted metal gate clanged open, and the stagehands hauled out trunks of costumes and props, pivoting them on their corners.

The Perrot Ballet was moving into the theater and beginning rehearsals for its fall season. Dancers ran up and down the narrow stairs to the dressing rooms and the rehearsal rooms. They experimented with the portable barres, accustoming themselves again to the feel of chipping black paint and the oil of thousands of hands on galvanized pipe. They chattered and complained about the length of time it took to travel uptown, about the terrible quality of expensive food in the neighborhood, about the cramped, dingy dressing rooms.

Achille Perrot watched the truck unloading. Scanning the activity, his eyes gleamed bright and nervous one moment, turned vague and dull the next. His black clothes blended into the black of the velvet wings. His face and hands were white and chalky. The dancers avoided passing too close to him; the stagehands maneuvering the trunks of costumes toward the freight elevators gave him a wide berth, as if the space around him were charmed and could not be breached.

Sumner Loewen, in an immaculate navy suit, stepped delicately in his lacquered shoes around the piles of rope and stacked flats that littered the floor. He and Perrot stood side by side and watched as three men wheeled the dingy blue death-leap scaffold from *Swan Lake* onto the tongue of the loading dock. The plywood edifice with its lumpy mattress clattered and trembled.

"The paradox of art," said Sumner Loewen. "Love and death every night and twice on Wednesdays and Saturdays. Pity and terror, catharsis, then out for a drink or a cup of tea."

"I despise that contraption," said Achille Perrot. "Although I have died there hundreds of times, I could never trust it, I could never believe it would support me."

"One never gets used to death," Sumner Loewen answered.

"One must. I have."

"How? You can't hold it in your hand like a rock and

turn it over and get the feel of it and see what it looks like. How can you get used to what you can't know?"

"By holding nothingness in your head. At the beginning it is intolerable. After a few seconds, the brain panics. But with each repetition, it becomes possible to endure for a longer period of time. It is similar to building an immunity to arsenic—small doses at first, gradually increased. It is also like staring at the sun."

"Is death bright?"

"Very bright, I think," said Perrot. "Unbearably bright, I hope. It is one of the few things I hope for."

"How metaphysical." Sumner Loewen laughed. "And I have gotten what I hoped for. Achille, I hate to change the subject, but with all the recent confusion I haven't been able to tell you: we have received a generous gift. I am sure you know who the donor is. Publicly, of course, he wishes to remain anonymous. He has given us our building, along with funds for its maintenance, generous funds. I'm very pleased. We will be able to expand to the top floor and refurbish the offices and the rehearsal rooms, and we'll have enough for the core of an operating endowment. I thought perhaps we could name one of the new rehearsal rooms after Dana."

Achille Perrot frowned. "You do not expect me to be happy."

"No. The donor said you wouldn't be. It was the only thing about the gift that satisfied him."

"And you think Dana would have liked to have a rehearsal room named after him?"

"He loved the company."

"He loved anything that would love him." Perrot turned away. Dana Coelho's death had not surprised him. Perrot had expected it and had used the boy as quickly as he could. It had been an inevitable unraveling.

The news had been an explosion of memory in his brain, a bomb, a flash followed by wailing. During the German occupation he had hidden with his mother in a barn. He slept with cows to keep warm; he stank of manure until he could not smell it on himself. He heard at varying distances the air raids and shelling—whistles, explosions, wails. At night in the darkness he had danced to the memory of music and to the stomping and snorting of cows. His mother could not remain in hiding; it was not in her nature to cower out of daylight or to live with cattle. On a spring day she had walked outside and had been caught and deported; he learned after the war exactly what happened, exactly to which camp she had been taken and how she had died. That day, when she walked out of the barn, the liens of love had been lifted. Perrot had stared into the sun through the cracks in the barn siding until his eyes glazed and ached. He forced himself to bear the brightness.

Perrot shook his head like a kaleidoscope to scatter the images. Until this summer he had resisted memories, hidden them in order to use himself better. He preferred invention, memory reordered and disguised, memory freed of obligations to his history. He understood Dana's death. The first time he saw Dana Coelho, Perrot had understood that the boy should not have to grow old. Dana had been like Perrot's mother as he had kept her in memory; Dana, with his golden skin and golden hair, even resembled her physically. He had been too light; he had not had enough ballast; he was fizzy like champagne, ebullient, afraid of growing flat, too much afraid of the dark. Perrot had already mourned him. He had reassigned his roles.

"Bring blue up to seven." The ballet's technical director sat at his board in the center of the auditorium. He spoke into the microphone, and his disembodied, amplified voice sounded over the rehearsal piano onstage in an absurdist narration. Company members sprawled in the orchestra seats, legs propped on the backs of the seats in front of them. Their woolly leg warmers made their feet look like pairs of hand puppets. The corps de ballet and the principal dancers were rehearsing Achille Perrot's new ballet, the Webern-Schoenberg arrangements of Strauss waltzes.

Perrot had decided to call the piece *Reductions*. He sat like a tangled spider on a folding metal chair on the apron of the stage, his long legs in their black trousers crossed, his arms folded. His head was bowed, and his white hair reflected the shifts in color as the stage deepened from warm incandescence to night blue. The dancers, oblivious to arbitrary changes in the stage's atmosphere, waltzed behind Perrot's silhouette. Rosalind Child, her hair wrapping her body like a fringed shawl, wore a red body suit and flitted through the other dancers like a precocious, decadent child. The lights brightened and dimmed irregularly. Dark, nervous music filled the theater.

Once Perrot stopped the dance to correct the corps, and in the silence the air continued to vibrate with anxious harmonics, like a mosquito buzzing. Caroline Harbison and Alexander Ives danced their tense steps, perfunctory turns and harsh lifts, a bitter waltz sliced by Rosalind Child's dizzy trajectories; they danced pain as binding as love.

At the end of *Reductions,* Perrot nodded, dismissing the corps de ballet. The dancers watching from the auditorium applauded and rearranged themselves. Perrot beckoned to Caroline Harbison. She stood in front of his chair and he talked steps to her. She marked the combinations. "Yes," Perrot told her. "Good. Something like that. You will need more to fill the measures. Add whatever steps you want. You know what to do."

She looked at him, uncertain. "I don't. I can't."

"Of course you can." He smiled. "It might be a bit too romantic and too old-fashioned, but let's do it. We will see if it works. We can always take it out."

Rosalind Child, electric still from her dance, flickered on stage, executing perfect little pirouettes, singing to herself. Caroline watched her and waited for her to light beside Alexander. But the girl seemed oblivious to him, entranced with her own pleasure, her own spinning. Harry Menard fished under the piano bench for his copy of the Schubert impromptus.

Alexander crouched beside Perrot. "I don't know how it will be," he said, "without Dana."

Perrot nodded. "It will be different. It might be better."

Alexander frowned.

"One must not give power to the dead." Perrot smiled

and coughed thick phlegm. "Forgive my cold. I cannot seem to get rid of it."

Harry Menard repeated several times the runs that ended the last impromptu. In the blue wash that lit the stage, Caroline Harbison's skin took on a greenish tinge, and her eyes, outlined in black, looked like a Siamese cat's. Kevin, the new dancer, was taller and slighter than Dana and to Caroline his red hair made him seem frivolous. She hardly knew him; she had no interest in him. He pulled off his leg warmers and squatted on the floor next to Alexander Ives. As he talked, he rested his hand on Alexander's forearm. Caroline took her place for the beginning of the ballet and gazed into the dim auditorium. She saw Rosalind Child settle into a seat up front, and a moment later Sumner Loewen entered the theater and sat near the back.

Alexander crossed the stage. He stood behind Caroline and rested his hand on her shoulder. His fingers cradled the nape of her neck, familiar on her skin. From habit, she leaned back against him in the old dance; she straightened, remembering that for him it was only a dance. Alexander nodded to the pianist. The music began, soft like a memory. Caroline bent in the slow pliés of the introduction.

Sumner Loewen turned sideways in his seat to stretch his legs. He crossed his feet at the ankle, and his shoes gleamed in the dim theater. Caroline Harbison's steps seemed dreamlike; the distance to the stage erased the visible effort of her muscles. The new dancer entered behind her, a tentative shadow. The blue lights dimmed, then warmed to violet. The technical director spoke numbers softly into the microphone.

Alexander Ives leapt onstage to the repeating theme, legs open, arms wide, a large bird flying low on the currents of music, rising and falling with the slow theme and arpeggios.

Self-absorbed, the dancers circled the empty center of the stage, their steps like filigree, intricate and flimsy. As the ballet went on, Sumner Loewen watched with increasing frustration and disappointment. He had hopes for Alexander Ives. Loving the future, he had devised the perfect, painless transition: Alexander would begin immediately to ease Perrot's choreographic burden and would assume control of the company upon the old man's eventual retirement. They had years before that would happen, but Perrot was tiring more easily, and Alexander could take up the slack. In his enthusiasm it had not occurred to Sumner Loewen that Alexander's ballets at first might lack the polish and the urgency of his dancing, that he might have to learn to make them, which could be as difficult as learning to dance.

However devoted to his dreams, Sumner Loewen was not blind. Not that Alexander's ballet was bad, but it suffered in comparison to Perrot's, and Alexander would always be seen in comparison to Perrot. From the audience it was impossible to see the dancers working, to see them strain. The music, he saw, needed that force, that muscular counterpoint. The dancers' isolation from each other onstage did not translate into longing; they seemed too much involved with the perfect execution of their own beautiful steps, impervious to the music's articulation of loss.

Sumner Loewen saw that Alexander had made changes, especially in Caroline Harbison's part, but he not altered the intent of the ballet as Achille Perrot had wanted. The dancers never touched; they remained aloof from each other; they spun cocoons. Caroline Harbison's arabesque at the end was perfect; her back, arms, and legs arched in an exquisite long line. Alexander Ives had given her time for preparation, disguised as a yearning reach—a token gesture to Perrot, which fell short and seemed to mock his intention. Harry Menard pounded the last chord, wiped his forehead with his shirtsleeve, and closed the music.

Sumner Loewen shrugged, shedding his disappointment. He was glad he had resisted Gertrude Stella's request to see the work today. A pragmatist, he understood that the elements of his design were sound, but he had to adjust the balance. He would have to manage carefully. To ensure that Alexander did not leave the company, he would have to be permitted to make ballets. Sumner would have to separate Alexander from Perrot, to minimize both the comparisons and the friction between them. That meant, he saw, that

Alexander would have to limit his dancing, which would immediately diminish Perrot's ballets. Perrot had relied too much on his dancer; there was no one who could take his place.

Beads of sweat on Alexander's face shone blue and red from the stage. He watched Perrot, who remained enclosed in his black arms and legs. Caroline Harbison walked in a small circle, cooling down like a horse. The new dancer, Kevin, flopped on the floor in front of the curtain. The spots came up, simulating yellow daylight. Perrot raised his head heavily and blinked as if he had just awakened.

"It's too bad they were still setting the *Reductions* lighting," said Alexander, resting his elbows on the piano lid. "I think this ballet needs something warmer, and maybe a painted scrim."

Perrot cleared his throat and coughed into his handkerchief. "I do not understand." The soft consonants sounded hard; he spat them out like pits. "You have not made the changes." In the brightness his skin looked like pale fired clay.

"I made lots of changes," Alexander said. "I thought you'd be happy."

Perrot stood and pointed at Alexander Ives, his arm a black rod tipped with an ivory hand. The theater grew silent, accused by his gesture. "You cannot see what you have done. You cannot see what this looks like. You should not be dancing in this. You are too close." He lowered his arm. He breathed deeply; the bones of his ribs showed against his thin black jersey shirt. "Alexandre," he began again, pronouncing the dancer's name in French, "believe me. Go. Sit in the audience, in the front row. Watch one or two measures. You will see what I am trying to tell you. I will dance your part. Let me show you the difference."

Harry Menard played a high trill on the piano, a frivolous bird. Alexander glared at Perrot, desperate to be right. Caroline Harbison continued to walk around and around in her circle.

"Alexandre." Achille Perrot took the dancer by the arm. Reluctantly Alexander tipped himself upright, and Perrot led him to the wings. He lowered his voice until it was barely audible. "Alexandre, I would like to use your ballet. I would like to use it in the repertoire this season. I have been tired. I have been unable to do everything I would like. This piece of yours makes an interesting program with the waltzes."

Alexander did not look at Perrot. His eyes were distant, mistrustful, focused on blackness.

Perrot continued: "I cannot use your ballet like this. It would not do you justice. I cannot put it on a program where people will compare it to my work. I know what you think. But I am not doing this for myself. I am not changing it to make it my own. If you can believe me, this is for you."

Perrot's fingers on Alexander's arm were hot. His breath was moist with mucus, rotten with sickness. Alexander closed his eyes and turned his head so that he would not have to smell it. A moment passed. Caroline stopped pacing and rose on pointe, her hands on her hips. "Are we going to do it again?" she asked. Alexander did not answer.

The lights dimmed blue again. "Five, three, two," intoned the technical director.

Perrot released Alexander's arm and went to the piano. He sat beside Harry Menard and opened the score. "Let's do," he said. "Let's do the last impromptu. That has the big problems, I think." His skin in the light from the music stand was white as bone.

Caroline Harbison bourréed to the back of the stage. Alexander stood behind the piano bench, his arms crossed. "Perrot, why? Why should we do this again? We've been over it before. I know what you're going to say. I know what you want to see. If you don't like what I've done, why don't we just quit?"

Achille Perrot half turned on the piano bench and glared at Alexander Ives. His glasses reflected two blue spots. "I understand that you are unhappy with my interfering. I have explained to you why I am doing it. I have tried to reassure you. I know it is not easy for you. One is always faithful to one's first love. It can be quite shocking when it proves not so beautiful." Perrot smiled. His teeth glistened against the bisque of his lips. He gazed at the dancer disdainfully, as if

Alexander were a petulant child. "I also understand that you have been talking about leaving the company. I have had to admit to myself how much I do not want you to leave. But if you are certain that is what you want to do, please do not continue to waste my time. I have many more dancers. Please, go. I assure you, I do not need this." He paused, coughed, and lowered his voice. "Yes, you will be a loss, another loss, but again, only of time. You do not perhaps understand what you are. You are not so different from Dana; you are an object of desire. You make people want my ballets now, but I do not need you. There will be somebody new; there is always another performer. It is a pity that you will not permit me to make you into something else, something more permanent. Because that is what you desire, is it not?"

Alexander dropped his hands, exposing himself to Perrot's words. He contracted, as if he were about to spring, or to shrivel into himself. The theater was silent.

Perrot banged his hands on the piano in a dissonant chord that resounded through the auditorium and, leaning on the keys, pushed himself to his feet. "Well?" He inclined his head toward Alexander in a gesture of invitation. His fingers trembled. "What is your pleasure?"

Alexander, his eyes as blue as the lights, was silent.

Caroline Harbison stepped downstage. She gave her hand to the old man.

"Let's do," said Caroline Harbison to Achille Perrot.

She turned to Alexander Ives and offered him her other hand. "Let's do," she repeated.

Alexander raised his eyes to her, but she did not look to see whether it was in gratitude or anger. It was done, all she could do for him.

"So," said Perrot quietly, turning toward the stage. "Let's do."

Perrot indicated the starting place in the music and walked across the stage to Caroline Harbison's side. He nodded to Harry Menard, who began to play the manic scales at the end of the last impromptu. Caroline marked a measure and then spun in quick turns away from Achille Perrot.

The choreographer took three small steps, following

her, then hesitated and bent into a brief plié. His hand out-stretched toward Caroline, he leapt. It was a perfect arc, high and light. The old man was suddenly ageless, his back held straight, legs extended parallel to the floor, arms echoing exquisitely the line of his legs. Caroline stood transfixed, watching him, forgetting her arabesque. The leap seemed to last forever; Perrot remained buoyant, less substantial than air; he flew higher than the music, into silence.

He descended and his right foot touched the floor. There was a crack, small and clear, sharp like a branch snapping under snow. His leg bent, at the knee, at the thigh, and Achille Perrot crumpled on his side at Caroline Harbison's feet. She wailed. Alexander Ives hurtled across the stage. Kneeling beside Perrot, he leaned over the old man and pushed his arms under Perrot's shoulders to raise his upper body. Perrot's eyes were open and unfocused like a baby's. His glasses had fallen off. One leg stretched in front of him; the other bent in the middle of his thigh. Alexander Ives pressed Perrot against his chest and cradled his head. Caroline picked up his glasses.

The shock waves of a subway train passing under the street vibrated through the theater. The dancers crowded onstage; those in the audience leaned against the railing of the orchestra pit. They waited, suspended in the moment of transition from performance to real time, as if they expected the lights to go up and the curtain calls to begin. They watched for Achille Perrot to stand, face the applause, and take his curt, confrontational bow.

Sumner Loewen snatched the telephone from the technical director's board, dialed the police emergency number, and asked for an ambulance. He ran onstage, skidding like a novice skater on his smooth leather soles. He knelt beside Perrot, opposite Alexander. "Achille," he called. "Achille." The choreographer turned his head, but his eyes remained dilated and bewildered.

"We should move him offstage," said Sumner Loewen.

"No," Alexander barked. "Wait for the ambulance."

Alexander Ives shifted his body so that Perrot rested between his legs. Perrot groaned from the movement. His head lay on Alexander's shoulder. Caroline crouched and slid his glasses on his face, more to protect herself from his naked eyes than to enable him to see.

She touched Alexander's arm, and he regarded her, his lips pulled back from his teeth, his eyes guilty and accusing. Caroline shook her head. She wanted to embrace him, for comfort and to comfort him, to absolve them both, but Achille Perrot lay between them. She reached for Alexander's face and stroked his cheek; it was wet with tears. The old man's leg remained skewed in front of him, loose bones in black trousers. Alexander Ives began to rock back and forth with Perrot in his arms.

"This is not how he should have hurt himself," Alexander said, afraid. "He could have twisted his ankle or his knee. This is not what he should have done."

Sumner Loewen took off his jacket and spread it across Perrot's thigh, hiding the injury.

An ambulance siren sounded outside, the cargo door slammed open, the siren invaded the theater. Two paramedics, in blue overalls, ran onto the stage wheeling a gurney between them. One carried an oxygen tank. Pushing Sumner Loewen aside, they started to pull Perrot from Alexander's grasp.

"No," commanded Alexander.

"You want us to revive the guy or not?"

"He hasn't had a heart attack. It's his leg." Alexander threw off Sumner Loewen's jacket.

"He needs oxygen for shock. Listen, I ain't got time to argue." He knelt and removed Perrot's glasses and clamped the mask over his mouth and nose. "There any light in this place?"

The spots blazed. The paramedics considered Perrot's leg. They detached the stretcher from the gurney and laid it alongside the old man. They reached for Perrot's shoulders, but Alexander shook his head and blocked them. "I can lift him," he said. They backed away.

Tenderly, Alexander braced Perrot's back with one arm and slid the other under the knee of Perrot's sound leg and maneuvered him onto the stretcher. "He's so light," he said to nobody. The paramedics lifted the stretcher and secured it to the gurney, and Alexander Ives and Sumner Loewen followed it to the ambulance.

The gray linoleum dance floor reflected the blue and red and white spots. The dancers began to leave the stage. Caroline Harbison remained until all of the others had gone. Rage filled her: fury at Alexander for his stubbornness—if only he had had the grace to acquiesce to Perrot—fury at herself, at her need to make peace, to interfere. "Let's do." It was not her place to say that; she was only the instrument.

Slowly, weeping, in the spot where Perrot had fallen, she crouched and rose and extended her left leg. She performed the high arabesque at the end of Alexander's ballet, controlling the difficult balance from her abdomen, the simultaneous tightening and release of pairs of muscles. Comfort, forgiveness, survival—all lay only in the permanence of repetition. She finished the dance; tomorrow she would start it again.

16

ACHILLE PERROT LIVED IN A CARAMEL-colored brownstone near Gramercy Park, a few blocks from the company's studios. He had planted the tiny garden in front with bright red geraniums, white alyssum, and blue lobelia. The garden amused Sumner Loewen, who considered it falsely naive. Perrot kept the flowers washed so that they always appeared shiny and new; in the morning on his way to the company, he uncoiled a hose and cleansed the blossoms of city soot. While he was away in the summer, his houseboy, Eric, kept them clean.

A flight of stairs bisecting the garden arched over the small ground-floor windows to the main entrance on the parlor floor, a deeply paneled oak double door in the center of a bank of tall windows with ornate lintels. A waist-high gate was locked at the foot of the stoop; beside it a short path of bricks laid in a herringbone pattern curved to a small door set under the stoop, plate glass protected by a lattice of wrought iron patterned like ivy. Although the brownstone was part of a block of similar houses built by a developer in the early twenties, it seemed different from its neighbors, more flamboyant, larger in scale and paler; the developer designed it for an actress who had migrated to Broadway from Wisconsin and had made her fortune from the men she met as a vaudeville performer.

Fanny Loewen carried a large carpetbag. The day was warm, Indian summer, and she had dressed in cotton, a voluminous dress of deep, autumnal red. The warm wind passing through it dried her perspiration. She paused to watch two fat, slothful bees in an end-of-summer stupor circle the geranium blossoms. She stepped sedately down the brick path and rang the bell beside the low wrought-iron door. After a moment, Eric, a compact young man with mahogany cheeks and ebony eyes, let her in. Fanny Loewen followed him through a low-ceilinged hallway with blank white walls and a polished blond wooden floor. Eric wore a crisp white shirt that billowed out of his black cotton trousers; he walked in Chinese slippers. His feet made no sound on the rubber treads of the steep chrome stairway that led to the ballroom off the original entrance. Fanny Loewen had always been somewhat jealous of Achille Perrot's house. She aspired to dramatic effect, but her husband limited her efforts to the facade at Arabesque; in the city he insisted on the restraint and self-conscious moderation of the middle class and mistrusted eccentric interiors. Perrot indulged himself with extremes—baroque excess during the winter and ascetic simplicity in the country. Fanny Loewen always ascended the ladderlike stairs slowly, the better to savor the room's surprise.

It was like entering a vast Italian piazza from a narrow side street; from the stairs, the only hint of dimension was a gleam of light. One entered it from a hole in the floor, looked up, and saw the ceiling, gilded plaster ornately molded into garlands and rosettes and interspersed with painted cartouches. In the central oval was depicted a watery blue cumulus-encrusted sky populated with putti like chubby pink airplanes, who dived and turned somersaults in the stratosphere. Perrot had concealed in the cornices theatrical spots whose beams bounced off the ceiling, producing a pale wash like the Venetian sun reflected off the canals.

Wreaths carved in relief from boxwood adorned the walls, and within the wreaths hung paintings of mythic triumphs. Plunging beasts were harnessed to chariots; bulls towed a golden cart; fantastic creatures, half-horse and half-dolphin, pulled a shell-shaped boat carrying nymphs and heroes wearing armor over their naked torsos. The room contained few pieces of furniture: six side chairs and two painted Italian wedding chests. On one of the chests stood a bronze of a woman and a bird: Leda and the Swan. Leda bent one knee like a Venus, and the Swan entwined its neck and wings with her limbs. Perrot had explained to Fanny Loewen that the sculpture's design had been taken from a lost painting by Leonardo da Vinci, a painting known only from copies. "An interesting variation on *Swan Lake,* don't you think?" he had said. "The sexes are transposed, but that is really not very important."

Fanny agreed. Gender had ceased to mean much to her after she married. She saw beauty as neuter; gender, at least her experience of it since her marriage, was irrelevant. At first she had expected to be disappointed, but she found that she was relieved. She confined love to art, where it was safe, frozen, and infinitely repeatable, although she maintained an affection for her husband. Her ability to divine the future made her discount love, which depended on the potency of the present. For Fanny Loewen, the present was not the primary tense.

"Mr. Perrot is in the garden," Eric said.

Fanny Loewen pushed a brass button beside one of the wall panels. It released a concealed door, which opened onto a flight of steps leading to a back garden. A high pink brick wall enclosed the garden. Red roses climbed the wall, and knots of precisely pruned boxwood hedge defined beds containing a profusion of annuals: marguerites, lantana, ageratum, salvia. Pots of red geraniums edged the brick terrace. The flowers were leggy, their woody stems visible between yellowing leaves. They continued to bloom, however, eking the last energy from their roots.

Achille Perrot reclined on a varnished deck chair as if he were taking the air on the promenade deck of an ocean liner. Pillows supported his back and his broken leg. Guy Pissarro sat beside him on a white-painted wrought-iron garden seat, a clipboard in his lap.

"My dear Achille." Fanny swooped down like a heavy kite and kissed Perrot. "And Guy, how nice. I hope I'm not interrupting anything." She settled into a chair fitted with white canvas cushions.

Guy Pissarro inclined his head in a sharp matador's bow. "We were discussing the season." He rose and brushed his fingers diffidently against the back of Perrot's hand. "I will see you tomorrow. You'll call if you want something?"

Perrot grasped Guy Pissarro's fingers and squeezed them.

"Well, Achille," said Fanny Loewen, "your geraniums are looking very well for so late in the season."

"I have been feeding them and covering them at night. I am nursing them along and prolonging their lives. But they will be dead in a month."

"Don't say that. Take them indoors. They're in pots. Keep them through the winter."

"That would be exploiting them." Perrot smiled. "They should be permitted to die of natural causes."

Fanny Loewen looked at him suspiciously. "You love geraniums. I thought you always took them in."

"I will not take them in this season. Geraniums are innocent and immodest, like dancers. But dancers do not last very long, either."

Fanny furrowed her brow at the allusion: "Sumner is still very upset about Dana."

"Sumner did very well with Dana," replied Perrot.

"That doesn't change how he feels." Fanny Loewen arranged her skirts and crossed her white legs at the ankles. She wore turquoise espadrilles whose strings wrapped around her feet like toe-shoe ribbons. Her flesh bulged between the crisscrossed ties. "So. How's the leg? Healing nicely, I hear."

Perrot rang a silver bell on a table beside his chair. Eric

appeared with a tray holding three stemmed glasses and a bottle of wine in a silver ice bucket. He filled two glasses nearly to the brim and offered them to Fanny Loewen and Perrot. The wine was the color of topaz.

Fanny Loewen tasted and smiled. "Achille, I've brought you all the latest gossip before Sumner comes."

"With all his latest plans?"

Fanny Loewen laughed. "Sumner always plans."

"And I do not."

"Sumner can't bear getting up in the morning unless he knows what he's going to do every day for at least a month in advance."

"You should not try to dispel my suspicions." Achille Perrot's dry brown lips drew away from his long teeth and pale gums.

Fanny Loewen interpreted his expression as a smile and returned it. "Well. Where to begin? You know about Alexander and that little girl?"

Perrot nodded. "I know what there is to know."

Fanny Loewen tilted her broad blond head. "What do you mean by that? Are you hinting that you arranged the whole thing?"

"The future is your business, not mine, Fanny."

"But what you did—you know, putting her in the ballet—happened in the past, so you have to tell me. I can't figure out the past, how we got to where we are. I never try; it's too murky. You didn't put her in *Swan Lake* just to play matchmaker and upset Caroline, did you?"

"Fanny dear, for me, romance is irrelevant. If you must know, Rosalind's smallness interested me. Alexander and Caroline are well matched. I was curious to see what a difference in size would look like."

"Achille, you're teasing. I don't know whether to believe you or not."

"Does it matter if you believe me? What has happened has happened."

"Well, anyway, I think Caroline has a beau. I'm not sure; it's a guess, but I hear that actor—you remember, from the summer? He was tagging after that terrible Eveline de

Charny. How she could pretend to be a dancer . . . I don't know how Sumner put up with it, and he didn't get very much, either." She shook her head. "But I hear that this actor calls for Caroline after rehearsal. I have no idea how serious it is, and she's the last person who'd let on."

Perrot nodded. "The actor, he was a clown?"

"He said he was, but he's much more than that. False modesty. I've read his reviews." Fanny Loewen smiled and reached for her carpetbag and extracted a small package wrapped in red foil and tied with a silver lace ribbon. "I almost forgot. I brought your favorites—griottes, dark chocolate with kirsch, to fatten you up." She unwrapped the box and offered it to him.

Perrot shook his head. He had only sipped his wine; Fanny Loewen's glass was empty. "You do seem a bit peaked," she said, plucking a bonbon from the box's plastic tray. "Well, I'm sure the hospital would do that to anybody. What a terrible time for this to happen, at the beginning of the season. When do they say you'll be back on your feet?"

"They?" asked Perrot. "Who are 'they'? The ubiquitous 'they.' "

Fanny Loewen laughed, but Perrot remained serious.

The brick wall muffled street noise. Perrot spoke softly, almost a whisper: "What do 'they' know? It has nothing to do with 'they.' "

Sluggish bees drugged with nectar flew in heavy arcs. Achille Perrot took off his glasses. Brown shadows circled his eyes; his parched skin had cracked like clay. His right hand, long and white, nails curved like claws, rested on his broken thigh. Fanny Loewen reached out and laid her hand on his. She felt the rigid cast beneath his trouser leg, and the sharp bones just below the skin on his hand. She withdrew her hand quickly, as if the bones had nicked her. Tears filled her eyes. "Achille," she began. "Oh, dear. Achille . . ."

Achille Perrot's eyes grew as sharp as his bones, warning. Eric appeared and refilled Fanny Loewen's glass. The loud bees buzzed.

"So," Perrot said after Eric had gone back inside. "You saw. You see. I am going to die."

Fanny Loewen shook her head vehemently. "Don't say that." She shivered in the heat of the afternoon.

"Why not? I have known—assumed—for some time, for months. I am used to it. Do you remember that I had a cold at the beginning of the summer? At your party I was not well. It did not improve, so I went to my doctor for medicine. The medicine did not help, and the doctor became suspicious that it was not a simple thing. They made tests and found early signs of an abnormality in the bone marrow. Abnormality—that is what they called it. Very early signs. They said it was not serious, not to worry. They assured me that I would have years. 'They,' Fanny. 'They' is so comforting, is it not? Even when 'they' are wrong, we believe them. This abnormality of theirs eats the marrow of my bones. It hollows them out. That is why my leg broke. It was a perfect landing. It should not have happened. My bone was hollow, and it could not take the force of the impact. They have begun treatment." He shook his head and smoothed his white hair. "Look at me. You see the treatment, the drugs, not the disease. And they want to begin radiation. The cure makes me sick. The disease never did. At least I have not lost my hair."

Fanny Loewen kept her small, compassionate eyes on Perrot while he spoke. When he finished she took a large swallow of her wine. "How long?" she asked. "How long do you have to live?"

" 'They' say that after this treatment I could be in remission. Perhaps not, perhaps they will have to continue the drugs. The cells may start growing again in three weeks, or they may not start again for years. 'They' cannot tell the future as you do." He shrugged and put his glasses back on. "Now you know. And you may not say anything to anyone."

"Not even to Sumner?"

"Sumner. He would feel less treacherous about what he is doing, but then he would not enjoy doing it so much. He guesses something, which is why he is so busy planning, but, as he often does, he guesses wrong. He thinks that I will recover. He thinks that I am angry at Alexander. His plan, you know, depends upon Alexander. Sumner thinks I will oppose him, but I am not sure I care enough to. Certainly I do not have the energy. I am not angry at Alexander. I only wish that he learned more quickly. I wish he made no mistakes; I am unreasonable. I suppose we must tell Sumner. He is entitled to know. But he will torture me with the future." He shifted in his chair at the scrape of footsteps. "Ah!" he said, as Sumner Loewen appeared, carrying his briefcase. His hard soles scraped the sand between the bricks. Eric followed him.

"Achille!" exclaimed Sumner Loewen. "How good to see you outside on such a beautiful day. You look much better this afternoon."

"It is Fanny," said Perrot. "Fanny always improves me."

"Has she brought you chocolates and eaten them herself?"

"Only one," Fanny Loewen said, pouting.

Eric presented Sumner Loewen with a glass of wine and refilled Fanny's glass. Absently, Sumner drank, and, surprised, paused to savor its taste. "A good white Burgundy, in the middle of an ordinary afternoon! How delightful! You must have known that we had something to celebrate today. Did Fanny guess? Has she been telling the future again?"

"Yes," said Achille Perrot.

Sumner Loewen, his skin buffed pink and shining, sat opposite his wife. "Well, finally we own the building. The arrangements took longer than they said they would; they always do. Evidently their lawyers had worked out some interesting tax angles, and I couldn't begrudge the de Charnys a small profit."

Perrot lay back in his chair and closed his eyes.

"Sumner," Fanny Loewen began.

Sumner Loewen took another appreciative swallow of the wine.

"I would rather have a dancer than a building," said Perrot.

"Roland de Charny was not there when it happened. He was not involved. You can't blame him."

Achille Perrot hauled himself higher in the chair. Fanny Loewen hastened to adjust the pillows. "I will tell you a story," Perrot said. "You have wondered about my life. During the war, my father could have saved my mother. She was Jewish, as you know. He did not save her; I do not know why. Perhaps he would have had to risk his own life, and that is too much to ask; perhaps it was not convenient; perhaps he did not care. He did not try to save me, either. I hid in a barn. I lived like a cow. I escaped only because I was lucky, and because I liked darkness. The barn was like a theater, always dark. That is one reason I am so fond of the barn at Arabesque." He smiled.

"Then, Achille, this is reparation."

Perrot laughed. "Do you believe in money for lives?"

"I am not sure I believe your story. I told Roland de Charny that I was not at all sure you were really his half brother. I said that you could easily have invented the relationship."

"That is correct. But does it matter? It is true that Ulysse de Charny was a collaborator. It is also true that my father could have saved my mother and me if he had tried. I see Roland de Charny and his daughter and I am angry, in particular or in general, at them or at whom they represent. What is the difference? A gift to me—or to you—does not justify the past. And furthermore it is not what I would have wanted."

"The gift was to the company. The Perrot Ballet."

"It was to you. You are the Perrot Ballet; I am Perrot. It is what you want. It is part of your scheme. I have no ambition for the future. I should not be alive. I should have died fifty years ago. Why should anything I do survive me? In my mind it already has. It has all been posthumous. You have been working with a ghost."

He reached for one of Fanny Loewen's chocolates, bit into it, and sucked the liqueur from the bittersweet shell. He smiled at Sumner Loewen with ironic affection. "Sumner, you are often bizarre in your judgment of people, but you are always right about how much money they will give. Enjoy your building and your endowment." The lowering sun reflected off the lenses of his glasses; he took them off. The sides of his nose were blue where the frames had rested against the cartilage. His eyes were round and unguarded.

"Please. I am tired. Fanny, take Sumner home and tell him about me."

On cooler days Eric moved Achille Perrot's deck chair inside to the large ballroom. He lay under the sunny painted sky and gazed at the putti. Sumner Loewen arrived for lunch; he had lent his cook to prepare meals that would entice Perrot to eat. Twice a day, morning and evening, Guy Pissarro came to see Perrot, bringing with him reports of class and rehearsals. Guy Pissarro scheduled visits from dancers, the older members of the company, although he protested that they would tire Perrot. But Perrot insisted. "The company is fragile," he told Guy Pissarro. "The dancers have not recovered from Dana; they are preoccupied and it weakens their dancing. You have told me that yourself. They must feel my presence."

Caroline Harbison came often. Perrot talked to her of the execution of steps, balances and turns, and of dancers and ballets. He described to her the dancers he had seen perform the classics before the war. He expounded on how technique had developed. He talked to her of the difference between Europe and America—the burden of the past and the burden of the lack of one, the burden of having to invent. "That is the curse and blessing of America," Perrot said. "Always to have to come up with something new."

"I cannot invent," Caroline Harbison answered. "Alexander can't understand why I don't want to make ballets."

"You can *do*. You do steps and give them a dimension I never imagined. Doing is invention," Perrot told her. "You do not see your luck."

"But I'm afraid of being still," she said. "I hate myself still. What will I do when I can't dance anymore?"

Perrot gazed at the painted clouds. "I taught you to dance. I cannot teach you how not to dance."

Alexander Ives never visited; Perrot never asked after him.

Finally, Perrot's leg had healed sufficiently so that he could be driven to the theater. Refusing crutches, he walked with two canes. Fanny Loewen bought them for him, ebony sticks with knobs of Meissen porcelain, one a maiden with bare rosy breasts, the other a shepherd boy with tousled blond curls and equally rosy breasts. "Thank you for your thoughtfulness." he said, smiling. "Only you would have the imagination to give me a choice." Fanny Loewen reflected on the implication of Perrot's words and decided that she would prefer to think that he was gallantly complimenting her good taste.

As Perrot entered the studio, he greeted Alexander Ives as if only a day had passed since they had seen each other. Alexander, watching Perrot hobble, winced at the canes' taps. Perrot ignored the dancer's distress. He sat beside the piano and watched while Guy Pissarro led the company class. Perrot took rehearsals of his new ballet from a chair, and he danced changes in the choreography with his hands. By the end of the week *Reductions* was set. Members of the company took the new work as evidence of the choreographer's improving health. Sumner Loewen began to speak of Perrot's recovery.

"Recovery," Perrot said to Fanny Loewen that Friday afternoon as he lay on his deck chair in his ballroom and she sat beside him, nibbling on her offering of liqueur-filled chocolates. "At the beginning of death, have you noticed how the truth is spoken in antonyms?" The company, even her husband, marveled at how Perrot seemed suddenly to enjoy Fanny Loewen's company. She, however, never inverted the truth; she never spoke in antonyms. Understanding the future, she never said, "When you are better." Instead she sat with him and gossiped and kept him enmeshed in life.

Still Alexander Ives did not come. This angered Guy Pissarro. His large black eyes were undefended by eyelashes and gleamed vulnerably at Perrot. "He is rehearsing his ballet, *Impromptus,*" Guy Pissarro told Achille Perrot. "He is using our dancers and our studio and Harry Menard. He has no right to do that."

"What do you think of his ballet?" Perrot asked.

"I have not seen it for weeks."

"I know that you have." Perrot smiled. "I know that you see everything."

Guy Pissarro bent his head. His scalp, with his monk's tonsure, gleamed as naked as his eyes. "I have to tell you, Achille, it is getting better. He has changed it."

"Is it good enough?" Perrot asked.

Guy Pissarro widened his melancholy round black eyes. "If you mean, is it what you hoped, the answer is no. Is it good enough for him? It is a beginning. It is not like your beginning."

"I was younger," said Perrot. "And free. I am a terrible burden for Alexander. I am his bad luck. Let him rehearse. We will use the ballet."

Guy Pissarro looked shocked.

"Oh, yes, everyone will talk, but I do not care. That is out of my control; I care only about my ballets. Sumner will be happy. He has forgotten the risk. People will be eager to see Alexander's ballet, but they will not be so eager to love him. They will love this one, because they think I have approved it. Later they will doubt if he is good, not because they doubt Alexander—they cannot judge; they have no faith in themselves. They will see many reasons for Alexander's ballets to be performed, and none of them will have to do with their merit. They will think of continuity; they will think that only Alexander Ives has the reputation to maintain the company; they will think that perhaps I was prejudiced in his favor and made the first ballet for him. The problem will be with the next one. He has not had enough time to learn, but I cannot give time to him. And the public does not know how stubborn Alexander is. If they knew, they would not like him from the beginning. He will have to learn to hide that stubbornness." Achille Perrot closed his eyes.

"Why does Alexander not visit?" Guy Pissarro asked.

"Because he thinks my injury is his fault. He thinks that it would not have happened if he had listened to me."

"It would not have."

"No, believe me, that is not true." Achille Perrot held out his hand, and Guy Pissarro took it. Perrot pulled the ballet-master close to his chair. "Is there anything you want that I can give you, that I can arrange for you?" he asked.

Guy Pissarro said no.

"I am giving you this house, you know."

"I do not need it."

"You might need the money."

"You are talking as if you are preparing to die."

"I will not live forever, and I thought that you should know what I intend to do. Being injured makes one think of these things."

"You are recovering," said Guy Pissarro, but his eyes shone with tears like an icy road at night. His emotion embarrassed him, and he excused himself and left Perrot alone under his painted sky that even in the evening radiated daylight.

Perrot began to spend his days in the bedroom; the hard slats of the deck chair bruised his bones and left black-and-blue stripes on his skin. Even padding could not protect him. A high white hospital bed was installed. The bedroom was plain, its elaborate moldings subdued with white paint. White linen curtains hung at the tall windows and at the door, which led to a small balcony overlooking the garden. There was very little else in the room: a bedside table, two small paintings on the walls, dark abstractions by the American painter Arthur Dove, which Perrot had Eric rehang so that he could see them out of the corners of his eyes as he lay in bed.

Late one afternoon, Alexander Ives arrived at the house. Eric led him upstairs. Perrot rested on a turquoise foam-rubber pad indented like an egg carton. His skin was tinged yellow by the low sun; lines like cracks in porcelain radiated from his mouth.

At Alexander's entrance, Perrot was struck by his beauty. Perrot over the years had reacted to Alexander in different ways: with possessive lust, with fatherly pride, with jealousy, with delight—and with regret. Alexander's beauty had, for Perrot, embodied his own decay.

Today Perrot saw the dancer differently, as if he had crossed a barrier of space—delight, jealousy, and sadness recalled, but from a distance. Perrot saw Alexander's beauty not only in terms of its physical elements but also in terms of its spirit. He saw the blackness surrounding Alexander—his fear, his desire—as the backing of a mirror, and he understood how he had always seen in Alexander those parts of himself he wanted reflected. Now he was too far away to be reflected in the dancer; he could see Alexander unobstructed, apart from him. Perrot could love Alexander selflessly.

Perrot said to Alexander, "They treat me like an egg, so I will not break."

Alexander had retreated to the balcony. Marigolds bloomed in window boxes hung from the balcony railing, marigolds as profuse and golden as fallen leaves. A faint odor of dried grass and compost rose from the garden below. For a quarter of an hour, Alexander Ives did not speak. Perrot removed his glasses and dozed.

"I'm sorry," Alexander said.

Perrot opened his eyes calmly, as if he had been waiting. "You should not be. You are not sorry for resisting me. You protected yourself and your ballet. You are not kind, but neither am I. And you have what you want. Do not regret anything. You could not know what would happen to me. Are we not like animals, an old lion and a young one? Why not?"

Alexander turned away from the balcony. He blocked the sunlight through the French doors and shadowed Perrot's face. He approached the bed, bent over—a prince bowing—and kissed Perrot's cheek. He held his breath against Perrot's sour odor of illness and concentrated on the texture of the old man's skin against his lips, dry and dusty as the surface of the moon, eerie, lonely territory. Perrot's eyes remained open. They were smooth and glassy, like basalt; they were meteorites hardened in cold, distant space. Alexander saw through their adamantine clarity into death, saw the diminishing incandescence of Perrot's soul.

Achille Perrot raised his long arm, and his black sleeve fell back from his wrist. The withered white skin, the veins blue, like mapped rivers, moved Alexander with a pity that made him moan. Tears filled his eyes. Gently, so that his hot touch would not startle Alexander, Perrot brushed back a loose strand of hair from the dancer's forehead and stroked his cheek. "You are still brown from the summer," Perrot said.

"Mostly it's faded."

"Kevin has learned your ballet?"

"As well as he can. Sometimes I look at him and expect to see Dana."

"Guy has been helping you?"

"He's scheduled rehearsal time. I haven't needed anything else."

"Guy can help. He has a good eye."

Fractionally, Alexander withdrew into himself. His blue eyes, cleared by tears, clouded again. Perrot noticed and smiled. "I forget," he said. "There is nothing we can tell you."

Alexander shook his head.

"That is too bad." Perrot patted the bed. "Sit down. I would like you to do something for me. I am not asking you to touch your ballet."

"Then anything," Alexander said.

"I have been thinking of a ballet, a simple one, a small one. It is not anything that you would perform—it is too small, too domestic—but I would like very much to see it. It is very simple; it would take no time. Will you come? Will you come here so that I can make it?"

"I'll come," said Alexander.

"Will you come with Caroline? I want to make it for both of you."

Alexander winced. "I will, but I don't know if she will."

"Of course she will. I will ask her," Perrot insisted. "She will come for me." He paused. "And she will be coming for you, too. Caroline is faithful."

In the early evenings, Alexander Ives and Caroline Harbison walked together from the ballet studios to Achille Perrot's brownstone to rehearse his ballet. They did not talk and they kept a careful distance on the sidewalk, yet they could not avoid falling in step with each other, anticipating each other's timing as they turned a corner or hurried to catch a light.

Caroline Harbison assumed that Alexander knew she spent time with Amos Furst. She knew that Alexander had been seeing Rosalind Child, although it hardly comforted her to know he saw her irregularly and that Rosalind was bewildered and complained. As they walked toward Perrot every evening, she thought that they were fools for not listening to their bodies; such physical sympathy must have significance. It was so honest, so evident, so different from the false starts of the heart. So perfect and rare. At night, afterward, Caroline thought about what she could say to Alexander, what she wanted to say—nothing and everything—and she kept silent.

For Alexander, it was a relief sometimes to see Caroline across a raked distance and to be able to keep that earth undisturbed, as serene as a Japanese garden; it was a relief not to be confronted with her knowledge of him. The force of her desire dissipated across that empty space. He was grateful for her silence. But beneath relief lurked emptiness. He told himself it was normal; it was part of the process of disassociation—regret, habit, patterns worn into the brain and body. Then Caroline would dash across the street as a light turned yellow, and he would leap beside her, matching the length of her jump, framing her energy, and he knew what she was thinking and what she wanted, and at that moment he wanted the same thing. But only briefly. Rosalind Child's desire demanded nothing from him; she took him lightly, loved him, and left him intact and untouched and alone.

Achille Perrot had Eric wheel the hospital bed against the balcony doors so that the center of the bedroom was cleared. Dressed in black pajamas, Perrot lay on his turquoise egg carton with a tape recorder propped beside him. He made the ballet from the bed. It was set to a trio sonata for two flutes and harpsichord by Bach.

Perrot watched Alexander Ives and Caroline Harbison enter his bedroom on the first evening, and he sent them out the door to come into the room beside each other again. "You need only to walk together to dance," he told them.

In the ballet there were few steps and a great deal of

walking: complicated patterns of walking. The dancers' paths, had their feet spun webs like spiders, would have knotted them together in an intricate lace. What steps there were Perrot took from eighteenth-century dances, an allemande, a minuet, little skips and turns, small relevés onto demi-pointe. The ballet depended not on spectacular lifts and balances, but on close timing, anticipation, and a counterpoint of movement.

"Listen," Perrot said to them, "listen to the music. There is also a version for cello, for one instrument. In the sonata, the lines of the two flutes are very close. You cannot always tell them apart; the first part is lower than the second, you know. That is what I want the ballet to be like; I do not want to tell you apart, but at the same time I want to know that you are separate."

They worked while outside it grew dark. Eric came in and turned on the lights; as everywhere in the house, the lights were recessed behind a molding so the room seemed lit by a distant source, an electric sun. Every ten minutes he returned and adjusted the rheostat, turning the lamps infinitesimally brighter, maintaining daylight.

They remembered the first ballet they had made together; it had also been to Bach. Those rehearsals had been charged with possibility, light-headed with the first shoots of love. These rehearsals were fraught with equal energy, charged with death, with the exhausting effort of ending. In their way they were as tender and as precious as the first rehearsals years earlier, as intimate with shared secrets. Their dancing had not changed; their dance had. This time they knew that it was something apart from them—a paradigm of love, a permanent shadow that existed before and after them, when they danced they joined their bodies to its perfect shape.

Caroline mourned; each step ached for the severing of what had been beautiful; each step trailed strings that Alexander could have picked up had he wanted to. But Alexander retreated; the ballet to him became steps to solitude. He defended his withdrawal, or Perrot gave him the steps to do so. Although it seemed as if Alexander began each step and

Caroline finished it, and it seemed impossible to unravel the line of one dancer from the other, each of Alexander's steps was complete in itself, round, beauty hoarded. It took great effort for Caroline to time her movements to his, to find the precise instant when their steps would be tangent.

They walked and walked around the bedroom, the two of them, while Achille Perrot lay on his turquoise foam-rubber egg carton and watched them and spoke combinations and punched the tape recorder—play, rewind, play again.

Often, after they had finished, Perrot rang for Eric, who arrived noiselessly in his Chinese shoes with a bottle of wine and three glasses on the round silver tray. Perrot insisted Caroline and Alexander stay. "I am drinking up my cellar, and I need your help," he said. He spoke to them—to Caroline it appeared that he spoke to Alexander—about his ballets, why he had chosen certain combinations of dancers, how he wanted them to look, what sort of technique the dancers should use to realize each dance correctly.

If he had not been in the process of dissecting it so eloquently in the ballet, Caroline would have thought that Perrot was ignorant of the situation that existed between her and Alexander. She marveled at how Perrot kept them together as long as he could, impervious to her unhappiness in Alexander's presence.

She tried to focus on the objects in the room, but there was not much to distract her—the two paintings, the array of plastic medicine vials on Perrot's bedside table, the turquoise foam-rubber pad. She studied Perrot; his face riveted her. His black pajamas made him look Oriental, like a withered, ancient sage, his body reduced to the economical lines of a Chinese painting. She tried to deny that his body was diminishing. As its flesh dissolved, its character emerged, like ridges of harder rock protruding in eroded limestone. Kindness and cruelty, concern and indifference, involvement and aloofness, anger and compassion—contradictions worn into intricate patterns.

After the fifth rehearsal, Perrot said, "Why do you pretend not to hear me and read the labels on my medicine bottles out of politeness? I am talking to you."

"Then can I ask you an impolite question?" She saw no reason not to be direct. This ballet he was making was causing her too much unhappiness to remain deferential. She watched his face compose itself into a pattern combining benign interest and suspicion.

"Of course," he said.

"Why didn't you make this ballet on Rosalind Child?"

Perrot smiled, his teeth as long as a skull's, his magnified eyes glittering with curiosity, watching not Caroline but Alexander. "That is not what it is about," he said. "What are Rosalind and Alexander doing with each other? Do you know?" he asked, still watching Alexander. "What they are doing is not what I wanted. They are colliding, Alexander and Rosalind. They are like those bumper cars at amusement parks. I used to be very fond of that game, did you know that? Years ago, Fanny and I used to go every summer to the fair in Pittsfield and ride the bumper cars. I preferred to avoid collisions, but sometimes they were irresistible. Are you not colliding, Alexander?"

"I don't understand," he said, embarrassed, pleading innocence, looking to Caroline to defend him or change the subject.

But she was beyond shielding him. She stared at him with her blue-gray eyes, wishing she could view him with Perrot's cold curiosity. She and Alexander had not collided; she was too soft for collision. She sipped her wine, a viscous red; it had made her dizzy. Eric had brought a plate of cheese, but she could not afford to be profligate with calories.

Achille Perrot's expression rearranged itself as he turned his gaze on Caroline. Suspicion vanished and was replaced by compassion and sadness and regret—not for what he had done to her, Caroline guessed, but for himself, for not having done more, for not having made more dances. "I am sorry," he said. "This ballet is painful now, but then you will have it. Both of you. It will be something. It will show you things, I promise. You will not hate it."

*   *   *

The geranium in Caroline Harbison's apartment hung on to life. It was top-heavy, and she had supported its immensely long woody lower stem by tying it like a vine to the living room window frame with string and thumbtacks, so its meager leaves could catch the available light.

"My neighbor forgot to water it this summer," she said to Amos Furst. "I've been trying to revive it. It would break my heart to throw it out. Perrot gave it to me twelve years ago."

"It's lived a good life. It must be the oldest geranium on record."

"I think Perrot is dying," she said. "Everybody says he's getting better, that his leg is healing as fast as you can expect at his age. But I think he's dying. There are too many medicines in his room. You don't have to take that much stuff for a broken leg. It's something else." She picked up a plastic watering can beside the geranium and poured water into its undersized pot. "He gave this plant to me to teach me how to dance. 'Dancers are like geraniums,' he said. I call it Achille when I talk to it. My mother says it helps plants grow if you talk to them."

"That would be an interesting piece, a talking plant, kind of a herbaceous Miss Lonelyhearts."

"Not much movement, though." Caroline went into the kitchen to put water on for coffee. Amos stood in the living room regretting his remark. He should have offered sympathy, not banter. He watched Caroline with her perfect gestures fill the kettle and put it on the burner, turn on the flame, bend to check its height. The coffee ballet. She stood with her hands on her hips, her brow arched as if listening for Perrot to correct her.

From her posture, Amos tried to divine what she was thinking. Considering, he thought; she was considering him. She was not sure whether she wanted to come out of the kitchen. Would it reassure her, he wondered, to tell her that he did not love her and did not expect her to love him? Would it relieve her anxiety or intensify it? He did not know how you loved someone who lived so much in her body. He was almost afraid to touch her; either it would mean too much or it would mean nothing at all.

She came out of the kitchen with a glass coffeepot and two cups on a tray, suddenly domestic, comfortably armed with coffee. She put the tray down on the table in front of the sofa. The room was simple, a sofa and a chair covered in beige nubbly cotton, prints of dancers on the wall by Degas and Picasso, Toulouse-Lautrec's cancan girls, a photograph of Nijinksy. Snapshots stood on a dresser in the corner: an elderly couple, complexion and hair like white bread and mayonnaise, gazed lovingly at their daughter taking the picture; a rangy young man, straight black hair, optimistically smiling—Caroline's brother; and Alexander Ives, his face strongly shadowed from above, photographed at noon in the summer. Amos recognized the barn at Arabesque— Alexander Ives, harshly lit and reduced to three inches by five inches, beautiful nonetheless.

Even though he was sitting beside her on the sofa in front of the coffee tray, Caroline Harbison was not sure what Amos Furst looked like. His features were too changeable, soft-edged, capable of recomposing themselves into different personalities. She did not know what to do with Amos. She did not even know how to begin; she had no idea of love if it was not danced first. The clarity of this thought startled her; she had had too much wine at Perrot's after the rehearsal and she was fuzzy. She wanted to ask Amos what he thought love was.

What shape did it have? What were its steps? How did you know what to do? A big jump? Small traveling glides? Fast dizzy turns? What kind of partnering? Precarious balances? Was it no dance at all? Was it without line and impulsion? Had it no music? She was afraid of that. What next? Amos had met her after the rehearsal at the Exuma restaurant and had walked her home. Caroline had asked him to come up. What next? The walls of Caroline's apartment were thin. They listened to the diesel hiss of delivery trucks, sirens, voices.

Amos heard the sound effects behind the snapshots of

Caroline's family—crickets, cars slowly cruising into driveways and garage doors rumbling open and shut again; the drizzle of sprinklers, lawn mowers, snowblowers, children's sneakered feet slapping on the sidewalk, dogs barking, the icy jingle of the Good Humor man in the summertime, meals where the loudest sound was the chink of knives against dinner plates. Not unlike the sound effects of his childhood, but without his overlay of voices, the Jewish percussion of anger, anger for its own sake, for the rush of adrenaline it offered, the high, the small surge of familial power. The Harbisons were polite; they said "please" and "thank you"; that was apparent from their faces. Probably they listened to each other; possibly they respected one another's opinions. They did not live in attack mode. They did not parry or twist words and turn them back against the speaker newly sharpened.

Amos thought that he might be too sharp for Caroline. He had survived despite irritation. He had taken the grit of his life—his parents' dissatisfaction, and his grandparents', for that matter, their aspirations, and the abrasion that they understood as love—and he had spun pearls around it; he had tried to make grit into art, into his monologues. At least that was what he thought on his good days; on bad days he thought that he talked compulsively because nobody would listen to him while he was growing up.

Caroline Harbison had had no irritations. Her sanity was alien to him. He had never known a sane dancer. But he had not known very many sane women, he realized, or men. He did not travel in sane circles. Caroline's balance was immensely attractive to him, though he did not trust its sturdiness and he waited for her to wobble. With someone like her, did one wait until one was married to have sex?

He had a big nose, Caroline thought, which seemed small when you looked at him face-to-face, and he had beautiful green eyes, edged and flecked with gold. The gold changed color according to the light; sometimes his eyes appeared murky, the color of pond water. Nothing about him was definite, but when she looked at his eyes she did not see distance; she saw curiosity and mystification. It amused her that she should mystify someone. She drank her coffee. She did not expect love now; she would have found it false.

She wondered if she should tell him that or if it would sound as if she was putting him off. She was not. She wanted to encourage him; she wanted him to stay, for what she did not know. There was a brightness about him, like a lit window at night through which she could make guesses about what she saw inside. It bore no connection to anything else in her life.

"How was the rehearsal?" Amos said.

"He lies there in his bed, on his foam-rubber mattress that's supposed to prevent bedsores, telling us what to do, and I can't imagine him not there. I cry every time I see him, afterward, leaving the house."

"I'm sorry."

"He's getting fainter. Oh, I see it in his face."

He touched her shoulder. She put down her coffee cup. "You don't have to comfort me."

"You never want comfort."

"I love him. Things are even between us. I gave and he gave. I don't want more than he's given me, and he doesn't want more than I've given him."

"That's rare. That sounds like something everybody wants but never gets."

She nodded. "I'm lucky." She corrected herself. "I've been lucky."

"Everybody in the company must be miserable."

"Nobody thinks about it. They think he's coming back."

Amos leaned back on the sofa. His eyes grew murky. "What about Alexander?"

Caroline looked away. "I don't know." Amos was not asking about Perrot and Alexander Ives, but about her and Alexander.

"You've been dancing with him almost every day."

He was not asking about dancing. Her instinct was silence; she could dance Alexander, not talk him. But Amos talked. "We dance. Sometimes I forget that we can't be what we dance, but we can't," she said, and felt exposed. "I don't know what else to say. I mean, what about Eveline de Charny? What did you see in her?" she retaliated.

"Nothing serious. I thought she was great-looking," Amos said, "and I thought her money was fabulous and it fascinated me. I thought she could really help, you know, shoot me into stardom like a satellite launch, believe it or not. It was the corrupt part of my nature. That's the truth."

Caroline tilted her head and regarded Amos quizzically.

"You wouldn't understand that," he said.

"No."

"You wouldn't have a beer, would you?"

Caroline shook her head. "I'm sorry. I don't have much in the refrigerator. Do you want more coffee? Mineral water?"

He stood and looked down at her on the sofa. She seemed prim—back straight, head high, knees together—but he could not decide whether that was due to her dancer's posture or her character. He tilted his head.

"You're imitating me," she said. She considered him—his jeans, his black sneakers, his shirt sleeves rolled up to his elbows. She liked his forearms, more slender than a dancer's, downy with brown hair. His palms were broad, but his fingers were narrow and tapered, surprisingly delicate.

He smiled. His eyes were a tropical green now, like the sun on thick leaves, green mixed with gold. "I'm trying to figure out how to play this. I've admitted my perverse lust for money and power. I've told you I'm corrupt, so you're wondering what you're doing with me in your living room. You've got more important things on your mind, like love and death. Your parents are perched on the dresser staring at you, and they might as well have little balloons coming out of their mouths saying how proud of you they are and what a bad guy I am. So I think, Is this the time to make a move, or should I just quit while I'm ahead and say good night and call myself a stupid jerk all the way home for shooting off my mouth?"

"Are you asking my advice or beginning a monologue?"

"Would you believe a dialogue?"

"So it's my turn?"

He nodded.

Caroline Harbison rose and faced Amos and stretched out her arm, a slow, graceful unbending, and placed her hand on his chest, at the neck of his shirt.

He stared at her, startled, and opened his mouth. She shook her head. "You tell me I have to be still. Now I'm telling you that you can't talk. I have something to say. I'm not sure I can explain, so if you don't understand, say so, and I'll try again." She felt his skin under her fingers and the pulse of the vein at the base of his neck. "What we're going to do—I don't know what it means. I don't know if it means anything except that we're both here. But I'm not in the habit of doing this. You have to know that."

She was flushed and her hand trembled. She added, convincing herself, "But it's something. Even if nothing else happens, even if we don't do anything else, it's something. Do you understand?"

He nodded.

She tilted her head back, and Amos put his hand on her chest and felt her breastbone under her taut skin and the ridges of her ribs. Her slow heartbeat vibrated beneath his palm, and he bent his head and kissed her. She led him into the bedroom. They felt each other's shape and dimensions and texture. The harmony of his proportions surprised her; the smoothness of her skin surprised him. She liked the taste of his mouth. He had expected her to be arrogant about her body, but she was gracious. In the night glare of the city, Amos watched Caroline's face to see if she grew afraid or changed her mind. She watched him, waiting for his eyes to close, and when they did not, she felt their light on her face and it infused her with warmth. They kept their eyes open.

Love was a dance, always a dance. But this dance surprised them both with simple steps and sure balances. They improvised together, and they stayed with each other easily. This dance led them in no secret isolating variations, but toward peace. Caroline surprised Amos, who had anticipated remorse, and laughed.

*   *   *

301

Every twenty minutes Eric wheeled Achille Perrot's bed a foot or two west, as the October sun through the bedroom windows shifted and lowered to the south. "This is my swan boat," Perrot told Guy Pissarro, "the prop I refused to use to carry the Prince and the Swan Queen away at the end of *Swan Lake*. Perhaps I was mistaken; perhaps we should put one in. I like the effect." He hummed the last measures of the ballet. "I must think about it."

Perrot was continually cold, but blankets pressed too heavily on his body. His black pajamas absorbed heat, and in the sunlight he covered himself only with a sheet. His bedside table, cleared of medicines, was littered now with photographs and folders containing costume and staging notes for his ballets, and with magazines and newspapers. Perrot grew irritable; he wanted to live more days, and he wanted each day he lived to last longer. For the first time in his life, he read the newspapers thoroughly, immersing himself in each day's trivia—local news, scandals, trials, murders, investigations of corruption—the endlessly unresolving random plots of existence.

Sumner Loewen arrived for his lunchtime visit. Achille Perrot pulled himself up straight in the bed. His eyes were black, angry and magnified. The day's paper was open across his legs. "Have you read your friend Gertrude Stella today?" He pointed to the paper. Without giving Sumner Loewen a chance to answer, Perrot began reading: "Sumner Loewen announced that the fall season will proceed as scheduled despite an injury to Achille Perrot. There has been much speculation as to the future of the Perrot Ballet. Loewen has just revealed that an anonymous patron has donated the building housing the company's offices and rehearsal studios; the donor has also established an endowment fund. "For the first time since our founding, we are in the process of developing a long-range plan to ensure the company's future," Loewen announced. "The time has come to define and identify both our financial assets and our artistic resources." Perrot, however, has always insisted that he has no interest in the company's outlasting him. When asked about this, Loewen replied, "Perrot is lasting. We are not discussing prefixes.""

Sources within the company, however, intimated that the dancer Alexander Ives is being considered to direct the company until Perrot recovers from the fall he suffered several weeks ago during a rehearsal. Ives's first ballet will be performed this season, marking the first time the Perrot Ballet has danced a work that its founder did not choreograph.' "

Sumner Loewen moved the visitor's chair into a shadow. He nodded familiarly as Perrot read with his uninflected French intonation.

"How was such a thing printed?" Perrot demanded, flinging the paper from his lap. It caught the current of sun-warmed air and drifted to the floor. "And there is a photograph of you, and one of Alexander. Nothing of me. It is my company. The Perrot Ballet."

Sumner Loewen shook his head. "Achille, I had nothing to do with this. There should have been a picture. Of course we talk, Gertrude and I. I told her about the de Charny gift—she has no idea that he's the donor, of course—and she imagined the rest. I don't think there's anything there that you and I haven't discussed."

"And Alexander? Directing the company? Now? She is crazy, or you are."

"The business about Alexander is pure speculation on her part. And she makes it clear that the appointment would be temporary."

"Did you suggest it?"

"I did not. It was a rumor. Who can control that? You know she sends the dancers little presents and mentions them favorably in her reviews, and so they give her bits of gossip. I can't do anything about that."

"She knew about Alexander's ballet."

"It has been scheduled. I know that you don't think much of her intelligence, but she can read. None of it means anything, fortunately. If you want, I'll write her a letter."

Perrot shrugged.

"You are much improved. You are getting better. That speaks for itself. The drugs are working."

"If you take them, they work," Perrot answered.

"Of course. What do you mean?"

"You know that I think of my dancers in terms of their usefulness to me. I also think of myself—of my body—in those terms. I am not at all useful like this." He lifted the sheet, revealing his wasted leg in black pajamas resting like a bandaged chopstick on the turquoise foam. "I am useless on crutches. I am useless in a wheelchair. I am useless if I cannot move. I do not want to linger. I understand endings. Art teaches endings, do you not think so? I, in any event, believe in endings." He smiled at Sumner Loewen. The smile was sweet and angry. He closed his eyes. "So," he said. "I will end."

There was a frost in late October. In the garden the leaves of the geraniums and lobelia withered and blackened; the geranium blossoms crumbled. The lobelia hung, blue pendants from stems that cascaded over the clay pots like charred spiderwebs. On the balcony the marigolds survived, but barely; overnight their gold had tarnished. Achille Perrot refused to give Eric permission to remove them.

The morning of the frost, Eric interrupted Perrot as he was studying his newspaper. "Rosalind Child is here to see you, but I told her you did not like to be disturbed in the morning."

Perrot put down the paper. "Ask her to come up." Against the morning chill Rosalind Child wore a denim jacket over her thin white shirt and white cotton trousers. Perrot could feel the day already warming. Indian summer would follow the frost, and the black flowers would remain, a reminder of capriciousness.

She held a plant wrapped in a white florist's sleeve. "I'm sorry to come without making an appointment," said Rosalind Child. "I was afraid to ask Guy Pissarro because I hardly know you, and I was sure he would tell me I couldn't come. He's like a watchdog. I'm afraid of him."

"There is no need." Perrot smiled. "He will not bite. But is that not the sort of thing people say about their dogs that are the size of bears? I am glad to see you."

She surveyed the room, its lack of surfaces. "What should I do with this?"

"Remove the paper so that I can see it," said Perrot.

Rosalind Child ripped the sleeve off a large yellow chry-santhemum. "I knew you liked flowers, and I wanted to get you something that would last. The florist said they were hardy."

Perrot patted the table beside his bed. "Pick up those pictures and put it here. I will look at it instead of my dying marigolds."

"What are these?" Rosalind Child asked, as she gathered the photographs.

"See for yourself."

Rosalind leafed through them. They were photographs of Achille Perrot when he was a young man, glossy dramatic studio shots from the thirties and the forties. One was a portrait, his shoulders entering the frame on the diagonal, one half of his face brilliantly lit, the other half in shadows deep as velvet. There were pictures showing him dancing: Albrecht in *Giselle,* Franz in *Coppélia,* Don Quixote. Rosalind Child pulled one out from the bottom of the stack and caught her breath. Perrot smiled and took it from her. He was cos-tumed in black as the Prince in *Swan Lake.*

"I thought that was Alexander," Rosalind said. "You look just like him there."

"I did, though I was not as handsome as he is. A coin-cidence. When I first saw Alexander I was astonished. He could have been my son, if I'd had a son." He put the pho-tograph down. "That is the reason you came, to talk to me about Alexander?"

She hesitated. "And I wanted to see you."

"Sit down, my dear." He gestured to the visitor's chair beside the bed in the sun.

Rosalind sat and took off her jacket. Achille Perrot could see the shape of her small breasts under her thin white shirt. He gazed at them. "You came to tell me you are in love with Alexander and to ask my advice."

Rosalind Child nodded. She sat straight and enjoyed his eyes on her body.

"So. Tell, now that I have begun for you. I know, of

course, about you and Alexander. I hear everything. I know you are not happy."

"But I should be. I feel so stupid sometimes."

Perrot nodded. "He is like a beautiful painting, or a statue. He exists and it is impossible not to desire him, because he is there. He possesses a magic that you want for yourself."

"It's not only that. It's that he's so—when I'm with him it's so perfect—I know I can't love anybody else after him. But when I think about him, I feel kind of empty. It's like I'm always expecting more and it isn't there."

"What do you mean by love?"

Rosalind Child shrugged. "I feel good, in my stomach. Actually, I feel bad in my stomach; it gets all tight. I can't eat; I feel kind of dizzy. I feel like I've swallowed all this bubbly air. Like I'm ready to take off."

As she talked, her hands swooped like swallows over the bed. Achille Perrot caught her left wrist in his long fingers. His nails curved over his fingertips like a hawk's talons. "Rosalind, I will tell you about Alexander and about myself, and possibly about you. You must understand. I know what love looks like. All my life I have been looking at love, to be able to tell my boys and girls how to dance it. Alexander learned love from me. He can dance love. So can you. I have been teaching you. You think it has been pliés and tendus, but it has been love that you have been learning to dance. For Alexander, the most important thing is to dance love. Knowing love, feeling it—that is not important. And for you, perhaps that is also the truth. You are intended to dance. You will have to see, but I think I am right."

"So it isn't real? That's a terrible thing to say." She tried to withdraw her hand, but Perrot held it. "It's so sad."

"Who is to know what is real? I do not know. To dance love is beautiful, and it moves us as if it were love—more so, often. Perhaps it is more real. Real love, whatever that is, can be sad and ugly and boring."

With the remnants of his dancer's strength, Perrot pulled at Rosalind's arm and tilted her body forward out of the chair, balancing her, pulling her to the bed so she had to sit next to him on the sheet. The sleeve had fallen back from his arm; his skin was white and hairless, sagging, wrinkled against the bone. "I always knew what love should look like," he said.

He leaned back against his pillows, removed his glasses, and closed his eyes. Rosalind Child stayed on the bed beside him as his grip on her hand loosened and he slept. The sun shone on his nose, making his nostrils red and translucent. His eyelids were veined blue, his lips, in sleep, were slack. He snored, he sniffled, the wrinkled hollow at the base of his throat fluttered. His chest rose and fell unevenly. His thin mouth twitched. Rosalind Child kept her eye on him, her hand twined with his. Eric came in and wheeled the bed west. "The swan boat." Perrot smiled, waking. "Love survives death."

17

IN HIS EXQUISITELY CUT DARK GRAY SUIT, WITH his pink skin and silky white hair, Sumner Loewen, blooming with satisfaction, stood in the lobby. He thrived on the press of the opening night crowd. His efforts over years had built this following; he had cultivated its loyalty. Achille Perrot had made the company, but Sumner Loewen had made the audience. This was his moment. The company was formed, fixed; Perrot had done his part. From now on, Sumner Loewen realized, the audience would become more important than the art; its cultivation would determine the future of the Perrot Ballet. The work now continued in front of the curtain; behind was maintenance.

It was raining outside, cold, sooty autumn rain, and through the open doors the splash of traffic in the street outside underlay the high-pitched greetings in the lobby, the gritty snare-drum scrape of shoes on the marble floor. Sumner Loewen loved the flutter of furling umbrellas and wet raincoats, the darting, kissing heads, and the cacophonous mix of perfume. To him it was prelude, like the sound of the orchestra tuning to a dancer.

Patrons and potential patrons greeted Sumner and Fanny Loewen, who shone resplendent beside her husband in a luminous bronze taffeta gown that seemed battery powered. Sumner greeted each according to a complicated formula that balanced potential donation, actual donation, duration of loyalty, and effort spent in cultivation. Beside him, Fanny Loewen was uniformly effusive, which added a tantalizing edge of ambivalence to each exchange and made all donors—large, small, and those whose gifts were not yet consummated—want to give more. In his head, as he greeted his flock, Sumner Loewen calculated the running totals of annual gifts and endowment gifts; he was proud of the figures.

Walter Mowbray shyly touched Sumner Loewen's shoulder. The young man wore a brocaded paisley jacket threaded with silver and gold. A stripe of golden glitter sparkled under his bleached eyebrows. "All these people. It's just too much, don't you think? We've never had an opening night like this, have we, Mr. Loewen? I can't believe the calls we've had for tickets—I mean, everybody wanted to be here. There just aren't any left! Not one. Sold out! And I want to thank you for dedicating this evening to Dana. That was very thoughtful. It means a lot to me."

Sumner Loewen nodded. It was a titillating reminder of notoriety, too. The networks, national and cable, as well as the local stations, had dispatched crews to the opening.

Walter Mowbray cringed as the crowd jostled him. He wailed: "My outfit is being destroyed. First the rain; now all these people! I'm crushed! You know, Mr. Loewen, I haven't slept in two weeks. It's been too much. Really, I need an assistant! And what do I say when people ask me if Mr. Perrot is here?"

"Tell them that his doctors felt the effort would be too taxing." Sumner Loewen promised to hire an assistant and patted Walter Mowbray's Lurex lapel with little sweeping strokes to dismiss him, and wondered if Walter, despite his skill at managing his own image, should become the assistant while the company hired an experienced public relations person. There were new critics to cultivate, new outlets for publicity, new techniques for shaping audience perceptions: tours, festivals, television specials; it was time to begin.

Although Sumner Loewen could not see above the crowd, like a sheepdog he had an acute sense of the whereabouts of those who were important to him. He tilted his head eagerly, and Gertrude Stella cruised to his side on a heavy swell of perfume. Sumner intended to kiss the air over her chapped, chubby hand, but she thrust her fingers against his mouth. A prong of the setting of her ruby nicked his lip. He resisted flinching.

"Thank you so much for the flowers, my dear," Gertrude Stella crooned. "They were—they are lovely. Orchids—so extravagant, and they've lasted so long!"

"You've been very good to us."

"I have every reason to be. And, Sumner, my dear, I would just adore the chance to talk to Alexander. An interview, very low-key, but very soon. I don't want anybody else to get him before me. Maybe a little dinner? Informal. What do you think?"

Sumner considered. "I will talk to him after tonight—if you promise me that you'll help him, teach him. Alexander is new to this. He doesn't yet know what to do. But I'm sure he'll be amenable."

Gertrude Stella smiled. Her thick yellowed front teeth, their edges smeared with lipstick, resembled carnation petals. Sumner Loewen kissed the air in the direction of her face, nudging her into the arms of his wife. Fanny Loewen thrust her pursed lips into the air next to Gertrude Stella's large-pored, powder-clogged cheeks and slipped her once again into the crowd's current.

The congested lobby had begun to clear. Sumner Loewen aimed his wife inside the theater. The lights flashed, and latecomers, like ducks, shook rain from their evening feathers and bustled inside. Sumner waited. The ushers closed the doors to the auditorium. Like Achille Perrot, who always remained backstage until the dancers had gone and he was alone to watch enchantment dwindle, Sumner Loewen relished the sudden emptiness of the lobby. He took pleasure in the mingling of atmospheres—indifference seeping in from the street to dilute the anticipation that lingered like perfume. Through the doors, Sumner Loewen heard the oboe sound its tuning A. He started inside.

A car drew up in front of the theater. Perhaps a lawyer, Sumner Loewen guessed, fresh from a closing, worried that his wife would be angry with him for arriving late. Curious, he turned to look. It was a woman, swaddled in a shiny black cape, wearing dark glasses. When she saw Sumner Loewen, she ran eagerly toward him. Her high heels skidded on the wet marble floor. "Sumner! Sumner! I was hoping you'd still be here!" She swooped upon him and enveloped him in the rubberized folds of her cape, mussing his smooth hair, annoying him.

Eveline de Charny removed her glasses. Her face was gaunt, her expression one of suffering. Sumner Loewen could see that she had emphasized with powder the shadows under her cheekbones, and she had left her lips pale.

"I thought you were still abroad," he said, returning her enthusiastic embrace with some reserve.

She shook her head. "Abroad? Oh, Sumner, don't be so delicate. Have you ever been to one of those discreet little dry-out homes? Of course not. It was obscene. They treat you like a child. Lights out at nine-thirty. You can't do this, you can't do that. No phone calls. They talk about God all the time; they're worse than my mother. Appalling, really too much. They had me making pot holders. Me. I've never held a pot in my life. Therapy, they called it. It was too ridiculous, Sumner, just too silly. Pot holders! Can you see me giving pot holders for Christmas? And my own children—they were desperate for nurturing. On the telephone they sounded so pathetic. Nobody was meeting their needs. With Atalanta gone—I cringe every time I think how I trusted her with them—and their father, you know, refuses to have anything to do with them. So I had my driver come and get me, just yesterday. I walked out; there was nothing they could do. And how could I stay away from the ballet?"

Sumner Loewen bowed briefly. "We are honored to have you."

Ignoring the perfunctory nature of the bow, Eveline de Charny bent down and confidentially took Sumner Loewen's arm. "I'm suing my parents, you know." She spoke quickly, breathless with manic energy. "And I've decided to go to law school in January—the law is so fascinating, so dramatic. I can't wait to get involved with the ballet company again, and to see Achille. How thoughtful of you to dedicate the evening to Dana. Poor thing."

"Your parents will fight you," said Sumner Loewen.

Eveline de Charny smiled. "But, Sumner, I'm in a no-lose situation. The trusts are in place. My parents can't touch the ones my grandfather Magnus Arbroath set up, which go to me at their death. If I don't win now, I just wait. How many more years do they have? My father hasn't been well. I think Dana—he hasn't gotten over Dana. Poor thing."

"Your father?" Sumner Loewen stepped back. "Or Dana? I beg you to excuse me. This is Achille's new ballet. You would hate to miss the beginning, wouldn't you? Perhaps I will see you later, at intermission."

He opened the door, letting a sliver of light into the dark theater, letting a measure of music out to the lobby, and, without allowing her to precede him, trotted down the aisle to his seat. His wife's dress crackled gently as he brushed its skirt from his seat. He pitied Eveline de Charny, but enough was enough, and she had nothing for him now. To give her her due, she was amusing. Pot holders. He had not been overly rude—if her case went to a jury, it might rule in her favor. Poor thing— He interrupted his own thought with a shudder of disgust for Eveline that was rare in his carefully edited repertory of emotion. To avoid judging himself, he rarely judged others. Because of her the company was on solid ground, and because of Dana. Poor thing.

Stagehands sauntered back and forth, bouncing on the heels of their sneakers; the electricians spoke softly into their headsets. Members of the corps de ballet gathered in nervous bunches and stretched at the barre. Two or three ventured onstage. As the stage lights shifted to red in preparation for the first ballet, one girl did a quick double pirouette, wobbled, and giggled. Another peered through the peephole in the curtain at the audience settling itself.

With Perrot absent, everything was different and nothing was. Caroline Harbison, in makeup for *Reductions*, wandered backstage. She had wrapped the shawl Eveline de Charny gave her over the red gauze skirt of her costume. During the last week her ankle had swollen again.

The audience's rumbling filtered muted through the heavy curtain. Caroline crossed the stage, shuffling in her ballet slippers; the girls stepped out of her way, deferring to her. She hopped onto her right foot, gauging the ankle's soreness. Always the bustle before a performance galvanized Caroline with its chain of emotions: nervous anticipation, then at the call a shiver of panic at the inevitability of going on, dizziness as the orchestra began, finally the physical surrender to the count of measures, obedience to the music, to the dance.

Tonight she felt inert. Without Perrot here, connections had been broken, lines cut. Figures moved backstage, appearing and reappearing between the wings. Guy Pissarro emerged onstage for a moment, tiny and erect, face ruddy in the lights; he pointed as he counted his girls. He wore black. Caroline turned away from the sight of him in black, dressed like Perrot; he prefigured mourning. "Ten minutes," the stage manager announced over the sound system backstage. "Ten minutes."

She picked up her new toe shoes and struck them against the cinder-block wall with all her strength, each one ten times, fifteen times, breaking in the wooden shaft along the sole. So they would not disturb her makeup, she swallowed tears. Perrot was getting better, everyone said. Caroline knew he was not. She tied her shoes, flexed her feet, ground the toe boxes in resin. The ribbons indented the flesh at her ankle. Amos Furst had sent her a geranium for opening night, not a simple flashy red one, but an old-fashioned scented geranium with tiny blossoms whose intricately lobed, fuzzy leaves smelled of spearmint. "What you wanted is out of season," the card said. "I hope this will do. Love."

"Five minutes," announced the stage manager, "five minutes."

Caroline tossed her shawl over a backstage barre. Rosalind Child was warming up at the far end. Caroline ignored her; she had wasted jealousy. The girl was not responsible for Alexander. Despite herself, Caroline at this moment wanted Alexander. His presence, his beauty, even that quality of his that had harmed her—his gift for gesture. She wanted that to reassure her now.

Rosalind Child smiled briefly at Caroline Harbison, expecting no response. She looked good, Rosalind admitted to herself, but a little worn out. She pitied Caroline for that, though it would not show to the audience. Rosalind leaned against the barre backstage and straightened the seams in her black stockings. The bodice of her costume for *Reductions* was cut low—it was little more than a silk camisole with strings for straps—and a short black organza skirt draped her hips. She passed her hands over her body, pleased with her perfect shape. She was flushed already. Her eyes were outlined with black makeup and her lips were red, matching her red shoes; her hair hung loose, gleaming even under the flat backstage lights. She stretched slowly, meting out her eagerness in increments, thrilling to her suppleness, stretching calm, preparing, as Perrot had instructed, to dance love.

The orchestra tuned. The costume mistress tacked a loose strap to the bodice of one of the members of the corps. In the wings Guy Pissarro arranged his girls and sent them onstage. Rosalind Child took her place. In the opposite wings, she saw Caroline Harbison. Behind her, Alexander Ives appeared, a red shirt bloused over his black leotard. The music began, and at their cue, Alexander opened his arms to Caroline.

Caroline Harbison and Alexander Ives entered together, bound in their close waltz. Rosalind Child counted, ten measures, eleven, twelve, and she danced on. There was a suggestion of waltz in her steps, like an old memory. She danced the seduction in the music, its demolition of the waltz's innocence, its mockery of the lightheartedness of empire. Her steps were condensed, echoing the implosion of open harmonies; she danced chromatic lust. Weaving between Caroline and Alexander, she felt no guilt for separating them, seducing Alexander, and leading him in her corrupt dance. She flaunted her flexible child's body, her winglike arms, her delicate thighs. Caroline Harbison's long knowledge of love seemed heavy and futile against Rosalind Child's sleazy brilliance.

But at the end of the ballet, Caroline Harbison danced her last solo, which Perrot had given her as an afterthought. "You know what to do," he had told her. "We can always take it out." He had never mentioned it again, nor had he asked to see the steps Caroline had devised. She had made up steps. Now, freed from her partner, she spun in a series of dazzling, quick waltz turns that kicked at the narrow harmonies of the arrangement, revealed its constriction and its disillusionment with gaiety. Rosalind Child, panting, aching from lack of breath, watched from backstage and understood Caroline's power. It was beautiful to watch, controlled and loose, not happy but hopeful; she danced with an expansiveness that permitted opposites, embraced them. Her technique was perfect, although Rosalind could see her compensating as she favored her right foot. Although Rosalind Child knew that her own steps were better than Caroline's, she worried that Caroline might detract from the impression she had left with the audience. This was her only chance tonight— another ballet had been substituted for *Swan Lake*—and Caroline was dancing in everything. But when Rosalind Child appeared for her curtain call, she saw that the audience had not forgotten her. The new dancer. There were shouts and stamping, and flowers tumbled from the balcony.

Backstage, Rosalind Child laughed, cradling her triumph like the abundant bruised flowers in her arms. The cheers continued. Caroline Harbison returned backstage with her armful of roses, but she did not carry as many as Rosalind. The curtain remained parted. Rosalind Child could see the dusty white shaft of the spotlight shining from the ceiling. Guy Pissarro motioned to her to go out and take another bow. She pranced forward onto the apron, and collided with Alexander Ives. He caught her in the air and embraced her and lowered her gently to the stage. Without thinking he found her balance. His hands rooted her and lightened her, and, clutching her roses, she stretched her neck and breast backwards in a white arc of joy. Her hair fell nearly to the floor. The applause intensified. Rosalind held her balance and her beautiful line. She was enchanted, enchanting. Perrot had been right. She had danced love. There was nothing more she wanted.

After the dancers' curtain calls, the spot shone a vacant halo at the place where Achille Perrot would have stood, where he would have come out to receive applause and take his reluctant, arrogant bow. The audience grew suddenly silent, taken by the image of absence. With a rumble of feet and a slamming of seats, the people stood. The applause resumed and there were shouts, and more flowers fell through the empty light onto the stage.

The house lights went up. The dancers scattered to their dressing rooms. Caroline Harbison peered through the peephole as the audience left for the first intermission. Despite the crowd, she felt as if the theater could have been empty for their performance. Nobody had watched them dance; nobody was really watching.

She went downstairs to her dressing room and changed into white tights for Alexander's ballet. She had time to rest; the next piece was a little divertissement for the corps. She rubbed the geranium's spicy leaves between her fingers. It perfumed the small room and masked the waxy smell of makeup. Amos Furst was not at the performance. He had a rehearsal himself; she hoped to see him afterward. That distance pleased her. She could not yet name what she felt for him, and she felt no urgency to know what it was; she knew its size and she could locate it. It was small—she could see past it—and so it did not eradicate unhappiness. It began in her stomach as an infusion of pleasure, but it did not make her light-headed; it clarified her instead. It loosened her shoulders, it made her unafraid to be still, it made her laugh, and she wondered what it would become.

"Places," came the voice of the stage manager. "Places."

To reach the stairs to the stage, Caroline Harbison had to pass Alexander Ives's dressing room. The door was open. From habit, she looked in, expecting him to have gone, to watch the corps dance; but he sat at his mirror, in costume. He stared at the glass as if he could not find his face. His eyes were frightened. Caroline entered the room. He looked up as she approached and saw her in the mirror. "I thought you'd be backstage watching," she said. "The rest of us need to think somebody's watching us. We can't dance without somebody watching. It has to be you."

"I had to change my costume."

"Maybe you shouldn't dance."

"What are you asking me to do?"

"To watch."

"And not to dance." Alexander lowered his eyes to his legs and raised them again to Caroline. "And what will you do?"

She shook her head, not knowing. "You'll have to find somebody else to partner me."

"Perrot is alive. It would seem like I was trying to take his place. It would be betraying him."

"No. He doesn't care. He says he doesn't, and that's the truth. He expects it." She placed her hands on Alexander's shoulders, on the familiar knobs of bone beneath the muslin shirt of his costume. Her thumbs pressed into the muscles on either side of his spine.

He closed his eyes. "I don't know."

"I need you to watch me," Caroline said.

"Places," the stage manager repeated. "Places, please." Caroline took Alexander's hand and led him upstairs.

The curtain rose in silence for Alexander Ives's new ballet, revealing a backdrop painted with a pastel landscape: a clearing in a forest of gnarled fairy-tale trees whose boles suggested the faces of gnomes. Flowers, variously colored lilies, littered the forest floor. The scene was bordered with a garland, like a faded tapestry. The audience murmured appreciation and surprise at this decorative departure from Achille Perrot's asceticism, and there was light applause. Harry Menard, in evening dress, entered and sat at the piano on the stage. His coattails hung over the bench like the tail of a swallow. He settled himself and glanced at Alexander behind the first wing. Alexander nodded.

Harry Menard raised his hands and Caroline Harbison inhaled. He began to play, and she entered on the first note and sank into her slow pliés. She was nervous; her breathing was too shallow. Kevin, the new dancer, began shadowing her steps. She strained for breath; her face reddened; she could not will herself calm. She thought she would faint. She was afraid for Alexander, afraid of failing him. Alexander entered with his wide, showy leaps. The audience interrupted with applause. Caroline caught her breath, relieved, reassured. Tears blurred her sight and black mascara ran in rivulets down her cheeks like a clown's makeup, but the audience could not see.

The dancers raced the music with quick intricate steps; they chased each other, unable to catch up with the notes. They danced in separate spaces, disjointed like memory, tantalized by memory, yearning for connection. They approached each other and retreated; they reached out, but they were too far away. Throughout *Impromptus,* the music, treacherous as memory, shifted too quickly for the dancers to maintain a foothold. Then suddenly, at the end, Alexander leapt and closed their distance, and they joined hands in a ring and circled, skipping—Perrot's image, Perrot's steps— the reconstruction of a child's dance, the memory of, or the wish for, innocence.

The last chromatic run: Caroline Harbison spun and crouched and rose into her long arabesque. Her foot trembled violently; her ankle ached. Alexander, alarmed, reached out to offer balance, but Caroline raised her arms and recovered. Finally she gave him the step he wanted; she balanced alone as the last chord vibrated into silence.

Alexander Ives came out for his choreographer's bow. He seemed disoriented in the bright light, out of character.

He looked over his shoulder and stepped back behind the curtain and, wanting to remain the dancer, tried to drag Caroline Harbison out with him.

"No," she protested. "Go. It's yours." Those in the first few rows of the audience heard her and repeated the story with delight; it appeared in all the reviews the next day. The entire audience understood Alexander's mimed confusion and laughed sympathetically. He was breathing hard from the dancing and from the applause. He bowed low and tripped; then he raised his head and smiled and stood still, his arms wide, accepting, holding on to the applause for balance.

Sumner Loewen clapped his hands over his head. "Bravo," he shouted. "Bravo!" The audience, taking his cue, cheered with him.

There were problems, still, with the ballet, Sumner Loewen thought, but on the whole it was fine, solid enough, sufficient for his needs. The audience was happy; he was happy. Friends and patrons crowded around his seat during intermission to praise the ballet and to offer him congratulations. Gertrude Stella, who was sitting just in front of Sumner Loewen, wordlessly offered him her hand, an accolade. Her eyes were wet with pleasure, her lips parted to reveal her red-rimmed yellow teeth.

"You are coming to the party?" he asked.

Gertrude Stella nodded. "And your Alexander will be there?"

Sumner Loewen promised to deliver. "So," he whispered to his wife, not without pleasure, "My Alexander. He has become my idea."

The program had listed the last piece as *Swan Lake*, Act II, but an insert announced that it would be replaced by *Sonata*, another new ballet by Achille Perrot. Sumner Loewen leaned forward and whispered to Gertrude Stella: "Achille did not intend this to be danced in public, but we are disobeying him. Alexander and Caroline wanted to do it, as a tribute because Perrot cannot be here tonight. He will pretend to be very angry when he finds out."

"He will be angry," whispered Fanny, overhearing.

319

"But it will be too late," answered Sumner.

The curtain rose on a stage that was bare except for a harpsichord, chairs, and a cluster of clay pots of marigolds on the floor. The musicians came onstage and tuned briefly before beginning the Bach. A fragile web of music shimmered in the theater. Against a white scrim, Alexander Ives and Caroline Harbison, in black, danced the ballet that Achille Perrot had made for them in his bedroom. They danced as one person; their feet sounded like one person's, the soft percussion part of the music. Her foot lifted, his touched the floor. They danced with a precious congruence. Caroline smelled their powder and sharp sweat; she could not tell herself apart from Alexander.

His blue eyes were wide open for her to follow. Dancing, she trusted him. Dancing, they could do anything. Loving the dance—during the dance—they could love each other.

Arms entwined, Alexander and Caroline took their curtain calls. They came out again and again, until Alexander asked the stage manager to have the electrician turn off the spot and bring up the house lights. Dancers, Walter Mowbray, Guy Pissarro, the whole company—everyone was already onstage waiting to congratulate them; Caroline saw Sumner Loewen's white head bobble as he stumbled over an electric cable. She stepped away from Alexander.

"What are you doing?" he asked.

"I'm going."

"You can't."

"I have to."

"You're going to Perrot?"

"No. Not tonight. It's too late. In the morning I'll go."

"I'll go with you."

She nodded. She was weeping again.

He reached for her to embrace her, but she moved beyond his grasp. His eyes darkened for a moment with yearning and with his desire for completion; his mouth opened as if he were about to ask for love or confess to it.

From the habit of desire—and from her habit of crossing to his loneliness—Caroline wanted to go back to him, but for tonight they were finished dancing.

She ran away, leaving Alexander Ives on the stage. Large and beautiful in his black tights and leotard, his blue eyes brimming with tears—they were tears of triumph, Sumner Loewen assumed, not considering what else they might have been—Alexander Ives returned embraces and thanked admirers for compliments. He told them that it was Perrot's evening, that the masterpieces were Perrot's, that his ballet owed its shape to Perrot. He was saying the right things; Sumner Loewen approved. He hoped Alexander would say those same things later to Gertrude Stella, giving her the opportunity to contradict him and anoint him successor. The older patrons of the company told Alexander that he reminded them of Perrot when he started the company. It was, Sumner thought, proceeding smoothly.

"Take your time changing. I'll send my car back for you," Sumner said to Alexander as he left for the party.

Alexander Ives shook his head. "I'm not sure I can come. I don't feel like celebrating."

Sumner Loewen smiled. "You should make an appearance. You are—" He hesitated, searching for the correct ambiguity. "You are the one we all want to celebrate." He lifted his hand for Alexander to follow. "But I understand how you must feel. It would mean a great deal to me if you would come. Only for a few minutes. Perrot never stayed longer than half an hour."

Alexander Ives paced the stage until the dancers had gone. He stopped still, precariously balanced at the center of the empty space, alone in its desolation and in its potential. The house lights went out. The stagehands lowered the asbestos curtain.

Alexander waited on the black stage, anxious until his eyes got used to the darkness and strange shapes resolved into the familiar apparatus of the theater: barres, cables, flats, trays of resin. He wished for Perrot, but there was only blackness where the choreographer had been.

Alexander raised his arms and beckoned. The shapes of

dancers entered from the shadows; their white shoes glittered like stars, and their white tulle skirts filled the stage like the milky mesh of the galaxy. He opened his arms wide into second position and the dancers jumped and streaked through darkness, falling stars burning white arcs of magnesium. Steps filled his eyes; whirling constellations over his head patterned the black velvet atmosphere. The dance stretched to the infinite edges of space, and Alexander Ives stood still at the center. The electrician came in and switched on the night-light.